I0534285

CHALLENGES OF
THE GODS

SOMETIMES, HEAVEN IS OVERRATED

CHALLENGES OF THE GODS SERIES
BOOK 1

C. HOFSETZ

CHRACATOA PRESS

Challenges of the Gods - Second Edition.

COPYRIGHT © 2025 by C. Hofsetz.

First Edition Published 2019.

Challenges of the Gods Series, Book 1

This is a work of fiction. Names, characters, places, and incidents are either the product of the author's imagination or are used fictitiously, and any resemblance to actual persons living or dead, businesses, events, or locales, is coincidental.

Print ISBN: 978-1-951832-02-5

Digital ISBN: 978-1-951832-03-2

First Edition Print ISBN: 978-1-5092-2432-6

First Edition Digital ISBN: 978-1-5092-2433-3

Cover Art: Samuel Florentino.

Cover Design: SGuerra Design.

All rights reserved. No part of this book may be used or reproduced in any manner whatsoever without written permission of the author except in the case of brief quotations embodied in critical articles or reviews.

Published in the United States of America

"Showing a genuine flair for originality, narrative story-telling, and the crafting of more plot twists and turns than a Coney Island roller coaster, C. Hofsetz's 'Challenges of the Gods' is a riveting great read."— Midwest Book Review

"Holy cow it has the most satisfying, beautiful, perfect eucatastrophe (Thanks, Tolkien) of an ending." — Erin, Wood Between The Worlds

"Throughout it all, readers are kept in suspense about how such a struggle will end." — Kirkus

"Hofsetz provides us with intelligent musings, reflections, and more than a little soul searching too."— Book Viral

American Fiction Award winner – Science Fiction: Parallel Universe/Alternative History category. American Book Fest.

Literary Titan Gold Award winner.

Reader's Favorite International Book Awards finalist – Audiobook category.

To Bere, Alice, and David

ACKNOWLEDGMENTS

I would like to thank my wife, Berenice Fuchs Hofsetz, for her patience and ideas on improving the book. She was the first one to read and edit it. She also helped me tone down the sexual innuendos. This is indeed a planet of prudes.

Thanks to Dutch Hixenbaugh for his help. I'm sure he must've been in shock when he realized the reason I don't write books for a living. A big thanks to Kisa Whipkey, who, among other things, helped me create depth and make the story more interesting. Also, thanks to Mica Scotti Kole, who helped me trim the story, name things, and work on the inner dialogue.

And of course, thanks to Dianne Rich from The Wild Rose Press. With her feedback, I was able to trim the word count and greatly improve my world building. In fact, publishing a book is far from being a lonely enterprise, so I also acknowledge here all the staff from The Wild Rose Press who helped with all the logistics involved in putting the first edition of my book in English in the hands of the readers.

David and Alice, my lovely kids, also helped me or tried to help me in their own way. Alice even suggested a few names and gave me some grammar tips, while rolling her eyes at the story.

Thanks to all the beta readers who read the whole manuscript or parts of it. Thanks to Madhav Deshpande,

Amirali Jazayeri, and Andrey Yavolovsky for help in defining names and expressions in their respective languages.

Finally, despite all the help, I'm solely responsible for any errors or plot holes in it. Although, to be honest, I'll be secretly blaming the editors.

PART I

*I distrust those people who know so well what
    God wants them to do,
because I notice it always coincides with their
    own desires.*

— SUSAN B. ANTHONY

1

HEAVEN

The first thing that comes to mind is that the afterlife is overrated. Even after death, everything I am, everything I went through, remains. The sadness, the hopelessness—the betrayal. No matter where I go, it'll always be there.

My last hours are fuzzy. I remember going somewhere, numb, just after I learned about my fiancée's affair with my best friend. What a cliché. A story that's been written over and over again. I thought my relationship was special. I should've paid attention to the statistics.

A bright yellow sky hangs over me where I lie, surrounded by odd diamond-shaped grass. My stomach feels lighter. I'm half-naked, wearing a hospital gown in an alien world. The situation is so bizarre it makes me smile. This cannot be real. And yet, everything is somewhat familiar.

As I stand up, I almost lose my balance. Gravity in the afterlife must be less than Earth's. The furry grass tickles my feet as I stumble through the field, squashing the fuzzy leaves. Spreading my arms wide, I touch everything, concentrating on the texture of the foliage, taking my time.

Someone definitely did a good job here. The level of detail is impressive. The wind, the air, the ridges, the trees —they all seem flawless, except for the pulsating purple trunks. Still, my mind is stuck on the fact that this is not real, that I am, in fact, dead. Whatever made this world— this place—is crafty. It looks perfect, but it doesn't feel real. It's as if the air is filled with electricity, connecting me to the ground, the vegetation, the surrounding area. It's uncanny.

Movement catches my attention, and I peer through the tall, skinny trees. In the distance, a dark-haired woman runs through the forest, making a lot of noise. She wears a pair of long, faded blue pants. Her white shirt is joined in the middle of her chest by small, disk- like objects in several equally spaced points, and I could swear she has a belt of some kind. It's an odd outfit. Really odd.

The forest floor is littered with dead lianas—or maybe vines—that were once attached to the trees, and the long, thick, black branches crack like fireworks as she steps on them. They should make running almost impossible, but she manages to do it all the same. A black man wearing a blue soccer jersey—I hate that team—and a blonde woman in a trendy one-piece tracksuit chase after her, though they're having trouble keeping pace.

The blonde stops running, crouches, and shoots several times, but misses. Great, I'm in a first-person shooter game without a weapon. This is not at all what I expected from Heaven. In fact, I didn't even believe in it.

Up above, in the sky, a flash of motion catches my attention. It's hard to see them through the trees, but two people circle us from above, observing the action unfolding below.

How interesting. If we can fly in this place, why are the others running?

The sharp crack of a branch breaking brings my gaze back to the fleeing woman. She's running toward me now. And it's too late to do anything. We make eye contact as she gets close, and she moves her arms up, as if protecting herself, trying to stop. But her momentum keeps her going and her foot is trapped by the vines. She crashes to the ground, face first, her body cushioned by the leaves.

I suppress a chuckle, but I can't hide a half-smirk. She notices it, frowning. I suspect I'm not making friends today. Maybe I should help her up.

As she tries to untangle herself, the man gains on her, grabbing her right leg. She kicks him in the face with the other leg, but he doesn't let her go. The blonde catches up and points her weapon at them, hesitating, but the fight is over. The fugitive stops kicking, and the man pulls her up, holding her arms behind her back. I notice he sports a visible face tattoo. They are so focused on her that they don't see me, just a couple of feet away.

Once she's secured, the blonde points her gun at their captive's face, ready to shoot. But the man leaps between them, pushing the gun away. They start arguing. Funny, the language they're speaking is familiar, but the words don't make sense. I should understand them but I can't.

The dark-haired woman looks at me and shouts. "Who are you?"

She speaks in an exotic foreign language that somehow makes sense to me, but I ignore her. Based on their "weapons," it's clear they're playing a game, but I have no horse in this race. Who knows which side I'm supposed to be on? Are there even sides to choose when you're dead? I mean, I do feel a little guilty—she tripped and fell because of me—but still. Talking to me announces my presence, which startles her opponents and brings their attention to me. She did that on purpose.

This time, the woman carrying the weapon doesn't hesitate. She points it at me and pulls the trigger. I blink as the leaves next to my head shiver. They must think I'm friends with their prisoner. My assumed "friend" kicks the device out of the woman's hand as she pulls the trigger a second time, making her miss the shot. Something grazes my arm, and I frown. I wasn't planning to start playing yet, but they're forcing my hand. Still, I'll enter the game on my own terms.

For as long as I can remember, my brain has been—or seems to be—faster than most. Don't get me wrong, I'm not necessarily smarter than anyone, just faster. When I was young, people stopped inviting me to volleyball games because I knew exactly where the shot was going to land, and I often collided with someone fighting for the same ball.

But this is not real life. This is not even life anymore, and I won't hold myself back. Running toward them, faster than they can react, I push the guy restraining the fugitive. When her hands are free, I grab them and look into her beautiful black eyes. She clenches her teeth and looks at me, surprised.

Since no one has told me what I can and cannot do yet, I do the obvious thing—I jump into the air, taking her with me, flying. In no time, we're through the canopies of the sparse trees and moving away from the forest. The blonde keeps shooting at us, but we're moving fast, and we're already too far.

The sight we had from the ground does not do justice to the view from above. It's a striking, albeit alien, landscape. An unreal sun near the horizon stuns me speechless. It's a red giant—that explains the yellow sky—though it seems like an odd choice for an afterlife mostly modeled after Earth.

"Are you some kind of angel?" the dark-haired woman asks me, eyes moving rapidly from side to side.

Her accent is strong; that's not how you speak this language. I have no idea how I know that, though.

"Slow down!" she shouts. "How are you doing this?"

"Anyone can!" I smile, which surprises me. Not the smile, but what I just said. How do I speak her language?

We stop on top of a hill. The woman stumbles away from me as soon as I let go of her hand, while tracing her left eyebrow with the palm of her hand. In spite of what just happened, she looks great. Yes, her clothes are unusual, but she's wearing a ponytail, a few strands of hair hanging loose and covering her face. It reminds me of my fiancée, the way she always wore her hair...and then my mood sours. Why do I do this? I want to start over! The past—my previous life—should stay in the past.

"My name is Jane. Who are you?" she says with both hands on her hips. "And, seriously, how can you fly?"

I laugh. Two bright points glint in the sky above the forest—the people I noticed earlier. "Look at them over there," I say, pointing. "They're flying!"

"But they're messengers. They're not humans like us."

"They're what?"

I don't think she hears me. Stepping closer, she stares at my left shoulder, and the cutest frown appears on her face.

"You're bleeding." She looks back at me.

Unimpressed, I peek at my arm. A trail of blood drips from a slash wound just under my bicep, where the blonde woman's shot clipped me. I wince, covering the wound with my hand. It's odd, but that doesn't mean it's real. If they can make the landscape so perfect, they can also model blood, right? I laugh nervously. It hurts a bit, but that may just be part of the package.

"That's...interesting," is all I manage to say.

The moment ends when Jane frowns again and looks up. The flying people, the "messengers," glide toward us. Except they're not actually people, like Jane said. I've never seen anything like them—all white and shiny, ethereal. They're hairless, albino humans in impossible, geometrically perfect bodies. It's as if two statues came alive and decided to meet us.

"We apologize, Ms. Engel, but your friend is not supposed to be here. He isn't here by choice. Not yet."

Who are they? Spirits, or angels of some kind, perhaps? Jane seems to know them already.

"So, you're saying it doesn't count," she says, her attention focused on the creatures hovering above us.

The nearest shining white entity takes hold of my arm. "My name is Hermes," he tells me. "Please, come with me."

Ignoring my protest, he strengthens his grip on my arm, and we fly away from Jane.

WE EXIT this incredible landscape through an exquisite round entrance that wasn't there a second ago, entering a long, straight, dark corridor. Playtime is over. It's time to learn about my responsibilities and chores, since I doubt there's free lunch even here.

The corridor reminds me of horror movies, where humans flee in the middle of a dark and foggy haunted wetland. There's no water, but the reflection on the floor makes it look like there could be, and the absence of—I don't know, buildings, walls, landmarks?—makes my stomach lurch. This place looks ominous.

After a few seconds of Hermes pulling me uncomfortably by my arm, he speaks. "There was a problem in the hypersphere. We'll discuss what happened later. For now, you're late to a major event."

The way he talks to me is so...human. He sounds like an old and loving grandfather who also happens to be the local mob boss. In statue form. As for me, I stay quiet as we walk through the hallway. There's plenty of time—maybe even all of eternity—to ask questions, like, "Why do they call Heaven a hypersphere?"

Then the nothingness in front of us shifts, transforming into another round entryway, and the noise of people talking breaks the silence. A little thrill goes through me as I watch them—all my mistakes and old relationships are history. New friends will help me restart my life with a clean slate.

"Careful what you tell them. They are not your friends. I'll explain later," Hermes says.

The next room is breathtaking. We are at the top of a large, granite-white flat circle floating in outer space, and I hold my breath for a second thinking I'm really in space. A massive Earth hangs above us in the center of the room, the continents visible beneath the familiar pattern of clouds. I have to give it to them—these designers of the afterlife— their environments are spectacular. But Earth is upside down.

People are coming in from other entry points, chatting and laughing out loud. Despite the spectacular scenario around us, I can't help but watch them in awe. What an odd group. Everything they wear is outlandish. Some have one-piece suits with colorful flowers, animal prints, or, I think, cartoon characters. At least three are completely naked, though they seem very aware of it and try to cover themselves with their arms.

Jane is also here, and she sees me as soon as I notice her. Uh-oh. What Hermes told me—about no one being my friend here—comes to my mind. Avoiding eye contact, I look down at my feet, only to realize that they're bare and I'm still wearing the hospital gown. I'm not butt-naked, but, you know, my butt is naked. Suddenly, that fact doesn't seem so irrelevant anymore. Jane walks toward me with a huge grin as I put my arms to my back, like it's something people do all the time. I blush.

"You are a little more prudish now," she says. "It didn't seem to bother you before," she continues, adjusting her ponytail with both hands. I stop looking at her to avoid bringing back more memories of my ex.

"Well, I'm not the only one who got brought here while I was in the middle of something." I gesture toward a naked girl. To my dismay, she hears me and blushes, giving me a death stare. I pretend I don't notice.

"So, is this your new friend, Jane?" a man next to Jane asks.

He sports a thick mustache on top of his lip and his tan skin stands out against the nearly all-white floor. It's clear from the way he saunters over, immediately crowding Jane's space, that he's feeling protective of her. They are more than friends. For no reason, I decide I hate him.

"Is it true you can fly?" he asks, looping an arm around Jane's waist. She goes rigid but doesn't fight it. Fascinating; his accent is different than hers.

"I was told that there was something wrong with the... system," I explain, trying to say as little as possible. I gesture toward...outer space, I guess.

"System? Does he know where he is?" the man asks Jane, pulling her closer. She bites her lip.

"I don't think so," she answers. "Where are you from?" she finally asks. "I can't place your accent."

She's not my friend. Or so they tell me. I must remember this.

"Do you know where he's from?" I ask, nodding at the man beside her, evading the question while keeping my backside covered. "He has an accent. And so do you, by the way."

Jane and the man glance at each other, puzzled.

"He's not thinking straight. I bet he's on drugs." The man laughs, pulling Jane closer.

"Stop it." She scowls, stepping away from her companion

Suddenly, someone speaks with a loud, clear voice, drawing everyone's attention. We all turn to find a humanoid standing in the center of the room, below the planet. It—she?—glares at me. It resembles Hermes but she's bright red instead of flawless white. The room goes quiet.

"Welcome! For those who don't know me, I'm Iris." She keeps looking in my direction, and I have the uncomfortable feeling that she's singling me out.

"This is an unfortunate step in this process. Some of you don't believe us, and have decided not to participate."

I'm off the hook, then. For the moment, at least. I don't know what's going on here. A few glance my way, as if accusing me of being one of the non- believers. I shrug, looking at Iris. She's shorter than us, though she must be on top of a pedestal of some sort, as we have to look up at her.

"But sometimes we must bring you all here, even against your will, to learn the stakes."

Interesting. What stakes? Where are we? And isn't everyone brought to the afterlife against their will? The room is awkwardly silent as we wait for her to continue.

"I'm sorry that you have to witness this," she concludes, and then turns her face up, toward the planet.

People shift uncomfortably and the rustle of murmuring skitters around the room. They are...shocked? No matter what the "messengers" show us, it's only fabricated. I mean, what are they going to do, destroy Earth in front of us?

Then I watch as they destroy Earth in front of us.

It starts to disintegrate inward, slowly at first. My left brain is thinking about how complicated—but still plausible—it'd be to simulate this, while my right brain floods with the emotion of billions of people dying. I realize with a sinking feeling of nauseous clarity this is not just a visual presentation. Somehow, I can sense their screams, their distress, their hopelessness. Whole families, whole cities, whole countries are disappearing. All lives fading in a couple of seconds.

This is real. This is really happening. My eyes fill with tears. People are crying around me; Jane and the man hug. Others cluster around the couple, trembling.

Who do these creatures think they are? Why do they have this power?

I hear what sounds like a girl scream, except that it's me. As I howl, I lurch forward, my inappropriate attire forgotten. The people around me seem to be pushed away by an invisible force as I'm crushed under the emotional onslaught feeding into my brain. I faint.

2

HELL

When I come to, my head is pounding. I don't know how long I've been unconscious. My vision is hazy, and I can't think straight. My augmented senses don't seem to be working anymore. Am I under the influence of painkillers? One thing is certain, though. I'm in a bed, in what looks like a hospital. Nearby, a woman is working on a bag of liquid, fumbling with some tubes.

Something seems off. Clumsy screens are scattered everywhere, and objects are larger than normal. It's like I was sent back in time but that can't be what happened. Yes, the computers are archaic but they don't just look aged. It's as if someone asked an art student to draw what they thought computers looked like forty years ago. My mind must be playing tricks on me.

A gnawing pain in my chest reminds me that something dreadful happened. And then it hits me—I just witnessed Earth disappear.

The woman wears blue overalls and an amusing contraption curiously resembling a wired stethoscope around her neck. She keeps checking the transparent bag of liquid while reading something on a pad. My guess is that she's a nurse, maybe a prison nurse. This room is certainly austere enough to be a prison, and I can't see any windows, though they may be behind me.

My train of thought is interrupted when I hear a loud, high-pitched beeping noise coming from the woman's scrubs. Almost as if she was expecting this, she pulls a weapon from her pocket. This is the moment we make eye contact. She must've known I was awake, and now she's going to kill me.

Too bad. She should've killed me while I was asleep. Using my left hand, I punch the arm that holds her weapon faster than she can react, and it scatters out of her hand, flying across the room. She screams as I remove the tubes and needles from my arm in a single quick motion and move away from her, stumbling and tripping on something on the floor.

In my peripheral vision, I notice the wannabe assassin has pressed a button next to the bed—security alarm? Getting up, I run as fast as I can to the door, but it takes me longer than I expect to reach it, and she's faster than I gave her credit for.

"Help!" she yells.

I stumble into the hallway outside the room just as two men yell at me from a lounge area on my right. Both of them also wear blue scrubs. They start chasing me, and I hit an empty stretcher as I try to escape. Pushing my hand against the wall, I manage to stay upright, but I'm still unsteady, feeling weak. It's too late, anyway. They grab me and pull me down. I fall to my knees. The woman that was trying to kill me sticks a syringe in my arm.

A wave of cold rushes from the insertion point, and I

sway in place as darkness descends across my vision. I lose consciousness. Again.

THE ALL-WHITE ROOM where I wake is so bright I don't see any depth at first. Indirect lights project on the ceiling from unknown sources, reminding me of the internal design of the latest jetliners. It's supposed to give you a soothing experience, but in this case, it does the opposite.

My vision adjusts as I stand up, and my legs wobble. Hermes and Iris stand a few feet away. I'm back in the same magical place where I met Jane and the others, where I watched the "messengers" destroying my home.

"I'm glad you are back," Hermes says, taking a step closer to me. "We have a lot to talk about."

And then I punch him in the face.

Hermes clearly didn't expect me to do that; he falls flat on the floor of this paradoxically soothing white room. To be honest, I didn't expect me to do that, either. A burst of pain rushes along my knuckles, but it was worth it. Iris is nearby, smiling, but she moves away from me after that.

Hermes stands with precision and grace, as if this happens all the time. This annoys me.

"I understand you are upset, human." He is not as grandfatherly this time. "Everything will make sense after."

Keeping his distance this time, he puts his hands on his hips. It doesn't look like I hurt him in any way. At least I caught him off guard. Small victories.

"You're saying there's a good explanation for why you destroyed Earth?"

Hermes is close enough that I can see his alien—I no longer believe these creatures can be anything else— skin in more detail; it's made of intertwined white wicker spread in a perfect sculpted mesh of human anatomy. I could easily confuse him for an android if it weren't for the pulsating blue veins visible in his joints indicating he's a biological being. And for the fact he talks like my favorite uncle.

"We did not destroy Earth. You must trust us," he says. His white eyebrows move, frowning, and his welcoming face gives me the feeling that perhaps I can trust him. I sigh.

"Then what planet did we just see implode?" I ask, hopeful.

"Earth."

Goddamn it, Hermes.

"But you just said......" I sound almost childish.

"We did not destroy it. Others did."

My heart falls to the floor. This is such a rollercoaster of emotions. Everyone I knew and loved, everyone who betrayed me, gone. Just like that. I take a deep breath.

"Who are you?" I demand.

"We are the messengers of the gods."

I glance at Iris to see her reaction, but her face doesn't tell me anything. She's still wearing a creepy smile. You've got to be kidding me.

"What the hell is going on?" I yell. "What...gods?"

Perhaps they abducted me. Yes, that must be it. This is an alien abduction, and they're playing with me. The room looks weird enough, like what crazy people describe when they explain their experience to the news. Maybe they weren't insane, after all. "And how do you even know they're gods?" I continue.

"It's simple, really. They created us." Iris remains silent, arms behind her back, unreasonably happy. "They created the Earths."

This is too much for me to process. Pacing around, my

bare feet are greeted by a warm, soft, rubbery floor. And yet, it's as shiny as aluminum. I get goose bumps just by looking at it. What I see and what I feel do not exactly match.

"Even if that's true," I say, although I don't believe them, "what makes them gods? How do you know they're not just an advanced alien civilization?" I immediately think of something else. "Hold on, you said they created the Earths, as in plural?"

"Correct," Hermes crosses his arms and looks down. He looks back at me. "Have you heard of the multiverse theory?"

Staring at nothing, I stop walking next to an invisible wall. Is it really there, or am I just losing my mind? How do I even know it's here? Extending my arm, my right hand touches a smooth, warm barrier, proving that I'm not crazy.

"Of course, I've heard of it. It's crap."

Bright colorful lights shine where my fingers meet the unseen boundary of the room, making me smile despite what's happening.

"The multiverse theory is partially correct," Iris says, looking at me with red eyes that never blink. "The planet you saw being destroyed was Earth, but not your Earth. We want to help you avoid this fate."

Relief washes over me, followed swiftly by guilt. Even if it's true—and I don't know yet if I believe them—billions of people still died before my eyes. I cannot forget that.

"So, there are infinite copies of Earth?"

"No, that'd be silly," Iris answers with a smirk that makes me cringe. Unlike Hermes, she doesn't behave or sound like a human being. She must've skipped the "totally not robots" training.

"There's a finite amount. But there is a major problem that will eventually destroy them all." She laughs, but immediately frowns. It's as if she can't figure out the right facial expressions.

"Your gods made a mistake?" I also laugh, humored by the thought of imperfect gods.

"Yes," Iris admits, jerking her head side to side, deflating my argument. I was planning to ask what kind of gods make mistakes, and they probably would've answered, "Why wouldn't a god make a mistake?" And this would've gone on and on. In fact, we should probably agree on a definition of "gods" before we discuss them.

"And we have to pay for that mistake," I conclude, a bad taste in my mouth. I'm angry at her in particular. Hermes seems to empathize with me better.

A planet materializes between us. I jump, startled. It'd be a disservice to call it a hologram, since it looks so perfect, but I can't think of any other word. These guys really are good with their audiovisuals.

"If your civilization is advanced enough, you can create a portal that connects two Earths," Iris says, gesturing toward the smaller version of Earth. The image of the planet zooms in, all the way down to what looks like a park in the northern hemisphere. It's daytime, and in the middle of the park a gigantic and transparent semi-circle the size of a ten-story building opens. It's a gate of some sort; the other side looks somewhat distorted.

"The portal is a bad idea," Iris continues in her out- of-tune voice. "At some point after the Earths are connected, the planets are quickly consumed by their own gravity, and they cannot turn it off."

The scene pans out as the planet begins to disintegrate around the interdimensional gate. Assuming that what they say is true, the implosion is caused by the portal. The planets are attracted to each other, drawn like magnets through that small passage between worlds.

As the mini-Earth is consumed in front of me, I feel nothing. No emotions come through my brain like before. I'm thankful they didn't replay them this time. I think they're afraid of my punches.

"Your Earth will develop this interdimensional technology within fifteen years," Hermes says, averting his gaze from the dying Earth. It's as if he's ashamed of it.

They stop talking, perhaps waiting for my reaction. I take another deep breath.

"How do we solve this problem?" Or how do I solve it? It definitely seems like I'm not just here for educational purposes. They've obviously singled me out for some reason. Otherwise, the people from earlier, the other witnesses, would all be here with me.

"It's simple," Iris says. "One of those Earths must be destroyed."

I close my eyes for a second, hoping to perhaps wake up and make everything go away. No such luck.

"Really? Your so-called gods can't conceive of a better way to fix this?" I shake my head in disgust.

"We have tried many options before. This is the only one that works," says Hermes, nodding, and I catch myself nodding back. Damn it, stop bewitching me, you old bastard.

"Have you tried telling them, oh, I don't know, not to create the portals?" It's time to be condescending again.

"Of course we did but eventually one of the Earths opens it anyway. They don't heed our warnings," Hermes explains. "And then everyone dies. We are giving a chance for at least one planet to survive."

I want to ask what I'm supposed to do here but I see

what's coming. After what they've said, it's so obvious. And much worse than I thought.

"You have been chosen," Iris says, guessing my thoughts. "You will infiltrate your Earth's counterpart and destroy it." She moves closer, and the contrast of her bright red body with our calming surroundings makes me step back.

"This is crazy. There must be another way. You're asking me to kill billions of people!" I plead.

It's one thing to watch and feel a planet die. It's orders of magnitude worse to be the one responsible for it.

"I'm sorry, but when you have to choose between billions or twice that number, you always pick the smaller one," says Hermes.

I'm not a killer. I can't do this. But what choice do I have? If I don't, or if I fail, my own Earth will be destroyed. Either way, the responsibility falls on me.

"But why me?" I ask. "I'm not special." A homeless guy who spent three days on a tree last month is more famous and more interesting than I'll ever be.

"You're right. There's nothing out of the ordinary about you," Iris says. "In fact, Hermes spent months trying to convince me not to pick you since you're so average." She nods with another unsettling smile.

Hermes avoids my eyes. And he seemed so nice to me. Now, I don't feel so guilty for hitting him, though I am a little uncomfortable with how they perceive me.

"Why don't you do it?" I change the subject. "Just pick one at random and destroy it. We don't have to suffer through this."

"We are not murderers," explains Iris.

"You say that, but you want me to commit genocide. And the people on the planet I'm heading to are none the wiser. That doesn't seem fair."

Hermes and Iris share a quick glance but say nothing for a moment. My knees quiver with dread. I risk a quick glance at the bed behind me, considering if I should sit down. But this is not the time to show weakness. I am so stupid. Jane, who I met earlier, is not from my planet, and she knows what's happening. She knows about the messengers. This is why they showed that Earth imploding today. Goddamn it.

"You know what?" I say, before they answer. "Your gods suck."

3

ALIEN

The hospital-prison almost makes me feel better. I don't know how long I was out this time. My head is fine—the drugs must've worn off—so I'd guess at least a day, maybe more if they kept me drugged for longer. The tubes are back in my arm, and I hear someone talking. I try to focus on what he says, closing my eyes to hear him better.

"You say you don't look like that child, but you'll have to take care of him if you're his father," the voice says, and people cheer. What type of place is this? I'd think this kind of discussion would be private, not done in front of a crowd.

"When it comes to four-week-old James, Billy, you are not the father," the man claims, followed by gasps and shouts. I turn my head and see a TV mounted above the bed next to me.

The TV looks old, almost fake, except it works. The computers and monitors around me are ancient. They're really behind in computer technology here. In a way, it's fascinating. And then I realize—this must be the other

Earth. The one where I'm supposed to kill everyone I see and meet from now on.

I wonder who I am supposed to be here. Did I just randomly appear in this bed? If so, Jane and the people from this Earth who know about a mole here will figure out my true nature soon, and the game will be over. I still don't know what to do but I must get up to speed as soon as possible. Otherwise, my planet will be destroyed. But I know nothing of this life, of this Earth.

A woman with long brown hair, wearing a white robe, comes into the room and turns the TV off. She acts as if she owns the place, and now I'll never know who James' father is. She ignores my angry stare and pulls up a chair.

"Good morning, Mike." So, I'm supposed to be "Mike" here. I guess that answers my previous question. "I'm Dr. Alice Hallan. How are you feeling today?"

"Uh......" I'm unsure of what to say. "Better, I think. Where am I?"

Alice frowns when she hears my voice. As Jane did earlier, she must've noticed my accent.

"You are in the Los Angeles Medical Center. You had an accident, and you were brought here, unconscious, three weeks ago. Do you remember anything?" she asks, slowly moving her pen in between her fingers. I always liked that trick.

"No," I try not to give away my mission the moment I start it.

"Okay. We're going to have to do some tests." She picks up a huge, thick tablet to take notes on, and the pen she has in her hands connects with that device with a subtle rubbery click.

"Let's start with the basics. Can you tell me your address?"

"My address?" I say, still admiring her tablet. The last time I saw one like it was in a museum. "I...don't remember."

She may as well just bring me my death warrant. I'll sign it, and everybody can move on.

"Do you remember anything at all? How about your full name?" She seems concerned. In fact, we both are.

"My name is...Mike?" I guess, hopeful, but she frowns again and takes more notes on her cumbersome pad. Somehow, this is not the right answer. Just kill me.

"You don't remember your last name. Hmm." She doesn't look at me. "Do you remember where you live, or any of your friends? Do you know where you work?"

"I don't remember anything," I tell her the truth.

Actually, the truth is that I'm a potential mass murderer, and I have no idea why and how I ended up here, or even how to do the actual mass murdering. But if I said that out loud, she'd probably think less of me.

"This is very odd. You have the symptoms of a stroke—you have amnesia, and your speech doesn't sound right—and yet, your body coordination is fine, and we can't find anything wrong in your MRI. I'd like to do a few more tests before we let you go."

Amnesia is a good excuse for what's happening. Obviously, I remember everything that happened to me, the real me—or, at least, most of it. I'm not Mike, but I can pretend to be him to fulfill my plan. Whatever that will be.

Thinking about it makes my mouth dry. I panic for a second, but I must remain calm. Nothing good comes from people losing their minds, especially in a hospital. Anytime someone freaks out in a movie, there's almost always a syringe that comes out of nowhere, and I've had my quota of needles for the day.

"I see you have no relatives in your file. Two people are asking for you, but we can't let them in since they're not family. They are"—Alice picks up a piece of paper from beneath her pad and reads from it—"Ravi and Linda. Do those names ring a bell?"

She looks at me. I blink, blankly. No bells ring nearby.

"You don't know these people? Interesting. Linda is your ex-wife, and Ravi tells me he's your roommate."

Mike has an ex-wife?

"Doctor," I ask, "how old am I?"

Alice gives me a brief stare and checks her pad. This is a question she must not have heard before. I quickly look around for angry-people syringes, but it's just us.

"You're...twenty-five." Mike and I are the same age. It makes sense.

"So," she says, "should we let them see you? Both of them?"

It's obvious that I need help, and I need friends. Linda's an ex, but Mike might be a jerk for all I know. I have to see them both so I can decide what to do.

"Yes, they can see me."

It's late afternoon when a thin, dark-skinned man and a tall, red-haired woman are shown inside and, once in, stay at opposite ends of the room. Based on the way they look at each other, it's clear there's no love between them. Linda has a half-smile on her face, but Ravi seems bitter.

"I'm glad you're better, Mike. But I can't believe you let... her...come here." Ravi clenches his teeth.

Linda looks around the bright room, as if searching for something—or someone.

"Calm down, Ravi," she says, looking up at the ceiling. "You're just upset because you were jealous of my relationship with him. You always wanted him all for yourself." Linda finally looks in my direction.

Staring at them, I ask, "Were we all…in a relationship?"

Interesting. I'm straight, but maybe Mike was not. Meanwhile, Linda's eyes glisten, as if fascinated by the sound of my voice.

Ravi snickers at me. "No, Mike. You married her, not me. And you hated her guts after what she did to you." He points at her, his thick eyebrows frowning.

Did she betray Mike? Maybe Mike and I are similar regarding relationships. Perhaps the gods—or the messengers of the gods—were trying to level the field.

"Come on, Ravi. Despite what happened, I never stopped loving Michael."

"What is marriage, anyway?" I ask. Maybe it means something different on this Earth. But you know when people look at you as if you're stupid? That's how they look at me. Except I think there's also some pity in the mix.

"What exactly do you remember?" Ravi asks, frowning.

This is going to be a long day. As I did with the doctor, I decide to spill the beans.

"Guys, I don't remember anything. I don't remember you, her, the accident, or anything about my life. I'm sorry."

Frustration fills my mind as the words come out of my mouth. I've lied more times in the last few hours than I have in my whole life. I used to be proud of being honest. How many moral codes will I have to break because of these so-called gods? At least I haven't killed anyone—yet.

"I'm your friend, your roommate. I'll take care of you." He stops talking and closes his eyes for a moment, visibly regaining his composure before continuing. "She gave up on you. She left a long time ago. We both hate her. We used to write songs and plays about how evil she is. She shouldn't be here."

Linda laughs. "Ravi always exaggerates. But how would you know, right, Mike? Maybe we can start from scratch. Come home with me. I did a lot of stuff I regret, and I'm sorry I abandoned you. But we were married, so you must have liked me sometimes."

She has a point. Still, the fact that they don't live together anymore, and that Mike is Ravi's roommate, makes me believe that he trusted Ravi more.

"I'm sorry, Linda. I want to go home. I don't remember anything, but if home is where Ravi lives, then that's where I'm going when they let me leave this place."

Linda walks around the bed, her eyes scanning the room as if it's the first time she's been in a place like this. Her behavior is so odd that it makes me look around for something strange as well. Everything is weird to me, though.

"Fair enough," she says, getting closer and touching my arm. "You know where to find me if you need me."

Her sudden movement and her cold hands make me cringe. Linda immediately stops touching me. Nobody likes rejection. She becomes cold and distant.

"Well, I'm swamped. I'm glad you're feeling better, but I have to go." She looks again at Ravi, and then back at me. "See you, Michael."

When she finally leaves, Ravi sighs, looks at me, and says, "We've discussed this many times, but I'll let this pass because of your amnesia. Even if I weren't straight, I'm way out of your league." He laughs.

I like him. I'll try to kill him last.

4

BRAINS

In the morning, I'm taken to what they call Dr. Alice's office. It's not as big as I would have thought, and it's styled with a sort of retro feel.

A few pictures hang on the wall, several exotic plants with long leaves perch in various corners and on shelves, and two plain chairs sit in front of an over- decorated desk with objects I don't recognize. Alice sits behind it in a larger, flamboyant chair with comically large armrests, though she doesn't use them. Instead, she's taking notes when I enter the room, and she stands up to greet me.

"Hello, Alice," I say, and her smile vanishes for a split second.

"Hello, Mike. How was your night?" She smiles again. Grabbing my hands with both of hers, she shakes them as if her life depended on it. This doesn't look good; maybe she figured something out. My skin prickles and my hair stands up as I sit in one of the empty, plain chairs.

"The best night I've slept in ages," I reply. A flat black rectangular object hangs on the left wall. I only notice it because she keeps stealing glances at it.

"That makes sense," she says with a soft laugh. "It was the first night where you weren't moving and jerking around while you slept." She sits on her comfortable chair, leaning forward, her fingers moving on top of a weird device with lots of buttons.

"Anyway, we unfortunately still don't have any idea of what happened to you. All your tests are clean."

She stands up abruptly before continuing, and walks over near the edge of the table, next to the black object on the wall.

She smirks. "I have something to show you."

The object lights up, like an old computer monitor. An image appears on it, covering the right half of the screen. It's a picture of a slice of my brain.

"This is the last MRI scan we took of your brain. It looks the same as all the others we took. There's no sign of trauma or stroke. Every brain is different, so at first, nothing stood out," she says, a smug smile on her face as she moves to reach for something on her table.

"You may not remember this, but you were here about two years ago." She picks up a chart. "You were in an accident after"—she looks at me, her forehead creasing—"you crashed your car and had a concussion. We took scans of your brain then, too. Here is one of them."

Another picture of a brain pops up on the other side of the screen, so we can compare both MRI images side by side. On the right, we see my brain as it is today, and on the left, we see Mike's brain from when he was here years ago.

"They are not from the same brain," she concludes, eyes gleaming with enthusiasm.

Unable to control myself, I leap from the chair and walk closer to the screen. Alice moves away from me, lowering her eyebrows for a second.

"Mistakes happen all the time," she continues.

"The brain on the left has a concussion, but, as I said, it's not the same brain as the one on the right. At first, this looks like a clerical error. Maybe we stored someone else's MRI in your files. These types of mistakes almost never happen, but no system is perfect."

Moving from one picture to another, I keep comparing the brains. This is fantastic. For a while, I forget my situation —where everyone on my planet is going to die—and I immerse myself in this puzzle.

"But, you see, as I looked into these brains, I found something that's impossible," Alice continues, now with a wide grin. She has noticed the same coincidence, and this is why she's so excited. Who wouldn't be? It'd be a major discovery anywhere. It's unexplainable.

"This part here"—I interrupt her presentation, indicating a spot on the picture—"is larger in both brains. These two other places are also larger than normal." Alice looks puzzled after I say that.

She crosses her arms. "Correct."

Those areas in my brain were always like that. I know them by heart. And yet, no part of two brains are completely alike. There are always some differences.

"These other smaller areas—here, here, and here— are also enlarged," I say, indicating the regions on her wall monitor.

"The fact that they're larger is not unheard of. People are different."

"Yes, of course," I agree, absorbed by the enigma in front of us. "But you said it yourself—people are different. The problem is that these areas look exactly the same—in both brains. They are a copy of each other. This is impossible!" I conclude, overjoyed with our discovery. She grins back at me. We're partners in this.

Except that I probably should not know that. How would Mike know this? My only hope is that he's a doctor of some sort.

Alice nods at my chair, indicating that she's done with my invasion of her work area. I go back and sit, less confident now, not knowing what to do with my hands.

"The use of MRI for identifying people is an active area of research. But this is not foolproof. I could not use it in a court of law—yet." She walks back behind the desk and sits down. "But having two pictures of two different brains with that degree of similarity is, as you just said, impossible." She sighs, leaning back on her tacky chair.

"People spend whole careers without seeing something like this," she continues, picking up a pen to fiddle with.

I stay quiet. I went too far. I know I went too far. She's eyeing me with suspicion.

"Mike, how do you know this?" she finally asks. "You don't even remember what you used to do."

"I don't know," I lie.

"You're not a medical doctor, and you didn't work with anything related to brains. It takes a trained eye to notice that."

I shrug. Nothing I say will make this better.

"I'm told you're a genius of some sort, so perhaps you are so smart that you noticed the similarities yourself." She seems unconvinced.

I'd also be skeptical. Even if I were the smartest man on Earth, how would I know that something was not normal in those pictures? A layperson in this area might have assumed that parts of the brain can be the same. Only a professional would know that they are enlarged. However, she doesn't have an explanation, either.

As for me, I know exactly what's going on. Those matching areas are the language centers of the brain. Therefore, those modifications must be what allow me to speak both their language and my own. Mike's original brain has the same thing. Somehow, they kept his brain and mine in sync, at least in the language areas.

How cool is that? He must be able to speak my language as well. And now that I think about it, the people who were running after Jane must have been my people. But if that's true, why couldn't I understand what they were saying? Perhaps we can only speak one language at a time.

"Mike, we cannot help you much here. You are free to go home." She gives me a quizzical look.

The room starts to spin for a moment, and I grab the bottom of the chair with both hands. I close my eyes and try not to throw up. I'm a huge idiot. The implication of this discovery is so obvious it makes me nauseous. Mike's also a mole. He must've replaced my body, and my planet is in even more danger than I thought.

"But I have one thing to ask you before you go," she says, clearly ignoring my discomfort.

Worse, she said Mike's a genius. He'll figure out how to destroy my Earth within a few days, execute his plan in a month, tops. Meanwhile, I'm here thinking people on TV are talking to me. Great. My planet should be proud of its champion.

"As you somehow know, what I just showed you is extraordinary. I want to write a paper about it."

Taking a deep breath, I try to remain calm. I don't know how things work here, but I think she needs my permission to go ahead and study that. Once her paper is published, the whole world would see it. Eventually, someone, somewhere, would make the connection, and I'd be dead.

I shake my head. "No."

I wonder if I should help pick her jaw off the floor. I just destroyed the world she must've created in her mind this morning, probably during breakfast, where she saw herself as some kind of hero.

"No?" she asks. "Mike, this is an amazing discovery. This shouldn't be possible."

"Give me some time to think."

5

THE RING

It's already night by the time I finish filling out the discharge paperwork and I'm ready to leave. Ravi is waiting outside. Everything in this world is alien to me, so I appreciate his help. Sure, I could figure some things out by myself but the more help I have, the better.

Meanwhile, I must figure out what to do. Iris told me I can go back to the hypersphere anytime but since Jane and her friends know about a mole on Earth, this would increase the chances of them recognizing me later. Maybe I should stay here for as long as I can.

"I'm glad you're feeling better," Ravi says. "We have so much to catch up on."

He takes me to what looks like a parking lot with several funny-looking cars. You can't beat the four- wheel basic design, I guess, but people went nuts here with many different colors, sizes, and models. It seems so tacky.

I wonder if they have motorcycles. Since I can think of a word for it, I bet they have them. This is a good way to find out if something here is similar to what I have on my planet, I realize. As long as Mike and I both know about it, I'll have a word to describe it. That means we both share a subset of words for our languages at the intersection of what we've learned in our lives. Fascinating.

"I want to thank you, Ravi. I wouldn't be able to do anything without you."

Turning around the corner, we search for his car. It's odd that he has an actual car in the first place, and that it was not waiting for us outside the hospital. I'm about to ask Ravi about this when I see it. I gasp and take a step back. Today is a day of unbelievable things.

"Oh...my...God!"

Ravi stops and looks back at me, a puzzled look on his face, but quickly turns ahead to see what I'm seeing. We both stare at it. I can only imagine his surprise. I wish I could see his face, but I can't turn my head away.

Low in the sky, above some buildings in the distance, there's a massive bright white globe. It's too close; Earth will collide with it at some point. Did the gods change their minds and decide to destroy this Earth anyway? My mouth is open.

When I finally turn to Ravi, he's looking back at me, but his face doesn't show surprise, more like amusement.

"Seriously, Mike. I get your amnesia, but you don't remember the moon?"

A moon. No, Ravi called it the moon. Their Earth has a freaking moon. And it's massive. Beautiful. Menacing. Instead of a moon, we have a ring of debris that can also look spectacular. We call it the Ring. The name of my planet —Jora—means the ringed temple.

There are many theories on how the ring around Jora was formed. The most prevalent one is that we had a moon. It couldn't be just any moon, though. It had to be a large one compared to the size of Earth. The idea seemed so far-fetched, but here it is. Astonishing.

"It just looks so pretty...tonight." I stumble with my words. Ravi looks at me, squinting.

My mother used to take me to church, where a sizable waffle, representing the large asteroid that existed before the Ring, was broken into pieces. The Book of the Ring tells us that its rocks are our angels, and each piece of the waffle is our own guardian angel. For some reason, we would eat them at the end of the ceremony. I know—creepy.

"I don't know"—I keep talking, thinking about what to tell him—"I could've died in that accident, but I'm alive, and that gave me a better appreciation for everything." I fake a smile.

No reason to draw further attention to the situation, so I force myself to stop looking at the moon, and we resume walking to Ravi's car. To my surprise, the door doesn't do anything by itself. Ravi has to open it by actually pulling on its handle.

"You must be hungry, Mike. How about we go out? Have your favorite food?" Ravi asks as we enter the car. "It might bring your memories back." I sure hope Mike liked steak, and not something weird like quinoa or, God forbid, anything from the produce section.

Funny, the car has a wheel that hangs just above Ravi's lap. What a weird contraption—and then it hits me. He's going to drive this thing. He, a flawed human like me, is going to drive this several-thousand-pound, man-killing machine.

All those historical videos of people driving their own cars and crashing start playing in my mind. I remember watching them as a kid, horrified, but filled with a guilty, morbid curiosity. They said that more than a hundred people would die in traffic accidents every day, and that was only in our country. Today, I may be one of them.

As he starts the engine, I try to remain calm. If I keep slipping up, even he may figure out that something else is not right, not just my memory. People drive their cars here, and I'll have to make peace with it. Even if this is my worst phobia, I have to let it go. I try to relax by doing breathing exercises. I hope Ravi won't notice.

We start moving and I grab a handle that conveniently hangs just by the window, trying to keep my composure.

"Motion is bothering me, but I'll be fine," I say.

His car isn't special. There are lots of people on the roads with us, all driving their own vehicles, hoping not to kill anyone today. They rely on colorful lights to decide who gets the right of way. Nice. My life depends on strangers not disrespecting, ignoring, or missing a bulb of red light. Savages.

Besides the moon, the computers, and the death wish everyone here seems to have, everything else seems similar to planet Jora. Humans are the same anywhere we live, after all. And then I think back to my "mission." How sad, how pointless it is. People will die for no other reason than some stupid aliens making a mistake.

Ravi keeps driving and, against all odds, we survive. Our car stops at another parking lot after he barely misses the red light. He doesn't speak much, and I don't know what to say. There is nothing in common between us, unless he's been to the hypersphere, and I'm not going to ask him about it.

"Ravi, you know that I don't remember anything. So you'll have to explain a lot of things," I say, and he nods, holding the door of the eating place for me. We step inside Mumbai Cave, a restaurant, and a dark-skinned woman greets us by name, taking us to our table. She hands us a booklet as we sit.

"For instance, what's my line of work? What's my background?" I look at the booklet—a food menu. I don't understand any of the words. That means our planets don't have a common word for it, so there's nothing like that in my place. "And what are those little red things?" I ask as I point at them. He makes a grimace.

"They are peppers. Choose the one with the most peppers, which is five. You love it." I go back to looking at the menu.

"You work at the California Institute of Technology," Ravi explains, "as a particle physicist. You finished your PhD at twenty-three, and everyone in the world wanted to hire you."

It's clear that I'll have to abandon that kind of work. I like particle physics as much as the next guy, but it's not my cup of tea. It would take years for me to relearn what Mike knows, and I would never be as good as he is, anyway. I think Ravi has figured this out already.

"In your spare time, you were working on a new idea to create artificial black holes," he goes on. "Before the accident, you told me you were near a breakthrough."

"And what do you do, Ravi?"

"I'm not like you. Yes, people respect me, but I'm just a regular Joe. You're the brilliant one. We worked together when you did your PhD, and we've been inseparable since then."

I look at him in concern, and he seems to realize what I'm thinking.

"Don't get me wrong, I was never jealous of you. I can't compete with that, and I never wanted to in any case. I'm just happy to work with you." He looks at me expectantly and says, "You're a genius, Harry!" But he's soon back to his gloomy self when I don't react to what he said. Harry must be my nickname.

I like to think I'm one of the best at what I do—and I am —but I would not call myself a "genius." Geniuses solve complex math equations with their eyes closed. I have to use my fingers to count the days of the week. Hermes and Iris spoke about fairness but I'm under- matched for this game.

One of the meals with five peppers sounds appealing, so I order it. Ravi asks Aditi—the server—to make it with extra chili, a word I don't know yet. My hope is that the food here is better than the hospital's. I could use a change for the better.

"I don't remember any of this," I confess. "My career is probably over."

Ravi looks through the window at the late afternoon traffic, avoiding my eyes. The person in front of him, the one who used to be his brilliant friend, is gone unless I get my memory back. However, I know this won't happen.

"Don't worry, Mike. You'll remember everything. It may take months, or a few years, but you'll be back to your old self. I'll take you to your lab, and you'll see."

I look outside as well, impressed with the number of cars, knowing what he said is impossible. And just like that, my mind wanders to the messengers' place. In hindsight, I should've asked Jane's people what they do, where they work, their addresses, and so on. But doing that would look suspicious, and I wouldn't remember all the answers anyway.

Besides, I still can't grasp the idea that Mike could destroy Jora at any moment.

"And even if you don't remember, you're still you. You

can start from scratch. You're a whiz." He smiles and looks at me.

The server brings bread and, for a change, I love it. It's fluffy, and it breaks apart in my hands. In terms of food, I like simple stuff.

Things get a little awkward in the silence, and Ravi tries to break the ice.

"I heard that you hit a nurse while she was grabbing her phone. Is that true?" He laughs.

It turns out that it wasn't a weapon at all, as I had supposed—she'd had a phone in her hand. They need actual devices for communication here, whereas we haven't needed them for decades. Biochips implanted in our heads do those things as soon as we start crawling. Our senses are augmented with computers. In fact, that's what I do—did— for a living. I'm a neurocomputer engineer.

The only place our devices don't work is in prison. If you're in jail, you lose your sensory privileges. It's awful. That's why I thought I was in a prison when I woke up at the hospital the first time. And the fact that their phones look exactly like a police-issued interceptor on Jora didn't help at all. I had to assume I was in jail and that she had a weapon. How could I not?

I regret nothing.

"My head was fuzzy." I force a laugh. "I thought she was going to hurt me."

Ravi bobbles his head side to side when I talk. This is a gesture that doesn't exist on my planet.

"It's fine; you taught her a lesson. She shouldn't be answering phones while taking care of patients."

Aditi brings our food on large plates—I've never seen so much food in my life—but I'm so hungry I'll be able to eat everything, and then some. The horrible food at the hospital had killed my appetite but I'm finally ready to eat something good. I pick a utensil that looks like a small bowl, fill it up with the largest amount of food I can cram into my mouth at once, and chew with my mouth open. You know, even in an alien Earth, we should have manners.

My mouth burns and my eyes water as I gag. This is not food. I look at Ravi in anger, feeling deceived. He's trying to kill me. Ravi's thick brows snap together as he gives me an evil look.

6

APRIL

Home is a small two-bedroom apartment, and only Ravi and Mike live here. I wonder if it's normal to live with your wife or friends in a small place like this. On Jora, it'd be easier to find out. I could just start several queries on the net using the biochips implanted in my brain. The information would be back in seconds.

We can do that in our sleep, and we often do it accidentally. I woke up one day with a list of the top ten cities to have cuddle parties blinking in my peripheral vision. I'm not going to lie to you—going to one of those parties was a mistake.

I miss being always connected with the network through my brain but it's great not to have those extra sensors in my body all the time. People need a device to do that here, which, at first, seems bad, but they're not bombarded by information every single minute unless they use it. If I go back one day, I'll try to be unplugged at least a few days a week. Right now, I can't stop thinking about death. And dying.

Ravi's upset, and I don't blame him. We haven't talked much since the police let us go. It wasn't a fun ride coming home, and not only because we could die at any moment due to reckless drivers.

"Ravi, I'm very sorry I got us banned from Mumbai Cave. Sorry I tried to hit you. And I'm sorry I yelled at all the customers that the cooks were trying to poison me."

He looks at me and sighs. "It's okay, Mike. If you think about it, I took a deranged person who had just assaulted a nurse straight from the hospital to a nice restaurant expecting he would behave like a normal person. It's my fault, really."

The living room is smaller than I'd imagined it, and the amount of books, electronics, and furniture is surprisingly high for such a small space. There are pictures on top of shelves and on the wall but there are also a few clear spots.

"Again, I'm sorry. I don't feel like myself. Since I don't remember anything, I'm always on the edge."

Ravi carries my bag to what I assume is my room. "How often do you think people are trying to hurt you? You have a disease!" he shouts from there. I say nothing and just wait. He soon comes back and sits on the couch near me, though not too close.

"Don't worry, you'll get over this. This is just the first day." He smiles thinly. Next, he stands up and leaps to his feet, startling me, and I instinctively guard my face with my arms. Ravi rolls his eyes.

"Mike, you should get a hold of yourself. No one is trying to hurt you. I just want to know if you want to drink or eat something. You must be starving."

Well, he should've known not to make sudden movements in front of a "deranged" person. My stomach growls when he mentions food, though.

"Yes. Do you have some bread? I mean, plain bread, maybe butter?"

His face cringes when he hears the word "plain."

"Sure, let me grab something for you," he replies with a disappointed look.

Ravi walks into the kitchen, and I realize that it's already been four hours since he picked me up at the hospital. At first, I thought we were going to spend the whole night at the police station but Ravi knows how to talk to people. They were also very understanding due to the fact that I had just left the hospital. What a great spy I am. I got arrested an hour after I started my mission, with no plan in sight.

The bread Ravi brings is made of square slices that are white in the middle with a brown crust, and it's stale. He also brings soda made from beer root that tastes awful but I promised myself I wouldn't make a scene because of the food. I'll eat and drink this crap even if it kills me.

As I chew it, I realize that, even stale, this is better than the hospital food. I swallow a little bit and look at Ravi.

"Ravi, what happened three weeks ago?"

Watching me enjoying the food, Ravi leans in the kitchen's doorway.

"You were driving west on State Route 2 and you lost control of your car. We don't know what you were doing there. You hadn't left this area since"—Ravi pauses for a second before continuing—"Well, you hadn't left Los Angeles for years. And all of a sudden, you were out there, driving and crashing your car."

I'm not surprised. A self-driven car wouldn't have crashed. These people are just asking for it, driving cars themselves. But maybe I'm being too harsh. We were exactly like that in the past, so who am I to blame them?

"You should go to bed," he says. "I'll stay around for about an hour and hit the sack."

"No," I protest. No need to hit any sacks. "I need to know more. You're hiding something from me."

Ravi turns away, avoiding my gaze. He must know something about me, maybe even about Hermes or Iris. This cannot be a coincidence. Maybe he didn't try to kill me at the restaurant. Perhaps he wanted me unconscious so he could tie me up and ask questions later.

But then again, what are the odds of him knowing about the hypersphere, him being that close to me? I doubt the messengers of the gods would be so careless, unless they're stupid.

After a few seconds, he clasps both hands behind his head and closes his eyes before speaking.

"Mike, it's late. You need a good night's sleep. We should do this slowly."

"I can't go to sleep with something like that hanging over me."

Ravi sighs, and walks over to the large apartment window. Staring at nothing in particular for a while, he bobbles his head almost imperceptibly.

"All right, Mike," he concedes. "You're only twenty-five, but you've lived so much. Don't you think it's odd you have an ex-wife already?"

On Jora, I was engaged and ready to be married, and people told me I was too young. I nod. Apparently, that was another thing we had in common.

"You've always been bright, ever since you were young. Usually, people like you—or me, for that matter—are socially inept. That's why we marry later in life, after thirty. Or so I hope."

That seems like a bad stereotype. For one thing, I know many bright and outgoing people. But I don't interrupt him.

"I met you when you were already married. You were twenty years old and had already been married for two years. I was told that when you two met, you were like fire and gunpowder. You were made for each other. You married when you were eighteen years old."

That's very early indeed. I wonder what happened that drove them apart.

"Why did they—I mean, why did we marry that early?"

Maybe it's normal on Earth. I don't want to ask if this is normal here, though. I should know. I'm from here, if anybody asks.

He walks toward a shelf next to a recliner, opens a drawer, and pulls something out of it. "You're right. Usually people don't tie the knot at eighteen."

The object he brings over to show me isn't a knot. It's a picture of a blonde girl in pigtails with food all over her face. My guess is that he's hoping to see a signal of recognition but I give him none. However, it's pretty obvious who she is.

"She's my daughter," I conclude, in a low voice.

Ravi smiles thinly.

"This is April. In this picture, she was four years old. You told me you got married because Linda got pregnant. But, then again, you also said that you'd have married her anyway. You loved her."

Ravi gives me the picture so I can take a closer look. I grab it with both hands but I don't look at it anymore.

"The year we met, Linda abandoned you. She said that you were working too much and ignoring her, that she was raising April by herself. You weren't helping her at all" He has a worried expression on his face. "She was right; I could see it. But she didn't even try to talk to you. You'd have tried anything."

"She took April with her?" I ask. Why didn't she bring her to see me at the hospital?

"No." He scoffs at my question. "She abandoned you both. We never understood why. She loved that girl as much as you did." He proceeds to sit on the couch again. "After she left, you became a single father, raising a one-year-old daughter, doing a PhD. It was too much for you to handle."

Ravi rubs his eyes for a moment. He's in a somber mood.

"This is her last picture," Ravi says. "She disappeared one day from preschool and was found dead soon afterward."

My eyes get watery, and I gather the courage to stare at her picture again. April is not my daughter but it doesn't matter. I thought I had it bad when my fiancée cheated on me, or when my mother abandoned me when I was ten. But that is nothing compared to losing a child.

"You were getting your PhD that month; you were only twenty-three years old. We had a party scheduled for later that day. April was supposed to spend the night with some friends. But the party didn't happen." He looks even more tired than before.

"Where was Linda?"

"It took us a week to find her and let her know. She didn't even come to the funeral," he explains with rage in his eyes. "We buried her after you left the hospital, the same one you were in today. You got in your car soon after you found out she was dead. You crashed driving west on State Route 2."

That explains the concussion. The MRI picture they have from Mike is from that time. These cars are death traps. Still, I can't help but think what a convoluted life Mike has had so far, and now he has to kill a planet full of people on top of it. My planet.

"How did she die?"

Ravi takes another deep breath.

"She d-drowned ..." Ravi stutters. "She drowned at the west fork of the San Gabriel River."

He looks at me as if expecting something but this information doesn't mean anything to me.

"You see, if you take State Route 2 west—" Ravi tries to help me, but I interrupt him.

"Okay, I get it." I raise my voice as I swallow a sob. I've heard enough. Ravi sits closer, his eyes wide, watching me. We stay quiet for several minutes as I process the story.

"Don't you remember anything from this?" He breaks the silence. He saw my tears, so he's a little hopeful. But I'm not Mike, and no matter what he says or does, it won't make me Mike. Yes, April's story affected me but you'd have to be a monster to not be saddened by it. I'm not a monster. Not yet.

"No, I'm sorry. I'm so sorry for her death. This must've been devastating but I don't remember anything."

The moment is over. Ravi gets up and tells me he's going to sleep. I can help myself to whatever food or drink I find, and I can get reacquainted with my room and paraphernalia. He tells me to stay home the next day and not to answer the phone, especially if it's Linda.

I stay on the couch by myself with April's picture in my hand, her light green eyes haunting me.

7

IMMERSION

Ravi is gone when I wake up. It's time to get myself together. So far, I've just been an unwilling passenger on this wacky train, with no direction whatsoever, and no control over my life. That ends today.

My first decision is that I'll stop panicking like a lunatic —I learned this word from Ravi, since, you know, we don't have a moon—and stop screaming like a little girl. I can do that, at least for a day. There will be no rash decisions from now on. I'll think straight, make rational decisions, and do some research. Next, I'll buy the largest, easy-to-conceal gun I can put my hands on.

As I sit on the soft and uncomfortably small black chair in my room, I look at the monitor for several seconds. I have no idea how to use it. It doesn't answer to my touch or my voice, and the thing asked me for a password.

A funny-looking object located just below the monitor grabs my attention. Its function is obvious. It's the same device Alice used to input commands into her computer. I wish I could take a picture and send it to my friends. There are so many buttons in one place, and I have to press them in the right order to get the computer to do my bidding. This is going to take forever. At least I can read, write, and speak English. This is probably because the language centers of Mike's brain and mine are identical. But clearly we store our passwords somewhere else.

I take solace in guessing that Mike must be doing worse than me. If my assumptions are correct, he's wearing my own body on Jora. We learn how to use our biointerfaces when we're toddlers. But he didn't grow up there. He'll have to learn it from scratch.

After about half an hour of failed log-in attempts, I get hungry and go to the fridge. On it, there's a handwritten note from Ravi with my password. So the fridge is used for notes, not for food, as there's almost nothing in there. But then, these people also brush their teeth in the same place they have their toilets, so I suppose I really shouldn't be surprised.

I go back to my room with several slices of cheese rolled around dollops of peanut butter, and it tastes as good as it sounds. Delicious.

After about an hour of clumsily typing, I figure out that the thing next to the keyboard that I'd thought was a fancy antenna is actually used to move an arrow- shaped object on the monitor. In no way is this faster than our biochips, but it helps me a lot.

As I search through Mike's personal information, I find that his name—my name—is Michael Pohlt. They have multiple names here. I remember Alice saying something after her name, but I'd thought I'd misheard.

We don't have last names on Jora, and all the other information we need we can query through our biosensors, even the name itself. If two people share the same name, our brains differentiate them based on the input data. Sometimes, we assign an emotion or even smells to a person, and that information shows up in our brains before we even see each other.

For instance, one of the last things I did on Jora was to change my ex-fiancée's bio-imprint from flowery love to sewer-tinged anger, so I could act accordingly when she showed up. If you are raised with a system like this, names are secondary. Linda and April share the same last name as me—Pohlt. This is Mike's family name, then.

Ravi's last name is Chandrasekhar. It took me an hour to find out, but I made it my most important job of the day. I decided that I wouldn't ask him what his last name was since he would be even more disappointed with my lack of recall. However, I'll probably forget it later today.

Michael Pohlt is even more interesting than I thought he would be. He moonlights at the Department of Aerospace. Looks like rocket science is a hobby of his. On top of that, he's also an amateur pilot. Boy, I will disappoint so many people here. He pilots his own plane, or should I say, his flight club's airplane. It's no surprise—if they drive their cars here, it makes sense that they would also pilot their planes. Bunch of daredevils.

A picture of Mike next to an impossibly large rocket sitting on its side, called Saturn V, brings my attention to Earth's space program. Unbelievable. They've put people on their moon. Clearly, Earth's way ahead of us in space exploration and weapons of mass destruction. With those types of rockets, the development of intercontinental ballistic missiles is a plus—or a minus, if you think about it.

On Jora, stockpiling missiles is useless. Our advanced computers can take them out even if a swarm of them is sent, so not much money is spent in this area of development. Here, though, they have so many they could destroy Earth many times over, with no way to stop them.

The blood drains from my face when I learn they had a world war with these modern weapons— airplanes, machine guns, tanks, artillery, even nuclear bombs. Imagine the horrors. Our last war had horses and old-style rifles, but after that, Jora soon became connected with the computer revolution. It explains why we have three hundred million more people than they do.

As for rocket science, I guess if you have a moon this close, it's an extra incentive to fly there. Having a ring of debris makes sending rockets into space harder, but we do have a few satellites in orbit, and we're sending probes to Mars soon. In fact, we were going to test a Mars rocket in about a year. It will be the farthest any man-made device will be from Jora.

Around lunchtime, I leave the apartment to look for food. There must be something out here that I like besides cheese and peanut butter, and Mike's wallet has this funny paper money. People won't believe me when I tell them that a society with paper money has been to space. It seems like one of those unbelievable plotlines you find in your below-average science fiction book. Also, I may be able to use the plastic cards he carries as currency; they do have a chip in them.

A blocky building that looks like an embassy of some kind catches my attention. Their country is represented by two large upside-down parabolas, both stamped on a red flag that flies high on a pole. The yellow twin curves, as tall as an average person, are proudly shown on the side of the building. Maybe I can gather some information there.

When I step inside, I realize my mistake. This is not the office of a foreign country. People take restaurants here too seriously. Here, I'm served a meal that's made for kings. Ravi must know this place; it's right next door. I'll bring him here to make amends. But it has to be soon. The rib sandwich is here for a limited time only, according to the signs.

While I walk, I think about my situation. There's a lot I can infer just by looking at the facts.

First, I can assume that none of my close friends have been to the gods' realm. That would be dumb. My mission would be over the first day. I mean, come on, amnesia would be the go-to excuse for any mole.

Second, I think that what Mike and I do for a living is highly relevant to completing our mission. There must be a way to destroy the planet that will make opening the portal impossible. The answer becomes obvious when I think about Mike's research. If he's right, we could create mini black holes with particle colliders. Of course, this is all hypothetical. No technology is able to handle the math needed to do that. Wait, that's not true. I should say, there's no computer powerful or fast enough on this Earth to do that. Mike could use any computer on Jora to do it, and the collider doesn't even have to be that big.

Great. Good for you, Mike!

I could do the math to see how long it'd take here, but I'm lazy, bad at physics, and I see a place that sells what looks like ice cream. Setting my frustration over Mike's good fortune aside, I duck into the ice cream shop, letting the problems swirl around my mind like the sugary confection swirls on the top of its cone.

After all that thinking and two soft-serve ice cream cones, a plan starts to form in my mind. There's no need for a gun anymore. Instead, I buy the weapons that will help me solve most of my problems—five cans of pepper spray.

8

CALTECH

After a week of resting and learning more about both this Earth and Mike, Ravi is taking the day to drive me to the Caltech campus. I'm going there so I can get Mike's things and say goodbye to his friends because his career is over.

Meanwhile, I don't have a plan about my "situation." Even if I did, it would become somewhat obvious almost immediately to whoever is looking for me. Worse, Jora may already be doomed. So I'm not the most fun person to be around at the moment. I'm surprised Ravi's still my friend after all my outbursts.

"In a way, I feel like I'm paying a debt to you," Ravi says, as he almost hits a gigantic car in the middle of what can only be described as a stampede of them. I don't understand why they have these huge vehicles but only one person inside. Is the rest of the car just for protection? They certainly need it, driving the way that they do.

"You taught me everything about football. You took me to a San Francisco game when they played Seattle in their new stadium. You even set me up on a blind date that day. It was me, you, Linda, and Hanna. We had the best time."

This past weekend, we watched San Francisco play Arizona. Mike's a fan of San Francisco but they're having a bad year. Or so Ravi says. There's nothing like this on Jora. The most famous sport consists of two squads of nine people trying to get a ball in the opposite team's net. You can only use your feet, so we also call it football.

"San Francisco won that game by a point when Seattle missed a last-second field goal. It was awesome!" He grins while honking at one of his road enemies, flipping them that special hand signal where you keep your middle finger up. I'm not certain what it means but I can guess.

"Our dates were a disaster, though. Linda was already acting distant, and Hanna and I had a big fight about politics. You should've told me about that beforehand. Judging by her upbringing, I never would've guessed she's a—" Ravi stops mid-sentence and pushes on a foot pedal. The car brakes hard and we're thrown forward against our seatbelts. The people behind him honk. He almost ran the red light. Again.

"That was close. Sorry about that," he apologizes. He's not trying to kill me. He's not trying to kill me. I repeat the phrase to myself over and over.

"Anyway," he continues, "I feared the return flight that day. Fortunately, Hanna and Linda decided to fly together, and you spent the whole flight explaining the rules of the game. I was hooked."

After we park, we take a set of empty boxes with us and walk toward Mike's building. It's a bright, sunny day, and there are bicycles everywhere. It almost never rains in Los Angeles, and if you have a bike here, it's easy to go anywhere. At least, that's what my research on the computer said.

"I don't get all those penalties. How can you be flagged for unnecessary roughness? All the roughness seemed necessary," I argue. Ravi just shakes his head. This either means no or that he's disappointed with something. I'm going with the latter. The head shake has a different meaning where I come from. There, it means someone is soliciting no-strings-attached sex. For a day or so, I'd thought that people here were really outgoing. Luckily, there are many other fast food chains I can still go to, although none of them have rib sandwiches.

Parking is at a premium here, and it takes forever for us to walk across the parking lot. If they had self- driving cars, they could have just dropped us off and driven away. Only a few of us own special vehicles to tow or carry loads. The rest are considered public, which means we can pick up any car, go home, and the next day, hop into a different one.

We finally get to a modest building with a small flight of stairs by a large tree. These structures are not as majestic as I thought they'd be. They're big, cumbersome, gray boxes with ugly windows. This is supposed to be one of the places where Earth does its most advanced science projects but it pales in comparison to their football stadiums.

Once we're inside, lots of people come to say hi and goodbye. Some even have tears in their eyes. Mike is the youngest assistant professor to ever work here. It's like I'm at my own funeral, and I'm being forced to get up from the coffin and shake hands with my grieving friends. I can't wait to get out of here and go back to just being paralyzed by fear.

Mike's office reminds me of his bedroom. It's bare, well-organized, and functional. As soon as we get there, I close the door. I hope to avoid chatting with anyone else, but people keep coming in, trying to talk to Ravi and me.

Everyone wishes me the best while eyeing Ravi. I'm right here, and I can see you, damn it! They move on from Mike's amnesia and start discussing physics. Unfortunately, it's all gibberish to me.

As we pack Mike's few things in boxes, one more person comes to the door. I'm starting to get annoyed. My career is over. I know. Just leave me alone.

"Hello, Mike," a tall, red-haired man says, interrupting us. "How are you doing?" His gaze drops to where I'm holding a picture of Mike and April. I'll save it for Mike, just in case he survives this.

"Hi," I reply. Curiously enough, he doesn't look straight into my eyes, approaching Ravi instead. Maybe he's hiding something. I get it. Mike went nuts and doesn't remember anything. Let's just hope he's not planning to kill us all.

"Uh. I'm Dr. David Schneider. I'm sorry you're not feeling well. We're all rooting for you to come back." He looks down. His hairline is receding, and he looks like he's in his forties.

"Thanks. But it'll take a long time before that happens." Ravi doesn't seem at all bothered by David's odd behavior.

"Nah, you'll be back to your old self in no time, I'm sure!" David consoles me, almost looking at me. "This is just an extended vacation." He laughs.

I say nothing, because I don't know who this person is.

"Mike, uh, you and I were working together in an experiment at a particle accelerator near Geneva, in Europe." David prompts me. Yes, I read about it—they call it the LHC. I remain quiet as I watch him.

"This type of collider is used to smash atoms together so we can study the result and test our theories." He fidgets and glances at Ravi. No one speaks for a moment. He looks directly at me for the first time. "Uh...an atom is—"

"That's okay, I know what atoms are." I sigh. I'm sure if I waited long enough, he'd end up explaining physics from scratch. They must be puzzled at my type of amnesia. I know some things, but I don't know a lot of others. It's almost like I have no amnesia at all, and Mike was replaced by another person.

David comes into the room, still distracted, looking around. I'm not sure if he's upset because of the situation, or if he's just figuring out what he can steal for his office, like a vulture.

"I thought that Mike's—I mean, my research was about mini black holes."

He smiles at me, a flash of amusement crossing his face.

"No, you were doing that on your own time." He opens and closes a few books, but doesn't really pay attention to them. "You have to have tenure here to do research in what you really like." He reads the side of yet another book. "You're the best of us, but you still have to start from the bottom like everyone else."

We keep packing Mike's things—mostly heavy books made of real paper. Since he wasn't much of a hoarder, we'll only need about three boxes. His whole life and research are stored on remote servers on a "cloud" that I can access from anywhere.

"As for your real job," David continues, "I'm taking over for you. It will take way longer for me to finish the project on my own, so I hope you can come back to it once you feel better."

David glances at me, then turns to Ravi.

"By the way, I'm flying to New York at the end of the week."

"Are you going to RNL?" asks Ravi, all of a sudden interested in what David's saying. I wish people would stop using acronyms. It's disrespectful to people with amnesia and impostors.

"Yes, that's the point," David acknowledges. "Why, do you want me to do something?"

Ravi looks at me, as if asking permission for something. I nod—which means yes here—but I have no idea what he wants from me. Unspoken communication is the hardest to learn. Ravi drops a book called "The Rest of Physics," authored by Mike, into his box, and walks toward the door.

"Wait here. I need to grab something," Ravi tells David.

While David waits, he helps me pack. As we work together, I can see that he's a real friend. He slowly tries to make eye contact once in a while. He, Ravi, and Mike must be close, but I'm a stranger to him. Clearly, David's worried about Mike. I'm bad at judging people—just ask my ex-fiancée—but even I can tell he's concerned.

"Mike." He finally breaks the silence. "I want you to know that you helped revive my career. If it weren't for you, I'd just be teaching."

David's avoiding my gaze again. He grabs a pack of four books from the shelf, storing them in the third box, and stacks them neatly by their sizes.

"You brought a spark that reignited my research. You're a great friend."

He stops what he's doing for a moment and puts his shaking hands on my shoulders, forcefully looking at me. I wince. My right hand goes inside my pocket, where I left my mace.

"Let me tell you something, Mike. If you need anything —anything at all—from me, please let me know. I'll do everything I can to help you." I let go of the pepper spray in my pocket, relieved. He's not trying to kill me.

"Thanks, David." This interaction reminds me of what happened with Dr. Alice, when she was puzzled because I didn't call her Doctor. "I mean, thanks, Dr. David."

David shakes his head vigorously and moves away from me, going back to his weird self. He grabs and opens a book that was already stored in a box.

"No, Mike. Don't call me Doctor. Just David." He eyes the book as if he's talking to it, not me. "Remember, we're friends!" He laughs, and I finally understand. This means Dr. Alice is not my friend.

Ravi comes back with a fat brown envelope, giving it to David.

"Here you go," he says. "Please deliver this for me."

"I certainly will." David grabs the envelope and grins at Ravi.

"It's not what you're thinking, you dirty old man," he complains. "This is for research."

"Research, sure! Why don't I ever hear about this so-called research?" David laughs, and Ravi's eyebrows rise. He's a different person when talking with Ravi.

"I'm sorry, Ravi. Geez, it's not like it's the end of the world." He looks down at the floor again.

Ravi rolls his eyes as he closes one of the boxes with some kind of "duck" tape. Meanwhile, David looks at his phone.

"Well, I have to give a lab tour to some suits. I'll see you later," David says, leaving the room before he finishes his sentence.

After about an hour, Mike's office is empty and almost everything is in boxes, except his mini-fridge, and we take two trips to get all his things in our car.

"Ravi, would you mind if I go back to the building and look around? I want to see it one last time. It may even refresh my memory."

"No problem. I'll wait for you in my office."

An idea is forming in my head, and I need to take a closer look at their technology. I may not be a physicist, but I can help them in other ways.

9

DEAL

My fear of impending doom has dwindled a bit and I'm finally starting to work on a plan that'll help me stay sane. There's no way Mike will be able to destroy Jora anytime soon no matter how smart he is, and he's probably having as much difficulty adjusting there as I am here. One does not simply destroy a planet overnight.

My first goal in all this mess is to stay alive. Despite everything, I still like myself a lot; I can be entertaining at parties. And to achieve this, I have to beat Mike to the finish line and complete the mission, even if it takes years. Eventually I'll have to return to the hypersphere to gather more information.

I don't want to go back there but there's no other way around it. I must also do it without being seen by Jane and her friends, so I can't go back there before I find a way to keep myself safe while on Earth and in the hypersphere.

It's been three weeks since I visited Caltech. During this time, I bought a lot of stuff. For an outsider—or Ravi—it may look like the early onset of an engineer's midlife crisis. My room in our apartment is overflowing with electronic gadgets; tanks of liquid nitrogen, oxygen, and helium; sensors; probes; batteries; transformers; dials; headsets; infrared transmitters; walkie-talkies; a 3D printer; wire cutters; several electronic boards with lots of extra components; wine coolers; and a coffee machine.

It turns out that Ravi doesn't drink coffee—he prefers tea—and the beer they sell here is bitter. Bitter beer is an awful idea; no wonder they're so behind in computer technology. I now have almost everything I need, except a cat. I miss Bebe. My hope is that Mike is taking good care of her.

I'm also lucky in that Mike's financial situation is stable. He had a great job at Caltech as a professor and researcher, and almost never had time to spend anything. I mean, come on, he's a professor who lives with a roommate. Also, both his parents died in an airplane crash when he was ten, leaving him a considerable amount of money. It was, until now, largely untouched. I don't have any moral qualms about using it.

I bought goggles and fire extinguishers after the incident two weeks ago. Ravi almost moved out after that but he ended up staying once I'd apologized profusely. He also asked me several times what I was doing with all this equipment. I didn't want to say anything until I had something interesting to show him. This is not helping our friendship.

In any case, today is the day I start the first part of my plan. Since Ravi is avoiding me, because of the incident, I use an app on my phone to get someone to drive me to the hospital. Soon a driver shows up in an ugly white car with no seatbelts. Crazy people.

When I arrive, I ask for Dr. Alice in the reception area. I

don't have an appointment but I'm sure she'll make time for me. She's been calling me these last few weeks, and I'm getting worried.

I'm told to wait in the lounge area they call a "waiting room," and I settle myself as best I can in the uncomfortable chairs placed in orderly rows. They have many brochures to entertain patients and I flip idly through them. There is one about contraceptives and sexually transmitted diseases, but to my dismay, no one in the waiting room is willing to answer some perfectly valid questions.

After I learn everything I never wanted to know about vaccinations, end-of-life options, Alzheimer's disease, brain tumors, multiple and lateral sclerosis, concussions, epilepsy, strokes, heart attacks, and Parkinson's disease, my left eye begins to twitch. I'm almost sure it's a disease I just learned called myasthenia gravis. At this moment, the receptionist calls me, and I'm told to go to Dr. Alice's office. I marvel at this stroke of luck and make a mental note to ask her about my new, serious condition.

She's already waiting for me when I step inside her office.

"Hello, Dr. Alice."

"Hello, Dr. Mike." She snickers at me, and we shake hands. "The receptionist told me you were harassing people in the waiting area."

Like the other time we were here, she sits in her fancy chair behind the desk, where she can lean back comfortably. I slide into one of the plain ones just in front of it. Maybe this is some type of power play.

"Sorry, I was only asking if anyone there uses withdrawal as a contraceptive method. It's very stupid."

Alice laughs. "Sexuality is not something that people discuss often, especially with strangers."

Her office has a large window where we can see the famous California blue sky above some ugly apartment buildings. If I had been here at night the first time, I might have seen the moon before I went outside with Ravi.

"Well, it's their loss." And Jane said I was prudish. This is a whole planet of prudes.

My experience today is different from the first time I was here. A month ago, everything felt off, and I was in denial. I still had not accepted the idea of genocide. Now, I'm in the wishful-thinking stage.

"I heard you have a proposal for me," she starts, getting straight to the point. She's busy—I get that. As far as I know, she left someone open somewhere to come here and talk to me.

"Yes, I do." I nod. "You may use my brain scans with a few conditions."

She puts her left hand on the desk to straighten herself while spinning a pen in her right hand. This is not going to be cheap.

"Of course. Go ahead."

"My first condition is that you wait two years to publish your paper. When you do, you tell people you acquired those scans from someone from another country who wants to remain anonymous."

Very few people can hide their emotions, and Alice is no exception. She takes a couple of seconds to reply, squinting at me.

"Wait a minute. You know something. You have to tell me. I can publish this paper with those scans without your authorization."

My left eye twitches again, and I fidget. I think she's bluffing, but I don't know for sure.

"But this is something that can change our lives," she

continues. "If you know something, you must tell me. If people can manipulate brains like that, can you imagine the diseases we could cure? We wouldn't need half the brochures you read today." The pen spinning stops, and she moves it between her fingers instead. I wonder if she's a surgeon.

"Here's the thing, Dr. Alice," I say, rubbing my eye. "I do know something. My memory is coming back a little." I lie. "I'm part of a dangerous project for the United States government."

This is going to be good. I practiced it several times in front of the mirror this week. "It's so secret that not even the president knows about it." I move closer to her. She stays behind her desk, tensing up. "There are certain people that cannot see this information. Not yet. If they do, we'll all be in danger."

"What are you saying? This is some kind of spy game?"

I pause. A spy program is way more likely than the fake story about aliens I'd prepared. In fact, you know what? I change my mind. I like her explanation better. I'm going with that.

"Yes. The government wants to create spies who can talk like native speakers. I volunteered for the project." This makes perfect sense considering the areas of the brain that are affected. "So you see," I continue, "if you publish those pictures, they'll kill us. Of course, I'll be killed first." In truth, I want her to feel guilty, just in case she does it anyway. It'd be a small bit of revenge, since she'll never know why they actually killed me. Nice plan, I think, smiling to myself. "But you'll probably be next."

She blinks, looking a little pale, and her pen drops to the table as she misses one of its turns.

"But...this makes no sense! Why would it be okay to publish it two years from now?"

Alice has a good point. Damn it. I didn't think this through. In hindsight, I should've told the alien story. It would have been easier to explain—she'd be able to publish once the aliens are gone. Instead, I'm digging myself into a hole.

Stalling, I stand and walk around to stretch my legs, trying to think.

"Because...two years from now..." I pause, stumbling on my words. My mind is blank. I don't know what to say. The special mental state, where I can act and think faster than anyone, doesn't work when I lie. Meanwhile, Alice squints at me again. I clear my throat before I continue, gaining some time.

Finally, I know exactly what to say.

"Because, in two years, a lot of people will know about it, but I'll make sure you're the first to publish. When you do, others will confirm your findings with their own information." I grin again. That was close.

Alice sighs.

"Okay. Let's pretend that what you just told me is true. Even though it seems like you made this up on the spot. How would you guarantee that I'd be the first one to publish it?" She grabs the pen and starts fiddling with it again.

Clearly, she doesn't give me much credit. Why would I create this story on the spot?

"In this business, there are no guarantees," I confide in a low voice, feeling like a secret agent. "But I do have my sources. I'll know when it's safe for you to publish. Besides, it's better to be safe, than sorry."

She glowers at me. "Mike, are you threatening me?"

I laugh, nervously. "No, Dr. Alice. Far from it. But others wouldn't be so kind. I'm not kidding; my life is in your hands."

We both stay quiet for a long moment, and then she takes a deep breath. I think I have her.

"Okay," she says. "What you're saying seems very far-fetched but the whole situation is extraordinary."

It's my turn to breathe deeply. I did it. I'm a master of manipulation. She rubs her forehead with her left hand. The pen spins for several seconds, mesmerizing me, as she considers my proposal.

"You have to answer one question first," she says finally. "How did they do it?"

I look down and say, "I don't know. This change must've happened over several years."

That's the first time today that I'm being honest. She nods. And, against all odds, she seems to buy my story.

"But how did you learn about the spy thing?"

"Well, soon after I left the hospital, I began investigating. I found a few notes and made some calls. People didn't like that. And here I am." This is the craziest lie I have ever told anyone, and it's so implausible it makes me cringe. How am I going to get away with it?

She squirms in her chair, shifting positions, pondering what I just said.

"What else, Mike? You told me you had other conditions."

"Yes," I say, happy that we're moving on. "My second condition is that I want a full digital copy of the MRI scans."

Alice thinks on it for several minutes, biting her pen. To be honest, she has no choice. I hold all the cards. Well, except the MRI scans; she has those.

"All right, we have a deal. I still don't believe you, but I agree to your conditions." She pauses and levels a serious stare at me. "But Mike, I have a condition of my own." She bites her lip before continuing. "You'll have to tell me what happened here at some point. And when that time comes, I want the truth."

10

HARRY

It's late at night and Ravi is asleep. Unlike me, who works late hours and has no discipline, Ravi always goes to sleep early, at about the same time every day. Based on what he tells me, this is another difference between Mike and me.

Most of my work happens in the living room. My own room is too small for me to accomplish anything. I try to clean it up every day when I stop working, but often, I don't have the time to do a good job. Ravi and I fight, a lot. We're not the best roommates.

However, this doesn't bother me anymore. After several sleepless nights, I'm done. I finally have a working prototype in front of me. Seeing the final product—or, I should say, the barebones prototype— gives me the impression that it wasn't that hard, though it certainly didn't feel that way when I started.

There are two reasons why Jora is more advanced in computer technology. The first is that we had an early start with mechanical computers when electricity was not yet ubiquitous. The second is that it took us longer to go digital.

At the time we created our first computers, we didn't have the right components and the right technology to work on digital circuits. When we finally were able to make digital parts, our analog computers were already taking over the world. Thus, the technology there is mainly made up of biochips and synthetic brain cells.

I hear something from Ravi's room and look up. Strange, he's never up this late, and it's impossible to wake him up. The neighbors complained about the noise a few times, but Ravi was never the culprit. I wonder if he's feeling well. He got himself unbanned from Mumbai Cave, and he's been there many times in the past few days. I warned him that eating there was not a good idea. But for some reason, people on this Earth don't value unsolicited advice.

With no further clue echoing down the hall from Ravi's room, I shrug and turn back to admiring my prototype.

Analog computers have a big advantage over digital computers. Brains are analog, and our machines are so advanced that they have the brain capacity of most animals. Some are even said to be human-like, conscious, though there's no consensus. Unlike animals, they're trained to do specific tasks, so they don't waste time looking for food or a mate, with some embarrassing—although some would say awesome— exceptions.

Unfortunately, I don't have any specialized tools with me, of course, but I can make and train a simple prototype. Which is exactly what I've done. I've created the proof of a concept.

Ravi comes into the room and sits on the couch, wearing extremely short red briefs with the San Francisco logo, and a ragged white t-shirt. He grunts, pressing his stomach with his hands, clearly feeling a lot of pain. We eye each other, and he makes a grimace at me, which highlights his three-day old beard.

I have a good idea what he thinks I'm going to say. Any other day, he'd be right. I keep saying that he should stop eating at that restaurant. But not today. We have bigger things to discuss.

"You finished your toy," he grumbles, keeping his hands on his belly. He's lost all the respect he once had for Mike. He told me that one day while drunk, including a few colorful and offensive swear words as well.

"I did. And I'm glad you're awake. I want you to see something."

A small, remote-controlled truck stands out in the middle of the room, a bunch of circuits and wires on top of it, and two little cameras that look like little white eyeballs are mounted on each side.

"Is that all? This new hobby of yours really sucks. You made the truck uglier." He grunts again in pain.

"Just wait and see."

I pick up a metallic, spherical object the size and shape of a golf ball. Nothing happens. Seconds later, the truck comes to life and runs closer to us. This startles Ravi. There was no visible or audible command whatsoever. I smirk. This is the reaction I was looking for from him. The truck did its thing by itself. It seems to be alive, its eyes tracking the metal ball in my hand.

"His name is Harry. You know, after my nickname." It's weird that no one ever calls me that, though.

As Ravi gives me a confused look, I lift the ball and move it from side to side; Harry's camera eyes follow it. Without warning, I throw it across the room. Harry's eyes track the motion, but nothing else happens. He stays in the same place, as if waiting for something. Then, just like before,

Harry accelerates out of nowhere and goes after the ball, avoiding obstacles on the way.

In less than three seconds, he finds it and grabs it through the electromagnets in his bumper, though he still doesn't bring it back. Ravi seems to be enjoying this, and neither of us say anything as we watch the modified truck. The show is far from over.

I hold my breath while we wait.

Finally, Harry comes back to life by himself and brings the ball back. He turns the electromagnets off and the ball falls by my feet.

"Harry's brain is an analog computer," I say.

Ravi seems to be more interested in my little truck now, but he's not impressed yet. Granted, it's harder to build analog systems but he's seen digital computers do things like this before.

"How did you control it?"

"I didn't control him, exactly. He drove himself."

"What? Are you saying it—he—has a mind of his own?" He eyes Harry, incredulous. "How'd you do it?"

"I trained him. I just have to let him know when to do the steps I want him to do. He learned to detect the ball, to avoid obstacles, and to go after it. He responds to my commands." It's simple once you know how to do it. The problem is getting the components; I had to make some from scratch. And I cheated—I still used lots of digital parts.

"This is unbelievable, Mike. Unbelievable! I shouldn't be surprised, since you've never ceased to amaze me. But this last month ..." He trails off. "Can I try it?"

I get up and sit next to him. So far, so good.

"Sure, but we have to recalibrate him for you. Put this on." I take off my headset and give it to him. His eyes narrow.

"Is this voice-controlled? I thought it was just on. I didn't hear you saying anything."

In hindsight, I should've removed the microphone from the headset. I can see why he thinks I was giving Harry voice commands. But I just didn't have time to remove it. I say nothing, and he grabs it and puts it on his head. Picking a circuit board up off the floor, I switch the first four buttons.

"I'm going to ask you to think four different words. The words are 'Harry,' 'Go,' 'Back,' and 'Stop.' Are you ready?"

"Say what? You're kidding."

"Trust me. Just do what I say."

Ravi seems to have forgotten his stomach ache, as he leans back on the couch, unconvinced. This is going to be good.

"Okay. I'm ready."

I pull the first dial up and wait for the board to be ready.

"On the count of three, think of the name 'Harry.' Ready? One, two, and three!"

After that, I pull the dial down and flip the first switch. Ravi bobbles his head a little, but nothing seems to happen. It feels anticlimactic, but it is what it is.

"Great, let's do it again," I say.

Where I come from, our biochips connect us to each other wirelessly, and we can share images, videos, data, and even emotions. I can be in the middle of nowhere and be in contact with my loved ones. In fact, we can watch the same movie at the same time on opposite sides of the planet. It's an incredibly connected life, where you can work, love, and commit infidelity anywhere you are.

Here, we only have this crappy headset.

We continue with the three other words, repeating the process several times for each command. After that, Harry's calibrated, his mind fine-tuned to respond to Ravi.

"This should be good enough," I say. I hand Ravi the little ball and move farther away from him. Then, I turn yet another switch before I drop the board on top of the little table. Ravi waits. "Ready? Think the name 'Harry.'"

He looks at me with a puzzled expression, but does as I say. Harry comes to life and moves closer to Ravi, who, in turn, searches my hands as if trying to find another device controlling the truck. I have nothing of the sort. Harry can read Ravi's mind. The truck stops in front of Ravi, his eyes watching the ball in Ravi's hand as if he were an obedient little dog, waiting for his turn.

Seconds later, Ravi throws the ball and it bounces into the kitchen. Harry does a quick turn in place as he follows it with his cameras, but he doesn't go after it, not yet. He waits for his master's command.

"Now, think the word 'Go,'"

Like before, Harry accelerates and searches for the ball. This time, though, he didn't see where it landed, so he takes longer to find it. But sure enough, he finds it and connects the tiny ball to his bumper. Harry comes back to the living room before I can tell Ravi to think the word 'Back.' I smile. Ravi got it.

Ravi is stunned speechless. I shouldn't know that much about computers. Indeed, no one on Earth should be able to do what I did. In my defense, though, Mike is supposed to be clever, so there's a perfectly plausible explanation for what Ravi saw. And letting him think that is way better than using words like "alien," "gods," and "genocide" to explain.

I let what just happened sink for a while, waiting for Ravi's reaction. It doesn't take long.

"You created a synthetic dog, Mike. A dog! I can't under-stand ..." He sits there, dumbfounded.

"Not really. This is all he does. He doesn't love you," I joke. "Yet."

Ravi kneels down next to Harry, looking at the components, and for a split second, I think he's going to pet him. He must be considering all the possibilities. This is a radical change in how the people on this Earth think of computers.

Time for my sales pitch.

"Ravi, I have a proposal for you." He turns his attention to me. "But first, I want to apologize for this past month." Ravi looks away, avoiding my eyes. "I'm not Mike anymore. The Mike you know is dead. And you've known that for a long time, I think. Something changed me in the accident."

"It's fine, Mike. I should've been more understanding." He looks at Harry. "Still, you're doing great, considering everything."

I sigh. At least we have this understanding now. I'm not Mike; I'm a different person, though he doesn't know the extent of it.

"Ravi, what you saw here is just the beginning. I can make circuits that can solve problems several hundreds of times faster and infinitely more accurately than the fastest and best computers you—I mean, we— have now. What you see here is not a dog." I point at Harry. "He's the next computer revolution."

I wish people could applaud me. Perhaps I should've used the word "magical." I bet no one's used that when introducing new tech.

"And I want the two of us to lead this revolution."

Ravi stands up and crosses his arms, reflecting on my words, looking concerned. This is a lot to absorb. I get it.

"But how? I don't know anything about...this." He gestures toward Harry.

"And I don't know anything about particle physics. But

you do." I stand up in front of him to make it clear that I'm serious about this. "I saw your equipment at Caltech. We need customers. We start small, enhancing those computers with our hybrids. After that, the other physics departments, laboratories, and particle colliders will begin to buy them. In a year, we'll be selling them to other institutions, governments, large companies." I don't mention the military industry but it's implied.

He looks at Harry, who keeps moving his eyes and wheels until he suddenly stops. Ravi must've thought the command, "Stop." His last doubts seem to be vanishing. If I had been controlling Harry with a remote, there's no way I could have known the exact moment he ordered Harry to stop. Good. Trust, but verify. Did I mention my ex-fiancée already?

"And in five years, we'll be all over the world," I say.

"So, you want to be the next Bill Gates?" He smiles.

"Yes!" I reply, grinning, though I have no idea who Bill Gates is.

Ravi paces around the room, thinking about it. If he joins me, he won't be an academic anymore. It's a tough decision. I'm asking him to be a salesman, to help me design these new, specialized computer brains. This means no more teaching or research for him.

"I need some time to process this," he tells me. I understand. It's not easy for him to wake up with a stomachache and have to make a decision that will change his whole life.

"You don't need to make up your mind today. Take your time. I won't be going anywhere."

I feel a pang of guilt. What he doesn't know is that analog circuits have another interesting property. Even when mass-produced, each circuit's different. Therefore, you can't tell everything it'll do, unless you're the one who made it. I just need one backdoor to take over any system. They'll have no idea or means to find out—not for another ten years, at least. I'm like a supervillain.

None of this makes me any happier, though. I hate that I must do this. But I'm fulfilling my first goal— staying alive, no matter what it takes, no matter how many feelings I hurt. Still, betrayal is an art. My ex- fiancée would be proud of me.

"I just have one request of you, Ravi," I finally say. "Please, don't ever call Harry ugly again."

PART II

One Year Later

Love is being a willing prisoner;
Love is serving the one who beats us;
Love is to be loyal to those who kill us.

— SONETOS, LUÍS DE
CAMÕES

11

PARIS

I look out the window as the jumbo jet gets closer to Charles de Gaulle. A thunderstorm approaches from the south, but for now, the sun is shining and a towering structure I recognize as the Eiffel tower stands out from the other buildings. This is my third time coming back from Moscow but my first going through Paris. Ravi wanted to meet me here so we could go back to New York together.

Despite my fear of human pilots, I've been in airplanes a lot lately. My first attempt to fly was in a small aircraft from Los Angeles to Sacramento. When the plane started taxiing out of the gate, I realized we were doomed and, in retrospect, maybe I shouldn't have yelled that we were all going to die. Napa Airlines won't let me near their planes anymore.

In any case, those outbursts never happened again. You can say whatever you want about me, but I'm a fighter. By sheer power of self-control, the willingness to overcome my fear, and the very potent prescription- only anti-anxiety drugs, I fly all the time.

The airplane lands with—surprisingly—no casualties.

My only plan after customs and immigration is to take a bath at the hotel. Our flight to New York is tomorrow, so we have plenty of time.

Ravi's coming back from Geneva to meet me here. He's in charge of deploying our Indiscrete computers at the Large Hadron Collider. The name Indiscrete Circuits was Ravi's idea. Digital computers only use discrete values— usually zero and one—while analog machines have a continuous range. It sounded silly at first, but it has grown on me.

You'd think that I'd love to visit Switzerland with him, but I specifically decided that I'd never set foot inside the largest collider Earth has. If there is an easy way to create a black hole to destroy Earth, it's there. That place must be swarming with people who know there's a mole trying to destroy everything. In fact, they're probably killing people preemptively, just in case, and I fear for Ravi. Nevertheless, Ravi finds it bizarre that I visit countries like Russia and China, which are outside of our sales target.

Indiscrete Circuits is so successful that he hopes we'll be able to have a fleet of small jets by the end of the year. No thanks. I'm already scared of flying commercial, and I don't trust those small things with semi-professional pilots who are still paying for their flight education. To be honest, I only trust pilots with nerves of steel who learned how to fly while under enemy attack in a war or something.

A limo takes me to a hotel at the Avenue Montaigne, near the Seine River. I was under the impression that I had already learned the ins and outs of this planet, but the rich here live in a completely different world than normal people. And this is France; it's even better in the United States. Or worse, depending on which side you're on.

My room in the hotel is huge, and I get lost in what looks

to be a vast closet while searching for the bath tub. Later, after a long and calming bath, I check my phone and realize that I may be a little late to meet Ravi downstairs. I quickly dress and go down to the lobby to wait for him. He must be here already.

Like everything else here, the lobby is majestic. The whole experience makes me feel like a king. An exquisite chandelier hangs from the ceiling, just above a large granite mandala on the floor. There are many places to sit around it, but instead, I march toward a window—or maybe a glass door—so I can see outside and enjoy myself while I wait.

Today, I'm completely relaxed, and I'm not going to feel guilty about the luxury I live in now. I hope the next few days will be pleasant, even the flight back to the States. I deserve a mini-vacation.

A woman on the one chair by the window is casually adjusting her hair, legs crossed, while looking at her phone. That's odd; I think I've met her. She's pretty, so it'll be easier to remember. This is all in the back of my mind, though, since I'm searching for Ravi. I wonder why he's late. This is not like him at all. Suddenly, an alarm goes off in my brain as I get closer to the woman. Yes, of course I remember her. Jane.

Freezing in fear, I realize I'm about to be caught. My life is in danger. She looks older, in her late twenties, but it's definitely her. Jane knows about the hypersphere, and if she glances this way, she'll definitely recognize me. My worst fears are realized when she turns her head in my direction. I must do something but I have to be discreet. Fortunately, I can think faster than anyone else. Closing my eyes, I concentrate, and time slows down in my mind.

First, I do a quick inventory of what I have. I'm wearing some nice social clothes. T-shirt and jeans are my daily

outfit but not when I'm traveling on business. I need neck-
ties, then. I hate wearing them; they make it so hard to
breathe. Why in the world did they decide that a suit and a
tie was the way to go? Really, it's so uncomfortable. And it's
even worse during summer. Today, I refused to wear one. It's
so nice outside, I opted for my preferred attire of—wait, this
isn't what I'm supposed to be thinking. Time is running out.

My phone is in my pocket, and I'm carrying a computer
tablet and its pen. Perhaps I can make a weapon out of the
pen, throw it at her. No, that'd be dumb. It would accomplish nothing, except maybe prove to her that I'm her
enemy, and that I'm stupid. Her face is already turning to
me. Do something!

Trying to act nonchalantly, I shove the tablet in front my
face but it's too late. She catches my eye for a split second as
I turn around and carefully start running like a mad man. If
I leave now, I can hop on an airplane back to the US as soon
as I get to the airport. In my haste, I hit someone just behind
me. We both fall.

No one screams—I'm getting better at that—but we
make a lot of noise. Everyone in the lobby stares at us.
Funny, the person on the floor next to me is Ravi. It turns
out he'll end up killing me, after all, though not directly.
Thanks a bunch.

"Mike, what are you doing?" he asks as I sit up. There is
still a small chance she didn't see me. If she has any
manners, she'll pretend this didn't happen and go back to
her pretty business.

"Uh...I forgot something in my room. I have to go," I lie,
panicking. We both stand up and I'm ready to flee again. He
grabs my arm before I'm able to react, and I stare at him in
disbelief.

"You can get it afterward, Mike. Let's have some tea." He

looks behind me, in Jane's direction, and nods. They're in this together. "I mean...you can get coffee, if you want," he mutters, still holding me in place.

"Are you guys okay?" I hear a female voice ask behind us. Damn it. Ravi is looking at her, but I don't look back yet.

"Hello, Jane, I want to introduce you to someone." Ravi turns me to face her.

My heart drops to the ground. It's over. How did they even meet? It doesn't matter. There's nothing left but to end this with dignity instead of punching him, trying to run, being arrested, and banned from yet another place. This is all too soon. I'm not ready to execute my plans yet.

Taking a deep breath, I glance at Ravi. I'll never forgive him for this. Jane raises one of her eyebrows when our gaze meets. She knows.

"Mike, this is Jane Engel. Jane, this is Mike Pohlt." She lifts her hand toward me. Luckily, she doesn't have a weapon —at least, not a visible one.

"Nice to meet you, Mike. I've been looking forward to talking with you." Her hand hangs suspiciously in the air, as if it were a snake ready to bite. I search my surroundings for an exit, but there's no way out, and they might have accomplices nearby.

Jane keeps her arm hanging awkwardly for a few seconds before looking back at Ravi. He shrugs and hits me hard in the back of my head, trying to kill me.

12

JANE

I don't lose consciousness, since he didn't hit me hard enough. Ravi is talking as I stare at him in shock, but it sounds like he's far away from me.

"Come on, Mike, be a gentleman. I'm sorry, Jane. He has a problem with flying. He's probably still under the influence." He smiles broadly.

Oh, I see. Ravi's hit was meant to be playful. He wasn't trying to kill me, which means he doesn't know who I really am and what I must do here. Smiling, I grab her hand and shake it, looking into her gorgeous dark eyes.

"I'm so sorry. I'm tired from my trip." Jane has her mouth open, bewildered. "Nice to meet you," I say, glaring at Ravi. I wonder why he's telling her about my phobias. We'll discuss this later. Or maybe I'll tell her he's afraid of little dogs. He's very embarrassed about this. That'll show him.

"So, you're the brains behind Indiscrete Circuits?" Jane asks. "You seem familiar. Have I seen you before?"

I try to hide a sigh of relief. She doesn't recognize me; I'm going to live. There was no mirror in the hypersphere, but I bet I don't look like Mike there.

"I'd remember meeting someone as pretty as you." I flirt, smiling. Ravi laughs, and I wonder if he and Jane are a couple. The fact that they're both here is not a coincidence.

"Don't pay attention to him. He's a dog," Ravi says.

It's funny he says that. After all, I haven't been with anyone on Earth. Ever since I learned about my grim mission, dating's been the last thing on my mind. Why would I get attached to someone if one of us is going to die? Jane is different, though. Maybe it was her visible confidence in the face of her enemies when I first met her, or the way she approached me in the hypersphere as if she owned the place.

"How do you know Ravi?" I ask as we walk back to the table. The monsieur glares at me from afar, shaking his head at the disruption.

"We've been friends for a long time," Ravi explains. "Jane is an engineer at the Rochester National Laboratory on Long Island. She was in Geneva with me, helping out with our new equipment as a consultant."

RNL was one of the first places we installed our new computers, and it's where we're all going tomorrow. Dr. David and Ravi paved the way for us there, and we couldn't have expanded so soon without their help. After we started there, and a few places in San Diego, the whole world learned about our little company.

"I'm technically your boss, then," I say.

"You wish." She scoffs at me. "We often fly there for research purposes anyway, so why not? But I wouldn't be able to afford this hotel. This is all you guys." She looks at the gorgeous pillars of the lobby.

We're about to sit when Jane walks to the main window and watches the street outside, deep in thought. There's no question about who's really the boss, so we wait. After a while, she turns and looks at us.

"Hey, how 'bout we go outside to have coffee? It's a beautiful day, and this is Paris!" I can't argue with that. Giving a final scowling glance at the monsieur, I recover my dignity and we leave the hotel.

Paris is indeed one of a kind. It's a large city, but its low-rise buildings give it the charming feel of a small town. It's my favorite place so far, aside from San Francisco and London. Maybe the fact that Jane is here and not trying to kill me will tip the scale in favor of Paris. Ah, we'll always have Paris.

"You're the famous Dr. Mike. I missed one of your seminars years ago," she says as we walk. She carries a black leather purse, hanging from her shoulder, her hand resting on top of it.

"Yeah, about that, I don't doctor as much as before. As I told Ravi, I'm a different person since the accident."

Perhaps I should not emphasize this?

After walking about two hundred meters, we find one of Paris's famous cafés. It's fancier than we expected—we need a reservation, which we obviously don't have—but Ravi manages to get us seated at an outdoor table after they realize who he is.

The café is a round structure at the corner of a triangular city block, surrounded by standard Parisian architecture. We're seated near a pair of short-trimmed green bushes and engage in the art of people-watching for a moment. It's a busy location, and in the background, Paris's entrancing language murmurs like rustling leaves. It's a shame I don't speak French.

Ravi's phone rings soon after we sit and he answers

while we search for a waiter. Jane takes this time to get her own phone out of her purse to check her messages.

"I'm sorry. I have to go back to my room to check a spreadsheet," he says as soon as he hangs up. "The guys in the valley are mixing up orders. I'll be back as soon as I can." Too bad. I want him to be nearby when I tell her about his irrational fears and have my revenge. I can't do it without him here.

"How long have you and Ravi been seeing each other?" I ask, as I watch him walk toward the hotel. Jane laughs.

"You misunderstand, Mike. We're just good friends, though we do have some history." She looks gloomy for a moment.

"How come he never told me about you?"

Jane reaches inside her purse to pick up a small, round elastic thing that she casually puts in her mouth.

"You know how Ravi is," she mumbles through the elastic band. "He's not an outgoing person. He only mentioned your company two months after you started." She gathers her hair with her hands at the top of her head as a ponytail takes form. Then, she picks the hair tie from her mouth and quickly wraps her bundle of hair with it.

"I see. So this is all a setup for our first date?" I grin, and Jane looks amused. After her hair-styling performance, she looks exactly how she did when I met her in the hypersphere.

"Ravi was right. You are terrible." She laughs.

The waiter comes, and we order pastries and coffee. People should've told me about French food earlier. It's the stuff of gods. How ignorant I was to ever think that fast food was good food. I will forever be ashamed every time I order a cheeseburger. Not that I'm going to stop.

"How did you become an engineer?" I take a big bite of a

beignet, the French version of a donut. Fried bread is the best food on Earth.

"My father was a science teacher, tinkering with stuff all the time. I was always fascinated by anything related to science," she explains. "Soon, I learned that I liked to mess with machines and electronics. I didn't like the theoretical parts; they were too abstract. I wanted to see stuff with my own eyes."

"And how did you end up at RNL?" Her face turns gloomy again.

"Well, less than two years ago, I had just finished my master's degree at the University of Michigan. I realized I might have to start a PhD and, after that, find a job as a professor somewhere. But that's not really what I liked. And then I met someone." She looks away. "He helped me get a job at RNL. And I love it there. It was the best decision I've ever made." Her face is still dark.

My mouth is in heaven as I turn from the beignet and start on my croissant. Perhaps we should open French restaurants in the States. Somebody should've thought of this already. The coffee here is also good— strong and foamy. I can't drink too much of this, though, or I won't sleep tonight.

"You had a sexual relationship with him? The man who got you the job?"

She looks at me in dismay, quickly opening and closing her mouth, but saying nothing. Right. I always forget that we don't discuss these things here. I assume she takes me for some eccentric person without boundaries, and I'm fine with that.

"We were a couple, for a while," she admits, apparently accepting my lack of apology for the direct question. "He's a scientist at the laboratory. But we're not together anymore."

The look on her face tells me they didn't end in a good way. I won't ask about that; there are levels of jerkiness, after all. We have to know each other better before I can be that rude.

"Does Ravi know him?"

"Yes. Can we stop talking about him?" She is clearly tense about this subject. It must be hard to work with your ex. I'd change jobs if I had to see my ex-fiancée each day.

"Sure. Let's talk guns, then. I didn't know an American citizen could carry weapons in France."

Jane gasps, and her hand quickly grabs her purse, as if trying to protect it from me. If I were her, I'd keep an eye on her pastries instead. I'm almost done with mine, and I'm still hungry.

"You looked inside my purse?"

"Accidentally. It's not like I'm paranoid and search for guns on people. Sorry." That is exactly what I do, though, all the time. It took me a long time to stop confusing cell phones with police interceptors from Jora.

"Enough about me," Jane says. She seems to be annoyed. "Why did you get involved with computers? You were a physicist, not a computer engineer." Instinctively or not, Jane moves her purse around, away from me. Okay, ex-boyfriends and guns are off limits. Maybe we should discuss religion and, while we're at it, politics.

"I don't know." I lie. "After the stroke, I just realized one night that we should be using analog circuits, not just digital. I decided to try it out and soon after that, I made Harry." Everyone knows about Harry at this point. He's in his third generation, and we'll start selling him as a toy soon. "The rest is, as they say, history. I never wanted this attention, but it's nice to have money to invest in computers."

Slowly, the awkwardness wears out. Jane and I chat for a full hour before Ravi comes back. We stay away from touchy subjects. We also take our time, since unlike in the US, people here like to enjoy each other's company while eating food.

"Starting tomorrow, Mike is going to spend several months with us on Long Island," Ravi says, after he orders chicken with curry and chutney, an unusual afternoon snack even for him. "Your laboratory has our most advanced technology so far." He sounds excited.

I nod at him.

"I have a few ideas I want to try. We may open something in New York State, so we can keep up with the demand," I say.

"We're also investing in security," Ravi adds, looking at Jane. "We don't want unauthorized people accessing those computers."

It's so easy for me to lie these days. Ravi thinks I'll help with security but I'll do just the opposite. My computers are Trojan horses. Yes, we'll create technology that's new to Earth but that isn't my objective. It'll be harder with Jane around, though. I'd probably already be dead if she knew who I was. If Godfather Hermes had any say in this, I bet he'd want me to kill her. 2

THE NEXT DAY, we all go together, tired and sleepy, to the airport. Last night, we went to a night club to have drinks, and Jane and I even danced. Unfortunately, dancing on Earth has almost no sexual innuendo, at least not in Paris. Sometimes I forget that I'm not on Jora. I hope I didn't embarrass her.

We board an English Airways flight that'll take us to the United States, seated in first class. Jane and I are next to each other, and Ravi is in the window seat just in front of us. Don't get me wrong; flying first class should be awesome, but in the end, it doesn't matter if you're pampered all the way they walk you to a guillotine. You still won't be thrilled about it.

A flight attendant wearing a dark business jacket, skirt, and a blue-and-red scarf startles us, appearing out of nowhere. Puzzled, we stop talking as we watch her bringing me a drink that I didn't order.

"Here's your strawberry daiquiri, Dr. Pohlt." She smiles.

My face instantly becomes red, and I stare at Ravi in disbelief. The flight attendant smile vanishes.

"I didn't ask for anything," I say, trying to hide my shame.

Jane raises her eyebrow and watches Ravi, a half-smirk forming on his mouth.

"I told her to bring it." Ravi laughs. "It's your favorite drink." He glances at Jane. "It helps him fly, if you know what I mean." He winks.

Resigned to my fate, I take the drink. Ravi will pay for this but this is not the time or the place to make a scene.

"I...I have a sensitive tongue. I like sweet cocktails."

Ravi laughs even harder at that. Since he learned that I don't like beer because it's bitter, he keeps making fun of me. According to him, daiquiris, margaritas, and other wine coolers are girly drinks. But why on Earth would someone sexualize drinks?

The flight attendant leaves us alone, and we all avoid each other's gazes for a while. Usually, I'm the one who does awkward things, but this time Ravi stepped up to the plate.

"You guys were very courageous last night. Especially you, Jane," he finally says, changing the subject. "I warned you that his style of dancing is, uh, unconventional." He tries to mimic my dance style, but ends up just bobbling his head a little.

"Shut up, Ravi. Everybody was having a great time," I say. Reluctantly, I take a sip of my stupid drink.

"Mike's right. Yes, he was clumsy when he fell on that table, and he did start a fight with that French guy over me. But other than that, everybody had fun."

As she says that, the airplane starts backing up. We're going to take off. Ravi looks at me.

"Shouldn't you be taking your pills?" he asks, nearly managing to hide his smirk. I glance at Jane, once again embarrassed. This is really bad timing. I forgot to talk with him about not sharing my phobias.

"Not today. It's time for me to learn how to handle this." Jane looks elsewhere, pretending that she didn't hear it or that she doesn't care. I know it's stupid, but I feel ashamed taking the pills in front of her.

While I search for videos of little dogs on my phone, Jane reaches into her purse, absentminded, and pulls out another hair tie to redo her ponytail. Her gun's still inside her bag, in plain view. When I look up at her, my mouth opened wide, I realize that she's holding the elastic band with one hand and locking gazes with me. She knows I saw it. Perhaps she was carrying it illegally in France—the weapon, not the hairband—but how the hell did she manage to board an international flight and still keep her weapon?

Jane glances at Ravi, who's checking on his own phone, unaware of what just happened. She shuts her purse and looks away. This is not going to be a fun flight.

13

RNL

I spend the weekend at a hotel in Upton, New York. Just like the Rochester National Laboratory, it's located at the eastern side of Long Island. The hotel is not as fancy as the others I've been on this trip but it's a cozy and functional. To be honest, it's a change for the better. I was tired of feeling like royalty, and now I can act like a normal person again.

It's early Monday when a limo takes me to RNL. This is something else that'll have to change. Next time, I'll ask Ravi to send a normal car with a driver. I'm tired of acting like I'm the head of a state. No more limos.

When I'm inside the ring structure of the RNL's collider, I'm astonished at its size. In my mind it was tiny, because everything is miniscule when compared to the one they have in Europe, but this place is huge.

A white corridor curves around a series of green metal panels that look like covered roller coaster wagons on their side, all attached to the inner wall. Nearby, two gauges next to a black phone immediately make me wonder what type of call people are expected to make there.

Today I'll be replacing the power circuits with several small computer brains that will make quick, autonomous decisions faster than any human and better than any digital software. If this works, we can add more like that, and then we can focus on the larger ring. Even if I disregard the attempt to destroy the planet, which is my underlying motivation, I'm still excited by the project as a whole. It took a while for Indiscrete Circuits to finish building and setting up two-hundred fifty analog machines but it'll be worth it.

Looking around a large pipe housing cables near the top of the ring, I take some notes. There's no way I can reach it without a ladder. This place is so large we can drive a truck through here. As I think about how to reach up there, a voice from behind me brings me back to reality. For a moment, I'm startled.

"Mike?"

I turn around and see Jane and two others watching me.

"I almost didn't recognize you with your hard hat," she says. Jane wears a dark skirt with leathery shoes and no jewelry, looking business-like. She's in stark comparison with my workman's jeans and t-shirt. Women's dresses always confuse me. It makes way more sense for men to wear them due to, you know, our anatomy. Despite this, she looks sexier than ever.

"The security guard threatened to arrest me if I didn't put it on. Everyone has to wear them but it seems you guys are exempt."

They're the ones who give the orders; they can do whatever they want.

"I didn't realize you'd be doing the work yourself, Dr. Pohlt." A short-haired, tall man joins the conversation. He seems to be in his late twenties. "I thought you'd just be supervising." He's wearing a loose blue shirt and hilarious khaki shorts. Except that, for some reason, he has a thick mustache. It's so odd.

"This is...beneath you," he says with a strong accent. After a year, I can tell the difference between the ways people speak English. And then it hits me. He's the one who was with Jane as we watched an Earth being destroyed. I glance at Jane, smirking, and she returns my gaze with a dirty look.

"Please, call me Mike," I reply. I hate last names. "The technology is in its infancy still. I like to be on top of research and deployment, since not even my engineers are aware of what's coming. Anyway, I'm sorry, I don't know any of you."

"Yes, right, I apologize. My name is Dr. Frederico Pezzo." I shake his hand with a half-smile. So, she had an Italian boyfriend.

"I'm Dr. Joshua Davis," says the third man. If Jane and Frederico know the messengers, Joshua must know them as well. Small world. We could have a barbeque and they could kill me just before Monday football starts.

After the introductions, Joshua speaks.

"We want to understand your work better. We're particularly interested in how safe it is." He's a large black man, dressed more like me than the others. A few strands of white show in his otherwise dark hair. If I had to guess, I'd say he's forty.

"What do you mean?" I ask, feigning ignorance.

"Dr. Pohlt, I'm going to be frank. Is it possible for someone to hack our computers in any way?" Joshua peeks at my notebook and looks around at the machinery. Frederico steps back, giving him space, and everyone stays quiet for a moment. He must be in charge here. "Can the components be damaged? These accelerators are powerful. You can easily hurt people with them if they're mismanaged," he finishes, adjusting his glasses.

Instinctively, I hold the notebook closer to my chest.

"I see your point. An attacker could damage and disable it for years, yes."

There's no need to mention the possibility of creating black holes. The idea is preposterous with Earth's current knowledge and computers, and I hope they don't realize how Mike's black hole research could work perfectly with my computers in a collider.

"But I can guarantee that I designed and verified every single circuit I brought here personally. It's impossible for anyone to take them over," I assure them, taking a step back, away from Joshua.

"Yes, and we trust you," says Jane. "But we also want a way to disable everything by ourselves. We need a kill button." She moves her index finger down as if turning an honest-to-god light switch, almost making me laugh.

"Don't worry. There's a way to disable them all at once," I say.

Of course, they could always cut the power regardless of the consequences to the equipment or people if they have a good enough reason—like, say, saving the world. But I'll be adding an extra power circuit as we get close to turning everything on, just in case I need it.

We chat for half an hour about the technical details. Since I was already immersed in the machine when they arrived, I'm able to point out to them where the brains will be installed and how they're going to improve the accuracy of the collider. My plan is to update one per day. As I get used to the process, I want to install at least four analog brains a day, maybe five. Ravi will help me, and even David may do a few when he flies in.

The trio looks more relaxed after my explanations, and let me continue installing the brains. Jane stays behind when the other two leave.

"Come have lunch with us. We have a lot to talk about," she says.

"I'll meet you there," I reply. "By the way, where's Ravi?" He isn't one to be late.

She glances around the green panels before replying, her face clouding for a moment.

"He hurt his leg last night. He'll be in late today."

I blink, confused, and pull my cell phone to check for any messages. There are none. Why would Ravi tell her that and not me?

"He didn't want to bother you on your first day here." She appears to read my mind somehow. Awesome.

"Thanks for the info. It'll be nice to chat with you. And, of course, Dr. Frederico," I say with a snide grin.

A look of offense crosses her eyes, and then, with a quick punch to my arm, she turns around and leaves.

14

PROTECTORS

It's the weekend, and I've been at RNL for two weeks. There is no creative job left to be done; all remaining work is mostly manual. Someone just has to do it. Therefore, there's no reason to postpone it anymore. It's time for me to go back to the hypersphere.

I told Ravi and Jane I'd spend the day hiking in the county park. To be honest, I was a little bit hurt that neither one of them volunteered to come with me, even though I was lying. Ravi's going to New York on business, and Jane will bike with her friends in Rocky Point.

The reason I plan to do this during the day is to avoid Jane. There must be people from all over the world, and they may do all kinds of day and night shifts up there, but my goal is to not meet her the moment I get there, at least. I have no idea who or how many of others will be there.

There is one problem, though—I don't know exactly how to do it. You know, how to go there. Hermes and Iris forgot to mention that part. I may have to spend a couple of days trying to figure this one out.

As I close my eyes, my heart rate goes through the roof.

When I built my analog computers, I was isolated from whatever's happening up there. It's been more than a year, now, and I have no idea what to expect. Will Mike, the real Mike, be there?

According to Hermes, the hypersphere is a place we go when we're asleep, and we must go willingly. So, with my eyes shut, I concentrate and think, Take me back to the hypersphere. I keep thinking this sentence over and over but it doesn't work. This is silly. We should have some kind of instruction manual. Stupid messengers.

I open my eyes and jerk, startled to find myself in a featureless white room, lying on a bed-like platform. It worked. A disk-like door is open to my right, waiting for me, and the only reason I notice it is because of the subtle shades of blue coming from the corridor outside.

Trying not to freak out, I climb out of the bed and stride in the direction of the oval door. Similar to when I was in the hallway with Hermes, it feels like I'm not moving at all. Thankfully, the door approaching me makes this less surreal.

After peeking through the oval opening and looking both ways, I enter a circular, large hallway bathed in blue light. Like the doors, the floor is made of a solid, cotton-white glossy material, but the walls and ceiling are a mesh of neon lights that constantly change intensity. It's as if they're blinking sapphire stars, while paradoxically keeping the same level of brightness. That's cool.

Above my door, there's a plate in Arabic numerals—12. There must be at least twelve rooms up here. In fact, the circle itself must be gigantic, similar to a collider ring, but wider, and if I look at the closest walls, it's easy to miss its curvature. It reminds me of the large hallways in one of those huge hotels in Las Vegas. They seem to go on forever, and the rooms here are way farther apart than in a hotel.

As I stand in front of my room, facing toward the hallway, I hear voices from the right. That worries me. Since I want to avoid whatever creature is there, I walk down the corridor to the left. Maybe I can find the entrance to the alien planet with the yellow sky without having to meet people. I hate meeting people.

Several inviting, equidistant entryways with numbers line the hallway. They're almost all open. The distance from entrance to entrance is about ten meters. The numbers on the doors descend as I pass them—9, 8, 7. I keep walking, trying not to make any noise. There's no one here.

Finally, after about one hundred meters, I hit a sparkling blue wall at the end of the circular hallway, just after door 1. If all these rooms are for people, then there are already at least twelve of them. There must be more on the other side of this ring. Even so, this wall intrigues me. Its purpose has to be to stop us from going to the other side.

The bright blue barrier shows my foggy reflection. As I expected, the blurry face on the other side doesn't look like Mike at all. Clearly, here I look like me, the real me. This is why Jane didn't recognize me on Earth.

Touching the wall, I close my eyes and explore it with my new extra senses. It's amazing. I can observe past it. My mind tells me that the hallway goes on behind the barrier, that there are more rooms on the other side, and, in fact, it's very similar to this side. Does this go all the way around and back here, like a giant donut? In that case, why would they have a wall here? I try to focus even more, wondering how far I can see.

"Hey, you! Don't move!" A female voice booms. Seriously, I'm the best spy ever. I always get caught. Not only that, I get caught while doing something suspicious.

Turning my head, I find Jane standing there, glaring at me, wearing a gray tank top and black shorts. Nice, though I shouldn't be thinking about that, considering she's pointing a one-barreled "something" that looks like a gun at me. It has a bubble of some sort, shaped like a small blimp, on top of it.

"Hello, Jane. Nice to see you, too!"

She doesn't know I'm Ravi's friend on Earth, co-founder of Indiscrete Circuits. The only thing she remembers is our first encounter here. Therefore, she'll definitely recognize me. It's not every day that a handsome stranger saves your life and flies like a superhero.

"It's you!" she shouts, increasing her grip on her weapon. She doesn't act as grateful as I expected. Maybe she doesn't remember the details of our encounter? "Where have you been all this time?"

"I wasn't going to come back here, but I got bored. I can't fly on Earth. And, to be honest, I missed you. How are you doing?" I grin but I don't move.

"You are a coward," she accuses me. "People are dying here, and we need all the help we can get." She purses her lips. I'm not sure if she's relieved at getting one more soldier for whatever is happening here, or if she's upset that I didn't show up earlier. Probably both. "What's your name?" she asks, keeping her distance.

I thought a lot about that before coming here. I knew they'd ask my name, so I had to come up with something. It took me a long time to get used to Mike, and Mike is a common name, so I'm going to go with it.

"You can call me Mike."

She pauses for a while and frowns. "What's your last name?"

"You know, I'm not entirely sure I can trust you," I say, avoiding her question.

"You can't trust me?" She raises her voice. "Who are you? You've never done anything to help us." She sneers. To tell you the truth, I don't like this Jane that much; she's so disrespectful. Although she does look sexy when she's mad; but maybe I should wait for the right moment to tell her that.

"I remember saving your life. If someone did that for me, I'd instantly become his best friend."

My hands are still on the blue wall, leaving me connected to everything, but I try not to make any sudden movements. She's looking at me with wide eyes. The wall lights up with bright colors where I touch it, interfering with the patterns of hazy blue that covers the rest of the wall.

"And where were you when all the other people died?" she demands.

I must look like a robber caught by the police— hands up and against the wall. This is humiliating, yet hilarious at the same time.

"I don't know about you, but I didn't ask to be involved in this chamber of horrors," I say. She paces around me, looking closer at the flickering lights on the wall, created by my hands.

"No one had a choice. We do what we have to, otherwise Earth will be destroyed. You know that. Why don't you trust me?" She appears to relax a little, maybe affected by my distrust, or by the beautiful lights emanating from my fingers.

"First of all, you have a weapon pointed at me." I nod my head in the direction of the gun as best as I can in this position. She looks at her hands and finally lowers it down. I relax and turn around slowly, hands up, since she can still shoot me at any moment.

"Also, people have a history of betraying me," I tell her. She should know, Ms. I'm-going-biking-today.

"Very well, Mike. I don't trust you, either, but we'll see if we can earn each other's trust." She puts away her gun on her vertical shoulder holster, and moves away from me.

I lower my arms and sigh inwardly. Sometimes, confidence is everything.

"Can I get a football gun, too?" I ask. She glares at me in anger.

"What part of 'I don't trust you' did you not understand?"

"Who put you in charge? I didn't vote for you."

I dash past her in the direction of my starting point. Since she's not going to shoot me, I want to keep exploring this place. Meanwhile, she looks at me in disbelief; I'm walking away from her as if she's not even there. Doing a quick stride, she follows me.

"No, you didn't vote. You didn't fight. It's almost as if you're our enemy." I freeze for a split second, and she catches up.

"Here, you have to earn everything by actually doing stuff," she continues. I look at her, offended. "And thank you for saving my life that day,"—she looks down—"but that's not enough. You're a protector like us, and you left everyone here to die after that."

Funny, they call themselves "protectors." I'd have chosen "guardians," or maybe "defenders." What do they do here? Are the messengers still around?

I walk down the hall again, looking at the door numbers.

"Why did you choose to come back, Jane? You had the

same choice as I. You could've waited for a couple of months."

Walking by my side, she says, "Because I'm not a skeptic like you. I know how bad this is, and I want to save my people. That includes you."

Like the bright white rooms, the hallway has a calming effect on me. The blue movement above and all around me looks like a blue nebula in constant movement, set against a backdrop of stars. I can't help but peek at it every once in a while.

"So, are you in charge here?" I ask.

"Yes." She glances ahead. "And I didn't want it at first, but the other protectors begged me. So now, here we are."

As we walk, we pass by my own room—door 12.

"Who was the runner-up? I may like him better," I joke.

"You are such a jerk!"

"Sometimes." This reminds me of something I was planning to tell her. "By the way, you're really sexy when you're mad." I grin.

She punches my shoulder, way harder than she did on Earth, as if intending to hurt me this time. Brushing my arm with my other hand, I look at her, hurt. She's a psycho! And I stopped checking on the doors; I think I was around 16 when she hit me.

It takes me a while to realize there are people in front of us now, as we get closer to a giant, arch-like gate looming over the hallway on our left. Several of these so-called "protectors" are nearby, and I remember some of them. Joshua, Frederico, and...nice! Ravi is here. Wait, what?

15

PANGEA

oddamn it, Hermes. Really, God freaking damn it. I hate those monkey-faced prophet-wannabe aliens. What the hell are they thinking? Ravi knows about the mole? Ravi's a protector? He could've killed me already. Those stupid, boneheaded, manipulative messengers. I want to punch Hermes again, and again, and again.

"You got a new recruit, captain?" Frederico says in a mocking tone. "We could use some help here."

Good. I dislike him and his mustache here, too. I don't think it's a good idea for him to bother me when I'm this angry, so I take a slow, deep breath and try to calm myself. If I don't, I might just punch him.

"Yes, do you remember him? He was here when that planet imploded last year."

"There've been a lot of people showing up here since that," Frederico says. "It seems the demonstration didn't bother him."

Three rooms stand out in front of the enormous arch. They each have wide, circular entrances, larger than the other human-sized doors, but not as big as the gate itself. Instead of numbers, their plates have words—Red, Green, and Blue.

The color of each door and room—the ones I can see inside, at least—matches the hue announced on their respective plates. And unlike the hallway, with its ever-changing, fluid-like appearance, these doors are made of a solid material, perhaps plastic. They look almost dull in comparison with the rest of this place. There are no visible knobs or hinges.

People are cramming into the doorway of the green room—the one in the middle—trying to look at me. The entrance to the right of that room—red—remains closed, as is the door on its left—blue.

Using my special senses, I count two people inside the blue room, and neither one of them has energy weapons. The green room must be some kind of headquarters. Looking around, I count about twelve people, and there may be more inside their own rooms.

Ravi is the first one to approach me. "Hello, my name is Ravi Chandrasekhar." He looks way younger here than on Earth. Ravi's wearing a loose-fitting green t-shirt, and indigo shorts with several pockets. In other words, his summer hiking clothes. This is so odd.

"His name is Mike," Jane says with a wry smile.

In any way, how come Ravi didn't immediately figure out that I'm their guy? As if the fake amnesia wasn't clue enough. I must be missing something. Unlike the messengers, he's not dumb.

"Nice to meet you, Ravi." I shake his hand.

"Just Mike?" He bobbles his head slightly.

All of them are carrying those guns with the small ellipsoids in holsters. An Asian guy has an even larger one, the size of a rifle, hanging on a strap like it's a guitar.

"He doesn't trust us," says Jane. "He wouldn't tell me his last name."

"What?" Somebody shouts. They start talking so loud and it's hard to understand them. I bite my tongue and try not to say anything stupid.

"He should be arrested." A short, pale man with red hair and a goatee shouts from the back. "We do have a jail here."

I snicker. For some reason, this reminds me of the Monopoly game Ravi taught me last year. We always ended up not speaking for days after we played it, since I'd spend most of the game in jail. And then I have a light-bulb moment. I sense a barrier in the blue room, as if blocking the people inside from leaving. Blue must be a jail, and they have two people in there already. Who are they?

"He's one of us. It wouldn't work." Jane glares at the man with the goatee to make her point. "As you know, Bob, we can't arrest him here. He'd disappear when he wakes up and, the next night, just show back up in his quarters." She elaborates, as if this were a first-person narrative where things have to be explained to the main character.

"Actually, I may not come back. You guys are no fun." I shrug.

"What do you mean? Once you choose to be here, you'll come back every time you sleep." She sizes me up as if I'm stupid. My muscles tense, and I feel a cold sweat taking over. I didn't think this through.

"We could always kill him," Frederico says, hate in his eyes. Jane and I are both shocked but probably for different reasons.

"We've already decided that we're not killing people unnecessarily, and we're especially not murdering our own,

Dr. Pezzo!" Jane says. At least she's on my side. What the heck is happening here?

"Well, Jane," he snarls at her, shaking his head. "He didn't know that. Sometimes, as a leader, you have to bluff." He hisses, almost touching Jane's face with his finger.

"And sometimes, bluffs get you killed," she replies, glancing at me. If I can fly, what else can I do? Maybe I can find another way out of here.

"Hi, Mike. I'm Dr. Louise Bellaire." A pale blonde woman introduces herself, drawing closer to me. Louise is thin and short, with gorgeous, perfect green eyes. Like Jane, she wears minimal makeup. "I work for CERN," she continues. CERN is where the LHC is located. "You sound American, but it's not night there. Where do you live?"

For a while, I think that she's speaking in French to me; I don't recognize the words at first. Louise's accent is thick, although it's cute when she says "American." I'll try to make her say it as often as I can, just for fun.

"I live in the United States." Jane raises her brow at that. Yes, I said I live in the United States, not that I'm an American. I'm going to be killed by a thousand words.

"Why are you in Pangea now, then?" Frederico asks, folding his arms.

"Pangea?" I ask, and they look at me as if I'm crazy. "I mean, aren't we in the hypersphere?"

"Are you dumb, or do you just think we're stupid?" Frederico replies.

"Everywhere here is Pangea. The messengers told us this is where all the worlds meet," Jane says, putting her hands on her hips. "The main hypersphere is over there, through the gate." She nods at the arch.

Just like he had on Earth, Joshua walks over, invading my personal space. I almost laugh. Besides looking twenty, at most, on Earth he wore glasses, and now, without them, he doesn't seem that menacing anymore. In fact, everyone looks really young, in their late teens. Pangea is a magical place.

"Why are you here?" Joshua asks. He doesn't tell me who he is.

With the exception of the Asian guy, they all look like a poor excuse for an army. It's as if they just gathered a bunch of random teenagers from the streets and gave them weapons.

"Well, I didn't know you were having a weekend get-together. Sorry, I forgot to bring salad," I say, hoping to change the subject.

A muscular woman with long brown hair and a flowery, full-body, and loose dress, steps in front of me and introduces herself.

"I'm Carmen Gomez." I shake her hand, looking at her arm tattoos. Lots of people here have accents. Carmen's is also heavy, but not as strong as Louise's. In fact, I wonder why Jane was bothered by my accent when we first met, since mine wasn't that bad. Since then, I've had time to practice it. "I'm an expert in antibiotic-resistant bacteria. Like you, I'm not allowed to tell people where I work, so I understand your reservation. But what exactly do you do?"

Nice try, Carmen. Knowing what I do is half the battle to finding out who I am. I bet anyone here can figure out where she works since she told us her whole name.

"I'm a computer scientist. I work with sensitive government systems. But I won't tell you more than that. It'd defeat the purpose of being anonymous." I evade her real question.

It's fascinating to learn everybody's work and research areas. The protectors are spread everywhere in the world, everywhere an attacker could cause havoc. I'd almost enjoy the camaraderie of this group, if I wasn't the one they're supposed to hunt.

"We can sort this out later," Ravi interrupts. "There is more important business to attend to right now. We're losing this one, again."

I wonder what kind of competition goes on in the hypersphere, and what the point of that is. They should be trying to stop me on Earth, not playing games here.

"I didn't mean to interrupt whatever you were doing. Please, don't mind me."

Turning around, I move toward the arch. The gate opens by itself and bright sunlight comes from inside, illuminating the hallway with white and yellow colors mixing with the hallway's blue. Once I get used to the light, I can finally observe the hypersphere's landscape. It looks different from the first time I was here. The sky is a cloudless blue now, and there's less green than I remember. As I take this information in, Frederico grabs my arm.

"Wait!" he says. Does he always have to be this loud? "Where do you think you're going?"

"Let him go, Frederico," Jane says. "The worst he can do is get himself killed."

I frown, for I can see how that'd be a problem for me.

"No." Frederico is at it again. "If he dies, we have one less able-bodied protector to help us here."

How odd. They're talking about me as if I'm part of their group. They really have no idea who I am.

"You don't have one less or one more," I interject. "I'm not playing this game. I didn't want to be here, and I won't follow your rules. Or theirs." I look around, hoping that the dimwit messengers aren't listening.

"You're going to let Earth die?" Louise says, wide-eyed. She has a nice approach, trying to guilt trip me. It'd work on anyone else, but not on someone who's technically from the enemy team.

"This isn't about dying. It's about not killing. You all seem happy to shoot people around here."

Louise spreads her arms. "If we don't kill them, they kill us. Isn't it that simple?"

"Them?" I wonder if they're talking about the messengers.

"Yes, the Jori," Jane looks at me with a puzzled expression. "How would you not know this? You're a protector! You even saved me from them last time." She extends her arm in the direction of the arch.

Oh no. So they're fighting people from Jora here, my people, in the hypersphere. The protectors that died are casualties of this war. I'm not only a mole, I'm also infiltrating their own army. And we all know what happens with spies when they get caught.

"I know who the Jori are, of course." I force a laugh. "But for a moment I thought you were talking about the messengers," I lie, swallowing hard. Why are they even fighting here?

Jane's brow creases and she paces around me, staring into my soul. Maybe she knows already.

"The messengers are on our side. We have no reason to fight them."

I gaze at the other protectors to gather their reaction to what she says, but no one bats an eye. This is what a cult looks like.

"And why do you believe everything they say?" I ask, not able to hide my contempt. "Most of you are scientists. You should know better than this."

"Stop badmouthing the messengers, Mike. We don't have an option. We must do this," Jane says.

We're going to have this argument many times, I can tell, but I don't want to do it here, not now. I'll try to be the better man for a change.

"How about this? Let me look in there, take my time. Later, I can come here and discuss with you what's going on. How does that sound?"

The summer-like air coming from the hypersphere warms my neck, and the hallway slowly heats up. For a second, I wonder if one of my best friend's mother, Dooria, is going to yell at me to close the damn door. If she only knew. Leaving the door open in the summer is an order of magnitude better than stealing his friend's fiancée.

"This all started with your trust issues," Frederico says. "This is about trust. How can we let you go if there is no trust?" This brings murmurs of agreement from the others. Really? His argument is weak. Are we in soft sciences all of a sudden?

Despite the warmth coming from the arch, the usual noise of crickets and cicadas is absent. This is what's bothering me now. What kind of environment do they have there?

"There is a major flaw in your argument, Freddy." I challenge him, giving the arch a furtive glance. He squirms. "You think you can let me do stuff or stop me from doing stuff. Alas, you can do neither." I love saying alas. It sounds fancy.

Focusing on what I have to do, I engage my fast mode, and time slows down to a crawl. Jane narrows her eyes at me, as if realizing that I'm about to do something, and her hand drifts near her gun. I'm totally going to mention that when we go to couples counseling.

They aren't fast enough. In less than a second, I'm through the gate and out in the field. I have some alien hunting to do.

16

HYPERSPHERE

As I cross the arch into the hypersphere, I realize that I may not have made the smartest decision. A large sand dune stands in front of me, blocking my path. The fantastic landscape from last time was replaced by a mountain of dark yellow sand.

There's no other way to go but up. If they're following me, they'll catch me soon. Unfortunately, Iris told me no one can see me flying again, otherwise the messengers will let the people from Earth know my real identity. So I force myself to go up the dune in an honest, old-fashioned way, climbing as fast as I can. But my feet keep slipping in it, so I barely move.

The gravity here is lower than Earth's. This doesn't help me much, though, since it just makes the sand looser. Taking a peek back at the entrance, which looks completely out-of-place in this environment, at the bottom of the dune, I see that Jane is there, looking up at me.

Although nobody is actually running after me, I panic and try to go faster, but this makes me lose my balance and I fall all the way down. With her arms crossed, Jane laughs.

It's too hot here. That's why she's showing so much skin —not that I'm complaining. I'm sweating all over and will have to consider dressing better next time. Shoes, jeans, and a long-sleeved shirt aren't ideal for desert weather.

Jane is carrying something on her back—a backpack. When she seems to realize I'm not trying to flee again, she walks in my direction. Nobody else joins her. All the same, I get up and try to wipe as much sand off as I can.

"Can I help you, ma'am?" I ask, waiting for her to stop laughing. There's a large ellipsoid that looks like a small football hanging on her shorts; she must've picked it up when she got the backpack.

"You're making a fool of yourself. What do you think you're doing?"

"I'm looking for Hermes. We have some things to settle." Yes, I have to settle my fist on his face again.

"He's probably not here. They almost never come to the hypersphere." She looks up at the blue sky above us. At least she's not pointing a gun at me again.

"Are you by yourself?" I take a quick glance at the arch to double-check. It's closed. No one else is around.

She nods. "Yes. I told them to wait there."

I turn around and start climbing the dune again. Jane joins me, and I look at her, puzzled. "Shouldn't you be meeting with the Avengers back there?"

"They can handle themselves. I want to know what you're doing." The brightness of the sun on her pale skin highlights how young she looks here.

"I told you already." As I think about what I have to do, I hit my fist against my palm. She disregards my gesture and grabs my arm. Seriously? I stare at her, annoyed, but this time, she hands me the kid-sized football and a holster.

There are depressions on one side of the football, two buttons, and a quarter-sized hole at its tip.

"You'll need this capacitor. It's an energy weapon."

I strap the holster around my waist and store the weapon inside it.

"Since you're coming along for the ride, can you tell me what goes on in here?"

We start climbing again.

"This is the hypersphere. We compete with the Jori," she says, watching me struggle my way up the shifting sand.

"You fight here? This is where people die?"

She isn't even breathing hard. I should start going to the gym; the gravity here isn't even that bad. Maybe if I take a few deep breaths, she won't notice that I'm almost out of breath.

"We always fight, though other times, we solve puzzles, too. I mean, there's always a battle going on, but it's not only between people."

As we take our time getting up the hill, she explains the situation in Pangea. It turns out that there's always some sort of competition or puzzle they must solve. Some of them take months to be resolved, others may be done in days. Every time the hypersphere resets, they have to figure out what to do, and do it as soon as they can.

They're trying to catch the moles on their respective Earths but fighting here helps Jane's people to take out the protectors that are after Mike on Jora. Of course, they don't know Mike on Earth is me, their mole, otherwise I'd be screwed.

"Why are you even fighting here? Perhaps you should stay on Earth, looking for the mole," I say, and immediately bite my tongue. I'm a dumbass. Why give them ideas?

"We can't." She shakes her head, watching the sky for a second. "If we win, one of their protectors goes into deep sleep while we recover one of ours. If we lose, the opposite happens." She moves her hands through her hair. The absence of a ponytail makes it messy and fluffy, and she seems self-conscious about it.

I scan the landscape around us. There isn't much to see besides a wall of sand and the indigo sky above but I want to catch my breath. The sand is so fine that it falls down the dune like water.

"What do you mean by 'deep sleep'?" I ask, concerned. Not many nice things are associated with the word deep. Deep ocean. Deep space. Deep web.

"Their bodies go into a coma on Earth. We don't see them here until we win again." Jane pulls her hair back, but there's no hairband in sight.

"And what's the score so far?"

She pulls her hair over her left shoulder, combing it with her fingers, and gives me a grim look.

"We've lost five times. We defeated them three. Two of our protectors are in deep sleep. And five of us have died in battle."

The sun is almost at its zenith, and my mouth is dry. I'm thirsty.

"How do people die, though? Isn't this just a dream?" I'm not as confident as I was before, considering how absurd it is to be thirsty in a dream.

"Pangea is created in our minds but this is not just a dream, Mike. If you get hit and die here but don't damage your brain, you'll wake up. But you'll go through the whole experience of dying. I'm told that it's not pleasant. And if you do damage your brain, you die. For real."

Her answer makes me shiver. Surely, she must be understating it. Experiencing your own death, even if it's temporary, must be terrifying, to say the least.

"If you're lucky enough to wake up on Earth again, you're sore for the rest of the day. And you can't come back here for several hours," she continues. "But you don't have to die to suffer. For instance, Ravi broke his leg two weeks ago."

So that's why Ravi was late that day, and why she knew about it when I didn't. Moreover, as I think about that, I recall his stomach trouble the night I introduced him to Harry for the first time. Maybe something had happened in Pangea. Now I feel guilty; I assumed his pain was caused by his favorite restaurant. When I wake up, I'll have to erase all those bad reviews I left for Mumbai Cave under fake aliases.

Reaching the top of the sand dune at last, we stop to enjoy the view. This place is too large to fit inside the ring that goes around it. It's massive in here, and I see dunes everywhere. Several short, cylindrical gray buildings that look like grain bins stick out of some of them, and a single towering metallic pyramid dominates the landscape far away.

"We have to conquer the pyramid," she explains. "But there's no way to get there without going through several of the smaller buildings first, and they're heavily protected." She waves toward the round, grain- bin buildings. "You get shot at if you try to go over the dunes."

Smaller towers with hollow tubes surround each of the structures, possibly housing weapons.

"The Jori have already taken three buildings on the other side. Here, we've only conquered that one." She looks at the one closest to us.

The wind starts to pick up, and sand hits our faces, so we start the descent toward the structure. Although it's easier going down the dune than it was to go up, I misstep and prepare myself for another embarrassing fall, but Jane grabs my hand.

When she lets go, my palm is suddenly cold, and I feel lonely for the first time in months. There's no one who can help me here, and this is too much for me to handle by myself.

When we get to the bottom, Jane picks up her gun and points it sideways, getting ready for action. She appears to be worried about Jori finding us here. I leave my own capacitor in its holster. I'm not concerned. No one's nearby—I'd be able to detect them based on their auras—but there's no need to tell her that.

"So, let me see if I understand you. We're connected to this place through our brains. There's some kind of upload and download of our minds. But the download fails if your brain has a fatal injury while here and you really die." She nods without looking back at me.

We're walking toward Earth's cylinder, getting closer, but I'm thirsty, so I pause to roll up my sleeves and dry the sweat on my forehead. Jane opens her backpack and gives me a bottle of water. Her explanation and my thirst must mean that this body is at least somewhat real. I thank her, and we start moving again.

"Can I kill myself to get out of a bad situation?" She looks at me, bewildered. "I mean, avoiding the brain, of course."

"No. The hypersphere doesn't allow it. The gun won't fire. Of course, you could ask a friend to shoot you. I don't think I'd be able to remain friends with someone who did that to me."

"I'll try not to kill you, then," I assure her with a half-smirk on my face, but Jane pretends she didn't hear me. She doesn't appear to be in the mood for my jokes today, though she has no qualms about laughing at me when the occasion arises.

The outside of the building is made of interconnected metallic plates that follow no discernible pattern, like a giant puzzle with non-standard edges. There are no windows, and around it, in the nearby terrain, some kind of heavy artillery protects it. Large pieces of hollow, white-washed tubes and broken machinery are spread all over, the remnants of whatever has been destroyed.

Although the farm bin look-alike seems short from afar, it's actually a three-story structure, and it's so large it's hard to tell it's cylindrical when we're right next to it. Its opening is also higher than I expected—at least three meters high, and wide.

Jane runs toward the outside wall, rushing to the entrance with caution. Clearly, she's trying to see what's ahead without giving away her position.

The buildings on Earth look different than on Jora but they're obviously human-made. Now, for the first time, I'm in front of something that is, without a doubt, alien. Large veins hide behind the smooth walls, pulsing a light gray. The structure must be made of a mixture of organic and artificial materials. As I dash past Jane, she grabs my arm and pulls me closer— unfortunately not for a kiss.

"Get your damn capacitor out, Mike. You're not taking this seriously!" she hisses, somehow both whispering and shouting. I couldn't be more in love. "I'll stay on the right. You go to the other side of the cylinder to cover me. There may be people inside."

I'm not in the mood for that. To be clear, I am in the mood for whispering, but not for the SWAT operations.

"There's no one here, Jane. You can calm down." She stops scouting and looks at me, a confused look on her face. "I don't know how, but I can tell."

Giving me a sideways look, she nods, but keeps her gun pointed ahead as we enter the building. I immediately regret telling her that. They'll make me come here with them all the time, which increases the chances of my people seeing me. Damn it.

Inside the structure, the high ceiling highlights the fact that it's mostly empty. The sand has done a lot of damage, but we can still see some of the alien equipment. Instead of monitors, dozens of diamond- shaped, brush-like objects hang from the ceiling. The bristles must work like beams.

Four spherical consoles with seats designed for skinny, tall humanoids sit beneath them, too high for either humans or messengers. A sizable cavity in the middle of the chair's backrest seems to indicate that the beings who sat there carried something on their backs.

On the top of one of the consoles, the reverse relief of an immense hand stands out. The aliens who lived here also had five fingers, but two of them must be thumbs. Despite what Jane told me, I can't think of any explanation as for why the messengers would leave this technology available in the hypersphere.

As I study the large objects, Jane jumps and sits on one of the high chairs nearby. I touch the panels of one console with my fingers. Unlike the walls, the console doesn't have veins.

"Mike, you have to tell us where you live. It's for your own safety." I try not to laugh. The enormous, thin chair makes her look like a short, fat kid with her feet dangling from it.

"I can take care of myself, thank you very much." And, as if to prove her right, the console reacts to my touch. Lights flicker under my fingers, just like when I touched the wall earlier, but this time, I connect with something. Startled, I leap away from it. The panel's interface has neuro-connections similar to the ones we have at home, on Jora. Earth doesn't have them, but I can easily interact with it. Jane looks puzzled.

"You don't understand. There's another problem you don't know about yet," she says. I stop what I'm doing and look at her. "If you get stuck here in the hypersphere, or become their prisoner,"—all levity is gone from her tone— "you also go into deep sleep. You will not wake up."

I have a sudden urge to go back to my quarters as a pang of dread hits my stomach like a punch. Jane smiles, as if she's happy that something she said finally affected me somehow.

"How many prisoners do they have?" I scan the chamber, checking my surroundings. There's no one here—I know that—but I have to double-check now that I'm second-guessing myself.

"None at this time, although they almost took me prisoner that time you saved me. We've got two of theirs. Turns out, we're better at it than they are."

So the two people in the blue room are prisoners, just as I guessed. Jane looks down at her legs, moving them back and forth. It doesn't help her look less kid- like on the humongous chair.

"How about the protectors that you lost? The ones in deep sleep?"

"They were taken to hospitals on Earth in a vegetative

state and appeared to be brain dead. The hospitals and relatives wanted to turn off the machines that kept them alive.
We had to intervene." I nod, understanding the implications. If I'm taken prisoner, my body on Earth can die. One
more thing to be worried about.

Jane jumps off the chair and steps closer.

"So, Mike, where do you live?" she asks, maybe thinking
that we've bonded, and that her angel's lips have gotten to
me. Fat chance.

"I know you're into me, Jane, but I won't give you my
phone number." An offended look crosses her face for a
brief second. "Even if everything you've said is true, I'm still
not comfortable with this. As Frederico said, it's all about
trust. And trust takes time."

Jane throws her hands on her hips and shakes her head.

"Have you made any progress on finding our Earth's
killer?" I ask, pretending that I don't care that much about it.
Jane sighs before answering me.

"Not really. He's either really good at hiding or he hasn't
done anything yet. We have people in particle colliders,
nuclear power plants, hidden military projects—you know,
the works. Our only hope is that if he tries something, he'll
be caught." Jane looks away.

"It's frustrating. We know nothing. Maybe he's a woman.
Who knows?"

"I seriously doubt he hasn't done anything yet," I
confess. Why did I say that? I often forget that my mouth is
faster and dumber than my brain. Which is quite a feat,
considering how fast my brain is.

"You're probably right."

After that, I close my eyes and focus so I can visualize a
3D map of everything. My consciousness is in close contact
with this place. I see everything—the aura emanating from

Jane's body, the structures, the main building, anything nearby. There are people kilometers apart from us, but I can't get that many details on them due to distance. I wonder if the real Mike can see everything the way I do here.

Jane was right about one thing, though. Hermes and Iris aren't here. I can't find them.

"So, what do you think?" She gestures around, meaning the building, obviously trying to change the subject and to avoid the awkward silence.

"How did you secure it? I saw the large guns destroyed outside."

"We had several causalities, but we managed to use AED grenades close enough to disable them for a while. It took us almost two months of trial and error to get our timing right," she says in a somber tone. "This time, no one was killed, but lots of us have PTSD."

"What's an AED grenade?" The acronym that comes to my mind is automated external defibrillator, but that makes no sense.

"It's just an anti-electronics device. When we drop an AED, all advanced machines are disabled for several minutes but the electronics still survive. Even guns stop working but only for a few seconds. The simpler the device, the faster it restarts. Anyway, the worst part is that we have four more of these cylinders to go, plus the pyramid. People die all the time, and they're weary of coming here. We're not soldiers, Mike."

I see. Each building they have to conquer is a different puzzle. If you're willing to die, and take the risk of actually dying in real life, you move faster. It's understandable why they're reluctant.

"But why don't you go through the underground

tunnels?" I ask. "You can bypass all the buildings. There's almost no security there."

Jane looks at me, open-mouthed, as if I just told her I don't like eggs or bacon for breakfast. It's exactly how Ravi reacted after he learned that about me.

"What underground tunnels?"

Uh oh.

17

EXPEDITION

Waking up in my hotel room feels hollow. As a result of my stupidity, I now have a date with the protectors to storm that place tonight. Nice. And there's nothing I can do about it. Once I sleep, I'll wake up in a snake pit.

At least my body is refreshed. It seems that uploading and downloading one's brain still works as sleeping. It's depressing when you realize you're not going to sleep for a long time, though, perhaps even forever. I like sleeping. I want to sleep intellectually, but I don't feel like sleeping right now.

It blows my mind that Ravi and Jane didn't figure out who I am. They're not idiots. I'll have to be way more careful. I may need to find a place at the laboratory to sleep and pretend I work late. There's also the problem of getting stuck in Pangea, or being seen by Jori. Everything suddenly got way harder than I expected.

The clock on top of the nightstand says it's one a.m. It's going to be a long day. I spend it rechecking my plans on

Earth. It's only a matter of time until they find out who I am, so I have to be ready when it happens.

Finally, I get tired again and realize that it's time to go back, meet the protectors, and help them win one of their silly games.

When I wake up in Pangea, I decide not to talk to them right away, though. It bothers me that I don't know how many protectors there are in total. Making sure that no one's close by, I leave my quarters, turn right, and walk through the gleaming blue hallway toward the arch. This time, I won't let anyone stop me.

People try to talk to me as I walk by, and Jane even calls me, but I ignore everyone as I pass by the immense hyper-sphere entrance and the red, blue, and green rooms. The last numbered room before them was 21.

The numbers restart sequentially at 22 next to Blue. No one follows me, and I keep walking. They must think I'm that odd friend who's just a bit nuts—every group has someone like that.

After a couple of minutes roaming the large corridor, I reach another wall. The last number was 42. There are forty-five rooms on our side. Our hallway is a half-circle of about 450 meters, so the full circle must be almost a kilometer long. This is impressive, especially considering that the hypersphere inside the ring seems to have no boundaries.

The three chambers in front of the arch are special. They are not quarters. That leaves forty-two rooms, of which one is mine, so there are forty-one quarters for the other protectors. Five were killed and they've won the game three times. Therefore, Earth should have about thirty-four active protectors.

As I walk to the main rooms again, people start to intro-duce themselves to me. Names are always a mystery to me because I tend to forget them, and I wish that they had name tags up here. This isn't a problem for them, since after a year, they must know everyone by this time.

The door in front of Blue vanishes unexpectedly, scaring me at first, and a large, extremely fit black man steps outside. He looks me up and down before speaking, the door reappearing behind him.

"Hello, Mike," he says with a deep voice. "I'm sorry I missed you yesterday. My name is John Tyson. I'll be leading the expedition today." He's in better shape than anyone else here. But more importantly, he sounds like someone who knows what he's doing.

"Are you military?"

"Yes. I'm an army major. I work at the Pentagon."

He narrows his eyes at me, sizing me up, as if processing whether or not I'm a threat. I must not give him any hints that I'm a mole. I'm sure he'd kill me on the spot if he suspects me of something.

"How many of you—?" I start to say. "Sorry, I mean us, obviously. We're on the same team!" I laugh, nervously. "How many of, uh, us"—I wave my hand around—"are soldiers?"

He frowns and pauses for a moment before answering.

"Three," he says, moving on, and I sigh inwardly. "Captain Vladimir will come with us, and Lieutenant Qi will stay here as backup. We don't want all our eggs in one basket."

Vladimir Sobiesky is Russian, and Qi Wong is from China. I met them yesterday at the end of the shift.

"Do you need to have someone taking care of the prisoners?"

Louise is leaning in the Green doorway, watching us.

"No," she interjects. "They have everything they need inside." She furiously bites her fingernails, staring at me as she does that. This is so odd. It's as if she doesn't notice what's she's doing with her hands.

"But don't you ever interrogate them?" I press, crossing my arms. Louise tilts her head, as if trying to hear me better, not staring directly at me.

"They don't speak any language we know. Plus, nothing they can say would help us," she replies. This sounds even weirder because she doesn't look at anyone in particular when she says it. I wonder if she's like Dr. David and doesn't like making eye contact.

Our conversation stops when the red door vanishes and Jane exits the room. She hands me a kid-sized, dull-green football, probably the weakest capacitor they have. Everybody else has longer, bright yellow cartoon-like rifles, except they have square barrels with lime-green double ellipsoids on top of them. Despite their power, the weapons' designs are awful. An enemy would be able to see them from miles away.

All the weapons came from Red, so if I need better guns, I now know where to find them. My toy capacitor should do for our mission today, though it doesn't make me happy. Jane smirks.

Today, they're only sending a small group into the hypersphere because the others don't trust me yet. Also, they don't want to all be wiped out. So only five of us are going, including me and Jane.

John leads us up the dune that blocks part of our entrance. His stamina is astonishing, and I bet he could swim up the dune if he wanted.

Everybody has their guns out, except me. There's no one nearby, and it helps to have both of my arms to balance myself as I go up. No need to give another show of rolling down the dune. My clothes are more comfortable today, although wearing sneakers wasn't a good idea. I don't have special ops boots lying around like John, though. And at least they're not asking me questions about how I click so much with this place.

After several minutes of going up and down the dune, we approach the short and wide cylinder. Like yesterday, there's no enemy around. However, I do sense someone moving up in the sky, and I stop to focus on that spot. It's too far away for my companions to see it; I wouldn't have noticed it either, if I didn't have extraordinary perception in this place. The auras of living beings in the hypersphere are as bright as lighthouses.

I curl my lips when I identify the object—it's Hermes, the bastard. He's up there, probably plotting against us. Oh, how he'll pay for making me live with Ravi, a protector, when I get my hands on him.

The people around me stare in the direction I'm looking, but they can't see anything.

"Is there a problem, Mike?" Jane whispers.

"Hermes is floating over there. You said they almost never come here," I say. John shakes his head.

"There's nothing there," he says. "And even if he's watching us, why should we care?"

John has a point, but as soon as he says that, Hermes moves. Something's wrong.

"Jane, where's the other gate?"

"It's over there." She points at a place far away, through another dune. "We can't see it from here."

I close my eyes and visualize the geography of this place in my mind. Hermes is flying toward a place that is the exact opposite from our arch. There's only one reason for him to do that—he's going to tell the Jori what we're doing. If they come here, our small party will be trapped under their fire. They'll overrun us in no time.

The solution is obvious when I think about it. I grab my awkward football-gun, point it, and click on the depression on its top with my thumb. A loud charging noise, like an airplane turbine ramping up, makes everyone stop and look at me at the exact moment my capacitor fires. This is not one of my proudest moments but no one can complain that I'm weak or indecisive.

It's impossible to hit anything at this distance with a long barrel, much less with a handgun in the shape of a half-sized football while having no practice using it. And yet, due to how my mind interacts with this place, my shot lands right in his lower body, where I'd aimed. Though they couldn't see Hermes at first, the explosion followed by a thin trail of smoke up in the sky is unmistakable. My shot hit something, and they look at me as if I'm from another planet.

"You shot the messenger!" Jane screams, distraught by what happened.

"He had it coming," I say, and chuckle at the way she said it. "Also, he was going to warn the others!"

John snatches the football from my hand and throws it down the dune like a quarterback, hitting the edge of the arch. The gun explodes into small, harmless pieces. Impressive.

"You warned the Jori either way, you idiot. They must've seen the fireworks, same as we did!" John barks. I thought he'd like my shoot-first approach. Still, he's right. I gave away our position.

"They saw something, but they don't know what or where. Hermes was ready to inform them about us. I did what I had to do." Apologizing is not my forte.

"This is the only cylinder we've taken so far, you moron. They're coming straight here!" John shouts so close to my face that I can smell his minty breath. How does he do it? I didn't see any mints around.

John barely finishes talking, and Paulo, an engineer for a Brazilian aerospace company, is already staggering in the direction of the cylinder ahead of us.

"We have to go. Now!" Paulo says, lurching ahead. His thin and tall body exacerbates how clumsily he walks toward the building, as if he's afraid that we're going to run into the enemy.

"Come on, run! No one's here yet," I say, sprinting forward. We don't have much time. They may still be mad at me, but there's nothing they can do about it now.

When we arrive at the structure, I get through the door as fast as I can. Aside from Jane, everyone seems to hesitate a little before stepping inside, but soon, we are all ensconced in the alien cylinder.

I close my eyes and focus, searching.

"They're coming. I can sense them, about three kilometers from here," I say.

"They'll be here in less than twenty minutes," Paulo estimates, spreading his long arms wide. We'll be sitting ducks if we stay.

"Mike, how to get to tunnels?" Vladimir speaks finally, with a quiet, heavy accent. He never says much, but the situation has apparently gotten to even him.

I concentrate.

"There's an entrance below the spherical console over there." It's well hidden, and unless you know about it, you can't find it. Very clever. Vladimir is already grabbing the console, trying to move it away.

"Console is stuck," he says, tugging at the large, round

foreign metal object. The rest of us disperse around it and help him, but it's clear this is not the right approach. Instead, we should interact with it, figure something out so it will move itself on its rails. It's one of the puzzles, I realize. But we don't have time for puzzles, and no one besides me is used to operating that type of interface on the spherical console.

It takes us several minutes of us all pushing and yelling to get the console out of the way. It seems stupid that we could move it like that, but the game makers didn't realize that someone could see through it, I guess. No one should know about the tunnels unless they'd solved whatever puzzle the console has. Destroying everything in the building looking for secret passages when you don't know they're here would indeed be silly.

"They're almost here!" I say.

Thin, dark gray fluid shoots up from fibers on the floor, where they had connected with the console above until just seconds ago. It's disgusting. It looks as if we just killed and gutted an animal with blue blood. In the middle of this mess, we find a trap door. John grabs the handle and opens it, ready to jump inside.

"Not yet!" I whisper. "Throw an AED grenade first. There are surveillance electronics at the beginning of the tunnel." Nobody seems surprised at my knowledge anymore. John grabs a spherical object from his belt, presses a button on it, and throws it into the hole. We hear a loud noise from inside, followed by the sound of footsteps outside.

Oh no. The others are Jori. They can't see me, or Mike will be in danger, so I push Jane out of my way and jump into the hole ahead of everyone else. John, Jane, and Paulo follow me. It will take time for the others to find the external door, but they'll find it.

"You selfish bastard!" Jane complains in a low voice. From her point of view, I almost screwed up the mission by shooting Hermes, and now it looks like I just want to save my own skin. She wouldn't understand but I desperately want to protect Mike. If they see me, they might recognize me and kill him, since he must be using my body on Jora, and I am very fond of my body. So, in a way, I guess I did just want to save my own skin.

"Should we go?" Vladimir asks, back to his calm and stable self, as if people weren't running after us.

I focus again. Everything is clear from here.

"Yes," I confirm, but Jane stops me.

"Wait!" she whispers. "Just one thing. Everyone, forget about everybody else. Just run as fast as you can and get to the pyramid, no matter what happens to the ones in the back. Is that clear?"

"She's right," John agrees.

"Go!" Jane whispers as we hear footsteps from above.

Running like mad, we advance through the weaving tunnel, but at four kilometers away, it'll take a long time to reach the main structure. John and Vladimir soon disappear ahead of us, followed by Paulo, who has to duck his head to avoid hitting the ceiling. Jane runs by my side.

Like the cylinder above us, the tunnel is made of the same dark gray alien material, and it pulsates around us. Every time we touch or step on it, it brightens up, as if bothered by our presence. If the walls and the floor weren't solid, I'd think that a giant silver anaconda had eaten us.

Ten minutes after we start running, I hear noises from behind. The tunnel curves, so they don't see us— yet. I'm not a runner and, if she wants, Jane can leave me behind, but she's keeping pace with me. I'm in worse shape than everyone here even if I am in my nineteen-year-old body. Needless to say, this does wonders for my self-esteem.

We keep running until we hear people getting close. Next, I slip, fall, and hit my face hard on the ground. Pain explodes in my head as I see stars, and something wet drips from my eyebrow. They're going to find and kill me.

Jane stops, turns around, and drops down next to me, shooting nonstop at the tunnel behind us. The whole scene looks professional and, yeah, I'll admit it, arousing—except for the part where we're in mortal danger and I'm the screw-up here. Her quick maneuver works, though, and the people behind us stop running so they can shoot back. Jane's buying time with this tactic, but it won't save us.

I can't think of a better idea, however, so I roll over and watch the shooting match. There are at least four people down the hall behind us, and more are coming. We can't hold out for too long, especially when I don't have a gun.

"Jane, you have to save yourself!"

Everyone likes the idea of being a hero, but it takes

a lot of willpower to not just dump her and run for my life.

"No. You are the most important person in our group!"

She's right, but not for the right reasons.

Being in a gun fight is not something I do in a daily basis, but we are on the defensive, which makes things easier. Still, they'll overwhelm us in no time. A bald, skinny guy is fool enough to try a suicidal run and Jane shoots him in his belly. He falls down, dies—I assume—and his body disappears. The Jori take this time to move even closer. We won't be able to deal with all of them.

This is bad. Thinking about killing anyone makes me nauseous, and I don't want to kill my own people. We're screwed. There's no escape.

Then everything fades out.

18

INTERLUDE

S weat covers my body when I wake up in my room at the hotel, and I have trouble breathing. It takes a long time for me to understand what happened. Did I die? Nothing is out of place, except that my head's hurting, a lot. That may be because I hit it hard on the ground when I fell in Pangea. It didn't feel like I died, though. Then again, it's not like I have much experience in dying.

Moreover, despite the fact that I somehow survived, it's possible Jane didn't. The clock says one a.m. again. I can't just call her, because Earth's Mike has no idea what's happening in Pangea, and if I talk to her this early in the morning out of the blue, she'll suspect I know something.

So, my next several hours are wasted in refreshing her social media page every few seconds. Morning comes with no sign of her presence. I get ready to go to the laboratory in a somber mood, and then, finally, something shows up.

"We did it! Smiley face!" she posts, and I allow myself to breathe a sigh of relief, even as I have mixed feelings about it. Don't get me wrong, I'm happy she survived but people who post vague statuses like that make me cringe.

"We did what?" posts a woman called Jennifer.

"Just something at work," Jane adds.

"I work with you, doofus. What is it?" And it goes on and on. I mark the "doofus" reply with a thumbs-up. That'll show her.

I can infer from this that Jane's Earth won the game, and Vladimir or John must've reached the place just before the Jori got to us. Perhaps once the game is over, everyone still in the hypersphere wakes up. That was close. I wish people would tell me things like that, instead of letting me freak out all by myself. On the plus side, we got another protector back who may also find and kill me. I still don't understand how they don't suspect I'm their guy. I should post, "Life is hard, sad face."

During the day at the lab, I avoid everyone. Things are getting complicated. There's no way I'll remember what they said when in Pangea and what they said to me here.

My efforts to avoid the protectors fail when Jane finds me near lunch time, sneaking up on me when I was distracted on my cell phone, downvoting a post about a petty revenge that wasn't petty enough. For a split second, I think about running away from her but this isn't Pangea. I have no powers here. Usually, she shows up with a bunch of people and I have advanced warning since they talk so loud. She's by herself today. Ravi's still in New York, visiting his sister.

"Ready for lunch?" she asks me with a radiant smile, even prettier than usual. I forget why I was trying to hide from her.

"Sure, why not?" I give a quick glance to the lunch bag I brought, hoping that she didn't see it. "You're so happy today. What happened?"

Jane laughs and avoids my eyes.

"Sorry, it's personal," she says, attempting to suppress her smile as we head out to the cafeteria.

It's cloudy today, and likely to rain. We may get wet when we come back. It's odd to walk and talk like everything is normal. One moment, people are killing themselves up there, the next, we're here enjoying ourselves.

"You said it happened at work." I move my hands around to emphasize where we are, referring to her online status. "Clearly, we're at work and yet, I don't know what you were talking about."

"Stop stalking me on social media!" Her words indicate that she's mad, but she can't stop grinning. "I just didn't want to tell people, that's all."

When I think she's not looking, I stare at her body, searching for any sign of pain or discomfort. She's wearing only a light, short, blue dress and her usual black purse, so it's easy to check her skin beneath it. No bruising. Unfortunately, when I look back at her eyes, she frowns. She must have misunderstood what just happened. I wasn't doing it in a sexual way. Still, she rolls her eyes when she catches me red-handed, making me feel like a creep.

As we have lunch, I keep wondering what will happen in the hypersphere. It's going to reset, for sure, and I can't wait to be there when the next game is up and running. I'm also worried about what Hermes will do with me after I shot him.

It drizzles on the way back to the laboratory, and Jane's hair is getting wet. When she's happy like today, she glows, and despite my self-preservation instincts, I decide to take advantage of her mood.

"Jane, are you free on Saturday? I'd like to take you out to dinner or something."

"You mean, like a date?" She snorts while she laughs. It's not very cute, but I'll let that pass.

"What? Is that so farfetched?" I feign surprise. "Is speaking a second language required?" I bite my tongue after that. I really should think before I speak. Her face sours.

"Really, Mike, you're making this very difficult."

"I'm sorry. I was kidding. I can't help it."

We walk in silence for a while after that. At least she's considering my offer. If she accepts, it'll be my first date in more than a year. Unlike my previous relationship, I'll be the one betraying her from the start. Awesome.

"Okay, but just as friends at first. And it has to be an early dinner."

"What? This is unfair. We just had lunch as friends. In fact, we do it every day." I gesture at the cafeteria.

"Yes, but we are seldom alone like today. You got lucky." She's smiling again. Her eyes are so pretty when she looks at me like that.

"No, you got lucky." I smile back at her.

THAT NIGHT, I'm a little bit gloomy. Nothing of what I'm doing is sustainable. This has to end soon but I need to talk to the real Mike first. And I still don't have a plan for what to do in case I get stuck in the hypersphere.

The work on the collider is going better than ever, but it'll take half a year to finish it, and I'll need some help to figure out how to create a black hole even after everything is functional. I hope I get more answers from the people in the hypersphere. Also, worrying if the real Mike is closer to getting his job done is useless, so I try not to think about it.

I fall asleep without noticing it, and I'm in Pangea when I open my eyes again. There is no peace in this way of life, no rest in sleeping anymore. I only change places.

Looking up at the ultra-bright ceiling, I stay where I am, lying down, trying to decide what to do next. Honestly, I don't feel like doing anything. It's clear that I must speak with the messengers but I also need to know what's going on after the battle yesterday.

Closing my eyes, I connect with everything around me. My focus wanders to the hypersphere. No one's there, and the arch to the hypersphere is closed. There are people in both sides of the habitat rings, bright bulbs of light moving about their own hallways. I like to imagine that the wall separating the protectors near my quarters in the inner blue hallway is south, while the other wall, toward Jane's quarters, is north. There's an outer hallway, but the passages to go there are all closed.

"Hello, 12, anybody home?" someone says from the corridor outside. I hate that my room is number 12. It reminds me of the Seattle football team, and I like San Francisco now. Once I get attached to something, I tend to be faithful to the end.

Opening my eyes, I stand up as Paulo, Jane, and John come in.

"Geez, I have no privacy here," I complain. They're all in a good mood, grinning.

Paulo closes in on me, towering over everyone in the room. Then, he bends over and wraps his arms around my back before I can escape.

"We did it, Mike!" Paulo hugs me hard. From behind him, I show my hands to the others, looking for some kind of help or explanation, but Jane only shrugs.

"We got Charlie back!" he continues, after what seems like too many minutes of hugging.

Jane joins the hug party.

"You were great back there."

"Well, you saved my life. Thank you." I say, remembering that she didn't thank me at first, although I try not to be sarcastic this time. We're all happy; no need to spoil it. "Where is Captain Vladimir?"

"This is not his usual time," Jane says. Her hair is again pulled into a ponytail. She must've remembered to sleep with a hairband this time. "He'll be back when it's night in Saint Petersburg."

John's been ignoring me since he entered. Instead of interacting with us, he paces around, checking my quarters as if he has a warrant. He walks to the other side of the bed and glares at the wall, touching it.

John finally looks directly at me. "What you did back there was very dumb." Several dumb things that I did and usually do come to my mind; therefore, he has to be more specific. "Don't do that again. If I'm in charge of an operation, I'll be the one telling you when you can shoot." He sounds angry, but he's also smiling, so I think he'll be okay.

"You shouldn't shoot the messengers," Jane says, looking concerned. I try not to chuckle.

"But he was going to tell them about us," I reply as we hear people laughing in the hallway. Everyone's in good spirits today.

"You don't know that." She stiffens. "Regardless, there may be consequences."

"No worries. Please just tell Hermes to come and talk to me. I want to, uh, speak with him." And I hope he felt that shot. "Anyway, I still don't understand why you're just following all the rules. Have you tried talking to the prisoners?" I ask. "They're just like you, but from the other side."

Jane and John exchange glances.

"We attempted teaching each other a few words and sentences," Jane says. "But they're not cooperating, and haven't been for a long time, so we stopped trying."

Looks like they're faithful to the end. It makes sense, since they're fighting for the survival of Jora. My planet. I wonder if they know me.

"What I am saying is that if the gods are telling the truth about everything, why are we playing these silly games in the hypersphere? How does that fit in the story?"

"The gods are observing us," John says, perhaps finally convinced I don't have anything special in my quarters. "You may be right about the messenger warning the Jori. It's possible that they favor one side over another." He looks pointedly at Jane.

"The gods can't watch us directly, Major," she says, standing her ground.

"I meant the messengers, obviously," John lashes out at her, almost yelling.

"Uh...what do you mean by that?" I ask before I even realize that I did it. Damn. If I continue slipping like that, they'll figure out who I am.

She purses her lips before answering.

"How much do you know about the gods?" she asks. I look around, afraid of what to say, but decide to be honest for a change.

"Not much. I've never seen them. I was told they created Earth."

Jane raises her brow, looking at me as if I'm a child.

She shakes her head. "You have to understand that the

gods are not like us and the messengers, who come from real planets. The gods have always lived in Pangea, but no one can see or talk with them because they're not corporeal."

"Uh...what?"

With more patience than I thought she had in her, Jane explains that gods are multidimensional sentient blobs of energy that live in areas of Pangea unknown to us. They're beyond smart but their thought processes can take several days.

More importantly, Earth already existed when the gods accidentally created the other, parallel Earths. They needed new parallel universes to increase the size of Pangea. Apparently, the bigger it is, the larger their narcissistic cloud-shaped brains—I'm paraphrasing— can be, and the smarter they become.

In the process, however, they ended up dooming several planets because their inhabitants would learn how to develop portals that eventually would destroy them. The messengers were created after that to minimize the damage by using moles, like me and Mike, and the pointless hyper-sphere games.

Multidimensional sentient jerks, that's what they are.

"The gods definitely follow what's happening here," she continues. "But they don't take sides. They gave us free will." Her tone shifts at the end, and I can tell she's now trying to convince herself as much as the rest of us. "I just hope we can win this thing."

"And we have our winning ticket right here!" Paulo says as he puts his long arm over my head and pushes me toward him. Seriously, Paulo, personal space. I look up at him, annoyed, but he's clueless.

Jane crosses her arms and sighs.

"I can't believe we've been at this for twenty months already," she says.

I wince, looking at her in disbelief.

19

BATTLE STATIONS

They've been fighting for almost two years but I only got involved with this mess about fourteen months ago. When I met Jane and Frederico, they had been the protectors of Earth for half a year already, while it was my first time in Pangea.

Ravi knew Mike from before, and when everything started, Mike was still Mike, not me. Therefore, his best friend could never in a million years be involved in it. When I woke up impersonating Mike, faking amnesia, the timing was so different, and they were so absorbed in their battles, they didn't think I could possibly be the one.

The messengers never told them that the people who'd try to destroy the Earths—me and Mike—would only start their mission six months later. And they have no idea that I —and probably Mike too—infiltrated the opposite teams in Pangea.

The best place to hide something is right under your nose. Ravi would vouch for me if they got suspicious of Indiscrete Circuits. Not only that, but one of them—a protector—is a co-founder of said company. There's no way his partner could be his sworn enemy, because if he were, the game would be over for him.

After some awkward silence, Paulo speaks.

"It's almost time. We should hurry up."

We compose ourselves and head to the arch. Someone from Earth—or me, the mole—has to walk to the gate to open it, but in times like this, we have to wait. A large digital clock with a countdown tells us we have less than fifteen minutes before the hypersphere finishes its reset.

People gather in front of the arch, creating a commotion. Major John takes us to Red so we can all get guns, and I finally grab a decent capacitor this time. It's not the largest they have, but at least it has a respectable size to it, with double ellipsoids on the top.

Louise walks toward Jane.

"Are we doing the reconnaissance first this time? How many should go?" she asks, biting her thumb.

I learned last time that the military guys are in command while in the hypersphere, but Jane is in charge out here. The protectors have both a civil and military hierarchy. Jane can call the shots during battle, but if lives are in danger, she may be overridden.

"John and a few others will go first. When everything is clear, we can go afterward and take a look. If this is a puzzle game, it could take months to finish."

Jane looks at me, deep in thought, maybe considering that it could be over much more quickly; they have an ace up their sleeve now, though she doesn't know the ace is from another deck. And clearly, I'm running out of good analogies.

"What if it's not a puzzle?" I ask. I find it funny that they call them games, but I can't think of a better word.

"It could be a battle game. They end sooner, with more casualties," says John.

"We always hope it's not one of those," Louise adds, leaning her head as if to hear me better. "Our numbers are dwindling." I watch John as he shakes his head. He may prefer the battles.

The countdown drops to zero, followed by a loud siren, and the doors of the arch vanish in front of us. John and Charlie are the first ones ready to go. Charlie Terry, the protector they just got back from deep sleep, is an experienced captain of the British army. John told me yesterday he likes to have at least two military professionals every time they go in the hypersphere.

No sunshine comes from inside when it opens. Instead of a landscape, which is what I expected, a large round hatch with a valve wheel replaces the gate. The arch opens, only to show a door in its place? No one talks about this oddity, and John eagerly grabs the wheel, trying to move it counter-clockwise. Nothing happens. He tries it clockwise—the correct way to do this on Jora—and it starts to turn.

When it swings open, it reveals a vast room with yet another hatch at the end. John hesitates, and we exchange looks. Charlie is supposed to come last, so he also freezes. Our plan just got a little more complicated.

Either way, Joshua takes the initiative. With his right hand, he touches his forehead, chest, left and right shoulders, and then runs inside, taking the lead. To my relief, nobody else copies him. I'm not sure if I'd be able to repeat the sequence.

John and Carmen are right behind him. Of all the women here, she's the one who most looks like a soldier. I'd probably lose a hand-to-hand fight with her. Or Jane. Or anyone, really.

While John opens the second hatch, I close my eyes and explore the place in my own way. It's easier and safer to do it like this. I must be careful, considering I'm not ready to meet the Jori. There's a huge object on the other side of that door. I can't tell its shape yet, but it's larger than a building. And— interesting—there's no air outside of this chamber and the attached building, no atmosphere at all. It's pure vacuum.

Three of the protectors are already inside and through the second hatch, and we wait for their return. Meanwhile, my focus moves to the other parts of the structure, and I try to grasp its significance. It's made of wide compartments filled with machinery. Engines, weapon arrays, computers, and even a command bridge.

We're getting inside a huge spaceship.

Normally, this would be very exciting, and I'd be looking forward to traveling in space—who wouldn't? But this is clearly a warship. I can only conclude this game will end early.

Several minutes later, the scouting party signals us with the all-clear, and we enter the ship. I'm in the second wave. By my estimation, we must be close to the middle of the hull.

The ship walls are made of a light-red, wobbling material, like the insides of a live whale. If they weren't completely straight with chambers and entrances, and thus clearly artificial, I'd think we were just swallowed by an alien creature. Despite its meaty-looking walls and floors, it doesn't feel slimy or wet when I touch it.

Near the second hatch and inside the ship, ten human-sized, black spacesuits are stored in a locker with see-through glass. My guess is that they're to be used in case we have to evacuate, which is why they're right next to the ship's exit.

"No one's here. It's a bloody spaceship," Charlie says.

"There's a bridge at the front, five floors above us. We can pilot it from there," John shouts. "We should all go there and learn the command interfaces as soon as possible. The Jori must be doing this right now, too."

As we walk toward the bridge, the hatch door closes by itself, rotating counter-clockwise. Paulo, who was behind me, jumps at it to keep it open, but fails. A loud clacking sound is followed by the walls slowly becoming brighter, and the ship jerks forward—we're moving. He tries to open the hatch.

"Warning. There is no atmosphere outside." A female voice comes over the com system.

Stopping in his tracks, Paulo looks at us, wide- eyed. I count ten of us, ten spacesuits, and if I remember correctly from when I sensed the bridge earlier, there are ten seats in there. The ship has decided that everyone is here and the game can start.

"To the bridge!" John yells, and he disappears ahead of us. Following him with weapons at the ready, we run as if our lives depend upon it. Carrying my gun like that won't help me in any way, but it gives me confidence.

A series of colorful lines, as thick as a fist, indicate where everything is. The yellow ones are marked 'bridge' in dark blue. If the signs weren't there, it'd take a long time to find the place since the ship is so big.

The gravity is, again, lower than Earth's, which makes it easier for us to move. This is the only constant every time I'm in the hypersphere. At least there's gravity here, other-wise I suppose that most of us would be emptying our stomachs. We're not astronauts.

As we go on ladders and through hatches toward the bridge, the walls flicker as if they're moving, but it's only the veins throbbing beneath them. The pulsation turns into waves when we touch them, brightening them, as if they're made of liquid, but all I feel is the cold, smooth surface of the wall.

An oversized, curved view screen stands out in front of the bridge stations, but it isn't actually there. It's just dark space projected from beams above it, similar to those we found in the gray-bin buildings. At first, most of the protectors stand motionless, staring at the ten seats arranged in a half-circle in front of a panel that looks like a giant horseshoe, but John and Charlie are already working on the consoles.

"This is bollocks! It's as useful as a cock-flavored lolly!" Charlie says. I'll need a thesaurus when I get back to Earth.

The surface of the stations looks like a black sheet of glass from afar but as I get close to one of them, sections on it move down, creating hollowed areas shaped like a place for hands. They're next to, oddly enough, two cupholders. I wonder if they have coffee here.

I touch the depressions with both palms and connect to the ship's system, which projects controls directly into my brain. I get it—this is the engine station. Feeling better about the game, I take my hands off and look at the others, but they don't seem happy.

"I don't understand how this works!" Jane shouts, moving her hands rapidly on top of her chosen console. Why can't they use the controls? They're so simple, straightforward. I know that I have a special connection with this place but these have your basic, run-of-the- mill neuro interfaces that anyone can use.

Oh, wait. They've never used them. Neural connections like that are only available on Jora.

"I can see and interact with them, but nothing works," Ravi rants. "This is just like every other time. We can't make sense of any of this."

A hypothesis starts to form in my head—the games are rigged. The messengers are aware that only Jora has this technology but it's the second time I've found them. Who knows how many times the Jori have had an advantage because of it.

Since my current companions can't do anything, I move around the stations. I put my hands on each of them, and learn what they do. I take Paulo's hands off one and he looks at me, visibly hurt.

Offensive weapons station. Life support station. Navigation stations one and two. Every time I touch the controls, bright lights show up beneath my hands, which doesn't happen when they do it. One of the navigation stations confirms that we are in space, several kilometers away from our entrance. It's right at this moment that something else catches my attention. There's another ship—about two thousand kilometers from ours—coming toward us.

"What are you seeing, mate?" Charlie asks me.

"Everybody, hold on to something!" I yell.

Using my mind while connected through the navigation station, I order the ship to do a hard to port—or starboard, who knows, I'm not a sailor—to get away from them. It may not help, but I can't think of anything else. We're thrown to the side as I forget to activate the inertia dampers. I need to watch more science fiction movies.

"How can you read the damn controls?" John asks. His low, guttural voice makes the hairs on my neck stand at attention.

I must think. They're going to get suspicious, but what if there's an emergency? We're in space, and therefore...we need space suits. They all look at me, hoping I have some ideas. Sorry, John, there's no time to explain.

"Everyone, go back and put on a spacesuit. Now!"

They obey me without hesitation. We leave the bridge empty for a while and run back to the lockers. The ship is immense; it takes longer than I remember to go back to where the spacesuits are located. Carmen opens the transparent locker, grabs a suit and tries to put it on. We all stop and watch her, since nobody knows how to do it.

Her feet and arms can't get inside it no matter what she does. Turns out, it's not easy at all. The holes are not large enough, and she fails miserably. Grabbing another one doesn't help. She hits the same problem. Finally, she takes off all her clothes, revealing a complex pattern of well done and tasteful tattoos in intimate places.

Trying to ignore the fact that she's naked, we all stay quiet, observing. When she tries again to put the suit on, legs first, the black fabric finally comes to life, somehow detecting her skin and moving itself over her body like a liquid, adjusting to her dimensions.

"The suit...is fucking eating her!" Charlie says, and the way he says it creates another phobia for me, as if I didn't have enough of those.

"Clothes off, everybody!" John yells.

While my mind happily flashes back to the last time I heard this phrase, we all strip naked. Meanwhile, part of my brain regrets not going to the gym more often. This is not how I wanted Jane to see me in my birthday suit. I was hoping that it'd be a dark place, where most of it would be in her semi-drunk mind.

Oh well, there's no room for imagination now. On the

other hand, Jane looks stunning. She peeks at me. Once again, I'm looking at her, but pretending that I wasn't.

"Where are the helmets?" Jane asks.

There's nothing else in the vicinity that could be used as helmets, and the suits are useless without them, obviously. I interface with my suit and try to understand how it works.

"The helmet automatically closes if it detects loss of air pressure," I tell them as I run back to the bridge. They follow me but I suspect I'll have to do everything myself.

"This is just like the other times!" Frederico complains as we run. "It's hopeless. We can't use these controls. John, you must do something!"

"Shut up, Frederico," John screams at him. "Mike can control the ship. We'll survive this."

Back on the bridge, they keep trying to access and work with the hollowed interfaces, but they don't know how to do it. They can see pretty graphics projected on their brains, but have no control over them.

Moving from station to station to identify them all, I find a second one for offensive weapons, and two for defensive weapons. Next, I jump to a navigation station at the middle of the fat half-circle to watch what's happening outside. I pause. Something's wrong. An alarm sounds, and a flashing red light illuminates the bridge. Red alert?

"Mike, what's going on?" Jane asks.

The protectors look at me. I realize they're frightened. The navigation panel interfaces with my brain and I can see everything, but I wish I couldn't. There are fifty missiles en route to our ship. Panicking, I look at Jane, thinking that we're all going to die. With no time to answer her, I leap to the defensive station and spread what looks like flak in the direction of the missiles.

To my dismay, the ship's computer detects another fifty

that were just launched. For a couple of seconds, I don't know what to do. I close my eyes and focus. My perception when I do this is way better than even the ship's sensor array.

The protectors are all around me. Paulo is crying. Jane also fights tears as Louise covers her face with her hands. John and Charlie are still trying to make sense of the stations; they never give up. I have to give it to them. On the other hand, Frederico is just standing there, shaking and speechless. The blinking red lights continue to illuminate the bridge, and the alarm is even more distracting.

Meanwhile, more than a hundred missiles are coming in our direction. They'll hit us in less than four minutes. This battle is designed for people to micro- manage their stations with almost no computer help. If we had all the defensive stations manned, we could avoid most of the impacts, but as it is, they're just firing at us, mostly undisturbed.

I'm by myself here. I cannot do this alone. Shrapnel will go through these suits like butter. We're all dead, and not just dead, like "dead and back to Earth." The ship will blow up into millions of pieces. We'll be dead, dead.

Two and a half minutes. There's only one thing I can do, and my heart sinks when I realize it.

Telling the ship to silence the alarm, I ask it to project a 3D visualization of the incoming missiles on the screen, using the beams on the top. As I predicted, everybody turns to it. The holographic screen displays hundreds of fast-moving red streaks approaching a larger blinking yellow object in the shape of our ship. I did this on purpose, to distract them. Unfortunately, Jane turns away to stare at me with her big, wide eyes. I didn't want her to witness what I'm about to do.

A flash of fear crosses her eyes as I point my gun at her, and kill her first.

20

BLOODBATH

The protectors fall like dominoes in front of me, and the only sound I hear is that of bodies hitting the floor. A silent capacitor is perfect for ambushes. Aiming low, avoiding their heads, I finish the job in less than ten seconds. Somehow, John manages to shoot back at me before I kill him. His shot grazes my right leg, and blood drips down my thigh. I should've shot him first, but I didn't want Jane to see this for too long. A burning sensation takes over, with almost no pain yet, but it's going to hurt really soon.

The scene is gruesome. My hands are shaking. I did it at very close range; there's blood all over me. I'm glad it doesn't take long for them to disappear, even though their bloody suits stay behind. Paulo is the only one left, shaking on the floor. He raises his hand toward me as I shoot him a second time. My job is done. All my friends are dead.

Two minutes to go. The shock of killing people leaves me frozen for a while, but I have to focus and brainstorm my way out of here. Chances are, I'm dead anyway, but I must try something. Unfortunately, the capacitors are designed to not work if someone tries to kill himself.

I can change the ship's speed and direction, but it cannot outrun the missiles, and flying toward them won't change the outcome. Instead, I shoot the hull with my capacitor at its maximum output. The area brightens for a moment, the veins stop throbbing—but it dims as soon as I stop, leaving no sign that I did anything at all. I cannot shoot my way out.

An idea forms. Standing in front of the life support station, I touch the console and order the ship to do an immediate decompression. Several warnings pop up in my head, and I bypass all of them. The ship doesn't like losing its life support. Next, I run toward the ship's hatch.

Lights flash all over the ship. I don't run as fast as I'd like because I'm limping. It hurts a lot, and it's starting to get hard to breathe. A transparent helmet closing around my face almost makes me trip, startling me. It popped from the upper neck of my suit.

While the suit is pressurizing, it detects a large air leak around my thigh. Warning sounds and visuals are all over my face. I try to ignore them. It tells me it's trying to patch itself, but the hole is larger than it can handle. It's a big gap. I'm not sure how long it will hold.

Forty seconds.

When I finally get to the hatch, I immediately try to turn the wheel. A voice in my helmet scares me half to death and I freeze, making me lose a couple more precious seconds.

"Warning. There is no atmosphere outside." There's no atmosphere inside either, you idiot! Pulling myself together, I continue turning the airlock wheel until it clicks and opens.

Twenty seconds.

Jumping outside, in space, I attempt a weak smile,

thinking about what I achieved and forgetting for a moment that I slaughtered all my friends. Somehow, I made it. I'm safe!

Except that's not true. This seemed like a great idea, but now, in hindsight, I'm just hanging around next to the ship, moving away at a snail's pace. Worse, I forgot that there's no gravity outside and I'm getting nauseous. It's either that, the loss of blood, or the decreasing air pressure; I'm not sure.

Ten seconds.

I don't want to die. Not dying was a big part of my plan. So I close my eyes and focus on the hypersphere, searching for our entrance.

Five seconds.

I stop spinning and start flying, pushing myself toward the arch as fast as I can. Flying in the hypersphere is like I'm falling in the direction I focus, and it's not a good feeling. I don't hear or see the multiple explosions behind me, but I know they're happening soon. The sudden acceleration makes me throw up inside my helmet.

Keeping a small profile, I point my feet toward where the ship is, moving away from it. Still, debris hits my legs, spinning me around, and soon afterward, something else whacks against the back of my head. I lose consciousness.

WHEN I OPEN my eyes again, I'm floating in space, wearing my leaking spacesuit. The nausea comes back with a vengeance, and I tighten my jaw.

I don't know how long I was unconscious, but it seems that if we pass out in the hypersphere, we don't automatically go back to Earth. We only wake up on Earth if we really die, and only if we have no brain damage.

On the plus side, the suits are self-cleaning, so the flashing warnings on my helmet are easy to read. If I don't do something fast, I'll lose all the remaining air pressure. Luckily, I'm starting to get the hang of this. I stop my spinning and scout ahead, finding our gate a few kilometers away.

The more I do this, the better I am at it. Just by thinking, I fly fast toward where the arch should be. A minute later, I slow my approach. Otherwise, I'll splat all over it. Flipping upside down, feet first, I edge toward the hatch.

To help with the nausea, I pretend that our gate is down, and when my feet hit the door, I can almost believe I'm standing up on it. My head feels like someone's drilling into it with barbed wire, but I've made it.

After straightening up in relation to the door and opening the outer hatch, I push myself inside and drop to the floor. It closes behind me automatically, air is pumped in, and the atmosphere stabilizes. I rest for a minute to catch my breath before I move on. The hissing from the leak in my suit stops, and when the clear helmet hides itself, I finally take the suit off.

There's a large wound on my thigh but the energy used to create it also cauterized it. My forehead is wet, and there's so much blood on my hands that it looks like I killed my friends with nothing but my bare knuckles.

The only thing left to do is to get to the habitat rings. As I drag myself to the inner hatch and safety, my arms and legs have had enough. They've used up all the adrenaline in my system, and it's time to pay for it.

Finally, I open the second hatch and throw myself inside. Lots of protectors are there, looking at me. I must be quite a sight. Shaking, bloody, naked.

Standing up, my mouth opens, but instead of saying

something, I throw up and fall to my knees. Someone—Rose?—puts her hand on my shoulder. "Are you okay? What happened?"

Using all my remaining willpower, I stand up again, but they move back this time. "Where are John and the others?" she asks.

A loud noise comes from the gate, and I turn around to see it closing. The game has ended. We lost. My mind is foggy, and I can't remember anything. Something bad happened, that's for sure, but what?

"Did anyone die?" she presses.

Rose must be the only one who looks like herself up here. At seventeen years old, she's the youngest NASA intern ever. It's funny what we think when our minds are not well.

I look at her, hard, trying to focus. Her eyes are watery, which makes me feel guilty. Are they dead? Yes, some bastard killed them. In fact, they died all around me, one by one. Jane was the first to die.

Jane...wait a minute, that's not possible. I think I killed them. But why? Why would I do that? Why would I betray them? I'd never thought about how it would feel to be on the other side of betrayal. It sucks. I'm the one responsible for the excruciating pain. They're all dead, and it's all because of me.

I look back at Rose, but this time, there are tears on my cheeks.

"They all died," I tell her as I remember that I'm the bad guy.

"What?" she blurts.

Anger grows inside me, and I clench my fists.

"You don't understand! I don't like this anymore than you do." I shout at her. She steps back, her eyes wide. "They were supposed to die, anyway." They're enemy protectors.

Isn't that my job, to kill them? It doesn't feel right, though. Why do I have to kill them again? I'm not a murderer. I mean, I wasn't a murderer. I guess I am one, now.

How odd. Rose weeps for some reason. I extend my hand and touch her dark-skinned face as if she's a child that needs comforting.

"Don't worry," I tell her, matter-of-factly. I want to calm her down. After all, Jora is going to be safe. "I killed them all." I smile.

This is the last thing I remember as I fall to the floor.

I WAKE UP ON EARTH, in my hotel room, hyperventilating again. Without making any movements, I open my eyes and breathe. My leg hurts, I'm sweating, and I have a headache, but I'm not nauseous. And yet, my eyes are filled with tears.

Then I remember their faces, the look of betrayal in their eyes as I shot them. I close my eyes again, trying to somehow erase my feelings, but it doesn't work. I see their blood splattering my suit as I mowed them down with my gun. Yes, they did die, and it was quick, but it wasn't fast enough. I remember their pain, their panic. I start crying, unable to hold my sobs in anymore.

Could I have taken them all through the hatch and to safety without having to slaughter them? Was there an easier, painless way to send them back to Earth? Maybe I should've stopped the ship while it was closer to the entrance and sent them all back, wearing spacesuits. That never occurred to me. On second thought, even if I'd suggested that, I doubt they would've just followed me. But would we even have had time to do that?

Unable to stop crying, I try to focus on something else,

accept that this was the best outcome. I didn't have time. There was nothing else I could've done. What if they really are dead? Maybe I wasn't fast or smart enough. Regardless of what I think, every time my eyes close, I'll replay the bloody scene in my head, over and over. I can't even imagine how bad it was for those who actually experienced their own deaths. Deaths I caused.

After several more minutes, the crying is finally gone and I feel something different. Anger. Purpose.

Someone will pay for this.

21

DRINKS

I t's going to look suspicious, but I called in sick. I don't want to face the people that I killed. When I'm back in my quarters in Pangea, the door to the inner blue hallway opens and I hear shouts. People are outside waiting for me. I close that entrance with my mind.

Jumping out of the bed-platform, I rush to the outer ring's wall on the other side, away from the protectors. It opens in the shape of a disk when I approach it. This place responds to me, and I'm not going to hold myself back anymore. Stepping outside my room, I enter the still unknown and empty outer ring. I don't think anyone knows about this door.

While the inner hallway has a fantastic neon-blue illumination, this one resembles the rooms we wake up in in Pangea, bathed in white light. The invisible lights projected on the ceiling make it look even more like a luxury airplane, albeit one made for giants.

As I walk toward what I think of as south—a part of Pangea that's still fuzzy in my mind—I think about what I'm going to do. The messengers will talk to me today, one way or another. My feet touch the rubbery metallic floor in quick succession, without making a sound, and yet the heavenly structures around me don't seem to move at all— an optical illusion of how intangible the Pangea rings are to our normal senses.

After about one hundred meters, the scenario dramatically changes, and I arrive at the southernmost part of the ring. Unlike the other ring, where I met the protectors, there's no wall here. Instead, the hallway deforms outward in a bubble shape. I count five oval doors on it. The sterile brightness of the environment surrounding the entrances— or exits?—reminds me of escape pods from science fiction movies.

There's something else beyond the hypersphere and the rings around it.

The middle door opens, obeying my thoughts, and I enter this new environment. The smell of the sea and the sounds of the crashing waves startle me at first. It's another hypersphere. Perhaps it's the same place we watched the destruction of that Earth. However, instead of the flat circle and the planet, I'm on a sandy, desolate beach with palm trees, large birds, colorful late- afternoon sky, and somehow my clothes have changed. I'm wearing only beach shorts, no shirt, and my feet are bare.

This must be some kind of a joke. We always keep the clothes we were wearing on Earth, and I have to be careful not to wear anything that Ravi or Jane have seen before. It's always a chore. So why has that changed?

The sun is almost setting, and the ocean breeze is stronger than I'd like, but it's still comfortable. As I walk, little crabs cover my feet, tickling my toes when the waves reach them. It's like a tropical paradise.

Near some thick bushes guarded by several trees, the

beach opens to a small clearing in the shape of a semi-circle, made entirely of beach tables and deck chairs. For a moment, I forget that I'm in Pangea, and I enjoy the seashore and the ocean.

It must not be a surprise to anyone by now that, more often than not, I'm that stupid. I'm not paying attention to my surroundings like I usually do. As a result, when I finally do see Hermes, he's just a few feet from me, sitting on a chair. This whole world is a trap made of water, trees, and sand.

He gets up, catching me by surprise. Still, I have quick reflexes and punch the messenger with my right arm, making him hit a tree and land on the soft sand next to it. This time, my knuckles aren't hurt. I'm learning how to live in this environment, getting faster and deadlier every day. If I wanted, I could've killed him.

Soon, he's back on his feet, and his face shows no particular expression. The messengers are never bothered by my punches.

"You should stop doing that," he says, sounding like his usual warm-uncle self. I feel guilty for a second. "We haven't even been introduced yet. My name is Mercury." He rubs his hands on his body to dust off the sand.

"What?" I gasp. "You look and sound exactly like Hermes. I'm sorry, I couldn't tell you apart."

I look back over my shoulder, checking to see if anyone else looms behind me. I also search for an escape plan, in case I need it. "Where is he?"

"Hermes was indisposed on his planet for two Earth days after you killed him in your hypersphere. He's trying to avoid you."

Good. He should know what it means to be killed. I hope he suffered more than Jane.

"Is he going to tell everyone about me?"

"Not yet. We wanted to talk to you first." He keeps his distance from me. "Why did you break the rules?" Mercury crosses his arms in a creepy, human-like way, almost as if a naked albino person stood in front of me.

"I didn't break any rules," I say, putting my hands on my hips. "Iris told me no one could see me flying in the hypersphere." I grin. "Did anyone see me?"

"Ah. You took it literally instead of following the spirit of the rule." He nods.

They need lawyers in this place. On second thought, they're just trying to commit genocide. Let's not make it worse.

"This is why rules have to be clear. I don't make the rules, and I'm not going to try interpreting them."

As if we're old friends, Mercury settles onto a chair next to one of the tables closest to the shore, and invites me to sit down. Beaches are my soft spot, so maybe they created this environment just for me. Since I can't think of anything else to do right now, I decide to entertain him. The view is impressive, that's for sure, and I need to gather more information before the next phase of my plan.

"Why are the messengers helping the others?" I confront him.

He laughs. "What do you mean, 'the others'? The Jori are your people. The real question is why are you not helping them?"

"Because I haven't decided to play your games yet. I'm just trying not to kill people. And you didn't answer my question," I say, pointing a finger at him.

"We want to help the gods' mission here of saving one of the Earths. Your people are more advanced than theirs, and it would be better for us if they survive."

I shake my head. His answer doesn't make much sense.

"So, why the charade? Why don't you just send me to Earth without any protectors and stop the games?"

The trees nearby tilt a little in a gust of wind, creaking. Sometimes, I wonder if Earth is the dream, and this is the real place.

"There's more here at stake than just killing people. The best must win, and not just the ones that are technologically more advanced. Furthermore, we are observing how you deal with your emotions."

Not very well, I guess, since I keep punching them.

"Is that why Ravi's a protector?"

"Yes." He clenches his hands and rests his right elbow on the table, just like a freaking human. "We don't want you to just destroy a planet with no strings attached. We want to see if you are willing to kill your friends for a just cause. And you must feel bad about it."

"What?" I ask, dumbfounded. I don't understand.

Mercury looks down at his interlaced fingers while he plays with his thumbs. Stop mimicking us!

"The gods created cold-blooded killers in the past, and they caused havoc. This time, we want people with a moral compass." He looks back at me. "Even if they are devastated when they kill."

"Your stupid gods are making a lot of mistakes."

The breaking waves make me think how much I hate these so-called gods. I would love to spend a week here, if it weren't for these dumb creatures, and I'm not talking about the sea gulls.

Another messenger comes over to our table. Like Mercury, she's all white, her skin made of a mesh of white strands covering her freaky blue veins.

"Do you guys want something to drink?" she asks,

moving her right hand over her head as if she's moving her hair away. Except she's bald, and the gesture just looks weird.

"Yes, Venus," Mercury says. "Please bring him one strawberry daiquiri. You know, the kind he likes."

This is so unexpected that it makes me laugh.

"What makes you think I'm going to drink it? What if it's poisoned?" It's creepy that they know so much about us.

"We're not murderers. Hermes made that clear to you," he insists. Venus leaves us for a while, and I follow her with my eyes as she walks, like a human woman. I wonder how many messengers are here.

"I was almost killed in that last game, Mercury. How would that work for your divine plan?" I came up with "divine plan" more than a year ago, as I imagined how this conversation would go. His reaction is anti- climactic.

"You were not supposed to be there. If you ended up being killed, it would have been on you. Jora would have lost."

They don't want stupid people to survive. The fact that I'm not yet trying to kill the protectors may seem unwise to some people. Idiotic, even. But does that mean I shouldn't live?

"I have one more question. Why do I have so much control in this place?"

The problem with mimicking humans so much is that you also let your emotions show. Mercury tenses, rubbing his neck.

"Pangea is as old as the universe. All sentient beings are attracted to it, and, sooner or later, they find their way here. Your mind became aware of it when you were in a coma as a child."

When I was five years old, my father was killed in a

freaky forklift accident with a chainsaw. Unable to deal with what happened, I was distracted and fell from a balcony. I spent a month in a coma, unaware of what was going on outside. But unlike most patients in this state, I was conscious, having what I thought at the time were lucid dreams. There, I created my own world to play in, exploring its hidden depths, traveling off the beaten path. That's where I taught myself how to fly. If Mercury is right, those weren't dreams. I somehow had access to Pangea at that time.

"What do you mean, aware of it? I thought our brains were uploaded here!"

"What happened to you is rare, but it happens," he continues, grabbing at his non-existent beard on his bare chin. "Since your mind was so young, you were able to teach yourself how to change your surroundings, just like messengers. Effectively, you created your own hypersphere."

A wave crashes nearby, louder than normal, the sound enhanced by our temporary silence, making this meeting—for the lack of a better term—even more surreal. My eyes follow a seagull diving in the water, searching for an unlucky fish.

"I'm a mole, Mercury. Your mole. The chances that I'm also the one who created a freaking hypersphere when I was young are close to zero."

The bird jumps out of the water without his snack, and for some reason, this makes me feel better. Some things happen—or don't happen—for a reason.

"You did this to me," I say. "Why?"

"The messengers experimented with many humans, from both sides. All of our efforts failed in one way or another. In your case, the coma made your mind faster, but clearly not smarter."

His statement catches me off-guard. I didn't see that coming. Instead of a witty reply, all I can do is look back at him with my mouth open. You know, my signature move.

"But the stakes are higher now. People are learning what you can do. We must intervene."

Interesting. If people from Earth know they're cheating, they may rebel against the gods. This is why they have to intervene now. And I know exactly how I can help.

"Mercury, I can't stop you guys from creating those games, but they must be fair. The Jori shouldn't have the upper hand here, at least not yet. And I don't want people dying, regardless of which side they're on."

I'm not going to make the mistake of just following orders.

"Very well," he concedes. "We'll make arrangements to make it fair. They can learn how to use the neuro interfaces."

"How will you do that?"

Mercury laughs. "We're not going to do anything. You'll have to teach them."

"They don't have the required biochips." I point at my head. "It wouldn't work."

He folds his hands on his lap and looks at me.

"Neither do you, or the Jori. And yet, they manage to use it."

Mercury has a point. Even though I don't have the bio-implants needed to interact with the interfaces, I was still able to do it. I hadn't thought about that.

Venus comes back with my drink and puts it on my table. Her beautiful smile accentuates her bright green eyes, in contrast with Mercury's—and Hermes's—coal black ones. Still, I scoff at her. What are they thinking? She looks at Mercury and signals him about something.

"We'll be right back," he says. Mercury gets up, and then both he and Venus go somewhere behind the trees. I'm left alone, looking out at the nearly setting sun. It hasn't moved since I got here.

When I hear voices nearby, I realize that I'm a moron. There are twenty-one white beach tables with two chairs each, for a total of forty-two seats. This is the number of quarters we have in Pangea. They're expecting both the protectors and me here.

Jane is the first one I see. Just like before, with me and Mercury, we are too close to each other, with no escape plan. She's wearing an extremely hot, small red bikini. I was half-smiling before, but now I'm grinning. She also appears stupefied, but probably not for the same reason.

And then it dawns on me what she's seeing. The last time we met, I killed her. Granted, it was not one of my best days. But now she sees me relaxing on the beach, looking at her lustfully with a drink by my side. Not exactly the picture of remorse.

"Mike!" she yells. "What the fuck were you thinking?"

This is the first time I've heard her swear, and I like it. But then she comes even closer and punches me in the stomach. I fall off the chair with my hands on my belly. Nothing comes out of my mouth when I try to explain. It's hard to say anything when you have the wind knocked out of you.

"You killed me. You killed everybody! Because of you, we lost the game. Peter Jenkins is gone!" I lift my right-hand finger, the other hand still on my stomach. I need one more second to be able to reply.

"And now, here you are, enjoying yourself on the beach. What an asshole."

22

LIES

"Listen to me, you God damn little prick," John says, getting right in front of my face. I instinctively move my arm to protect myself. "The next time you even point a gun in my direction, son, I will shoot you in the head." He pushes me back hard, just as I was trying to get up.

"Let me talk!" I yell, but it comes out high-pitched. I take some extra breaths, and they wait for me to be able to breathe again. As I'm getting better, I get angry.

"Haven't you been paying attention?" I shout. Dumbasses, I think, but I don't say it out loud. I'm afraid that John might hit me. "The game is rigged. The hypersphere is filled with neuro-interfaced machines that only Jori can use. We had no chance."

"Then how do you use them?" Jane asks, as I slowly push myself to a standing position.

"Jane,"—she cringes when she hears me say her name and I'm suddenly glad it's Earth's Mike who has a date with her this weekend, and not me—"you know I have some kind of connection with this place. I don't know why, but I do. When we got to the ship's bridge, there were more than a hundred missiles already coming to destroy us. We were dead anyway. What would have you done?"

"I don't know," she concedes, "but I probably wouldn't kill everyone in sight, and definitely not my own fucking friends!"

To be on the safe side, I back away from her; otherwise, I'll likely get punched again.

"Maybe not. Do you imagine it was an easy decision for me? I spent the last few hours trying to figure out if there'd been another way, but I don't have a way to redo it. And yet, it worked. We're all alive, and that's what matters." I look at John, feeling the urge to be petty. "In fact, nobody has really died on my watch, Major!"

"Mike, how are you alive?" Louise asks, her soft, jade green eyes glowing. I feel even worse that I hurt her. "You didn't die and wake up. Rose told us she and the others saw you coming out of the hypersphere."

"Did they tell you in what kind of state? I thought I was going to die, literally." I flinch when I remember what happened. I almost didn't make it out alive. "I wouldn't have been able to save everybody. If I hadn't killed you, we would all be dead."

With a puzzled look on her face, Jane sits on the same chair Mercury was on just minutes ago. I try not to look at her bikini and focus on Louise nipping at her cuticles instead. Jane seems confused, and not because I'm not looking at her bikini.

"But if you're right, the gods...why would they do that?" Jane asks. Weird, she's okay with me betraying them, but not the gods?

Hermes—the real one, I think—interrupts our conversation, requesting that everyone be seated for some announcements. Venus and other messengers graciously take people to the tables and start bringing beverages, but I stay seated next to Jane.

Nearby, Ravi's staring at my drink, frowning. He glances in my direction, as if guessing I was watching him, and we make eye contact for a second. I look away, trying to hide my thoughts as he sits with Louise at a nearby table. Shit, this was not an accident.

Hermes is at a podium located at the center of the tables. Everybody is quiet, waiting. I can't believe they just keep doing the gods' bidding like that, without asking questions. Zealots, that's what they are.

"We're all gathered here today to talk about some changes," Hermes begins. His odd cult-like speech makes me cringe.

"First of all, the rules are being abused. Starting today, the only way to go back to Earth will be if you are in the habitat rings. If you get fatally hurt in the hypersphere, you will not wake up on Earth anymore."

I hear gasps. The games will become deadlier with this new rule.

"That's not fair!" John shouts. Frederico looks at me in shock, his face indicating that I was responsible for this change. They forget that I don't make the rules. They're angry at the wrong person. I shrug.

"No, you're wrong," Hermes states. "What happened yesterday wasn't fair. Many of you shouldn't be alive today, and yet, here you are."

Avoiding my eyes, Jane asks, "Is it true that the Jori can interact with the interfaces we've been seeing inside the hypersphere?"

"Yes," Hermes admits.

John stands up amidst the hubbub that follows.

"Damn bastards! You want them to win!"

And yet, the messengers are mostly unfazed by the humans' reaction. Hermes calmly waits for the commotion to die down, and then raises his hand.

"No. The Jori are no different than you, and it was our belief that you should've been able to access the interfaces. It's clear that we were mistaken, and we apologize for that." John crosses his arms, but he doesn't sit back down.

I get him. Apologies are not enough; people have died.

"From now on, there will be a mix of interfaces that will be familiar to everyone in every scenario." Except, if they have computers that connect with their brains, the Jori will always have the advantage.

Nevertheless, the messengers just made a big mistake. Some of the protectors may believe there is a gray area and the messengers, who are aliens, are not lying. The poor guys acted in good faith. However, I know they're lying. Mercury told me so. This is a game changer.

"You can relax here during the next few days. The hypersphere won't open for several weeks. We'll have the same discussion with the Jori." He makes a gesture to the other messengers and they bring donuts. These evil bastards know too much about me.

Hermes turns to leave but many protectors go after him. They have a lot of questions. I ignore Jane—who remains in her chair, looking at me—grab my drink, and stroll toward Mercury. He's the one who told me they want the Jori to win, while Hermes just said that this is not true. The messengers can and do lie to us.

I stop in front of Mercury with one hand on my hip, the other holding my drink. He waits, not making small talk. I'm furious, but enough with the punches. I want to make a point.

"The messengers have broken our trust," I say with a smug look.

Mercury shakes his head.

"It was a misunderstanding. Hermes just explained that." Either he doesn't comprehend what I'm talking about or he's afraid that the others may eavesdrop on us.

"People say that trust is a finicky thing. Do you know why?" I ask him.

"No, but I'm sure you're going to tell me." He narrows his eyes. Yep, they do that as well—human- like facial expressions.

"When you trust someone and they lie to you, every-thing else they said or did..." I move closer, to about an inch away from him, but he doesn't step back. "And I really mean every little thing..." Pausing, I shoot a quick glance at Hermes for dramatic effect, and then face Mercury again to finish my small play. "Everything is now questionable."

And then I throw the drink in his face.

To my surprise, Mercury doesn't react. He just lets the pink drink drip down his face, looking at me with a blank stare. This worked way better in my head, but in reality, what I did is pathetic. I should stop watching those Mexican soap operas.

I turn around to go and almost bump into Jane.

"Uh...I also punched him earlier."

I'm not sure if she believes me, but regardless, I'm done for the day. And pissed. I slink away from her and walk toward the water so I can go back to my quarters.

Jane stops me by grabbing my hand. Really? Planet of grabbers, is what they are.

"Wait. I want to say that I'm sorry." She grabs my other hand, too.

"This is very difficult for me. I watched—" She stops and swallows, stares at the sunset, avoiding my eyes.

I look down, and for the first time notice a discreet feathery wing tattooed on her left ankle. It's better than the ones I've seen before where the wing is so big that it takes over the leg.

"I still wince a little bit when I see you," she admits, raising her head and looking back at me. "But, Mike, you saved us. I understand that. The logical part of my brain understands it but it'll take some time."

Jane doesn't have superpowers in Pangea but she has a lot of power over me. My anger fades away, and I grab her hands tighter.

"And I'm sorry I had to kill you." My face twitches as I try to hide a smile. This is not something anyone would say, ever, except here.

"Thanks for killing me first, Mike," she murmurs, her face inches away from mine. The proximity of her face triggers my memories of killing her, and I let out a strangled sob. Jane lets her guard down for a change, and I hug her while she silently weeps.

After a while, things get awkward, and not in a good way. We separate. People walk toward us but I wish I could stay by myself.

"Mike, I want to ask you something," Ravi says. It takes a while for me to understand what he just said, because one of the two people with him distracted me. Louise is on his left, always looking at me, but not directly at me—I still don't know how to explain this— and a young Linda is on his right, frowning at some trees.

Yes, Mike's ex-wife Linda is a protector. The woman who abandoned him and their child, April. I should be surprised but I'm not. For all I know, David and Dr. Alice will show up here at some point.

"We need your help," Ravi presses. Linda smiles next to him, looking down at a tiny crustacean, and then up at the seagulls. "Is it possible for you to teach us how to use the devices? You know, the ones where you interact with your mind?"

I hadn't thought about that before but since Mercury mentioned it earlier, I think it can be done.

"Yes, I think I can teach you."

"Well, let's hope that the next environment in the hypersphere gives us time to learn, then." He bobbles his head.

Linda takes this opportunity to introduce herself.

"So, you're the one everyone's talking about, Mike." She raises her hand toward me. "My name is Linda Pohlt." I shake it. "I'm a reporter working for CBS in Los Angeles."

Like Jane, she looks pretty decent in a bikini but I can feel only contempt at her for bailing on Mike.

"Are you going to interview me?" I joke, but I can't make myself smile.

"Of course not. We must win first, right?" She giggles. And then she stares at the water, frowning. I do the same but there's nothing there.

"I didn't know we had media people up here," I say. Linda smiles again, looking back at me.

"There's also Becky from the BBC." She nods at the group of people talking to Hermes. "You really should meet everybody. We're a small group, after all."

"I've never seen you here," I tell her. "Have you met her?" I turn to Jane and Ravi, pretending that I don't know the answer.

"Yes. She's one of the cowards who avoids Pangea," Ravi says.

I'm not sure how all of this started, but the original forty-one protectors were told the same story they told me. They had the choice to stay on Earth and never come back here—except, apparently, for announcements like this—or return to the hypersphere every single night.

This helped to hide the fact that I was drafted about six months later than them. The protectors made a mistake in guessing I was in the original group and had just avoided Pangea. Otherwise, they would've figured out that Mike on Earth is not who they think he is because of his pretend amnesia.

"We're really good friends on Earth," Linda jokes, looking at Ravi. He rolls his eyes but says nothing.

"Why are you not helping the protectors here?" I ask her.

Linda laughs, watching me intently.

"The real question is, what are they doing here in Pangea?" All of a sudden, she paces in between me and the others, and stares at the messengers. I don't think she's in her right mind.

Jane's face flushes red, and she walks around Linda, giving her a side look.

"You know very well that they can win every game and send us one by one to deep sleep," Jane says.

A loud squawk from a seagull nearby makes Linda jump. And just like that, she's back to smiling. The others don't seem to be bothered by her erratic behavior.

"You misunderstood my question, darling." Linda giggles again, touching Jane's shoulder. Jane frowns, eyeing Linda's hand as if it were a snake. "Yes, someone has to be here, protecting our side, but why does it have to be me, or you? We're not soldiers!"

Linda walks closer to me and leans forward, looking directly at my eyes. I shift, uncomfortable with her attention. "After all, the mole cannot be here," she finishes.

I freeze, and my heart forgets it's supposed to beat for a couple of seconds.

23

DATE

After a couple of busy days back on Earth, I buy a house near RNL on Long Island. Nobody knows this, and I'm not using Mike's name to buy it. I created another private company just for this purpose. If I get stuck in the hypersphere, my body may die here, so I want to be prepared, just like the others.

It was difficult to explain to Julie, the nurse I hired, what I wanted. She'll have to come every day to check on me. I'll be paying a lot of money, so I hope she's going to mind her own business even if she thinks I'm a pervert or something.

People should still believe that I live in the hotel because I'm keeping my room there. And I can't have a nurse going every day to my hotel. It would look suspicious on too many levels.

As I wait in front of the hotel, a black limousine comes by and stops in front of me. That's unusual. We haven't used limos for some time, by my request. I always have this feeling that I don't belong in them, especially if I'm wearing sandals, like today. I'm also dressed with black shorts, a baggy t-shirt, and a nice pair of sunglasses. I wish I could wear my cowboy hat, but Ravi told me no sane person wears them on the beach.

The door opens, revealing Jane, pretty as always. She's wearing a bikini, but this time, she also put on a semi-transparent beach skirt. I can't help but grin as I get in the car, but once I turn around, I realize that I've made a huge mistake. She's not alone.

Ravi and Louise are also in the car, sitting opposite from her. This is why she wanted the driver to pick her up first—to set a trap for me. They know who I am, thanks to Mercury and Venus. It's almost funny. I'm going to be killed because of a strawberry daiquiri. My smile fades away and I frown, looking at them.

Ravi laughs. "You could try to hide your feelings once in a while."

Louise and Ravi both wear beach clothes, like me, and sit next to each other, holding hands. Jane is the devil; she's taking us on a double date. I chuckle.

"Hello, Mike. I'm Louise. Nice to meet you!" She's much older than Ravi, maybe in her mid-thirties. Her spectacular green eyes are hidden behind a pair of sunglasses. Louise tells me what I already know—she works for CERN at the LHC, and this is where she and Ravi supposedly met.

"So, you got backup," I say to Jane. Ravi and Louise hooking up is no surprise. In fact, this is true for all the protectors. They spend a lot of time together, risking their lives. There are no better friends than soldiers.

Jane blushes. "They were both around, and it's not easy for them to have some nice quality time together because they live so far away. Plus, we don't know each other very well, and you've known Ravi for a long time. I thought this would make you feel better."

The last person I wanted to see today is Ravi. And yet, I

understand why she did it. She's afraid of being vulnerable. Perhaps she wants more people to vet her relationship to see if she's doing the right thing. One thing is certain, though— she must stop holding hands with handsome guys who save her life once we start dating. That's not cool, even if the other guy is me.

"Jane wants me to check on you," Louise jokes, smiling, but she looks straight ahead. Jane and Frederico hooked up due to the closeness that's forced on them in Pangea. They were spending every single night together, and that created intimacy. One would be surprised, I suppose, that Jane is now dating outside that pool, but I know she tried that and got hurt. "She didn't listen to me last time," she concludes, as if reading my mind.

"I'm sorry Frederico cheated on you," I tell Jane. "But I'm not him. I promise." It's true that I have a horrible secret, but it's not sexual.

She cringes, and the mood in the car suddenly becomes grim. People on Earth don't like to be this straightforward.

"How...did Ravi tell you?"

Ravi's eyes go wide for a second, but his expression quickly changes to anger.

"No one told me. But it's kind of obvious, isn't it?" I shrug.

Really, I didn't even know him and I could tell he was up to no good the first time I saw his pretentious mustache. But who am I to judge? I can't even pick a fiancée who doesn't cheat on me.

With the exception of Louise, who doesn't seem to care, everyone looks outside, as if admiring the trees on Connetquot Avenue, and waiting for the awkwardness to dissipate. It doesn't work like that, though. Someone has to get the ball rolling.

"How long have you two been together?" I ask Louise.

She pauses before replying. "About a year, I think."

Louise obviously has a problem looking at people's eyes, but today, she's not even trying. She fidgets with a folded stick that reminds me of something but I can't quite place it. I hope it's not a weapon.

"What?" I cry, feigning offense. "Ravi never told me anything." I look at him, pretending to be hurt.

"We try to be discreet. We work in the same area, and people talk. I mean, they're buying our computers at CERN," he elaborates.

I almost miss something. I forget that I'm not supposed to know what happens in Pangea. Even though I know the answer, I have to ask him, otherwise it'd look suspicious. God, it's hard to keep track of these things.

"Wait, how's that even possible?" I pretend to be confused. "You barely see each other. She works in Europe, for God's sake." I want to see how they dig themselves out of this.

Ravi looks outside, clearly leaving Louise to the job of explaining this abnormality. In my peripheral vision, I notice Jane shaking her head. Louise will have to fabricate some lie. I wish I was recording this so we could all watch it and laugh together when they learn who I really am. Good times.

"We're in a long-distance relationship, that's true." She nods. "But we talk every day. It's all about intimacy." Well, she didn't lie. And she's right, intimacy is what makes or breaks a relationship.

"I know what you're thinking," Ravi interjects. "Long-distance relationships are hard but we're making it work."

Louise nervously folds and unfolds her stick a little, playing with it, and I finally remember where I saw it.

"It's a walking stick!" I shout. "Louise, your stick reminds me of the blind superhero. Have you seen it?"

If everyone in life had one shot—and only one shot—at lassoing our words and pulling them back down our throats, this would be my chosen moment to do it.

THE LIMO DROPS us off at the resort in front of a private beach. I wanted to take Jane to the Indian Island County Park, which is a nice place for us to ride bikes and walk on the beach. However, the media has caught up with me and Ravi staying around here. We don't have privacy anymore.

During the ride there, Louise was extremely polite about my faux pas—ironically, a French phrase. She was born with a condition where the eyes do not form. Since she was a baby, she's worn prosthetic eyes so her face doesn't deform around the lack of eyes. How interesting. Louise is blind here, but not in Pangea.

Ravi helps Louise toward a wooden gazebo with a straw roof that has a beautiful view of the ocean and the beach. Jane walks ahead of me, and I can't help but admire the mixture of sun and shadows delineating her curves. She catches me staring at her and looks at me with an amused smile. The lack of punching is progress, I guess. I take her hand and lead her to her seat.

The resort staff brings us some snacks and drinks. Jane gets a glass of Merlot, her favorite wine, while I decide to avoid the suspicious drinks and ask for a glass of Riesling. I wanted white Zinfandel, but that'd be too close for comfort. Moreover, I'm told drinking Zinfandel would make me look trashy. Who makes these stupid rules? Ravi and Louise are also drinking Merlot. We are so different, the three of them and I. We can even tell by the wine we drink. I'm sweet and semi- transparent; the protectors are bitter and dark.

It's time to break the ice. I ask Louise why she chose physics as her line of work.

"I grew up in Marseille, a city on the Mediterranean coast. The tides always fascinated me. You may not believe me, but the low and high tides sound different, and I wanted to understand why." Louise somehow manages not to chew her fingernails.

On Jora, tides are almost unnoticeable, since we don't have the moon. When I found out about them here, I was in awe.

"My father told me that the moon caused the tides. But that didn't make any sense. How did the moon affect the oceans, being so far away? So I learned about gravity. I was twelve years old when I modeled the solar system for a science project." She smiles, peers over at Ravi even though she can't see him, and finally bites her thumb nail. "The rest is history. I was lucky to get a job at CERN. It's very competitive there."

It's late afternoon and although it's cloudier than I'd like, I love the soothing sounds of the breaking waves and the ocean breeze. The tropical place in Pangea gave me the idea for the setting of this date.

"She's being modest, of course. There was no luck involved. She's just that smart." Ravi compliments her, and they kiss. I take advantage of their moment and try to kiss Jane but she pushes me back; not yet. At least she laughs when I try to do that, so no harm done.

After a few hours of enjoying the company, the view, and the view of the company, I grab Jane's hand and take her for a walk. The water is cold on our feet but the sun is warm on the skin, and most of the clouds are gone.

The only thing that doesn't let me enjoy this as much as I could is the fact that I'm hiding my real nature from her. And, if you think about it, so is she. I wonder if she likes piña coladas.

"So, do I have to ask Louise for your hand in marriage?" I joke, and she snickers at me.

"She's just a good friend. She doesn't want me to get hurt, again. And Ravi's the best thing that's happened to Louise. She used to be a chain smoker but stopped because of him, you know?"

Well, good for her but I'm here because of Jane, not Ravi and Louise.

"Why are you so distant? Are you afraid of me?"

"There is just so much about you that I don't know," she answers. "Heck, there's so much about me that you don't know."

This reminds me of her black purse that's always glued to her like an extra limb. Fortunately, she left it in her chair.

"Since you mentioned it, you seem very attached to your...purse." Jane steals a glance at the gazebo. She knows exactly what I'm talking about. "Any other reason to carry it, besides the gods—" I stop myself just in time.

Jane immediately frowns, stepping back a little.

"How do you know...?"

"The God's right to keep and bear arms?" I interrupt her. "You know, the second amendment?" I give a nervous laugh.

She takes a few seconds to answer. Maybe I'm going to die today, after all.

"There's no 'God' in the second amendment, Mike."

"I know. I was just trying to make a silly joke. Sorry."

She looks again in the direction of Ravi and Louise, biting her lip.

"It's because of something that happened years ago. It's

the only way I feel safe. As I said, we barely know each other." She sighs, staring at the ocean.

"No. I know a lot about you, Jane. You're a successful, smart woman. You have a master's in nuclear engineering. You work at one of the largest particle accelerators in the world." I advance toward her and grab her hands. "We all have our little secrets. What matters are our actions. Love is not what you say; love is what you do." I laugh at myself, and Jane laughs with me.

"That's so cheesy," she says, as I put my hands on her back and pull her closer, looking into her eyes. Then, I lean in and kiss her, and this time, she lets me. This is what Heaven is, the real one, not Pangea. Jane's lips taste salty and wet, like the ocean. Her warm body envelops mine in a passionate embrace, and she puts her hands on my neck. Ravi whistles and claps from a distance. I'll definitely throw sand in his face when we get back.

We walk side by side in silence then, our arms on each other's backs. I know what's in her mind—it's the same thing I'm thinking. We both have our second life in Pangea. How can we be together if we hide that from our partner? Our secrets are too big to be hidden. Either way, we deserve to be happy. At least for a day.

I stop and look into her eyes.

"Jane, I want you to come home with me tonight. And by home, I mean the hotel, of course."

She raises her eyebrow in amusement and punches my arm.

"This is only our first date. Who do you think I am?" she asks with a sly grin.

What a weird planet. Sex is so complicated here.

"You're saying next date we're good, then?"

24

OTHERS

I t's time to speak to the Jori. My language is still here, buried in my brain, but something happened to it when I showed up on Earth. I've been thinking about that for a long time, periodically looking at the MRI scans Dr. Alice gave me, trying to make sense of it.

Brains are my specialty. My major could've been neurosurgery in school but I studied neurocomputer science because I often get squeamish. As a result, I spent years in college drinking booze, partying, and analyzing my own brain, so I could learn how to install neurosensors.

True, I don't have an MRI scan of my head from when I was on Jora. My brain here is, in a way, damaged. The messengers destroyed the connections that allowed me to speak my language, and created other paths in there so I could speak English.

The second MRI image was taken when I was already on Earth and, like the old Mike, the new me only speaks English. I'm not very good at remembering...well, almost anything. Dates and names are gone the moment I get distracted, sometimes even while I'm in the conversation.

However, I excel at memorizing anything related to my work. So even though I don't have a scan of my brain from before I came here, I remember with great clarity what it looks like in the places that matter.

It turns out that Mike's brain and my old brain are almost identical in the language areas but Mike's has an extra, tiny connection in one specific place. I believe this is just a switch that turns those areas on and off. My hypothesis is that, if I add my old connection back to my new brain, I'll speak both languages, and who doesn't like to experiment on their own brain?

I knew that the moment I took the scans home but there were still a few problems to solve before I could restore that connection. First, this is all just a guess. If I'm wrong, I may cause damage to my own brain. The injury may be imperceptible, or I could start babbling movie names in alphabetical order. I may even die if the surgery goes wrong. Second, and most importantly, even if I am somehow able to do it, I'm known to be a coward. I've been talking myself out of doing this since the beginning.

Since I spoke with Mercury, I've started paying more attention to what I can do here in the hypersphere. Yes, my connection to this place is strong but it goes beyond what even I thought possible. Our bodies can be changed. And because we can be killed when we have brain damage, our brains can be altered, as well.

When I wake in Pangea, I make sure my door is closed. Then, I walk back to the bed and sit on its edge, admiring the whiteness in front of me. The amazingly bright and soothing room I always find myself in may actually be of some help, after all.

I'll first try it out on something less vital. My goal is to damage part of a nerve in my left hand and see if I can make my pinky stop working. If this doesn't work, or if I can't reverse it, it should still be okay. It'd be like

a battle wound that will fix itself when I get back to Earth, albeit with some nerve memory. I can live with that.

I concentrate on the nerve right after it forks to the pinky. With a quick thought, the connection at that point is cut, just like that, and I scream. I didn't even know it would hurt. It's like a whole bee hive just declared war on my finger. Damaging any nerve in our bodies will do that. Bringing my left hand closer to my eyes, I try to move my pinky but fail. It worked.

While I massage my hand for a bit, I consider my next step. This part of the operation worked. Next, I'll try to reconstruct the damage by recreating the nerve connections where I detached them. This is going to be harder than I thought, though. The wound is too deep, I cut too much to prove a point, and I'm not sure if I can reconnect everything.

Concentrating on my hand again, I find the right place and add the nerves back. It doesn't hurt this time, or at least, not any more than it already was. I don't do a good job, though. My pinky has some movement but it wouldn't be possible to reconstruct everything exactly the way it was. It's just too complicated. Fortunately, the area in my brain that needs repair is just a handful of neurons. Even if I add more to the mix, it's not going to matter. My belief is that this area works as a switch, and, as long as it's on, it should work. At least, I hope so.

It's time. Taking a deep breath, I focus. My heart rate goes through the roof as I investigate my brain from the inside. It's amazing; if we had tools like this, surgery or diagnostics would be so easy to do. It takes a while for me to get used to traverse a live brain due to the change of perspective. I'm inside my own brain. I know what I should do but I need to find it using a different map. No, not a map —it's the real thing—and it looks way different than an MRI scan.

After about ten minutes of searching, I find the right spot in my brain. Then, to be on the safe side, I restart the search from scratch and double-check to see if I end up in the same place. I do. This is it. I just have to add that connection, which I'm doing...right...now. Goodbye, world.

I open my eyes, afraid, feeling nothing different. I must say something.

"Hello, world!" I shout. Looks like I'm not insane yet, or at least, not worse than I was before. But this is English. Can I do it in Dïnisc?

"Äle mîndu!" I sing.

Excited by my success, I jump out of my bed, open the door to my room, and run outside, ignoring everyone else. People watch me from their rooms as I race through the blueish—almost sapphire—hallway.

When I get near the arch—it's closed, with no countdown yet—I notice people inside Green, where the protectors have their headquarters. They see me outside and walk toward me.

"Finally, Mike, you're here. Can we talk to you, Your Majesty?" John asks. "How did you manage to avoid coming here to Pangea for so long?"

I sneak a glimpse at Blue, the prisoners' room, eager to talk to them. This is not the time to chat with the protectors.

"I was here. I just wasn't in the mood to open the door. There's been too much yelling and punching going on."

John studies me with his eyes, as if looking for something. Jane stands next to him, scratching her furrowed eyebrows.

"Well, ignoring how, exactly, you kept your door closed,

we have to talk about our strategy. We don't know when the gate will open but we must be prepared," John continues.

Vladimir rolls his eyes at that, shaking his head.

"Plan what?" I say. "There's no telling what kind of environment will show up."

After a quick, angry glance at Vladimir, John moves closer.

"We had our asses handed to us in less than an hour last time, Mike. We need to work on some kind of plan, even if we're grasping at straws."

I cross my arms. "As a matter of fact, I have my own plan. I don't think you'll agree with me, so I'll do it alone."

John crosses his own arms in response. "Try us."

"Well, we're fighting the wrong adversary," I say, studying the abnormally large muscles that stuff his jacket to bursting. I gulp before continuing. "Our enemy is not Jora. It's the messengers." I gesture at the hypersphere entrance as if they actually stood there.

"Are you out of your mind?" Jane says, glaring at me. "They're the ones trying to save us, or one of the Earths, at least."

"As I said, you would not agree with me. Now, if you'll excuse me, I'm going to try to communicate with the prisoners."

As I begin walking toward the jail door, Jane jumps in front of me, blocking my way. This is not going to be easy.

"Please tell me you're joking. Are you really going to fight the gods?" She puts her open palm on my chest.

"If he wants to be Don Quixote, let him," Louise says, coming up behind her. "We may as well get some information from the prisonniers."

Jane eyes her for a second and finally nods, moving away, allowing me passage.

"Don't be stupid," Jane warns me. Funny, she says "stupid" like "stoopid," and I'm the one who has an accent.

Taking a deep breath, I step inside the room. The room is painted a lighter blue inside, which is great. Having a whole room with a hard and saturated blue would be hard on the eyes. As it is, though, it has a calming effect.

Jane enters the room behind me. The blue door's not back yet, since no one told it to reappear. While the arch is always closed, automatically opening when someone from the right team is nearby, the red, blue, and green doors respond to the thoughts of anyone in their vicinity—except prisoners, of course.

"Excuse me?" I tell Jane. I want to be alone.

"I want someone else in there with you." She guesses what I mean. "We don't exactly trust you— yet."

"Tell me about it. But no, I need to get their trust, and the fewer people here, the better."

Jane takes her time to decide, but, after a while, she nods. Once the blue door is finally back, and I'm alone with the prisoners, it occurs to me that one of them may know me. I turn around and finally look at the two people in here.

They're strangers. I breathe a sigh of relief. Before me, a black woman with wavy and short hair wears a single blue înofärmu. She's sitting on a white, blubbery couch behind what looks like a glass barrier. A bearded man in a purple vustodä is beside her. Unsurprisingly, they both look to be in their late teens.

The jail contains everything they need to survive. A discreet bathroom is located at the end of the room, next to some white laundry machines, a treadmill, and a stationary bike.

As I get closer to the prisoners, an area of the see- thru barrier vanishes, opening a disk-shaped passage through it.

The man moves in front of the woman as I step inside. Maybe they're afraid I'll torture them, or worse, but what happens next will shock them. I clear my throat and start singing in Dïnisc.

"<The girls in my town are easy; they like to show their booties.>"

To my dismay, I can only sing in my language. Worse, it's a trashy song that was popular just before I showed up on Earth. What the hell? In hindsight, I realize that I also sang when I first tried to speak Dïnisc. "<Hello, world>" is part of a popular song that I hate. I made a poor choice of words to try my language, and now I'm making a fool of myself.

25

INTERFACES

Their names are Katon and Talaia. I had to practice until I was able to sing more than just popular sleazy songs, but while I did it, they were rolling on the floor, laughing.

Jane comes in, and I shoo her away. She sees them laughing with tears in their eyes and looks at me with a grin. I tell her there was a misunderstanding, and they found it funny. Jane seems to be amused but she leaves us alone.

Despite his first instinct to protect his friend, Katon is the shy one, staying far away from me. Talaia, on the other hand, doesn't look like someone who needs protection. She marches toward me as if she's not a prisoner, holding her head high. I like that.

On Jora, most people have some type of stick-on jewelry on their temples that delineate the side of the eye. On Earth, they'd look like complex temple piercings that require minor surgery to stay put. We have technology to keep them in place without making holes in your skin. So they're easy to exchange and wear, like clothes. Or earrings.

Talaia's jewelry is a pattern of small swords that starts on her left temple and ends at her cheek, while Katon's is an octagon made of little triangles. The ornaments on the left temple almost always have religious significance, even if the person isn't religious, while jewelry on the right temple represents family or partners. Neither Talaia nor Katon have anything on that side. Swords, ironically, mean "peace in Heaven." Octagons represent victory. Or bananas. I was never into it, so I'm not exactly an expert on face adornments.

They want to know how I'm able to speak their language. I sing that the messengers helped me, which is not a complete lie. Talaia complains about some of the people here, or specifically, Frederico. According to her, he's a creep. I explain, in song, that we're just like them. Some of us have dubious morals—a few even root for teams with blue jerseys—but most are just good people trying to save Earth.

They refuse to tell me who their leader is or any other names of people in their group. I'm fine with that. I just wanted to see if I could actually speak the language, and I can, in a way. Anything else I gather would be useful, but it's not necessary. What I need is to talk to Mike—the real one —and I can't just go around asking about him. I could end up killing him if someone there recognizes me.

When I leave the room, I meet Vladimir in the hallway. Every time I see him, he has this look of mischief, as if someone just told a joke to him, or he's about to tell one. The fact that he's wearing only an undershirt with large arm holes, and a pair of blue pajama pants with white stripes, makes the situation weirder.

"Did you get anything, *priyatel*?" Vladimir asks once I'm outside.

"A few words here and there. This is going to take a while," I lie. I'm glad Vladimir is here, though. I have a favor to ask him.

"Captain, can you help me out?" I ask. Vladimir doesn't say anything. "Could you go to the armory and bring back the largest weapons people can carry? Bring as many as you can, please."

Vladimir is in the Russian navy. He's as tough as they come, and I think it's going to take a while to convince him to do it, which means I may have to do it myself. He smirks, as if thinking for a brief moment about what I asked. Finally, he looks back at me with a large smile.

"Sure, *drug*," he says, disappearing into the red room.

This surprises me. I was expecting some resistance but he didn't ask me any questions. What an interesting fellow.

After that, I walk inside Green, the one they call "the war room." Whenever I'm here, they're either interrogating, intimidating, or punching me. So when I'm in Pangea, I'm either in my room, the hypersphere, or some other place as far from here as possible. This is the first time I've ever been inside and not in a hurry, so I take some time to look around.

Like the other main rooms with colors for names, the walls and ceiling match their namesake, but the shade of color—in this case, green—is less pronounced inside. Despite the calming effect, it resembles a hospital room from old World War II movies. It looks tacky. Since the first time I visited Europe, I have a penchant for those movies.

A large mahogany table in the middle is surrounded by eighteen luxury leaning chairs with high backs, which are often used for meetings. The table's dwarfed by the size of the room, though, just like everything in Pangea.

Several smaller tables with their own orbiting chairs are

scattered everywhere. The protectors play cards at some of them. Yesterday, I tried to suggest a game that's similar to strip poker but the idea was quickly shot down.

The sides of the green room are filled with rows and rows of lockers. With the exception of guns, all their supplies are here. The lockers contain packaged food, drinks, tools, backpacks, clothes—the protectors are as messy as a bunch of high school kids.

Jane and Ravi are seated next to each other, with John and Carmen at the opposite side. Frederico is also here, but he sits several chairs away from them, not playing cards. Louise is casually smoking an electronic cigarette, leaning on a locker closer to the entrance. Joshua is next to her, discussing something, but they stop talking when they see me.

"I'm glad you could join us, Mike," Jane says. I walk over to the table and sit, placing my feet on top of the table, just like I saw in a movie. It's time to play ball. Or for a Hail Mary. I'm not good with sports metaphors from Earth.

"Please don't interrupt whatever you're doing. I can wait," I say, putting my hands on the back of my head.

Jane drops her cards on the table.

"How did it go with the prisoners? Seems like you're universally ridiculous," she mocks me, taking a sip from a mug. An aroma of citrus tea destroys my expectations of having any kind of coffee until I'm back on Earth.

"It's a gift," I admit, smiling. "I didn't learn much, but they told me their names. The man is Katon and the woman is Talaia. Also, it's not pronounced Jora. It's…" Then I sing, "<Jora.>"

"Interesting," she says, raising her eyebrow and smiling. "It's more than we have ever learned from them. Good job."

For the first time, she's not joking or mad at me.

"It's my charisma," I say.

"I don't think they're going to be much help," John says. "They don't know anything about the new hypersphere game, and they know nothing about the Jori's plans." John's always killing the mood.

"You're right," I concede. "But I just wanted to learn to communicate, not gather intelligence." I nod at Jane. "In fact, my goals and yours may have a lot in common but they're not the same."

Jane purses her lips and lowers her eyebrows.

"He's gone rogue," says Ravi, looking amused.

"I always was a rogue, Ravi." I chuckle. "I'm sorry if I like to find alternatives that don't involve killing people."

John stands up, walks next to me, and pushes my legs off the table. Ouch. Then, he puts his hand on the table, and eyes me with suspicion.

"We need to meet you on Earth. You must help us find our Earth's killer," John says, as if he hasn't just assaulted me. On the plus side, they still think that the mole cannot be here. I hope it takes a long time until they figure it out.

"I'll get to that, eventually. First, I want to help you with something here," I say.

Vladimir's timing couldn't have been any better. He comes in with a pile of weapons in a bag and drops them on the table, almost on top of John's hand, scratching the top in several places, and scrambling the cards everywhere. The pile of weapons makes me realize the irony of trying not to kill people by bringing lots of guns into the room.

"What the hell are you doing?" John barks at him.

A metallic smell fills the room, even though I believe most of the material used in the guns is some kind of black carbon fiber. Or maybe it's just a different type of steel.

"You should ask your tovarishch." He chuckles. I suspect

that he likes to piss John off. That explains why he obeyed me without hesitation, the sneaky bastard. What a team.

"Jane, pick up the large, double-barreled capacitor next to Carmen," I request.

Jane hesitates for a second and looks at John, who shrugs. Then, she stands and grabs the football-powered rifle.

I stand up as well. "Now, strap it on your shoulder, and turn the safety on." I don't want people shooting at each other by accident. She does as I ask her, and nods. I point to the top of the gun. "There's a screen here, in the middle. Can you see it?"

"I see something that looks like a mini football goal."

"You mean an American football goal," blurts Louise, but her face indicates that she regrets saying it. I snicker, and Jane frowns at me. I should stop doing that. She already told me it's not funny, so I clear my throat.

Jane cringes when I walk behind her but soon relaxes. From there, I move my left arm and grab the back of her hand, near the trigger. I pull her closer as I do this, and she doesn't complain. Her neck is near my face, and her hair touches my nose, making it itch in a good way.

Her perfume of Eau de something—she told me about it, but I forgot how it's called—survived the transition to the hypersphere. Who would've guessed? She smells great, even here. Grabbing her right hand, also from behind, I pull her even closer. I know she's smiling, though I can't see her face. I bet she forgot that I can sense beyond my eyes in Pangea; otherwise, she probably would try to suppress her grin.

"Okay, now I want you to close your eyes and concentrate," I say, and she obeys. I direct my attention to the weapon. It's trying to use her own nerves to communicate with her brain. If you're not used to it, it feels eerie. Her body instinctively tries to disconnect it, over and over again. It doesn't like anything using its own nervous system.

Because of that, her hand keeps moving away from the contacts. They've never felt anything like this before, but they must trust the interface, instead of fighting it. At the moment, I'm trying to keep Jane's hands relaxed and on top of the interface, but she's fighting me without even noticing.

"Relax, Jane." Then, pressing her hand more firmly to where we hold the gun, I cheat a little. If I can change my brain in here, I can do other tricks as well. With my mind, I create the connection for her, so she can learn to do it herself.

Startled, she opens her eyes, trying to jerk away, and drops the gun. It only falls to her belly since she had it on a strap. Meanwhile, I hold her arms, not letting her move away from me. It's not time to give up yet.

Turning her head around, she brings her mouth close to mine, as if surprised at what happened. We're both overwhelmed, though for different reasons.

"I saw...something there. This isn't just used for visually aiming at targets," she says, looking at me with her pearl-black eyes. "These are smart weapons!" I'm holding both her hands from behind and we are so close we could kiss. Time seems to stand still.

"Ahem!" Ravi clears his throat, and Jane jerks away from me, her cheeks growing red. I can't help but laugh.

"Please ignore the prude and try again," I say. She puts her hands on the gun and does what I said, but this time she stays away from me.

"I can see it again. But how...?" She looks at her weapon in awe. "It's detecting everyone in the room, calculating the odds of killing them. I think it can do more than that." Jane immerses herself in the view screen. All the projections Jane sees are in her mind, not on her real field of vision. Soon, they'll learn that the weapon also responds to their thoughts, but that will take some time.

John is next. I help him from the front—there's no need to get that intimate with a US Army major. My experience with Jane taught me that they only need a jump start to begin playing with it. It doesn't take long for them to learn the basics, and they all seem to love their new toys. For a while, it's like I'm not even in the room.

"We've been losing for so long," John remarks.

"It's amazing that we actually won even a couple of times."

On the other hand, I'm feeling a little bad. I just taught them to be more effective in killing my own people.

"I'd appreciate if you shoot only when necessary," I say. "I still want to talk to the Jori, and people tend to be upset when they get killed."

26

CHOICES

It's been a couple of weeks, and the hypersphere should open soon. We're all on edge, worried about what the messengers are preparing for us. Meanwhile, my new daily routine on Earth is more complicated than ever. I don't want anyone knowing about the house I bought.

Every day, I walk to the hotel and go inside through the back entrance, gathering anything I need from my room. Next, I go down to the lobby to wait for my ride. At night, my driver drops me at the hotel and I walk back to the house. I give generous tips to the porters and the other employees, asking for discretion.

And yet, where there's secrecy, there are rumors. I overheard them talking about me having an affair with a local married woman whose husband is often away. Nonsense. I'm certain I'll read about that on the gossip websites sometime in the next month or so.

At night, I sleep in a hospital bed with a special mattress because of my bed sores. It turns out we don't move our bodies when we're in Pangea—our brains are not actually here. It's a mystery how we can breathe without assistance.

The mattress helps, but if I spend more than one night like that, I'll need someone to move me around. This is another good reason to have Julie, my nurse. Since she doesn't have any kids, and her husband travels for business a lot, she almost always spends the night. In a separate room, which is ironic. On Jora, everyone in a marriage has their own room, even if you are a couple, a trio, or a foursome.

I bought all the equipment, fluids, and drugs to keep me alive in case I'm trapped. I've asked her to not take me to a hospital if I don't wake up. My best guess is if this happens, she'll wait one or two days. If I'm trapped in the hypersphere for more than a week, there'll be worse things to be worried about than explaining myself to hospital staff.

The operation I did on my brain in Pangea worked better than expected. I thought I'd have to do it every single night I'm back there, but it turns out that any brain changes that happen there are copied to our brain on Earth. This is probably what happens to the new memories we acquire in Pangea, as well. More importantly, I'm finally able to speak D'inisc without singing. The last thing I want is to be part of an impromptu musical when talking to the Jori. Not again.

At RNL, our work is going faster than we thought. We're finishing ten analog brains a day now. The job will be done in two months at this pace. David's here with several of his graduate students, and progress has been steady. The work is even helping his social anxiety. He seems happier and more relaxed, and even looks into strangers' eyes once in a while.

Everybody is excited about the new capabilities of the accelerator. Even I'm looking forward to it, though I have other, ulterior motives.

Jane hasn't talked to me since our date, however. Last

week, I went to a charity event organized by the Speck Foundation in New York, where I finally met Becky and Carmen in "real" life. Becky even tried to set up an interview with me but I don't give interviews. Anyway, I wanted Jane to go with me, but she never returned my calls.

Paradoxically, our relationship in Pangea is getting better by the day. We can't get enough of each other. So I stopped trying to contact her here. I'm a grown man, at least on Earth. I know when I'm not wanted. Still, this doesn't make me any happier. It's hard to date after I spent so much time with my ex-fiancée, even after a year has passed. You keep second-guessing yourself.

When it's lunch time, I walk toward the cafeteria. Ravi isn't here. He flew to Los Angeles this morning to spend a few days at Caltech. They were the first to have our technology, and it's worthwhile to go there once in a while. Still, it's weird that he's there while David's here.

Someone calls my name while I'm outside, looking up at the moon. It's awesome. We can see it during the day sometimes.

"Hey, Mike!" Jane says.

She catches up with me, though she doesn't look at the moon. I don't like what's coming up.

"I'm happy to see you, Jane. It's been a long time," I say, faking a smile.

Today, she's wearing a black business skirt that barely reaches her knees, and a sleeveless turquoise blouse covered by an informal gray jacket. As always, her hair is neatly arranged in a ponytail.

"I'm sorry, Mike, but we have to talk."

Yeah, I saw that coming. "It's not you, it's me."

"We've grown apart." "I'm going to concentrate on my

career." I know all the hits. I wonder which one she's going to pick.

She looks down, hesitating. Ignoring her, I start walking toward the cafeteria again. The clicking and knocking sound of her heels behind me indicates she's trying to keep pace. This will be a dreadful lunch.

"I was confused about my feelings," she begins. "And I think about you a lot. But I must be honest. I'm falling for someone else."

Ah, yes, it's the "I have feelings for someone else" track. How odd. Usually they go with the other excuses when this is the real one. I take a deep breath. I can take it. I bet it's Steve, from the cafeteria.

"Well, Jane. I'm upset about this, but I'm glad you told me before we were serious." I try to be the better man—uh, person. "Do I know him?"

"No, you don't. This is hard to explain," she tells me. "You two are so alike it's spooky."

"Please don't tell me that if we knew each other, we'd be friends. It's easier if you just kill me," I beg with a weak smile.

"Well, now that you mention it, you probably would be friends." She nods, thoughtfully. Did she just tell me that when I specifically asked her not to say it? Damn it, Jane. That's mean.

"It's understandable, really. You found someone just like me, but better," I respond. This seems petty, but I told her to kill me instead, and she didn't, so it's her fault.

She looks away, rubbing her forehead. I'm not going to make this easy for her.

"I know it sounds bad. There's nothing I can say or do about it, though. It's not that he's better than you..."

"You just have more things in common," I finish for her.

"I'm really sorry. I didn't see that coming."

There is something odd about this, though. A thought comes to my mind.

"Wait a minute, how come I don't know him? We're around each other most of the time," I ask.

"Uh...it's a long-distance thing. I mean, it'll be a thing, I hope," she says. Funny, just like Ravi's relationship with Louise. Actually, exactly like that, I think, realizing what's going on.

"You haven't asked him out yet?" I grin. I know who he is.

"Well, this is awkward. You're taking this better than I expected," she says, adjusting her ponytail even though it looks perfect.

"Go ahead and tell him how you feel. Life is short. I'm not going to be your plan B, though, just so you know." In fact, I'm both plan A and plan B. I never thought I'd be in this position.

"I understand. But I still want us to be friends."

This is not how this should work. If I wasn't the other guy, the right way to do this would be to cut any and all contact. Not for too long, just something like ten to a hundred years. Otherwise, your heart never heals. But this is not your regular break-up, and I'm okay with that.

"Sure, Jane. I'll always be your friend." I smile. "Want to join me for lunch? I heard they have steak today. It's a gorgeous, sunny day, and we can even see the moon!" I point at the sky. I'm always flabbergasted by their moon. "Flabbergasted" is one of my favorite words. Too bad people don't say it much.

Jane glances at the moon but she doesn't appear amused by it. People don't often value what they take for granted.

"Really, Mike. I thought that you would be at least a little bit upset," she complains. I find that amusing. Like me, she sometimes says things that are better not said.

"I'm sorry. I was already expecting that you would dump me, though. You didn't answer my texts." I don't know what else to say. Anyone watching our conversation would think I'm acting like a jerk. But she is the one breaking up with me, and now I'm feeling guilty. How does she do that?

We both stop walking and look at each other.

"I won't have lunch with you today. It'd be weird." She then kisses me on the cheek while avoiding my eyes and heads back to the laboratory. I watch her go but she doesn't look back. Guess I'll be eating alone after all.

Still, Jane did something admirable. She's not the type of woman who dates more than one man at a time. She has boundaries, and she doesn't leave other people waiting for her. Jane knows what she wants and goes for it, with dignity, unlike someone I used to know.

After all the crap I've been through, this is the number one quality I look for in a woman. Number two is not wanting to kill me, but that's negotiable.

27

SUPERDOME

When I next open my eyes in my quarters, I hear loud noises coming from outside my room. I jump out of my bed and run to the hallway. People are crowding around the arch. The large digital countdown says fifteen minutes. I'm even more worried about it this time. The messengers must be pissed, and I'm afraid they'll start retaliating.

In front of Red, I find Paulo giving out capacitors. He hands me one and nods. It's a big, double-barreled weapon, with a circle of small ellipsoids to power it, like a giant-sized nerf gun. I think he's forgiven me for shooting him twice.

Jane's inside Green. She waves at me and slinks around the other protectors, heading in my direction. Like everybody else, she's back to her desert clothes— in her case a tank top and shorts. As for me, I decided on black running pants and a navy-blue t-shirt.

I'm not going to let her die today. I'll be in the first wave this time, where, with any luck, I'll figure out a way to keep everyone safe. She doesn't say anything when she reaches me; there's no need. We kiss for a long time, surprising no one around us. I think the other protectors pretend they don't see us.

"That was unexpected," I lie, looking into her eyes.

"I wanted to do this today, before we fight," she blurts with a sudden grim look. "One of us might die. I'd never forgive myself." I kiss her again, pulling her closer.

"I will not let that happen."

"We never know what the gods' plan is," she says, looking at the gate.

Screw the gods. I don't care what their plan is. I have my own. And today is not a good day to die. We wait while the countdown goes to zero.

When the door opens, Joshua does the sign of the cross. Louise explained it to me when I asked about it the last time. It's odd that he's so self-assured, yet he still needs to do this. Meanwhile, John leaps inside like a gymnast. Vladimir, Joshua, and I are behind him.

A large, bright red structure dominates the view less than one hundred meters away. It's a dome about eighty meters tall, and it'd look like a covered soccer stadium from afar, except that it has no windows. The whole structure reflects the sun like metal. The sky is yellow again, with no visible clouds, and it feels like a warm summer day.

John walks ahead of us. There are no Jori that we can see —the gates are always far away from each other—but we must keep an eye out for booby traps. We take our time walking toward the structure, keeping distance between us.

John and Vladimir arrive at an entrance that must be at least four meters tall. A smooth and thin door slides open, and we stare at dim wall inside it. After a quick pause, they enter the building, aiming their capacitors toward the wall.

Meanwhile, I walk outside, around the dome, exposed. If there are guns or mines, I'll be able to detect them. Looking at the surrounding landscape, I notice that there's nothing higher than this building. It's on the top of a hill. The hill itself is covered with large arrays of guns all the way down, aiming outward, away from us. There are ten—no, twenty. No, more than that. Dozens of multi-barreled turrets line the hill, diamond- shaped grass in between them.

When I'm near the front of the building, I stop for a while to focus. There are still no enemies nearby, and no armed weapons of any kind. Breathing a sigh of relief, I walk to the front.

Several six-wheeled, armored vehicles with missile launchers of some sort are parked there. They must fire artillery energy shells or something heavy like that. The whole back of the truck is a giant vertical football, as if it's waiting for a god's foot to kick a field goal, making me smile despite the situation.

A winding road downhill begins just after the trucks, and it's protected by even more turrets. This place is a fortress. There's another hill in the distance, maybe ten kilometers away. It looks very much like ours, but it's too far for me to tell.

The vehicles are made for three people, and one of them must control the absurdly large capacitor. Reaching inside the nearest one, I grab a pair of binoculars, and use them to look down the hill. They have powerful optics and, like every other machine we've found here, they respond to my mind.

Several windowless, multi-sided structures are located in the middle of the hills—the messengers must have something against windows. There's no way for me to check what they have inside.

Another winding road goes up the other hill. It's hard to tell, but they seem to have the same vehicles on the Jori's side, in front of a massive blue dome. I don't know the goal of this game, but given the number of guns, this is going to be bloody.

John exits the building behind me. When he gets closer, I hand him the binoculars, and he gives me a headset.

"We'll use this to communicate," he explains. "Everyone's grabbing one inside the Superdome." Nice, they named it already. "Go in there and take a look. This will be our home for some time."

Turns out the "Superdome" is some type of headquarters. There are several rooms with all kinds of supplies, which indicates that we're going to spend a long time here. In one room, I find armored suits, weapons, ammunition, and neat smoke bombs. Another one has food, bottles of water, and what I hope is some kind of alcoholic beverage. The peculiar room next to that contains several pods with computers and screens with a handful of chairs each. A command area.

With a cup of coffee in my hand—the gods have heard my prayers—I meet Ravi in one of the hallways. Louise is next to him, having an honest-to-god real cigarette, and I cough several times. I almost don't recognize her because for the first time since I've met her, her blonde hair is tied into a bun.

"Mike," Louise says. "I can smoke here. It's awesome!" She grins, ignoring my discomfort. Not counting the effects on her brain, everything will go back to normal when she wakes up on Earth.

"Good for you!" I say. I hate this expression—my mind always finishes this sentence with, "but not for me." It doesn't sound that empathetic.

"There are even barracks and fully equipped bathrooms

in the back," Ravi explains. "This may take a long time to finish."

I almost laugh at his camouflaged clothes. He seems so proud wearing them, but it won't do any good here. There are no trees.

"This is a battle game, Ravi," I say. "They tend to end quickly, don't they?"

"Not this time. Look at how many weapons we have, and all the static defenses down the hill. And we've used up all our AED bombs."

He keeps surveying the place with me, and we find Jane in a room on the second floor of the fort. Unlike everything else, this one looks like one of the quarters in the habitat rings. The large, flashing red circle at its center contrasts with the all-white round walls and convex ceiling. It's as if we entered a video game in real life. In fact, this is exactly what I feel every time I show up in my quarters in Pangea.

"They must get here to win," Jane explains. "We have to protect it."

So, it's a capture-the-flag kind of game. Perhaps we should just let them win. Is saving one protector worth people dying? I want to avoid bloodshed but they want to protect Earth, and one of them may go into deep sleep because of that. We have different goals.

Paulo shows up from below, running up the stairs, panting.

"We have to go, now," he commands. "The Jori are moving!"

Oh no. The battle has already started and we're here doing nothing, enjoying ourselves.

28

CONTACT

We run down the stairs and outside the dome, in the direction of the trucks. There's no time to get better armor. Really, we should've done that from the start. There's no telling what gifts those structures in the middle of the battlefield have, and they'll get there first.

John is in the first vehicle. He stands up and yells, pointing at his ears.

"Everybody, put on your headsets!"

Since his vehicle is the first one in line, my intention is to ride with him. However, Joshua is already seated next to John, and Vladimir is on the weapon, so there's no space.

"Joshua, I have to be first. I can see better than everyone here."

Without hesitation, Joshua gets up and leaves the truck. He taps on my shoulder as he passes, and gets in another vehicle behind us. Now that we know each other, Joshua's acting less aggressive toward me. Once you're in his circle of friends, he defends you like a hawk.

As soon as I sit next to John, he starts driving in the

direction of the road. These trucks are equipped with advanced computers and could drive themselves—we only have to think where to go—but John likes to be in control. Since I'm just a passenger, I let him do whatever he wants so I can scout ahead.

"This is John," we hear in our headsets. "I'm leading the line. Let's identify ourselves. Mike is riding shotgun, and Vladimir is the gunner."

"Louise, second in line. Jane and Ravi, here." I can't help but grin when I hear her say that. Of course, she'd be the driver.

In front of us, the Jori advance toward the midpoint of the battlefield. They're already on the third curve down their road. Our mission has already failed. We're in damage control mode but maybe we can still do something even if they win this race.

"We have to go faster!" I tell John. The strange yellow sky doesn't help at all. It makes me more anxious. Yellow alert.

"Carmen, third. Joshua and Becky." Carmen's voice booms in our headsets.

Our truck starts the second curve on the road, and I choose this time to focus on the buildings below. They're too far away, and the ride is making me a bit sick, which affects my senses.

"Paulo, fourth. Charlie and Rose."

As we move closer to the buildings in between both fortresses, we can see them better. They're large brown hexagons as large as warehouses, with jagged sides, as if they were taken out of a giant honeycomb. Perhaps they contain supplies, or weapons that'll help us in this campaign. Or maybe they're just traps.

"No one else?" says John.

Moving my binoculars to the far right, I find a tall

lookout tower looming above the buildings, and another one just like it on the other side. Both towers are far apart from each other, at the extremes of the valley, and far away from the buildings at the middle. They don't seem to be important but they provide a nice panoramic view of the battlefield.

Our convoy is on the third loop of the road, while our enemy on the other side of the hill is down to their fifth. Jori don't drive their own cars, so they must be using the on-board computers, which should make their line of trucks move faster than ours. Somehow, though, we're keeping up with their speed. Earth has some crazy people, and they're good at their craziness.

Several seconds later, we finish the fifth loop of the road, while across from us, they're on their seventh. I still can't sense the buildings. They're made of material that doesn't let me see inside from afar. We need to get closer for me to sense anything.

"Amrita, do you copy?" John talks in the headset. It looks like John told her to stay behind. I'm glad he thought of that. "Can you can hit their side with our guns?"

Amrita Singh is a physician who works with India's Ministry of Defense. We chatted a week or so ago about how Pangea and our brains interact, and I think she got a little suspicious with how much I knew about the subject. I avoided her after that.

"We can't hit their side, John, or even the structures," Amrita replies. "The guns were designed to avoid them."

"Thanks, Amrita. Please keep listening to our channel," John replies.

After a while, our convoy reaches the eighth loop, and there are no more turrets nearby. The good news is that now we're close enough that my mind can finally reach inside the buildings.

The structures have several rooms packed with hardware. Their contents are large, egg-shaped capacitors, and there are lots of them. Worse, each of them stores an outrageous amount of energy. Anyone who puts their hands on them will vaporize the others, and maybe even themselves in the process.

Two of our enemies' trucks stop about a hundred meters after the bottom of the hill, and six Jori jump from them, running toward the closest structure. They'll be there in less than a minute, and we're still working our way around the second-to-last curve down the hill. The rest of their vehicles are positioning themselves in a defensive line on the last curve of their road.

"They're going to shoot!" I shout in the headset, so everyone can hear me. John glances at me and jerks the wheel to the left; it's harder to hit a moving target that keeps changing direction. There's nothing else we can do—even retreating is not an option anymore. A loud boom followed by a small shock wave hits us from the back, though our truck is unaffected by it. The noise is followed by that of tires screeching and screams.

Behind us, a plume of smoke rises.

"Oh god, Carmen's down!" Paulo yells. "What do we do?"

I glance at John, frightened. "Major, we must keep going!" I say. "We can't let them take what's there." John looks back at me. The last time I was like this was on the bridge of that battleship, so he must know I mean business.

"Paulo, let Rose help them. After you drop her, keep driving toward the front. Everybody else, stay on me," John yells.

There's just no time. We still have one last curve to go,

and they'll get to the nearest hexagon before us. Looking down at the steep hillside covered in sand, I make a snap decision and jump out of the moving truck.

I hit the ground running at first, but soon begin sliding downhill toward the same structure we were already aiming for. A normal person would start rolling, but I focus and keep myself steady, almost like I'm floating.

Behind me, John has to drive down the road for a while and turn back from the last curve. I can get there faster this way. The Jori will reach the building first, but I will be in through one of the doors on our side soon afterward.

"John, everyone has to cover me. Don't let people near any of the buildings. You don't want them getting what's inside," I say, as I reach the valley, running.

"Louise and Paulo—turn your trucks around and start firing."

They follow his orders, and soon both sides are firing at each other. The Jori had a lucky shot earlier; it's not easy to land a hit from that distance, and the large guns don't have computer-aided aiming. The shooting scares some of the Jori who tried to run toward their friends, making them run back to their trucks. They didn't think this through. Having six of them running to this structure seems like the smart thing to do but they should've left someone manning the truck's guns. Due to the heavy fire, no one's able to go there, grab the main gun, and shoot at us.

In the meantime, I have my own problems. It's just me against six. I can take on six, right?

"Joshua is dead!" we hear someone say in our headsets. It's Carmen, and she's crying. "I'm sorry, guys. I couldn't save him."

I almost fall when I hear that. Joshua's not supposed to be dead. I took his place in John's truck and sent him to his grave. He died because of me. He's the first casualty in the hypersphere since the rules changed. My mind schedules some time to feel shitty later, if I survive.

Like the doors in the dome, the hexagon's nearest doorway opens by itself, sliding to the left as I get closer, and I run inside. Catching my breath for a second, I concentrate. The Jori are already in here with me. They have no idea what's coming. Based on their auras, I know where each one of them is inside this thing. At the moment, they're splitting up, trying to find me. Big mistake.

"I'm positioning my truck to the right. It'll cover the two buildings there," Louise says.

The inside of the jagged structure is made up of smaller hexagons. Each room has six dark gray walls with doors that slide open when I'm close. In the middle, a single, larger chamber, surrounded by twelve hexagonal rooms stands out, its indented sides looking very much like an inverted version of the building. It's a honeycomb labyrinth. They have no chance against my mental map.

"Paulo, do the same on the left. We'll stay in the middle," John replies.

Trying to make as little noise as possible, I enter the third room on the left and go around a large pile of boxes. The walls pulsate if I touch or get close to them, illuminating the area. I avoid them to hide my position.

"Should we go down and help Mike?" Jane says.

"No one goes in there. That's an order!" John replies.

Their battle plans are just background noise. I run through at least six rooms and wait right next to one of the doors, as someone gets ready to enter. I take the first man by surprise, hitting him with the back of my gun. A bit smaller than me, the man goes down without a sound. I throw his gun away and grab his headset.

"Jane, stop!" I hear John say, distracting me. What the hell is she doing?

"Mike, I'm coming!" she says.

"No, stay there. Are you crazy?" I say.

"It's too late. I'm almost there!" Shit. Jane's going to get herself killed.

After I go around a curious double-sided forklift with no visible crew area, another enemy goes down when I hit him from behind. Meanwhile, Jane shows up inside the building in my mental map.

There is no need for panic, I tell myself. I can do this.

All of a sudden, the building shakes violently as we hear a loud explosion, and I cover my ears with my hands. The explosion messes up my ability to concentrate, and I don't know where everyone is anymore.

"John, who the fuck is shelling the building?" I ask, trying to regain my bearings. If they hit the weapons, this place might just explode entirely, and everyone around it will die.

"It's the Jori," he says.

"They have their own people in here!" Maniacs, that's what they are.

"It doesn't seem like they care."

My plan has changed. Jane and I are facing four enemies, and we're not together. Thus, my goal is now to find Jane and keep her safe. I try to focus. Everything starts to form in my mind, and it seems like I'll be back in the game soon, but another large boom shakes the building. They haven't stopped shooting at us, and I can't concentrate while they're doing that. Jane could be anywhere, and I won't be able to tell friend from foe at a glance. I'm blind and powerless if the bombardment continues.

My luck runs out as I round a corner and enter the large

room in the center of the labyrinth. Right in the middle of it, the tip of an enormous ellipsoid pops up from the ground. I don't understand its purpose. It must hold an immense amount of energy. But this is not why I'm screwed; the problem is that I'm suddenly faced with the last four of my pursuers, all at once, and all pointing guns at me. They must've realized their mistake and regrouped.

Shots are fired—not from them, but from Jane, who shows up in the far left corner. The Jori fall back behind a crane, taken by surprise. She runs back into the room she came from, but one of them is running after her, shooting, while the others focus their fire on me.

Still, Jane has put me back in the game, and even if I can't concentrate, I'm faster than they are. An idea forms as I run to the back and into a dark hallway. Removing my headset, I put on the one I got from the first guy I knocked out.

"<Everybody, retreat!>" I shout, in Dïnisc, relieved that I'm able to do it without singing. "<There are at least ten of them entering the building!>"

"<We have to run!>" someone replies. The three of them turn around and start falling back. I shoot some energy rounds behind them. There's still someone in the other room with Jane. As I look in that direction, I hear the buzzing sound of an energy shot, accompanied by bright lights.

"<What about Nia?>" I hear someone say in my headset as I sprint. Nia? My head spins. For a moment, I forgot I was listening in. What a sick joke.

"<There's no time! Run!>" I shout again.

They finally run, fleeing through the smaller rooms and out of the building. Pieces of the ceiling fall, and I have to hop around to avoid them.

"<Nia is trapped. There's no way out!>" I hear someone cry. "<All the entrances are blocked by debris!>"

At last, I'm able to get into the room where I saw Jane last. The sight before me now brings my world crashing down as surely as the ceiling. A woman with short brown hair is kneeling, holding Jane in her arms, blood pooling on the floor beneath them. Someone's crying, and it's not Jane.

"<I'm sorry. I didn't want to kill you,>" the woman mumbles in Dïnisc.

Uncertain of what to do, I stroll around them, trying to understand what I'm looking at. I point my gun at the woman in case she decides to fight. She looks up at me, tears rolling down her cheeks.

"<I killed her. I just wanted to stop her, not kill her,>" she sobs. Ignoring her, I look at Jane. Her belly is a red mess, and the growing pool of blood beneath them both is definitely hers.

Nia finally has a good view of my face. She gasps.

"<What? How?>" she asks, her brown eyes piercing mine. I have no words. I just watch as my ex- fiancée holds Jane as she dies.

29

NIA

Jane is unconscious after being shot in the gut. She must've turned back to face Nia and tripped backward on an alien forklift the moment she was hit. I kneel next to Nia and touch Jane's wound. The Jori keep shooting at the building. They have to stop. I won't be able to do anything otherwise. I change headsets.

"John, Jane is bleeding to death. I can't concentrate to help her. You must stop them from shooting at us."

"You got it, Mike," he replies. He doesn't even ask me how I'll help Jane. He just seems to trust my powers. As for me, I'm not so certain. Nia looks at me, incredulous.

"<What are you doing here? I thought you were...>" Nia says, but stops mid-sentence. I still have my gun in my left hand, pointed at her, while I take her headset off. Her eyes are wide, as if she's seeing a ghost. I'll deal with her later.

"<Not now.>" I apply pressure to Jane's belly with my right hand. I focus on her lower torso, exploring the inside of her body. She has a hole in her intestines. The energy exit point is more toward the middle of her back, but her lower spine is destroyed. If this had happened back on Earth, she wouldn't walk anymore, even if she survived.

The hexagon trembles with another shot.

The rules to not wake up on Earth with this kind of trauma are only valid outside the hypersphere. Jane has to go back to the habitat rings to survive. In there, she should wake up on Earth, safe, albeit with a lot of pain, but she'll be able to walk again. However, if the bleeding doesn't stop soon, she'll die. The wound is so bad that she would bleed to death even if I was able to grab her and fly to the arch.

Another blast hits our side of the building, causing dust, debris, and a foul brown liquid to fall down on us. Nothing major hits us, but Nia and I start coughing at the wet, powdery fragments falling from the ceiling. This last shot is followed by a long period of silence.

Seconds later, we hear a series of loud explosions, but none of them hit our building, and all is quiet again. John must have stopped them somehow. We're in the clear, at least for now. This is great, since Jane doesn't have much time.

"Enemy is pulling back," John tells me. "We destroyed two of their vehicles, and we control the ground nearby, but we can't go in yet."

I consider what I have to do to save her. This is more complex than just adding a single connection to my brain. On the other hand, my goal is just to stop the bleeding, so I can be rough on her. And I'll do it from the inside, in the same way I fixed my pinky, but on a larger scale. I'm glad she's unconscious, because that wound must hurt—a lot. I close my eyes, concentrate, and detect the damaged arteries. The larger one is the first to start closing, albeit not as fast as I'd like.

"How's Jane?" Ravi asks, but I don't reply. This is going to take a while. Nia keeps holding Jane's head and stares at me. The scene must be unbelievable to her.

This is not going as fast as I'd like. There's more damage than I thought. Focusing as much as I can, I work on her front and her back at the same time, using both hands. Nia doesn't go for the gun I left by my side. I'm glad for that. My hands are full.

After several minutes moving my hands around her belly and back while I close the wounds, the bleeding finally stops. Feeling relieved, I fight hard not to cry. Not in front of Nia. Jane's going to live as long as we take her to the habitat rings, which still depends on John and the others getting us out.

"<How did you do that?>" Nia asks, and I finally have time to look at her. She's so different. She sounds older, even though our bodies are kept in this young state here. Her hair is short, something she said she'd never do, and she changed her left-temple jewelry. In the past, it was almost always a feathery angel wing, symbolizing flight and freedom. The one she wears today outlines a complex black-fractal flame that starts on the top of her eye before reaching to her temple and down to top of her cheek. I don't know what it means.

"<This place is not real, Nia,>" I murmur while I look at my bloody hands. My heart aches as I remember that this was one of the first things I told Jane when I met her.

I grab the headset.

"I stopped Jane's bleeding but you need to get us out of here. We have to leave the hypersphere."

"We'll work on finding a way to get to you," John assures me.

"John, I'll be offline for a while. I have one of them here

with me. Please don't let anyone get close to any of the other hexagons, no matter the cost," I say.

"Roger that."

After I grab all the guns and the headsets, I take Jane away from Nia. I don't want to risk anything, and I can't trust her. Then, I look at Nia, thinking about what to do. My arms shake after the adrenaline rush, but I try to hide it. So much for pretending to be tough.

Nia and I remain seated on the smooth floor, and we both look at Jane, now sleeping.

"<How do you speak their language?>" Nia asks. She's wearing a sports version of the bämbêchê du prundê, which is sexier and easier to wear than the traditional one—great choice for a sandy battlefield.

"<It's a long story. We have more important things to talk about.>" And just like that, the sadness of the night I learned about her and Bodan comes back, followed quickly by rage. How could she do that to me?

"<I didn't know you were a protector. Why didn't you tell me?>" she asks.

My eyes try to grin at her, but the smile doesn't reach my mouth.

"<Why should I tell you anything?>" I reply. I thought I was over this, but you never get over having your heart smashed into millions of pieces. Just like that night, I can't hide my tears, but they're not from sadness this time. They're tears of anger. Nia, on the other hand, only tilts her head.

"<What do you mean by that?>" Nia says.

Really? I can't believe I have to spell it out for her.

"<So now you forgot you cheated on me?>"

She gasps. "<You know? Who told you?>" Her cheeks burn red, and she covers her mouth with her hand.

"<What are you talking about, Nia? You know exactly what happened. Bodan told me, and you confessed when I confronted you.>" I cringe every time I remember it. To make matters worse, never in a million years would I have thought that she would be the type of woman to cheat. Not Nia.

"<But...but you have amnesia. Did you just remember everything?>"

What the hell is she talking about?

And then it dawns on me. Nia thinks the one that took my place on Jora is me. The real Mike doesn't know about my life. He's living in my body, and he's none the wiser about her shenanigans. She and Bodan must've lied to him about how our relationship ended.

My guess is that he woke up with what they thought was amnesia, just like I did, and they had some time to craft a reasonable alternative story. Nice touch. I mean, why make me—or, in this case, him—suffer with the truth?

I ignore her question. Since we got to this subject, I have something to tell her, something to get off my chest. It's the same thing I said that night to that poor old woman when I was drunk and thought I was talking to Nia. The message may be delivered in a nicer way this time, though. No need to call her names. I can do better than that.

"<Nia, you destroyed me. You both did. It changed who I was, who I am, and I'll never forget that or forgive you. I hope it was all worth it.>"

All of a sudden, I want to go away, disappear. But I can't. I'm trapped here. Moreover, my reply seems hollow, rehearsed. They made me a cynic. I'll never be able to trust someone like I trusted her, not even Jane.

She remains quiet for a moment, thinking, and I take a few more breaths. My hands aren't shaking much anymore.

"<Since when do you remember?>" she asks, ignoring my last comment. She still thinks I'm the one with amnesia, and that I just remembered everything in a blazing flash.

"<You misunderstand me. I'm no protector, Nia. I'm the mole on their Earth.>" It's going to take a while before she's able to grok what happened. She's not seeing the big picture.

She folds her arms. "<You've been here since the beginning? Why didn't you tell me?>"

"<I was only drafted after the night I found out about you and Bodan. And once I ended up on an alien Earth, we never spoke again.>"

If you think about it, this is a confusing story. The mole looks like himself in Pangea, and like someone else on Earth. This, plus the time it took for us to enter the game, is a perfect explanation for why our closest friends didn't suspect us.

"<The guy with the amnesia, the one you probably told your fairy tale version of how you and Bodan ended up together, he's not me.>"

This is a lot for her to process. I get that. Her former fiancé, the one who's on Jora right now, is not me. In fact, he's trying to destroy it. Mike's a stranger in a strange land. The amnesia that helped them cover their illicit affair wasn't really amnesia. Like me, he's just pretending.

You should see her face when she finally understands.

She shakes her head vigorously. "<No, that's not possible. The fights here started a long time before your accident. That can't be true.>"

"<Why not?>" I ask. "<They never told the protectors that the Earths' destroyers wouldn't start the same time as them, did they?>"

"<The messengers didn't tell us they'd be here with us,

no,>" Nia admits. It makes sense. They'd thought that only protectors would fight in Pangea.

"<I know. It fooled people on Earth as well.>"

She now knows everything, and her eyes move side to side while she absorbs it all. She's going to do something, I can tell.

"<I must...warn them.>" Nia moves closer to me and tries to grab her headset, but I don't let her take it. She squints, confused.

"<What are you doing? Aren't you supposed to be on my side?>"

"<Ironic, isn't it?>" I chuckle. This should make me feel better, but it doesn't.

"<I don't understand. You're Jori!>" she replies. She's not stupid; she understands the irony, but not why I don't want to warn them.

"<I don't think Jora and Earth should be fighting each other.>" I look at Jane. "<They're not our enemies. The messengers are our enemies.>"

"Mike, do you copy?" I hear in my headset.

"Go ahead," I say.

"They're trying to flank us on our left. I dispatched one of our trucks and our own version of infantry. We have the high ground as a result and shouldn't have any more problems. We control the situation for the time being."

"That's great. We have to get out of here, then."

"Charlie is taking some of us down there to clean up the debris. We'll keep you up to date."

I congratulate him, and then sigh. Jane'll live. I look back at Nia and she takes it as a sign to restart our conversation.

"<You don't understand what I went through when all of this started,>" she says, trying to explain the unexplainable. "<I couldn't tell you anything about Pangea. I could only

talk about this with Bodan. You'd have thought I was crazy.>"

They bonded, just like Jane and Frederico, Ravi and Louise, Carmen and Becky, me and Jane, and who knows how many others. Pangea should sell subscriptions to singles. It's better than any dating site out there, although you still find your share of creeps.

"<There's no excuse, Nia. You should've ended your relationship with me first.>"

Nia instinctively touches her elaborate fractal flame, moving her fingers over it just like she used to do when she was annoyed with something. Or someone. Mostly me.

"<You should've been more open-minded,>" she insists.

On Jora, polyamorous relationships are the norm, and Nia and I were the exception. She's blaming the victim. How nice.

"<People in poly relationships don't cheat on each other. They still have rules.>"

Nia folds her arms and nods, seemingly in agreement, but her expression indicates she's conflicted.

"<I know, and I'm really sorry about that. Anyway, it didn't work out. After your accident and amnesia, Bodan and I grew apart.>" I guess he doesn't like it once he gets it. It's not forbidden anymore. "<What I did was foolish, and I can't repair it. But I miss you. I want to go back to where we were.>"

The idea of getting back together with Nia makes me look at Jane, and I put the back of my hand on her mouth, just to feel her warm breathing.

"<Do you love her?>" Nia asks, also looking at Jane.

Unfortunately for Nia, there is no way to go back for me. During the first few months on Earth, I had a lot of time to myself. I kept trying to brainstorm a way to fix things, to somehow be able to undo it. It was like I had a loop going on in my head, looking for a solution. But this loop has no exit. It'll never halt. There are some things that just can't be changed, and we must accept them and move on.

Although, to be honest, I'm still working on the moving on part.

I smile weakly. "<We just started seeing each other. It would be creepy if I loved her already.>"

This reminds of the first time Nia and I slept together. The first major step in a relationship on my planet isn't sex, since people there aren't that prudish. Instead, it's when we literally spend the night together, sleeping.

Even after marriage, people still have their own rooms, so sleeping together is, in a way, more intimate than sex. I was so happy that I couldn't sleep at first. Instead, I just lay there, spooning, thinking about how lucky I was.

"<No, I know you. You love her,>" Nia says, looking sad. "<But you can't be with her. One of you has to die, or both of you will.>"

When she turns her head to face me, the fractal flame on her left temple shines red and orange for a moment, reflecting the light. A cool effect, I have to say.

"<Not if it's up to me,>" I say.

"<Even if you both survive, how are you going to stay together? You live on different planets, and we can't build a portal between them.>"

I hadn't thought about that. Or maybe I had, and brushed it away. We might never see each other again. But time is running out, and I'm an expert in not thinking about stuff I don't like. There are other things to discuss before John and the others get here, and Jane's life is still in danger.

I stand up and walk next to her, but not close enough she can reach me.

"<Nia, I have a request for you.>" She listens, looking up at me, but doesn't say anything. "<I don't want you to tell all the Jori about Mike yet. When you get back home, can you send him a message instead?>"

She scoffs at me. "<Why would I do that?>"

I bend over, my hands on my knees.

"<Because I'm asking you to do it. I need you to trust me. I don't think it's a good idea to kill him. I have my doubts about whether I can go back to Jora if my body is dead.>"

Nia gets to her feet quickly, using the nearby wall as leverage, and we both stand upright, studying each other. She takes a step back.

"<And what if I warn them, instead?>" she says, waving in the general direction of the Jori dome.

"<Then I'll find another way. Mike isn't stupid. He can take care of himself.>" Mike must have a plan in place for if he gets caught. I do.

She tenses, frowning. "<He may try to kill me.>"

"<He wouldn't do that. Mike knows I'm close to his friends here. And I would just expose him if you were killed.>"

"<You don't know that.>"

Shaking my head, I suppress a chuckle. Here we are, arguing like old times. Two years ago, she made me invite Bodan and his dates to Saint Plehr's dinner wake to watch the fireworks. They were already together, but I didn't know. It's my turn to force her hand.

"<Nia, Mike's a good person.>" You can have a good idea of what someone is like by meeting his friends. "<He could've exposed me just by letting the people from his Earth see him in the hypersphere, but he hasn't done that.>"

Nia moves away from me, watching the destruction around us. She paces back and forth, thinking. As far as I'm concerned, she has two options. If she refuses to do it, we'll take her prisoner. If she agrees, I'll let her go, and then she'll have to decide if she wants to betray me again.

Finally, she stops and stares at me. I hold my breath for a second.

"<I'll do it. It won't fix what I did to you, but it's a start.>"

30

EXIT

John and the Earth protectors are taking the debris off one of the entrances outside. I keep Nia's headset near my ears, on mute, to check if the Jori are coming back. So far, they haven't done anything.

After I explain to Nia exactly what to tell Mike, we leave Jane behind for a moment to search for the injured Jori. Nia's worried about her friend Jal, whom she thinks is down in the rubble.

"<You didn't answer one of my questions,>" Nia tells me. "<How did you save your girlfriend?>" She says the last word in a sarcastic tone.

A large piece of wood and a pile of rocks sits on top of a black man lying on the floor in the next room. Nia's worried about him but I let her know that although he's hurt and unconscious, he'll live. We begin moving the rocks.

"<Since the first time I was here, I've known that this place isn't actually real,>" I say. "<It's created in our minds, like a vivid dream.>"

After I remove a large piece of debris that was on top of his head, I realize that I've seen him before. Even though blood stains his skin, almost covering his tattoo, I recognize him. Jal protected Jane from that bloodthirsty blonde when I first showed up in the hypersphere.

Jal doesn't have temple jewelry. Instead, he has a face tattoo, which is a sign he's in the military or law enforcement. It's a drawing of several lines, starting from a single point at the right temple, going around the bottom of the ear, and meeting again near the top. The lines are criss-crossed everywhere by circles and concentric patterns.

"<Jal's always so excited, always wants to be the first one in,>" Nia says with a smile. "<He's a lancer in the third battalion near our city.>"

Nia wraps her arms around Jal's body and moves him away from the messy floor. After he's in a more comfortable position on the floor, she lets him go. I crouch down next to him to have a better look.

"<It's a bad concussion but he'll be fine. No internal bleeding. In less than half an hour, he'll be awake, albeit hurting,>" I say.

"<You still didn't answer my question,>" she protests.

"<It's going to be hard to believe, but I can physically change things here. In fact, I just learned that I can do surgery. Isn't that awesome?>"

"<Can you kill people?>" she asks, apparently accepting my fantastic story without a qualm. She always did have an open mind. Too open, some would say. Okay, I must confess —I'm that someone.

"<I guess.>" I look at her in an odd way. It's a strange, but valid question. "<Why would I want to do that?>"

"<Would you have killed me with your magic hands if Jane had died?>" she presses, and I laugh. Nia's an artist on Jora. Unlike the latest, overused trend of developing only virtual pieces that are sent directly to our emotional centers,

Nia is one of the few that still works with her bare hands, painting and sculpting, while at the same time bombarding our brains with emotions. If anyone has magic hands, it's her.

"<No. I would've shot you!>" I stare at my own hands as I say that. I can joke about this now, but it still leaves a bitter taste in my mouth. "<I wouldn't have killed you. People were shooting at each other. It happens, and you seemed pretty upset about it. That would have helped your cause when you asked for mercy.>"

Jal is in the clear, so we walk in silence toward the other room where I met the first of Nia's group.

When we get there, Nia's other friend is nowhere to be seen. His body should be here, but instead, we see only a large broken beam in his place. There's a lot of blood on the floor, mixed with gray fluids. Nia weeps, kneeling by the beam.

"<His name was Omari. He left five kids, two wives, and a husband behind,>" she says.

"<Why are our people so trigger happy?>" I complain. "<You almost killed ten of us outright, including me, in one of these battles.>"

"<This is a war. You may not necessarily agree on how we fight it, but we do what we have to do,>" she argues.

As I think about her answer, a question comes to my mind.

"<Nia, who's in charge of our forces?>"

"<Oh, right...you don't know...>" Nia jerks her head, staring at me for a moment, and then looks down. "<Bodan.>"

Bodan was the kindest person I had ever met, and our friendship goes years back. While I was selfish, quick to anger, and often lazy, he'd always push me to help people and make new friends. And now, he's a ruthless, blood-thirsty jerk. I'd use more adjectives, but I'd run out of commas.

"<Bodan doesn't seem the type to do that,>" I say. "<But then again, I wouldn't have expected you or him to betray me like that, either.>"

When trust is broken, you recognize you don't really know someone.

"<He changed. He's an asshole now,>" she says, moving her fingers down the fractal flame on her temple.

"<And yet, you were still his girlfriend.>" It's my turn to be sarcastic.

"<Yes, but I was about to end it when you learned about us.>"

This is hard to believe. What are the odds that they were wrapping up their fantasyland just when I found out about them? It's the go-to excuse when people are caught. I was hoping for something less cliché, like mind control, aliens, or messengers of the gods.

After that, we head back to where Jal is so we can take him with us. I want to ask Nia when it started, her relation-ship with Bodan, how many times they slept together, if she loved him more than me, but it doesn't matter anymore. There's nothing to gain in asking these questions, and I'm not a masochist.

"<When did you first hook up?>" I blurt.

She looks away. "<Things were very chaotic at the begin-ning. We weren't used to not having our sensors on us.>"

I remember my first time in Pangea. The fact that all my biosynthetic senses were inoperable was one of the reasons I thought I was dead. I wish. At least the superpowers were cool.

"<We started losing the first battles, and I lost a good

friend of mine, Gytha. She was my rock here,>" Nia continues. "<Gytha was right next to me when she was killed. Something hit her on the head. We couldn't tell if it was a direct shot or shrapnel from a nearby explosion. I ended up crying in Bodan's arms in the habitat rings, and soon after that, we kissed,>" Nia says with a faint smile.

Her smile quickly vanishes when she notices my look of anger. Really, people who've never been betrayed are so clueless.

"<How often did you sleep together?>" I ask. Please just kill me. I don't know why I asked that.

"<I don't know.>" Liar. "<But I promise you we never had sex on Jora. We were always here when we did it. It was more like a fantasy to me that way. To us.>"

This is the Pangea version of not doing the deed on the marital bed at home. It's a virtual relationship, so it doesn't matter. It's amazing the stories people tell themselves to make them feel better. I want to tell Nia that my fantasy is to smash Bodan's face in when I see him, but we're entering the room where Jane is now, carrying Jal on our shoulders, and Jane seems to be awake.

"<Again, I'm sorry,>" Nia says.

Well, sometimes being sorry just isn't enough. What she said doesn't make me any happier. In any event, Jane can now hear us, so we'd better stop talking. Touching my mouth with two fingers pointing sideways, tongue out, I signal Nia to be quiet.

Jane's hair is messed up, her clothes and skin are covered with blood and dirt, and she looks weak. The room is filled with a sweet, metallic smell. She tries to lift her head, but I'm sure she doesn't see us yet, and doesn't have the strength to roll over to where we are.

I sit by her side and touch her forehead. Her body's

responding to the trauma with a fever. She looks at me as if asking me what happened, while her hands move to her stomach. That's a mistake. She moans in pain.

"It's okay, Jane. People are clearing a path for us now, and I'll take you back to the habitat ring."

She smiles thinly but her expression changes to one of fear when she sees Nia and Jal behind me.

"They won't bother you," I assure her. Jal sits up. It looks like he's feeling a bit better, though he also seems agitated when he sees me and Jane. Nia gestures for him to calm down and he complies. The fact we're not shooting at them is helping.

Nia takes a bottle of water from a side bag and gives it to me. I grab it and hand it to Jane, who hesitates for a split second, but ends up drinking it with loud gulps.

My headset vibrates. I put it on.

"Mike, we're almost there. Are you ready?" John says.

"Yes, give me a minute."

I feel somewhat clumsy carrying all our guns strapped to me, like an action movie hero, along with all the headsets, but someone has to retrieve them. Meanwhile, I pick Jane up with both arms, carrying her like a bride. The lower gravity makes it easier to carry her and all the weapons.

The light from outside illuminates the dark room once most of the debris blocking that entrance is gone. I make a hand signal to Nia and Jal that means wait. They'll stay inside for the moment.

Moving in the direction of the light, we finally get outside, and our rescue team is waiting for us. Ravi is covered in sweat, his shirt dripping wet. Paulo uses his own shirt to dry his face. Charlie and Rose stand below some large, plastic-looking pieces of the wall, trying to stay away from the suns. I hadn't seen the second sun yet. It must've appeared when we were inside the hexagon.

As I carry Jane and the weapons out into the light, everyone claps and hoots. Earth's team isn't losing anymore. We managed to retake the building and trap the Jori up their hill, though at a high cost for both sides. I have to take Jane to one of the trucks so it can drive her back, but first things first.

"Okay, you guys, listen to me," I announce as they stop clapping. "I've made a deal with a couple of Jori inside." Their expressions change to anger but I plow onward. "They helped me save Jane. In exchange, I'll let them go."

An awkward silence follows as they eye each other. Charlie is the one who speaks first.

"Bollocks! We can't do that," he yells. "They killed Joshua!"

"Their friend is also dead. He left a whole family behind," I say. Sure, Omari was killed by the others and not by us but telling them this wouldn't help my plan at all.

"We should take the Jori prisoner," Paulo argues.

"No. I promised them I would let them go," I say.

"You can't promise such things, Mike. You don't have the authority!" Paulo presses, glancing at John. It's funny, the ones who are in charge of this operation—John and Vladimir—don't say anything. Anyway, time to be badass.

"Let me be clear—if any of you shoot at them, I will hunt you down every single day in the habitat rings and kill you."

Walking with Jane in my arms—the lower gravity makes it easier than it looks—I stare at each of them in turn. Jane eyes me with a puzzled expression on her face. When I'm next to Charlie, I look him square in the eye.

"I'll kill you every day in different ways." The word "you"

must feel way more personal when the one who says it is shouting it in your face but Charlie doesn't even blink.

I turn to Paulo, and he moves one step back. He's at least five inches taller than I am, and it's hard to intimidate someone when you have to look up.

"You'd be surprised at how creative I am. You will suffer."

Becky is my next target, and I do the same dance with her that I did with Paulo.

"After a couple of days like that, you'll be begging me to really kill you, and not just Pangea-kill you." I hope she doesn't use this quote in any article she publishes. The news can take things out of context. Sad.

The silence that follows speaks a thousand words, so I walk to the damaged hexagon once more.

"Nia!" I yell.

They emerge from the rubble, taking small steps. Jal has his arm around Nia, who helps him move. Meanwhile, I watch everybody else, searching for any sign of them grabbing their capacitors. No one does. They got my message loud and clear. Nia and Jal slowly walk around the building and limp toward their hill. This is going to take some time.

In the meantime, I turn to John. There's one more thing I have to do before I leave the hypersphere.

"John, I've asked you for too much already. I'll never be able to repay you."

"You got that right," he says in a confrontational tone, but his smile indicates that he's not actually upset.

"But I have one more request. Please destroy all these buildings and what they have inside."

"Why? What do they have in them?"

"They're powerful, and extremely unstable capacitors. The messengers were hoping we would all kill ourselves trying to get them out. The one in the largest room doesn't seem to have any purpose except to blow itself up."

Talking about the messengers reminds me of the unseen blobs of energy, the so-called gods, the ones that are truly responsible for these deadly games. They live in Pangea, somewhere-but-not-here. From their point of view, things happen too fast in the hypersphere, and we might as well be microbes to them. How much do they care about the people dying here?

John looks at the partially destroyed building while rubbing his neck, deep in thought.

"The Jori attack didn't destroy the ones in your building," he says.

"That's probably on purpose. The messengers didn't want the arsenal to blow up that easily while we fought for them. You should shoot your projectile in an arc that reaches the center of the building on its downward trajectory."

John turns his face toward our trucks, studying the situation.

"I see. I'll have to shoot from the side, reposition our trucks," he explains while watching the enemies' vehicles in a distance. "This may expose some of us to them." After what feels like a minute or so, John sighs.

"All right, Mike, we'll do it."

Without any more delay, I nod and carry Jane to one of the trucks in the back. Instead of sitting in the driver's seat, I position myself on the passenger side. I want to keep Jane on my lap, and she can lay down sideways, while I embrace her back with my right arm. She snuggles with me, putting her head on my shoulder, and goes to sleep. Touching the truck sensors with my left hand, I tell it to go back to the arch.

31

TRUST

It's been almost twenty-four hours since I took Jane out of the hypersphere. At RNL, both she and Ravi were nowhere to be seen. Jane must've stayed home to recover from last night's ordeal but Ravi should be back from Los Angeles already. I wonder if he missed his flight, or if it was canceled.

Things are going to start happening really soon, and I'm getting worried. Nia made a great point. Maybe Jane and I never can be together and one or both of us may die. The thought of us not being able to stay in a relationship never even crossed my mind, though I do think—all the time, in fact—that I may not be alive at the end of this. I don't know what's going to happen but from now on, I'll be in the driver's seat. That's a bad analogy, because I prefer cars to drive themselves, but you get the point.

That night, in Pangea, there are few people in the habitat rings, so I walk through the enormous arch and head for the superdome. No protector guards the back entrance, since no Jori would be able to get here without going through our hill teeming with artillery. Earth's protectors must either be inside or scouting the front of the building. It's not like there are many of us here. We have fewer and fewer people as time goes by.

Once inside our fort, I find the large room holding the surveillance equipment. John nods at me when he sees me. Anyone who isn't on watch is here, looking at the monitors. This room is a bump in my plans, since I don't want anyone looking at what Mike and I are going to do.

Instead of the hexagons, the surveillance screens show only four large craters in their place. This brings a smile to my face. John apparently has no love for the messengers, like me, and I think he likes to mess with their plans.

"What an interesting day we had yesterday," John says. "You were right about those weapons. The first one that exploded blew everyone back, but most of the blast energy was absorbed by the ground. I'm so glad we could go back to Earth and get new eardrums."

"The messengers wanted to annihilate us," I say, still looking at the craters.

John grins, folding his arms in a way that shows off his green army jacket, with an eagle insignia and the word "airborne" above it. "Mike, I like your ideas, but be warned that the minute I don't like them, I'll stick them up your ass."

Yeah, yeah, he always says that, but he has a heart of gold underneath his incredibly strong body, death threats, and foul language.

"You know who the real enemy is, John."

I hear the sound of light footsteps behind me, and I turn around to see Jane. Her smile makes her glow. There's something different about the way she acts, so confident, almost boastful.

Her hair is loose for a change, and she's wearing denim shorts, an off shoulder white top, and sandals. Even though nothing stands out about the way she's dressed, she moves with grace, as if there's a spotlight on her. Nearby, Paulo looks at me, grinning.

"Shut up, Paulo!" I tell him, even though he didn't say anything.

She's so alive today, way better than the last time I saw her. Moving her black shoulder holster to the side, I put my hand on her stomach to check on her, and I'm so happy to see that she's fine. I can't help but sigh. My skin crawls when I remember the strange sensation of her body disappearing on me when we got to the habitat ring. For a moment, I thought we didn't make it.

We stay close, looking at each other. Even her holstered capacitor touching my biceps doesn't bother me.

"I missed you," I say, unable to hide my happiness. She looks so much better.

"I knew you would," she teases.

"Hey, I'm the one who's supposed tell jokes here."

She silences me with a kiss. Then she takes my hand off her belly, holds it in her own, and pulls me out of the room. Louise is leaving another room in the back and smiles when she sees us.

"One day, Mike, you'll have to explain to me how you do it. Are you my angel?" Jane asks, her eyes gleaming. I laugh.

"No, you're my angel. Plus, I don't feel like doing angelic things to you right now." She tries to hit my arm, but I dodge her this time. I learned my lesson.

"If it weren't for you, I'd have died, again."

"True, but you did the same for me."

And yet, she used a weapon to save me. She has no idea how I saved her.

"How did you save me yesterday?" she asks, as if reading my thoughts.

"It's this place, Jane. It answers my mind."

She takes me to the room that Louise just left, right next to the wing we call the barracks, and locks the door behind us. This room is smaller than the others, and it has a couple of wide shelves with iron-gold armor shells and pulse cannons, but most of it is empty space.

"But even if you had the power to do that, you're not a physician. So, how?" She'd be right, but she doesn't know my real background.

"I just concentrated on closing the wounds so I could stop the bleeding. It seemed to work."

We kiss each other again, this time with a different and clear purpose. She pushes me back and takes her shirt off. We don't have an audience, so we can be ourselves.

When we move to the floor, I'm delighted to find that there are blankets there, which means she planned this. Her smile broadens. I have to give it to her, I wasn't expecting this, not this early. What happened to the first-date rule? On the other hand, she has no idea what I have in store for her. Plans within plans.

As we make love, I manage not to think of Nia. Of course, the contradiction that I'm mentioning her name and, thus, thinking about her, is a bit ironic. Nia was my last, and I didn't have that many partners. But, truly, Jane is all I have in my mind at this moment. This is not just for me, it's for Jane as well. I want to make her happy.

On Jora, sex isn't taboo. We often go through several partners before settling down, and in some cases, multiple partners in the same night. In fact, we should be selling tickets to my world if we ever open a portal. Maybe the sexual freedom would make up for the fact that both Earths would be destroyed soon after.

Anyway, I had a one-night stand once, and it felt empty.

The physical act itself was great, but I learned that night that I need the emotional connection. I know—go ahead, call me a girl. For me, when I have sex with someone I love, it means that we belong together, that we have each other's back. I'm just wired like that. Other people can separate sex and love, and I have no problems with that.

Moreover, I can only feel like this with one person and one person only at a time, this connection that goes beyond sex. I'd never be able to hurt her. Nia is so different from me in this aspect. My definition of love includes trust, respect, and fidelity. I would move Heaven and Earth to be with the one I love and to never hurt her, no matter what happens, even if I'm told to fight in a secret war. This is another reason why I prefer monogamy. I don't want to share this intimacy with anyone else. The world fades around us. It's only us.

Afterward, we both lay, naked, and spooning on the floor. Our breathing has slowed down. I love this sensation, just after love. It's like she's so fragile, and I must protect her from any harm, especially her heart. We both have deep secrets but how I'm dealing with mine doesn't put her in harm's way. I will fight messengers. I'll literally fight gods for her. Her heart is safe with me.

Well, not really, because I'm a mole.

She turns around and looks at me, smiling. I wish this moment would never end but we're in the middle of a war. I can only hope that we'll get past this and be together someday.

"You're unbelievable. Have you never done this before?" she asks. Obviously, she doesn't mean sex.

"No, I was a little busy fighting," I confess. "You were my first. I mean, my first like this."

"You touched me...everywhere, but your hands...I was

holding your hands the whole time. You do only have two of them, don't you?" She closes her eyes, and I guess she's back in the moment. I know; I'm awesome.

"I had no idea that I could do that, but I can. At least here," I admit. She looks at my hands, still puzzled. I feel a little bad. I've spoiled her forever.

"Mike, do you trust me?"

"I trust you."

I turn onto my back, and she embraces me from the side. My left hand plays with her backside, her curvy legs, her shoulders.

"All right. Let's start from the beginning, then," she presses. "I've never slept with someone when I didn't even know his name." She gives me an intense look. "Mike, what's your real name?"

Turning around to face her, I move her hair away from her eyes with my left hand. We're on our sides, looking at each other, on top of the soft blankets on the floor, and she wraps her arms around me. This is the happiest I've ever been in my whole life. Too bad it's going to end.

For me, love implies trust, respect, and fidelity, remember. The only thing currently missing is trust. In order to fix that, I have to tell her, and pray that she'll forgive me.

"My name is Zeon," I say.

PART III

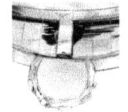

Even if I spoke the language of angels, without love, I would be nothing.

— I CORINTHIANS 13:1

32

TRUTH

Her forehead wrinkles in confusion, and my heart pounds faster. Not because I'm watching the beginning of the end of our relationship but because how much I'm going to hurt her.

"Zeon? What a strange name." Jane considers it, probably trying to figure out which country on Earth would have a name like that. "Sorry, I like the name. I've just never heard of it."

"My name is uncommon even where I'm from," I say, taking a deep breath. The reason I lied was that I didn't want to be killed. Jane might not see it that way, though. She may think I lied so I'd be able to kill.

"How about your last name?" she asks.

"I don't have one."

Jane frowns even more at that, our perfect moment gone.

"When can we meet on Earth? How far are you from Long Island?" she asks. This is a not-so-subtle way to ask for my address.

"We've already met," I answer with my eyes closed for a moment. "I'm sorry I had to deceive you."

It's hard for me to say this. She might never want to talk to me again after today.

"Really?" Still on her side, she pulls back from me and covers her naked breasts with her arms. "When?"

"On Earth, you also call me Mike. We had a date the other day, with Louise and Ravi."

I meet her gaze again and she squints at me, confused.

"How would you know that? You can't be that Mike. Did he tell you to say this?" She raises her voice, sounding angry. "Are you both playing games with me?"

At least we're making progress. She has a lot of good arguments for someone who has no idea what's going on.

"You told me it was weird that we were so alike. You're right. We're the same person, but on Earth, I look like him," I confess.

In a split second, she sits up and looks at me, concerned. I do the same, keeping my hands on the floor behind me for support.

"I don't understand. Aren't you a protector? But you don't look like yourself..."

"I'm not a protector, Jane. The messengers sent me there to destroy Earth."

The shock on her face feels like a knife in my heart, and it doesn't take long for her to act on her anger. Jumping to her feet, she starts to dress herself in a hurry. That's not a good way to end a date but I didn't want to wait anymore.

"You must think I'm so stupid," Jane snaps, and her New York accent gets thicker. "I feel like I'm fucking Louise Lane here."

Her mispronunciation makes me cringe, despite everything.

"That's not her name." I shake my head. "And our situation is not at all like that." This is another thing that we liars don't realize. I had more time to get used to the lie and the fact that I lied. Jane has barely started processing it. "Come on, Jane. In their case, the only difference is the glasses. I'm more like the spider guy." I nod for emphasis. The hero and the alter-ego are completely different.

Jane rolls her eyes at that. "The one who killed his girl-friend? Is that what you're going to do to me?"

Did he? That doesn't seem right. I spent the last year catching up with Earth's pop culture, but everything I learned about superheroes is from just a few movies. Does Tarzan have a girlfriend?

Adjusting the ugly gun holster around her shoulder—it looks like suspenders—the ellipsoid- powered handgun thumps to the floor. In a smooth and quick movement, she crouches and snaps it up.

"I can't believe we're discussing comics right now," Jane says, with the capacitor now in her hand. She stares at it a long time, as if deciding what to do with it. To my relief, she shakes her head almost imperceptibly and holsters the weapon. "I have to go. Are you going to let me leave?"

She crosses her arms and gives me a defiant look.

"Jane, please, don't tell the others yet." I'm glad she doesn't even ask about the fact that I wasn't in the game until very late. Mike had pretend-amnesia months after the real protectors started. She's smart, and she knows the messengers are not straightforward. She'll figure it out, which is good. I'm tired of explaining that part.

"You're here to kill us. What did you want to do, play with us first?" She mumbles through her teeth, biting an elastic band she grabbed from somewhere, her hands behind her back to make a quick ponytail. I love her ponytails.

"Killing people was never my plan. You know that."

"How would I know anything? You're a liar."

She's right, I am a liar. This is the price liars pay for lying. Everything that comes out of my mouth is under scrutiny now. It's odd to be on the other side, even if I did have my reasons.

"I had to lie, otherwise you or the others would have killed me."

Jane is now fully dressed and ready to leave. Still, I hope she lets me explain. There's so much I want to tell her.

"Please give me some time to talk to you before you leave," I plead.

She glances at the door. I'm naked and defenseless, but in Pangea, I'm not like them. Maybe I can make her disappear, or transform her into a frog. Who knows?

Without saying another word, I nod toward a long silver bench on the side of the room, hoping she'll stay to talk to me. She reluctantly sits and waits for my explanation, as if there's something left to explain. Giving her plenty of space, I sit nearby.

"I had to lie," I say. All liars think they have an excuse for lying, and I'm no exception. "Think about what I did here, Jane. Actions speak louder than words. I've always valued life. I saved yours many times."

My story is foolproof.

"Oh yeah? If you don't want to kill us, why are you installing your devices in our particle accelerators?"

Crap. I completely forgot about them. This is a very good question, and one that, in her eyes, just proves I wanted to kill them anyway. Too bad, I can't explain them until I'm ready.

"What do you think I'd do with them?" I try to avoid answering her question.

"I don't know, create a black hole? The real Mike theorized that we could do it. You must've read his papers about it, and you want to create one to destroy Earth."

Yes, Jane, it's everyone's childhood dream. I roll my eyes before answering her.

"They weren't papers yet, more like notes. But yes, I read them. It may be possible."

"So you did want to try it out. You're contradicting yourself."

I am, she's right, but this is everything I can tell her without disclosing my plans.

"It's hard to explain. Destroying Earth wasn't what I wanted to do, though. I had them installed so they could help with my real goals."

"What are you trying to do?" she asks, rubbing her eyebrows with both hands.

"Stay alive."

"But at what cost?" She's debating me as if I'm the bad guy. I never wanted to kill people. I didn't create the rules.

"You should ask the messengers. Their price tag is way more expensive than mine."

Jane stands up and crosses her arms, still tense, but looking more relaxed since I haven't moved to kill her yet. Also, if I wanted to destroy Earth, why would I tell her who I am?

"Well, Zeon. I thought you were special. You flirted with me several times, but only with me. I liked that. It was so different from my previous relationships," she continues. It's odd, but cute that she's thinking about that. Damn you, Frederico. "But it turns out I'm just a trophy in your little game."

Jane ends the conversation without giving me a chance to stop her and walks toward the door. When she gets there, she turns around slowly and looks at me one more time.

"Your friend, Nia. She apologized to you. Why?"

Right, this is everything that I wanted; my wildest dreams coming true. I'm not ready to discuss my past relationships with her, especially not the one with Nia.

"Nia is my, uh, ex-fiancée. She's the reason we broke up."

No need to go into more details. We can talk about Bodan and Mike some other time, after she's processed all of this, assuming I'm alive and not in jail.

Jane seems puzzled by my answer but then she steps out of the room, leaving me alone. I hope she doesn't tell anyone yet, though she can't stop me. No one can. Nobody can beat me in Pangea, and I have my own safety net on Earth.

This didn't go how I planned but I'm still breathing, so, considering everything, I call that a win. One of the few advantages to being a liar is that once you confess, you lift your burden, but you end up passing it to someone else—in this case Jane. This is why I can't help but feel bad. We had the greatest experience two people can have, even more so because of what I can do here in Pangea, and I destroyed it for her. I'm officially an asshole.

Thinking about what I did and what I have yet to do, I put my clothes on. The other protectors will know about me soon. It can't be done here, though. They must learn why they can't kill me on Earth. Granted, this will be way more dangerous, since I have no powers there, but I can only show my cards on Earth, not in Pangea.

To my surprise, Louise is waiting for me outside the door, steaming mad. Oh well, Jane must've told everybody already. I was hoping she'd take a couple of hours to decide if and when to tell them but I was wrong. As a result, I'll have to fight my way to the habitat ring before someone kills me.

"Mike, what did you to Jane? She just ran away, crying!"

This is not what I was expecting, and it distracts me for a moment. Before I can defend myself, Louise hits me in the arm. Seriously, what's up with women hitting other people's arms? This is abusive behavior. I'm about to protest when something else comes to mind.

How did Jane understand what Nia was saying?

33

CONSEQUENCES

My house in Long Island is always so quiet. The only noises I can hear are the birds and the wind rustling the leaves outside, way better than the apartment we had in Los Angeles next to the highway. It's too bad that I must go to the hotel every day, instead of enjoying this place.

Most of the rooms are bare, and the obscenely large windows on the beige walls give me the impression of an even larger house. To be honest, I like having so much space for activities. The only areas that have furniture are the bedroom, the kitchen, and the living room.

Yes, I'm a bit nostalgic. If you think about it, I may not be able to come back here at all, or anywhere I've been to for the past year. Soon I'll end up either in jail, dead, or sent back to Jora—or a combination of all of the above.

There are only a few things left to do. Everything else is in motion. My hope is that Mike will be on my side when I talk to him. This uncertainty ends tonight, or as soon as we meet, at least.

It's too early for anything, though, so I take a long

shower and get ready for the day. There's no way I'll be able to go to the laboratory again. In truth, there's no point in going there anymore. Everything that had to be done was done, and Jane might get me arrested or worse.

When I get out of the shower, someone is knocking at the door. Only Julie knows I live here, and she has a key. I wrap a towel around my waist and walk to the living room. Even if Jane had told the others, it would take them several hours to learn about this house, more likely days. I grab two pepper sprays, one for each hand. This may be the moment of truth.

My front door has side windows, and I peek through them to see who's knocking. The sun has not yet risen but it's already bright. Ravi is outside, with a day-old beard and the classic red eyes, and I assume he just came back from Los Angeles.

His grimace is a sign of anger, a lot of anger, so Jane must've told him. I wonder how he found me so soon. Maybe he has me under surveillance. Either way, I guess I'm about to find out. Ravi's my best friend, and it's better that I talk to him first before I address the other protectors. I make a quick decision and unlock the door.

The door slams against the wall when Ravi storms in, pointing a gun at me. He didn't come here to discuss football. This is bad. All my plans to protect myself are worthless now, and I was still curious about how many San Francisco quarterbacks were inducted into the hall of fame in the last century. Furthermore, I'm pretty sure my pepper spray won't work on Ravi. He has some kind of tolerance to pepper. He'd probably even like it.

"You fucking traitor! You lying piece of shit!"

It's good for him to air his feelings like that. No need to suppress them. However, I wouldn't advise anyone to do it with a gun in their hands. That's a little dangerous. Heck, anything you do with a gun is dangerous, but being angry is close to the top of that list.

"Nice to see you too, Ravi. Do you mind if I put on some clothes?" I ask, trying not to let the towel around my waist fall.

"Why, so you can go somewhere, press a button, and kill us all?"

I can see he's not in his right mind. Why would I wait until I'm naked and under the threat of a gun to do that?

"Ravi, if I had such a button and wanted to kill everyone, I would've pressed it already, wouldn't I?"

"Ah-ha! So you admit you're trying to kill us."

Ignoring him, I turn and take a few steps toward my room. The whole situation is getting out of control, and I confess, I'm getting rather tired of it. If he wants to shoot me, he'll shoot me, but I bet he wants answers first.

A shot hits the hardwood floor right next to my leg, making a loud noise—I hate the noise guns make—and spraying a few splinters into my leg. In movies, they sound so faint in comparison to real life. My ears are going to be ringing for the rest of the day.

Turning around, I eye his gun while covering my ears. The words Austria, 10mm, and auto, are engraved on its side, and it'd be cool if it weren't deadly.

"What do you want from me, Ravi?" I say, except with the ringing, maybe I'm shouting. "I'm sorry I had to lie to you but I had no other option."

He puts his left hand in his jacket pocket, takes a pair of handcuffs out, and throws them at me.

"Put these on, over there," he demands.

Carrying the handcuffs, I walk to the table where, if necessary, I can pull the table up and take them out from its legs. Ravi seems afraid of me. Maybe he's mistaken me for the real Mike. I can do no magic here.

"Not the table. The heater!"

Giving up on my planned exit, I do what he says and handcuff one of my hands to an old-school radiator. He relaxes after I'm trapped.

"All this time, how did I not see it?" Ravi asks.

I shrug—it's a rhetorical question anyway—and wait for him to vent. People always need some time to resolve these kinds of issues. Betrayals are hard.

"We thought we had a good plan," he continues with a forced chuckle. I think he wants to tell me the whole story. Good, let it out. "We researched patient data on any people acting strange during the month we became protectors."

The 10mm is still pointing at me as he moves around, making me uneasy. For a while, his eyes are looking at nothing as his mind seems to wander, but he snaps back to the moment.

"We believed we were so clever." He laughs. "We always hand delivered the data in envelopes."

They didn't use the internet or even snail mail to send the data? I knew the protectors were paranoid, which is why I was surprised they let me in like that, but still. Hand delivered seems a bit much. In fact, this is what bothers him, I realize. They were blindsided.

"I can't believe how much time we wasted on it," he says.

"You should blame the messengers," I say, nodding.

"Shut up, Mike!" he yells. "And how about that," he continues, "the icing on the cake. You're both named Mike, here and in Pangea. Unbelievable. Hilarious! Did you do that on purpose just to rub it in our faces?" He bobbles his head slightly.

"I liked the name Mike."

Also, in my defense, I never said my name was Mike; I said they could call me Mike. It's a subtle difference. But this won't help my case here, so I don't say anything.

"Where's the real Mike? Was he sent to Jora to destroy it?" he asks. I nod, confirming his suspicions, and he laughs. "The Jori have no idea what's going to hit them. You're not half the man he is."

Since he's steaming angry, I'm handcuffed, and he has a gun, I let that one go. But don't get me wrong. We will discuss this someday. I get defensive when I'm compared with Mike.

"How did you figure it out? Did Jane tell you?"

This is going to take a while, so I sit down and try to get comfortable. I mean, as comfortable as I can be while being naked and handcuffed to a heater.

"Wait, what? Jane knows about this?"

Great, I just threw her under the bus. Nice touch, Romeo.

"Well, uh…it's a long story. She just learned it last night."

Ravi's face changes from surprise to a deep frown.

"What the hell did you do to her? Is she okay?" He points his gun at me again.

"She's okay, Ravi. I didn't touch her." Actually, I did touch her, but not in the way he's thinking. Moreover, I am a gentleman, and I don't kiss and tell— at least, not yet. "How did you find out about me?" I ask again.

Ravi squints, probably still thinking about Jane. She isn't off the hook. I'm sure she'll hear from him.

"I got suspicious when I saw the drink you had in Pangea."

I scoff at that. "Yeah, about that. It wasn't an accident. Some of the messengers were setting me up. They don't like me there."

Despite the fact that the strawberry daiquiri was my best friend during many sleepless nights, I stopped drinking it for a while after that happened. But, if you think about it, the drink is innocent. No one should blame alcohol for his problems.

"Then I flew to LA to talk to your doctor," he says, ignoring me. Dr. Alice and I had a deal but I guess we just can't trust anyone these days. "Dr. Hallan didn't tell me anything, of course." Who the hell is Dr. Hallan? I wonder. She must work in the same hospital as Dr. Alice. "Even when I made it very clear that her life was in danger, she said she couldn't disclose anything about her patients."

Whoever she is, she must've realized my life would be in danger as well if she told him. Good for her. And also for me.

"But I didn't actually need her," he continues. "We've had access to all hospital databases since this started. I got a copy of your scans in no time and had a doctor check them. Do you know what he found?" He smiles thinly.

"They're not from the same brain," I say, rolling my eyes.

"They're not from the same brain," he repeats, with emphasis this time. His eyes are ablaze. Part of me likes to see this passion in Ravi. Louise would love seeing him like this. On the other hand, he does look a little crazy.

"So the only explanation was that you were a different person," Ravi keeps going. "Everything else fell into place once I realized that. It's now clear that you didn't start at the same time the protectors did, so it would be harder for us to find you."

Yes, I know. How many times am I going to hear this? I should start handing out pamphlets with the basics so we don't have to go through them over and over again.

"How did you find this house?"

My lower leg itches and spots of red blood appear at the base of the splinters, reminding me that fragments from the hardwood floor damaged by the bullet scratched my lower leg. Oddly enough, I start thinking about who I should call to fix it. As if it still matters.

"That was the easy part. Once I was back here, I just bribed the hotel staff. You're not James Bond, you know."

Ouch. What a cheap shot. I guess I let myself go when I wasn't caught for so long.

He left the door open when he came inside. The morning sun starts to appear, shining behind him, blinding me for a second and turning Ravi into a black silhouette. It feels as if I'm being interrogated under a bright light.

"Ravi, I'm not your enemy."

"No? You used me, Mike. You made me help your little schemes. And by the way, we'll disable your devices at the laboratory as soon as possible."

It's a shame. I think about all the work I did there—we did there. "There's nothing wrong with those brains, Ravi. It's not like—"

"I don't care," Ravi screams, interrupting me. Then, he kneels down, and I can't help but notice his finger trembling on the trigger. "Your time has run out."

And then it happens. Shots are fired, and Ravi's eyes go wide. Blood splatters all over me. I scream, thinking that my life is over.

Obviously, my first thought is that Ravi shot me but I don't feel any different. Instead, his gun drops to the floor and he falls on top of me. Embracing him with my right arm, I watch in horror as his life drains away and his breathing stops. There's nothing I can do for him. He's dying.

For a while, everything is fuzzy. I don't yet know who

shot him, but he's definitely dead, and it's all because of me. This is not Pangea. I can't save him. Tears roll down my face as I sob, dampening his dark hair, and I don't even consider my own safety. Poor Louise; she'll be devastated. She's another one who's going to hate me. I'm even starting to hate myself.

Ravi's assassin is hidden behind his body, and his murder is a mystery to me. They should be trying to kill me, not the protectors. I move Ravi's head around my shoulder, hugging him, to have a better view. Then I look up at her, wondering what the hell is going on.

Nothing makes sense anymore. She looks stunning in a long white dress that delineates her body well, and the brightness from the early morning sun bleeding into the room makes her appear like an angel, highlighting the black threads of her hair. Except she's holding the gun that killed my best friend.

34

DEMON

L inda, Mike's ex-wife, stands in front of me, crying. The gun shakes in her hands. The brightness behind her makes her dark red hair look black, creating an optical illusion. My ears are ringing again from noise of yet another shot, and I'm not sure if I should grieve for Ravi or yell at her.

"Linda, what did you do?" I ask, sobbing.

"I'm so sorry. I'm sorry!" Linda keeps saying. "I didn't want to do it, but I had to."

"What the fuck are you talking about?" I yell.

Linda walks backward and sits on the couch, her legs trembling, pointing the gun away from us. A pool of warm blood forms on the floor beneath me, wetting both my towel and my legs, soaking me. Oh my god, Jane will blame me. I'm blaming me.

"I was ordered to do it. They asked me to do it," she says with a quivering voice.

"Who, Linda?" I know who they are but I want to hear her say it.

"The gods!" she answers, looking at the ceiling with wide eyes.

She's nuts. Insane. This is beyond your normal craziness. What does she mean by the gods?

"The gods themselves?" I ask her. That's impossible.

"No, Mike. The gods are just...energy." Linda is shaking a bit less now. Her mouth shows a timid grin, and tears come down her face. "The messengers told me to do it."

"The messengers," I begin, trying to grasp the situation, "they told you..." I take a deep breath before I continue. "They told you to kill Ravi?"

Pushing Ravi's body to the side, I close his eyes. He died mad at me. Gods, what have you done?

"You don't understand, Mike, or whoever you are." Linda dismisses me, waving the gun around. "The messengers have talked to me since I was little. They're my whole world!"

Mercury told me they had made other experiments. Maybe Linda was one of them.

"I was one of their angels. They loved me, and I loved them." All of a sudden, she jerks her head in my direction. "Did you know that they ordered me to marry you?" She smiles, meaning Mike, of course. The way she looks at me makes me feel awkward.

I have to get out of here. Ravi's pockets should have a key somewhere for the handcuffs.

"I hated the idea at first. Mike wasn't my type. But they were right! They're always right. I love Mike with all my heart." She sighs. "We were made for each other."

Linda's distracted and talking to herself. I take this opportunity to look for the key. It's not in his right pocket; maybe it's in the other one. Too bad I only have one available hand.

"And then...one day...they blessed us with April. Oh, dear April." Her face becomes grim, and she glares at me as if waiting for some kind of reply or acknowledgment. I need to say something.

"But Linda, you abandoned her. Both of them. Why?"

She gets angry, stands up, and points the gun at me. It's the wrong thing to say, but in my defense, I'm not known for common sense. I can't believe she's mad at me and not the messengers. Either way, I really should think before I speak. One should never anger a crazy woman holding a gun.

"Because the gods told me to. Don't you understand?" she screams. I nod, quickly. I understand everything. Please put down the gun. She'll hurt more people if she keeps doing that.

Her anger fades and she continues talking, walking around the room, as if I didn't interrupt her.

"And then one day, they asked me to do the impossible."

I flinch as I hear that. Oh my God, she can't be serious. The realization of what she's about to say makes me stop looking for the key.

"Did you...?" I say. A knot forms in my throat, as if my body doesn't want me to say the words out loud. "Linda, what did you do?"

"The gods..." She stumbles on her words. "The gods ordered me...to kill her," she cries. "I thought...why would they ask me this? I thought they were just testing me." Her eyes fill with tears.

"What kind of gods would ask you to kill your own daughter?" I blurt, glaring at her.

"You fool!" she shouts, turning in my direction, threatening me again with her gun. It's common knowledge that discussing theology with a mentally disturbed fanatic carrying a deadly weapon is frowned upon, but I keep forgetting.

"The messengers know what's best for me, Mike, for us." Her eyes lose focus for a moment, and her arms drop, the gun pointing down again. "They know. What is best...," she mumbles.

She murdered her only child. What kind of mother would do that? And if she was able to kill her daughter, what will she do to a stranger?

After a while, she takes a deep breath.

"It's stupid. I thought they'd stop me." She laughs nervously. "During all the time it took me to drive her there and kill her, I knew in my heart that they'd tell me not to do it at the last moment. I was so sure about that."

"But they didn't." I finish it for her, and she starts crying with loud sobs.

The more I think about this, the more certain I am that these gods are not as powerful as they seem. Everything that has happened on Earth has been done by human hands, except the brain changes. They need us humans to do their bidding, and we do it eagerly.

Taking advantage of her crying, I continue my search for the key, but my behavior is no longer subtle. Her free arm rubs her eyes to wipe the tears that keep coming. She stops crying and looks at me again, catching me in the act. I'm busted.

"And then I made my major mistake." She restarts her story, ignoring what I'm doing.

"You mean...your major mistake was not killing April?" I ask, dumbfounded.

"I was stupid. I blamed the gods. This is how angels fall; they think they know better than the gods. I screamed at them once because of April and they disappeared from my life. I was left alone, no gods and no Mike."

Maybe the key is in his wallet. It's tricky to search inside it with only one hand.

"I should've known, Mike. They know better. They are the messengers of the gods. It's all part of their plan. I should always leave everything in their hands. But I doubted them, and they abandoned me." She shakes her head. "No. I abandoned them."

She sounds like an abuse victim. They think everything is their fault even when it isn't. A sane person would never try to kill their own daughter. But the messengers took advantage of a young girl, molded her to what they wanted her to be. They're disgusting.

"And then one day, I was chosen as a protector," Linda continues. "I still didn't want to see them or go back to Pangea. I loved them, but I hated them, too." She gestures with her gun as if it's not even there, like she's just in a normal conversation and not a cliché supervillain's monologue.

Taking Ravi's wallet from his pocket, I open it and check inside. The key's not there.

"But even the times I had to be in Pangea, the messengers didn't address me. They were right to avoid me, because I had broken their trust. But I didn't know how to fix it."

She clearly sees what I'm doing but I don't care anymore. The weird thing is, she doesn't seem to care either. I don't understand it. I guess I didn't have to be so careful about it at the start.

"You know, it takes a long time to rebuild trust," she explains. Tell me about it. I could teach classes. "But thanks to you, Mike, they accepted me back into their hearts." She grins.

"What did you say? Thanks to me?" I'm trying to keep her talking. She can see that I'm looking for something, but she may have not yet processed that I'm handcuffed to the heater.

"That day, at the hospital." She chuckles. "I knew you weren't Mike. I was going to tell Ravi about it, but the messengers talked to me that night. It was the first time they'd spoken to me since April…"

Wait, what?

"How did you know I wasn't Mike?" I interrupt her speech. No one else ever figured it out.

"Mike would never react to me like that, indifferent, no matter how much he's forgotten. So I connected the dots. You were here to destroy our Earth. You pretended to have amnesia to trick us!" She laughs. "Isn't it obvious?"

If it weren't for the fact that she just killed Ravi, this would be astonishing, maybe even funny. The only person who figured it out was a lunatic. My so-called mission could have ended before it started.

"What did the messengers tell you?" I ask.

Linda is lost in her own thoughts for a while. The key is nowhere to be found, and I give up. Either she'll kill me, or the police will show up. This scene will be very hard to explain if it's the latter.

After what feels like minutes, she says, "They told me who you were here and in Pangea. They promised me that if I protected you, I could live on your Earth with Mike, and they would never leave me again." She smiles. "And just like that, I'm an angel again!" she says, broadening her grin.

I want to yell at her, part of me wants to hit her, but she's a broken soul. She's been brainwashed by these so-called gods since she was a child. Their own messengers talked with her. I wonder if she visited Pangea and the hypersphere when she was young; my guess is that she did. How would you not fall for that? Even I thought it was Heaven the first time I woke up there, and I don't even believe in Heaven.

Linda was raised under that, and this is a fundamental part of who she is. The alternative, where everything they told her is a lie, where everything she does is on her, it's just too hurtful to comprehend. At the end of the day, it's easier to trust in those gods than to take ownership of her actions.

Dropping the gun on the coffee table, she comes around it and bends down near Ravi's body, next to a shiny object on the floor. She picks it up and hides it in her hands, but not quick enough that I couldn't see it. The key must have fallen to the side when she shot him. I wouldn't have been able to reach that area.

Then, she walks closer me, stretching out her arm, the key in her hand. It's within my reach, almost as if she's trying to give it to me.

I frown. "I don't understand."

"You should go. As soon as you leave, I'll call the police, but you must hide. The protectors will figure out who you really are soon," Linda explains, as if it makes any sort of sense.

"Linda, why do you believe the messengers? What if they're not who they say?" One should not look a gift horse in the mouth but I can't help it. "What if you just killed Ravi for nothing?"

She wipes her tears and grins at me.

"Don't worry about that. The gods will take care of Ravi the same way they took care of April. They're much happier where they are." She smiles. "You should also be happy! You'll see Ravi again. He'll thank us. You'll see!"

This is not how I planned this. No matter what I tell them, the protectors won't believe I didn't have a hand in this. To be honest, I have a hard time believing I didn't cause this, and I was here the whole time.

After grabbing the key and removing the handcuffs, I walk past Linda, toward the bathroom. It looks as if being naked and covered in blood is becoming a habit for me. Either way, I can't walk out of the house like this, so I take a quick shower to rinse the blood off me. I do it as fast as I can, get dressed, and then go back out to the living room. Linda is still there, happy, her mission completed.

"You didn't have to kill him. He wasn't going to shoot me," I say while closing the clumsy buttons of my shirt, wondering why they always have to make things so hard on this Earth.

"I couldn't take that risk. I didn't want to disappoint the gods. I want to see April again."

Linda watches me as I walk toward the door, shaking my head. But just before I leave, something else crosses my mind, and I turn back to face her.

"Linda, how many messengers talked to you all these years?"

"Just one," she replies.

"Which one?"

"Hermes."

35

LEVERAGE

When I get to the hotel, I'm numb and have a lump in my throat. Sirens in the distance seem to announce to the world that my best friend is dead. Don't take this the wrong way—I was never a fan of death—but since my father died when I was a kid, death seems to affect me more than other people. Ravi's is no exception.

This time, though, I'm also filled with anger. It's so unfair that the messengers picked me. I did nothing to deserve this, and I thought this was dumb from the start. Now, the people that I love are dead. It's time to put an end to this.

Avoiding the backstabbing staff, I get through the lobby and into the elevator. They've never seen me like this, ignoring everyone, and they keep their distance. They know what they did. As for me, it's as if I'm watching myself in an out-of-body experience. It doesn't feel real. Nothing feels real. The sights, sounds, and smells that seemed fine just yesterday, are now off- color, out of tune, out of place.

My best friend was just killed on top of me by a delusional woman who loves the body I wear that isn't even my own. Perhaps I could've avoided this somehow and Ravi would still be alive, but I can't think of anything I would've done differently.

Once I'm in my room, I take a deep breath. Yes, Ravi is dead but Jane and the others are alive. Even if they hate me, I still want to save them. If it's up to me, no one else will die.

I make a phone call to a specific number, hanging up after it rings once. The message is sent. The wheels are turning.

Next, I pause for a bit, mustering up the courage to call Jane. The news of Ravi's death will destroy her, and she'll hate me even more. Hesitating, I pick up the phone and do it. My hands shake as I wait for her to answer.

"Hello, Zeon. What the hell do you want?" I'm glad I don't have a last name. Based on what I've learned about them in this world, she would've used it for emphasis.

"Jane, I'm so sorry," I sob. There's no good way to tell her what happened. It's interesting how we lose control of ourselves when we have to give bad news to those we love, isn't it?

"What happened?"

She sounds frightened, and less confrontational, reacting to my tears.

"Ravi is dead. Linda killed him," I deliver the bad news between sobs. The line goes quiet but I can hear her silent and heavy breathing. There's nothing for me to do but wait.

"What did you do, Zeon?" she says, her voice cracking.

"It wasn't me. The messengers told her to do it," I explain.

"I don't believe you," she shouts. Her voice lowers then, as if she's trying to regain control of her emotions, hide them from me. "Where did it happen? Where are you?"

Anger is an easier emotion to deal with than sadness, and we often go there to protect ourselves. Moreover, after seeing people die in Pangea all the time, she must've learned to deal with death, at least a little.

"Ravi was murdered at the house where I spent my nights," I say. "But I'm at the hotel. Please come, and bring John. We have a lot to talk about." Without replying to my request, she hangs up.

The wheels of my plan are in motion, though this is not at all how I imagined it. When I first thought of this, I pictured Ravi fuming at me beside Jane and the others, but he's not here, and ultimately, it's my fault.

With the door unlocked and ajar, I sit on the silver L-shaped couch and turn on the TV. It's always on CNN, though I've never watched it. They're discussing the First Lady's dress. This all sounds very banal at this moment. News here is more like entertainment. They say that her dress was a little bit revealing, but from my point of view, it wasn't revealing enough. Planet of prudes.

Half an hour later, the protectors arrive. Even though the door was already open, it slams against the wall as they come in, reminding me of the way Ravi entered my house. The show has to start. There's no time to grieve anymore.

Jane storms into the room with her gun pointing at me, stupid Frederico at her side. Next, to my surprise, an old guy in a wheelchair follows them. My jaw drops. The handicapped man, with a full head of silver-white hair, enters my hotel room. Carrying a holstered gun on his hip belt, he's none other than Major John.

Four soldiers in battle gear and carrying rifles follow them but I can't think of anything except John's situation. Despite his handicap, he's still the best one of us in Pangea, while I could barely climb a sand dune.

"Why did you murder Ravi, Zeon? He was your best friend!" Jane says, and the way she speaks creeps me out. The tone of her voice is too normal. It's as if she's asking me why I left the toilet seat up. "And what about Louise?" Her voice trembles on her friend's name, and she lets her anger show a bit.

Not all the protectors are here, which makes sense. In case I try something and kill them, they still have many of them left. But if I'd wanted to do that, I would've already done it, so I don't think they're afraid of me. It's just a precaution.

"I didn't kill him. Linda did. He was my best friend." I manage to hold back my tears.

John is not wearing any armor, while Jane wears jeans and a white blouse behind a bulletproof vest that looks like it was put there as an afterthought.

"Yes, Linda confessed to the police. But she was at your house, Zeon. Obviously, she was working for you," John accuses.

They all pace toward me with caution. Except for John. He doesn't seem to care, maneuvering his wheelchair to position himself in front of me.

"I'd never do that. John, you of all people should know what the messengers are capable of. They have a lot of influence on people."

Jane's distraught, and the puffiness under her eyes tell me that she's done a lot of crying. It breaks my heart. She must be seeing the same thing in me, though, and I can tell she's a little bit puzzled. At the end of the day, we're all people who were hurt, though sometimes we misplace our anger.

"Don't insult the messengers!" Jane snaps. "They're trying to help us, you son of a bitch!"

I hear her loud and clear, but I do not avoid her eyes. Her faith in the messengers is misplaced.

"Jane, Linda told me she was some kind of angel of the messengers," I explain. "She was following their orders. Not mine." Jane shakes her head. I think she's still too emotional to see the big picture.

"And yet, you were betraying us," John says. "Why would I believe you?"

"Because I told Jane who I was before Ravi died. Why would I kill him after that?"

John glances at Jane, who remains quiet. He seems to know already. She must've talked to him on the way here.

"He had a gun. He was probably threatening you," John speculates. Jane's weapon is still pointed in my general direction but not directly at me anymore. I'm not on a murdering rampage yet.

"Yes, he was pointing a gun at me, but we were friends! I'd never kill him, or ask someone to kill him." Turning to face Jane, I say, "I'm not a messenger of the gods, and I don't work for them."

Her emotions are a puzzle to me. It's clear that she has mixed feelings about what happened, and she doesn't know how to react to them. She's angry, confused, and miserable. I wish I could comfort her, but in her eyes, I'm the enemy. And, well, I am the enemy.

"Why don't we just kill him right now?" Frederico asks, threatening me as always. I eye him with disdain.

"Why don't you just try it?" I ask, my mouth always faster than my common sense. "You coward. Vaffanculo!" I take this opportunity to exercise the Italian swear words that I learned on the internet as soon as I met him. I knew they'd come in handy.

This is too much for Frederico, who jumps to hit me, but

faster than I thought John could react, he rolls his wheelchair in a tight circle and blocks Frederico just in time, hitting him on his lower legs. Frederico screams and moves away. As impressive as this is, I wish he hadn't done it. I was ready to punch him back.

"Okay, boy, tell us what's really going on here," John demands.

He's the only one who has his emotions under control. He must know that I wouldn't call them here if I had nothing to show for it.

"Can you send your bulls out of here first? There's a lot for us to discuss" I say. John looks at the heavily armed men and asks them to leave. They look like they don't like it at all.

"Are you sure, sir? What if you are harmed?" a sergeant asks.

"I can take care of myself. Leave. If I need you, I'll call you," John says. Both John and Jane are carrying weapons. They can handle me. "One more thing, Sergeant. If anything happens to us here, you kill this bastard on the spot." He ignores my shocked stare.

With a final glance at me, the sergeant orders his troops to leave the room. It's just me and the protectors now. No more lies.

"Frederico has a point, Zeon. Why can't we just kill you?" John asks. "Have you done something at the particle accelerator than can kill us all?"

I'm still on the hotel couch. Jane refuses to sit, but I'll not stand up. I'm tired of this.

"When I read Mike's notes, I assumed that was what the messengers had planned for me. To create a black hole or something to destroy the planet. But it was all gibberish to me. I wouldn't know what to do with it. So even if I wanted to use it to destroy Earth, I wouldn't have been able to do it."

I pause for a second and look at Jane. "And I didn't want to do it, in the first place."

"You're saying that whatever you did to the accelerator is not harmful?" John asks.

"It's not completely harmless. I can easily hack into every piece of hardware I shipped. But there's nothing practical I can do with the ones in the colliders. Whatever you're getting at RNL is actually good for science, and it won't destroy the world, no."

"Are we supposed to just believe you?" Jane scoffs.

"You're the experts. I'm just the computer guy," I say, and she twists her lips. Closing my eyes for a second, I take another deep breath. "And yet, if you found out about me, you'd kill me. I didn't like that at all."

It's been about an hour since I made the call. Things are happening as we speak, and we'll soon learn about it on the news. They have no idea what's coming.

"My real objective was to get my computers connected to the military complex," I tell John. "And it was easier than I expected. After RNL and other places deployed them, the armed forces of several countries were all trying to buy our hardware."

Usually, it would take hours for the news to learn what happened. However, as a wealthy man on this Earth, I have connections. It was clear to me in the last couple of months that it was time to act, so I placed reporters on the carrier and warned them about something big. It should be on TV soon.

"Stop with the charades, Zeon. What the hell have you done?" John shouts, losing his cool.

I nod toward the TV. I don't think they noticed it yet, even though it's been on the whole time. It's like when you're in a bar and don't pay attention it because you think golf is boring, or because you don't care about the traffic on I-495. Jane and Frederico look at the large flat-screen on top of a wooden stand with convenient sliding doors, but John doesn't take his eyes off me.

"In a couple of minutes, you'll hear on the news that a Russian submarine has fired a nuclear missile that barely missed the aircraft carrier USS Theodore Roosevelt. Luckily, the missile was unarmed."

Shock is replaced by fear as they understand the implications. First, if the missile was armed, it would create a nuclear explosion. Such an event right next to an American aircraft carrier would mean a nuclear war between Russia and the United States. Second, they know that somehow I'm involved in it, since I warned them beforehand.

"Why would you believe anything he says? He's bluffing!" Frederico says.

Jane glares at him, clearly angry. There's no lost love between them.

"Zeon, you have to stop this. You're about to start a nuclear war," she argues.

"No, I'm just threatening one." I like to think this is better.

There's nothing on TV yet. If my call failed, I'm screwed, and they might just kill me on the spot. John soon gets tired of this and begins to slowly explore the room, watching me and sometimes typing on his phone.

Jane moves some tacky gold pillows off the couch and sits on the other side of the L-shape, crossing her legs. Frederico, on the other hand, is pacing the room nonstop, breathing hard.

While we wait, John also probes my behavior in the hypersphere, asking if and when I contacted the Jori, trying to guess what happened on his own. I'm about to explain my plans to meet Mike when the TV finally answers my prayers.

"This is CNN Breaking News. We are sorry to interrupt this program. We have just received information that the USS Theodore Roosevelt, deployed in the Persian Gulf, was attacked by what seems to be a submarine-launched missile. We don't have any further information at this time, but we'll keep you up to date as more information comes. Again, we just heard that..."

I breathe a sigh of relief.

"I'm telling you, we should kill il figlio di puttana!" Frederico shouts.

Seriously, sometimes I think I'm dealing with amateurs.

"Shut up, Frederico!" Jane yells.

"I assume we can't kill you, Zeon," John guesses. Frederico looks puzzled. Maybe he wants me to draw him a diagram.

"You're right. As of now, I have control of Russia's entire nuclear arsenal and one fourth of the United States'." I try to hide how relieved I am that it worked. "Have you heard of something called a dead man's switch?" They nod. "I must ping the system once a day, and every time, I use a different method, a different time, and a different password. It will take months for you to undo this, and you will run the risk of accidentally launching the missiles." I glare at Frederico. "In case you don't understand, that means that if the missiles don't hear from me in a reasonable amount of time, they'll launch automatically. Capicci?" Frederico stares back at me in disbelief.

"You'd start a nuclear war to save yourself?" John asks.

"No, I'd start one to save my planet. Actually, both of our Earths."

Less than a day ago, everything had seemed to go so well for this Earth. Now, all of a sudden, Ravi's dead and they're under threat of nuclear Armageddon. All because of me.

Jane gets up from the couch and walks next to John.

"But, Mike—I mean, Zeon—even if you destroy our Earth with a nuclear war, Jora can still be destroyed by the portal. Our Earth will still be around when you open it," Jane says, coming closer for the first time. "You must implode Earth to actually save your planet, or it doesn't work. What's your plan here?"

She's right. They all guessed that the attacker would use the particle accelerators or something like that. Making this Earth a nuclear wasteland doesn't make sense, since it doesn't save Jora in the long run.

"I don't have the knowledge to implode anything, Jane. This is the most I can do. It makes you wonder how much the messengers really know about what they are doing, right?"

Jane and John exchange a concerned look. They must make a decision but they're cornered, and there aren't that many options.

"Very well, Zeon," John says. "What exactly is your plan?"

36

SMOKE

We meet again in the hypersphere in Pangea but Jane is nowhere to be seen. I don't blame her; there is so much betrayal going on. She told me earlier that my plan is nuts and she won't help me. I hope that someday she'll understand my actions.

We discuss our mission at length in the command room at the superdome. This was not what I had in mind but it works out for the best. At first, I was going to do all of this by myself by creating a distraction in one of the towers and waiting for Mike in the other one. Since everyone's helping now, there's no need to disable the cameras in our fortress. Everyone knows who I am.

Even Louise is here but she's avoiding me. No matter what we think of it, Ravi is dead because of his involvement with me. I've heard that she's smoking again on Earth, not just in the hypersphere. Also, many suspect that I ordered Linda to do it.

"John, I can talk with Mike by myself. There's no need to put others at risk," I say.

His extremely fit chest impresses me even more now

that I've seen him on Earth. How does he do it? And why can't I have a six-pack here?

"No. We want to see the real Mike." I give him a quizzical look for a second, but I figure it out—he's worried that I'll defect to my own side and kill Mike. I'm too valuable for John. However, I could've gone there anytime I wanted when I was in Pangea, so he's wrong to fear that outcome. Ever since they learned about my real mission, he's positioned lookouts for me, as if they could stop me.

"Zeon, what happens if you're killed or captured?" Paulo asks me.

"That won't happen," I assure them. "I can do things here in Pangea that even the Jori can't." True, this doesn't mean I can't be killed—far from it—I just have an edge over everyone else. But, to be honest, I'm more worried about other people dying, and I'm happy that Jane is not going with us today.

We step outside our giant red dome and get in our tall six-wheeled trucks. Earlier, it wasn't that bright out—the red giant was near the horizon—but now, it's brighter. The hypersphere never ceases to amaze me. The giant star is still low, and the smaller sun is rising on the other side of the hypersphere. It's never night here.

"Get in your vehicles," John shouts. Time for the show to start.

Everything has to be done quickly, because the Jori can see what we're doing. I'm in the leading truck with John driving and Vladimir on the gun, but this time, it's our trucks that are going down the hill first.

John tries to drive as fast as he can. Like we planned, the Jori start their own convoy in response. We must be quick to avoid them shooting at us when we get down there, but today, we're prepared. Everybody's wearing armor and the gunners have had practice with their equipment. Moreover, today they're using the neural interfaces in their weapons for the first time.

As we go down the hill, we pass through the gun turrets that protect our fortress. This battlefield was designed to kill people, regardless of which side you're on. With the powerful energy weapons gone, it becomes a deadly stalemate.

There is no way we can go up the hill and not be butchered by these guns. They're controlled from the domes. Our trucks are no match for them. For some reason, none of the weapons systems are operated by advanced artificial intelligence systems.

My mouth dries as we get closer to the bottom of the hill. There's so much that could go wrong. Time is of the essence. The Jori may start shooting like last time. I don't want what happened to poor Joshua to happen again.

Through my binoculars, I focus on the leading truck. Nia's temple jewelry flashes twice under the double-suns, and Mike is by her side. I'm not worried about us being recognized; it's impossible to tell who we are from this distance. I just know it's him because I'm expecting him to be there. This is part of the plan I discussed with Nia the last time. Once the smoke is in the air, nobody will see us anymore. Still, it's odd that they're in the first vehicle.

Another thing catches my eye, then. They're not by themselves in the truck. The gunner is a black man with a face tattoo, visible even from this distance. Jal's the gunner. Somehow, they'll have to get rid of him before they meet me. Maybe they didn't have a choice. There's no reason to go down with only two people.

Their pace down the hill is not as fast as it was the other time. Nia's vehicle is slowing down the Jori's convoy, and they must be upset with her. Meanwhile, I brought one of their headsets with me in case they start talking. If something goes wrong, I can warn the others, but so far, they're in radio silence.

Our truck is the first to hit the valley below. Assuming that our entrance is east and theirs is west, we start going south, and Vladimir shoots the first smoke bomb. This is not your run-of-the-mill smoke— it's impervious to any surveillance technology.

"Number one out!" he says into his headset.

Paulo's truck, just behind us, swerves north. The deception has started. We split into two directions under a blanket of smoke, like airplanes in an air show. Except that we're hiding in it.

"Número dois deployed!" Paulo replies.

Since they can't see us, they must make a tough decision. They can't split and send half their numbers to the south and the other half to the north. If they do that, our convoy could slaughter their divided force because we have more trucks. We already destroyed two of theirs last time, and their only advantage is that they have more protectors.

"We're out and turning," Carmen yells. "Good luck to you guys!" They also go north. In fact, our whole force is going north except us. But the Jori don't know that.

One alternative is for them to try to guess the direction we're going. They can always turn back if we're not there, but they have no idea why we're going there in the first place. They don't want us to win whatever we think is there. The prize may be deadly, and we could perhaps destroy their whole force just because we got there first.

Of course, it's all a ruse. I'm the real prize, though I don't think Jane would agree with that. I just want to talk with Mike, but they don't know that, either.

Right now, Paulo should be leaving a small hole in the smoke screen, apparently by mistake. They should see our trucks moving north and, with luck, they'll think we screwed up and start following our main force. This is the distraction.

Meanwhile, Mike's truck should be going south toward us. We plan to talk to them before any shooting starts, and by then, it'll be too late for them to catch us. It's weird that they're in the first truck, though. How will they pull this off?

The main problem is that we can't see if it worked. We just have to execute the plan and hope for the best. I wish everybody on our team was helping us, but not all of them agreed. Several stayed behind, Jane and Frederico among them.

After riding for about fifteen minutes, we stop at the south tower, far away from the ramp where we left. We don't shoot any more smoke bombs. We dropped the last one about five minutes ago. They'll see us on their monitors now, unless Mike took care of them.

"A truck is coming," Vladimir shouts, looking through the binoculars.

"Just one?" John asks, hopeful.

"Da!"

"May I take a look?" I ask Vladimir, and he hands me the binoculars. Three people are on the truck. I recognize Nia and Mike, and I'm surprised to see that Jal is still manning the gun. This doesn't look right. He must know what's going on, which makes me wonder who else knows. Dread forms in the pit of my stomach.

Suddenly, our headsets vibrate.

"John, uh...we have a problem," Paulo says, and I can feel doom approaching. I wish at least one of my plans would work the way I drew it up. Damn it.

"Go ahead," John replies, while Vladimir positions himself on his gun, aiming at the oncoming vehicle. He can't shoot it, though. Mike is there, and he's on his side. We try to see what's happening behind Mike's truck, but we're too far away, and the smoke is in the way.

"Nobody followed us," Paulo explains in our headsets.

Crap. If nobody's following our main force, they must be following Mike. I glance at John and Vladimir, panicking. We can't take them on with only one truck. They shouldn't have come with me. They'll die because of that mistake.

"John, do you copy?" We hear Louise this time. Her voice is stronger than we're used to, and her accent less pronounced. "I'm in the last truck. We're driving back to check."

Earth's protectors are smart and autonomous; they don't need people ordering them around. They take the initiative.

"Be safe, Louise," John warns her. "If they shoot at you, go back to the main force. You can tell us what's going on later."

Mike's truck is within five hundred meters. I don't want to use their headsets and give away anything. Perhaps I should've been listening in more often.

"Wait, I see them," Louise says. I hold my breath, preparing for the worse.

John tenses. "Go ahead, Louise. We're listening."

"They haven't left the hill. Their vehicles are waiting at the end of the road."

"Why?" John asks.

"Va savoir pourquoi!" she says. She sounds irritated. I think it means she doesn't know.

Mike's truck stops right in front of us, and he jumps out of it, looking at John and Vladimir with a big smile. I confess I'm a bit spooked. I've been used to being him for more than a year now, and the only difference between me on Earth and him here today is the baggy bämbêchê and the small pänchä that is too short to cover his hips. This is uncanny. And I'm not talking about his hips.

"<Hello, Mike.>" I say in Dïnisc. I shake his hand. "<Nice to finally meet you.>"

With a strong grip and a big grin, he studies my face in detail. For a moment, it's like I'm in front of a mirror on Earth. Mike must be feeling the same weirdness, except he exudes confidence, and I feel small when I meet him.

"Hello, Zeon," Mike says in perfect English. "It's so nice to finally meet you in person. And a bit creepy."

37

MIRRORS

Nia and Jal stay in their truck, while Mike introduces himself to the others.

"You all know who I am, I assume?" He addresses them while shaking hands with each man, in turn.

"Dr. Pohlt, I presume?" John grins. "I'm Major John Tyson. Do you know why they didn't follow our trucks?"

"They know about me, Major Tyson. You did a great job with the smoke, but it wasn't necessary."

My suspicion is that Mike has done something similar on Jora to what I've done on Earth in order to stay alive. However, we don't have an arsenal of nuclear bombs there to threaten people with, so perhaps he figured out how to create a black hole. I'm sure Bodan would've killed him if he could.

"Why didn't you tell us, using white flag or something, you cyka blyat?" Vladimir asks, pissed. It doesn't matter how much you fight, you're always scared to death, and it would have been nice to not go through that.

Mike hesitates and looks at me, as if asking something

without words. He can read between the lines, but he probably wants to double-check, just to be sure. I nod.

"We weren't sure if you knew about Zeon."

So he doesn't want to kill people, just like me. The messengers made a mistake in creating two moles who think so much alike.

"We have to talk, Mike," I interrupt, tilting my head at John and the others. "But we need some privacy first."

John walks in between us and grabs me by my arm, as if protecting Mike.

"Why the secrecy? We are all friends!" he exclaims.

"I don't know who I can trust," I say. Really, if this doesn't make John and me best friends, nothing will.

"You don't know?" he rages. "Mike, your friend Zeon here has control of our nuclear arsenal and it's under a dead man's trigger protocol!"

Mike looks at me, puzzled, maybe weighing what John just said. I shrug, suppressing a grin.

"And he didn't destroy Earth yet?" he asks, not missing a beat. Of course not. If I had, none of John's team would be around, if I understand how Pangea works. But then again, I didn't read the manual.

"No, not yet."

Mike nods. "That's good enough for me."

"Vat?" Vladimir interrupts, his accent suddenly stronger. "Vat if he kills you?"

Mike looks at me again, as if searching for something.

"He doesn't have any weapons on him."

"Zeon doesn't need guns to kill. We're on your side, Mike. You should trust us. This should be obvious to you," John insists.

Mike pauses to think. This isn't going the way I wanted. I

didn't want to tell him this today, but he can't just trust people, even if they're from his Earth.

"Maybe you can be trusted," I tell John, "but I wouldn't be so sure about it." I turn to Mike, dreading what I must tell him. "Mike, you remember Linda, your ex-wife? She and Ravi were protectors here." This gets his attention instantly. He gives me a concerned look. He heard it, the past tense. "Linda killed Ravi today."

"What?" He glowers at me.

"Ravi found out about me and came to my house. Linda said Hermes asked her to protect me, so she shot him."

I hate that he had to learn it like this but John forced my hand. This is the first time that Mike's confidence cracks. I wear my heart on my sleeve, but, like John, Mike seemed like a rock from the start. The news that Ravi is dead has broken that façade. But then again, I just met the guy.

"And you...you let her do it?" Mike says.

I shake my head. "I'm sorry, Mike. When she shot Ravi, I was handcuffed."

Mike's hands tighten into fists.

"We're not exactly sure if Zeon had anything to do with it or not," John interrupts. I wish there was someone in the universe who had my back. I mean, really, just because I'm blackmailing them with nuclear annihilation doesn't mean I'm the bad guy.

"I'd never kill Ravi," I say. "I had plenty of opportunities, and I never did it. And, to be honest, I don't think he would've killed me, either. Linda is not in her right mind."

This is not the moment to talk about April. It's too much for him to take.

Mike stays quiet for a few seconds as we wait. He just learned his best friend was killed, and he doesn't look sure who's responsible for it. After what feels like forever, he finally puts his hands on his hips and sighs.

"I'll take my chances, John. He can't kill me for the same reason you can't kill him." I knew it. Like me, Mike has a plan. A whole planet dies if either of us dies. I just don't know how. Not yet.

John concedes, however, and lets me go. Mike and I walk toward the tower, leaving John and Vladimir behind.

Soon we start the long and hard climb. The tower is at least ten-stories tall. There's an unending zig-zag staircase that goes all the way to the top, and once we're there, we'll finally be out of earshot.

"Zeon, what day is today on my Earth?" he asks, as if making small talk. Puzzled, I tell him the date. The day and even the season might be different between our Earths because Jora doesn't have a moon. Still, I find it strange that he's asking me this kind of stuff. My guess is that he's trying not to think about Ravi's death.

Climbing the stairs is harder than I thought. Like the hexagons, the staircase and the tower are made from the same continuous, metallic-warm, gray material. The handrail gets brighter where we touch it. Also, like everything else in Pangea that's indoors, it's never dark. Unseen light sources illuminate our surroundings with almost no shadows, making it look like a poor man's videogame.

At the top, we're greeted by large windows with no glass, giving us a nice, clear view of the valley and a refreshing breeze to cool our skin. There's no time for sightseeing, though.

"Why would Linda do what Hermes asked her to do?" Mike says, breathing normally. The climbing didn't affect him. "She's not a killer, Zeon." I avoid his eyes. There is so much that he doesn't know, and this is not the time to tell him.

"She said she was some kind of fallen angel. And that she wanted redemption. She's nuts, Mike. Ravi died in my arms."

Saying that makes me relive his murder, and tears come to my eyes again. This is so tough. Mike closes his eyes for a while, and I can't tell if he's angry or just grieving. Maybe both.

"I'm glad Nia got a hold of you, and that we're finally meeting," I say, trying to change the subject. Mike looks at her and the others below.

"You know, Nia's not so bad. I know you guys have...a history, but most of the victories they've had here were due to her planning," he says. I frown, thinking about the violence. "Well, not the killings, just the strategy." He shrugs, as if apologizing for her. It makes sense—she's one of the most creative types I know.

"We must end this, Mike," I say, giving a furtive glance at my ex-fiancée below. "I saw your notes. Will you be able to create a black hole in one of our accelerators?"

"No," he admits. "Maybe in a hundred years or more." He smiles. Focusing on his work is helping his mood. Perhaps, if he concentrates on what we have to do, he won't think that much about Linda and Ravi.

"What did you do?" I ask, worried.

"Do you remember the mission to Mars that Jora was preparing?" Yes, I do remember. They were developing the most powerful rocket engine ever created in order to carry out that mission. Our ring of moon-debris is always a problem, getting in the way of our rockets. "I helped them develop and launch it," he explains.

"How would that help? You could only destroy a few blocks with it. Nothing more," I argue.

Mike touches the warm wall of the tower before answering.

"Do you play pool, Zeon?" he asks, and I fold my arms, thinking he's lost his mind. However, this is Mike, and he wouldn't be asking me that if it wasn't relevant, so I shake my head.

All of a sudden, he gives me an odd look and I realize that, by now, he must have learned the meaning on this gesture on Jora. "I mean, no," I add, trying to save face. "But I know the game. You bounce a cue ball off the other balls so they fall on some rails."

"Exactly. It turns out that if you have a large amount of computing power and advanced sensors, you can do some really interesting things. You can aim that Mars rocket at one of the rocks in your planet's ring, and there are a lot of them there. But if you hit the right one, at the right place, at the right speed, and from the right direction..." He pauses. If you calculate everything just right, he can make most of those rocks fall, causing major havoc.

"You're playing space pool with the Ring!" I finish, grinning. And then I'm sad. We're talking about destroying my planet.

Smaller pieces of the Ring fall all the time on Jora, but they're usually harmless. Once in a while, a big one gets unstable and falls. When this happens, we have tsunamis and earthquakes. However, if most of them fall at the same time, we're screwed. Even if we disregard the actual impact of the rocks, dust and ash would be thrown into the atmosphere, which would cause a new ice age and famine.

Nevertheless, even considering all of that, you'd have to be some kind of a genius to set it all up. The math would be impossible with Earth's computers, but perhaps doable with the advanced computers we have on Jora.

"What was the point of sending us to each other's planets in the first place?" I ask. I don't want to keep thinking about how close Mike is to destroying my home. "We can't create a black hole on either planet. Even if we decimated both civilizations, the planets themselves would still exist, no matter what we did."

"Correct. I realized that from the start." Of course, he's the smarter version of me, and it was his theory that, if true, would have allowed us to create a black hole and implode a planet. "But the messengers were lying," he continues. "After they talked about the portal, I researched it. Last month, we discovered how to create one. It's the same science needed to create a black hole, but it's much easier. Everyone's excited about that on Jora. We should be able to open it in about five years." He smiles. "There's only one tiny little problem with it. The portal only works if both Earths try to open it at the same time."

I consider what he just said. He looks at me, as if waiting for me to get the punchline of a joke. It doesn't take me long to understand the implications. I may be dumb, but I'm not slow.

"But the odds of both Earths opening a portal at the exact same time, with no communication between them are —" I begin.

"Astronomical," he says, interrupting. "It's further evidence that the messengers were lying." He leans back on the weird balcony, excited. He's not finished yet.

"It takes too much power to establish the initial connection. We can't keep trying it every single day. There's not enough energy on Earth to do that. We can't open a portal unless we agree on a date." He smirks.

"Wait, what if they want us to create the portal so we can destroy ourselves?" I ask, doubtful.

"I thought about that, too, but no. It'd be much easier to just bring everyone to Pangea, explain what a portal is and why they should open one, and let both of our Earths work out the details. They could just lie, tell us that the portal is harmless, and we would trust them and happily destroy ourselves, with the help of the gods."

If it were any other person saying that, it'd sound arrogant, but not Mike. He has so much charisma that it somehow feels right.

"In that case, what do they want us to do?" I challenge his conclusion. "If it's impossible to create a black hole, if the portal will not destroy us, then why are we having these games?"

"They expected us to do exactly what you and I did," he says, looking up at the strange yellow sky, as if the gods are up there.

Funny, I had to hear him say that out loud to realize what's happening, even after all the explanation and cues he's given me. I couldn't figure this out by myself because I'm not a particle physicist, and, more importantly, I'm also a moron. I always guessed that creating a black hole was possible, and that I was just too stupid to do it by myself. But if we can't create one at all, then there's only one possible explanation for all of this. The truth hits me like a ton of bricks.

"The messengers want us to kill everyone on both our planets," I conclude. But not with a portal. They want to destroy Earth with a nuclear winter, and Jora with a shower of rocks.

38

CIVIL WAR

W e're doing exactly what the messengers wanted—destroying both our worlds.

"But why?" I ask.

"Maybe they don't want us to help each other."

Walking near the edge of the tower, I watch our people. Nia and Jal have left their truck and are standing near John and Vladimir—not too close. My hope is that we can make peace today, but there's still a lot of distrust. The current situation is like a powder keg just waiting for a spark.

"Did you know they were cheating, trying to help the Jori win? If they want to destroy all of us, why bother with that?" I ask, trying to remain calm.

"There is so much we don't know, Zeon. Somehow, connecting the Earths with a portal is a threat for them." Mike seems to be taking this in stride. But then again, I just learned about it.

"And why do we have the games in the hypersphere?" None of this makes any sense.

"We may never know. The only ones who have all the answers are the messengers."

We must have a plan, though, even with all this uncertainty. It's time to turn the game.

"We have to attack the messengers. We must take the war to them," I say.

It's sad, in a way. I've never wanted to kill anything in my life. When I look at Nia from afar, I remember that I wanted to hurt Bodan. I want to beat him up, drag him behind a car, waterboard him, break both his legs and arms, and tie him to an ant hill. But not kill him. But if I have the opportunity, I'll kill the messengers and their gods.

"They have a lot of power. How can we overcome that?" Mike asks.

For once, I understand something better than Mike. He has no idea what I've been doing here.

"It's true that they told us lies," I say, still looking at our people below. "When you mix lies and truths, it's hard to tell them apart. And yet, I believe one particular thing they told me." I turn around to face Mike again. "They cannot directly kill us."

"How do you know that?"

"They told me they're not murderers," I say. Mike scoffs at me, shaking his head. "Yes, that could be a lie. But no one was killed, either here or on Earth, by a messenger." Mike's expression becomes grim. He must be thinking of Ravi.

"Mercury told me the gods made a mistake once," I continue. Those stupid gods made lots of mistakes, but this one stands out. "He said that they created a race of murderers at one point, and that it backfired. I think that they lost control of those aliens and replaced them with the messengers."

Mike puts his hands on the window's rail, and I could swear he and Nia lock eyes despite how far away we are from them. I wonder what they have gone through since I left Jora.

"You know, even if we save our planets, we may both end up dead," he says. He doesn't look at me. This is not a question. "I don't even know if we can revert back to our own bodies."

"We just have to stop this nonsense. If they need us to do their dirty work, then we should just stop doing it," I say.

"And yet, we'll have to convince everybody else of that. What if they have others like us that we haven't met yet?"

"We'll worry about that later. There's nothing we can do about that now."

After that, Mike and I discuss our plan for tomorrow. It's simpler than the one we just did—we're going to go to the messengers' place armed to the teeth, with as many people as are willing to help us, and attack them. They can't kill us, if our hypothesis is correct, so they'll fall. This will be our final battle in Pangea.

WHEN WE START the long trip down the staircase, I decide to ask a question that's been bothering me since he first talked to us.

"Mike, could you speak English since the beginning?"

He laughs. "No. I was only able to speak Dïnisc. I probably did the same thing you did." He points at my head. "There was someone on Jora who was shady enough to try stuff without asking questions. We tried several possible solutions until we found one. It took months." Mike didn't have the luxury of remembering his own brain like I did. He didn't know where the switch of his language was in his brain. It's amazing. They did it by trial and error.

"The hard part for me was finding a way to do it without being detected by Jora's protectors," he continues.

So it seems that he can't do what I do here in Pangea. I'm unique.

"The question is, how the heck do you speak Dïnisc, Zeon? Jora has neural gun injectors, but Earth doesn't."

Our steps make no sound when we descend, and the areas we touch brighten, just like the handrail. We noticed it on the way up, but it's more visible on the way down. It's like we're walking on a silent piano, the keys lighting up when we play them.

"I was lucky," I admit. "I had the right training, good memory, and super powers in Pangea." I laugh. "I did it myself, while I was here." He looks at me as if I just told him that the Beatles suck.

"You did it yourself," he mumbles. "Unbelievable!"

I give him a summary of how my mind can interact and change everything in Pangea due to the messengers' experiments, and he finally understands why John was worried about leaving us alone.

When we reach the bottom of the tower, the others are waiting. I walk over to Nia, who plays with her fractal flame on her hands, temporarily removed from her face.

"<Thanks, Nia.>" I don't know what else to say. This is all very awkward.

"<It's okay, Zeon.>" She still looks beautiful, but somehow tainted. I'm glad I had a year to get over her, otherwise I'd probably do something dumb and try to be together with both of them. I'm a sucker sometimes, especially when it comes to women.

We're interrupted by the sound of gunfire. Lots of it, from everywhere. Explosions flash on the hills and the roads. The horizon quickly fills with small mushroom clouds of smoke and debris. Jal and Nia grab their weapons and point them at John and Vladimir, who are also ready, pointing their guns back at them. This is getting out of control fast.

"<Saint Plehr!>" Nia yells, staring at the dust that's growing like a doomsday cloud.

"Wait!" I shout, making the wait sign so Nia and Jal understand. At least they're all still confused and not shooting at each other yet. All headsets are buzzing as people from both sides try to contact us.

"John, do you copy?" It's Louise.

"What the fuck is happening?" John replies. Mike and the others are also hearing the status through their sets.

"The guns on the hill on their side started shooting on their own people. Mon Dieu! It's a massacre," she cries. Mike's face is one of shock; he must be getting the same news.

"John," Paulo speaks in the headsets. "Our own turrets are shooting at us! We're out of range if we stay in the middle, but it hit one of our parked trucks. Luckily, there was no one inside, but—"

"Mike, tell your people to move to the middle," John yells, interrupting Paulo. Mike relays the message, but they must've realized that already.

The turrets cannot be shooting by themselves. Someone took control of them in both of our domes. Suddenly, it all makes perfect sense. The messengers have their own people among us, like Linda, and these traitors must be manning the guns.

Mike and I stare at each other with matching shocked expressions as we realize what's going on. We're a pair of bozos. If we die, both planets will be destroyed. And no one will make it up the hill alive unless we deactivate the turrets.

"Mike, do you have AED bombs?" I ask, afraid of his answer.

"No." He shakes his head. "We used them all up a long time ago."

John talks to Mike next. "Let's meet in the middle, next to the craters near the end of the roads. Maybe we can fight our way up if we join forces. Can you tell the Jori to not shoot at us?"

Mike nods and speaks into his headset. John is a fighter —he won't ever give up, but this battle was over before it even began. The range and power of any single one of those weapons far surpasses our truck guns. This is a meat grinder.

They get in their trucks, but I stay back.

"You can't stay here, Zeon," John yells. "You're too important to die."

I ignore him. It's time for me to think, to focus. Time slows down around me. Perhaps I could try to grab some people, fly all of them above the domes and toward the arch in several trips, but no, the guns would eventually hit me in one of my flights. They can shoot in any direction, including up, so that won't work. I could catch whoever is attacking us by surprise the first time—they don't expect people to fly here—but not a second time.

Fighting them on each dome is a possibility, but despite my powers here, I'm only one person. I'm not sure if I'll be able to handle all of them. In truth, there's no telling how many are in each dome. Also, Linda, Jane, and all of Earth's protectors are aware that I can fly, so I can only assume that they'll expect me to do that.

"Come on, Zeon! What are you waiting for?" John shouts again.

There isn't much time; people are dying. I've made my decision. I run toward Mike's truck so he can hear me better.

"Mike, we'll still go with our original plan. We'll all meet at the place we agreed tomorrow." He nods, puzzled. Even if we get back to our trucks, even if we join forces, we can't fight our way up the hill. There are too many guns.

They're all looking at me, probably thinking that I'm from another planet, and maybe I am. I give a last glance at each of them and jump into the sky, fist first, my other arm by my side, like a superhero. I wish I could see Nia's face. I know—this is childish, but I just can't help it.

My goal is to reach their blue dome, not mine. If I fly to our superdome, I won't be able to end this charade. I also fly low. Flying too high would give more time for the turrets to zero in on me.

They don't even see me for the first fifteen seconds. But midway there someone notices, and a few guns aim in my general direction. The rounds fly nearby, missing me by inches, but it's not like they're experienced gunners. I'm just too fast for them. I feel like a superhero! Maybe Jane was right when she compared herself to Louise Lane. I'm not invincible, though, so we need to find another hero for comparison.

While I mentally browse the rosters of all the super heroes I've seen so far, a shot explodes near my right arm. My trajectory becomes erratic, and I almost plummet. Seriously, I should stop thinking about stupid stuff and concentrate on what's important.

After an agonizing wait, I'm out of range of the enemy's artillery. I kneel when I touch the ground again, but I immediately stand up and start running. The domes are a mirror of each other—I hope—and I know where I have to go. Too bad I forgot to bring a gun. I'm inside the dome before anyone realizes.

Bodan is the only protector in the building. His punchable face is impossible to miss, with his gorgeous, long blond hair and stick-on jewelry made of red diamonds and emeralds. Untraditionally, both of them represent his rich family's coat-of-arms—winged lions.

The face he makes when he sees me brightens my day. Adrenaline makes me grin as I run, but there's no real joy in what I'm doing. People are dying. He must've been taken by surprise; there are no weapons on him, either. He scrambles toward a nearby table as I hurry to the stairs on the side of the room.

When Bodan finally grabs a capacitor, he shoots. But his shots are clumsy, missing me by a lot. He's too slow, and I'm too far away. I wave at him from afar, teasing, but that's a mistake. Screaming, he sets his weapon to automatic fire and by sheer luck, one of his shots hits my hip.

I fall and start to roll down the stairs. He stops shooting, smiles broadly, and runs after me. Okay, I have to concentrate. No need to screw everything up.

Luckily, there's no major damage in my upper leg and the pain hasn't struck yet—just like the other time in the hypersphere. Energy blasts must destroy nerves, and it takes a while for your own body to comprehend the damage.

Taking advantage of that, I rise and stagger toward the second floor, throwing myself to the right at the top of the stairs to avoid another shot. Their game disk flashes in the middle of the room on the second floor.

The rules of battles like these are simple. They end when one member of one team touches the flashing disk of the other team, like a traditional capture-the-flag game. More importantly, the moment this happens, the hypersphere shuts down and everybody wakes up on their own planet, unharmed. Supposedly. Well, the disk is right next to me, and I can end this, but I just can't help myself. Bodan must see me one last time.

He comes running into the room, panting, an incredulous look on his face. Grinning, I give him a thumbs-up with both hands and jump into the disk. Thumbs-up is an offensive hand sign on Jora, where, with one single gesture, I manage to offend him, his brothers and sisters, mothers and fathers, pets, and any livestock he owns.

"<You tickle-fucker!>" He screams the worst possible insult in our language, points his gun at me, and shoots, but I dive into the flashing light.

The game is over. We won.

39

EVE

The sight of my hotel room has never been this inviting. Everybody who was in the hypersphere should be back on their own planets. We'll get a protector out of this, and they'll lose one—as if we care at this point. I'm getting confused about who's them and who's us. It'll take several hours until we can be back in Pangea. And then, as the gods are my witnesses, this will end, one way or another.

The room is not as quiet as it used to be. Maybe I forgot and left the TV on, or my bathroom fan is malfunctioning. When I walk to the window, the source of all the noise becomes obvious, but the movement outside puzzles me at first. The parking lot and adjacent streets are filled with news vans and a crowd of protestors. I forgot about Ravi's death, and it hits me again like a truck.

Things have become way more complicated. The messengers want to kill us, regardless of where we are. I thought I had planned for everything, but before they killed Ravi, I didn't realize that they could turn people outside the hypersphere into assassins.

Since they want both me and Mike dead, I'm not safe here anymore, even with a dead man's trigger. I must do something about it, or I may be killed before I go back to Pangea, or even while I'm there.

Though I'm not in the mood for breakfast, I still need coffee, so I order some from room service. There's no need to turn the TV on. I know what's on the news today. It turns out I'm involved with both major stories, though one of them happened in the Persian Gulf. And my friends thought I'd never amount to anything.

The coffee makes me appreciate the simple things. Before the domes, there was no coffee in Pangea, and I missed it every time I was there. This is my favorite part of the day on Earth but it feels hollow today. Everything I've done this last year is lost. All the relationships I created, destroyed.

There's a knock on the door earlier than I expected. John could not be here that fast. The messengers must be trying to finish the job they tried to do in the hypersphere. Perhaps I shouldn't answer.

"Dr. Pohlt?" someone shouts. "This is the police. We have a couple of questions for you."

I breathe a sigh of relief. There's nothing to fear from the police. In fact, they might protect me. This must be standard procedure. Nothing I can say will help them. Ravi's murder is pretty much an open-and-shut case. Linda, the crazy woman, killed Ravi. I let them in, happy to see them.

"Hello, Dr. Pohlt. I'm detective Ken Mortinson, and this is my partner, Samuel Washington," Ken says in a deep voice, both his hands in his belt.

"Please, call me Mike," I reply, holding my warm mug of coffee.

"We're sorry about what happened, Mike. It must be devastating to lose a close friend like that," Ken continues.

"It is. Thanks."

Police uniforms are always fancy, but American cops take it to the next level. While most countries typically use plain shirts with a few fabric insignias, here they have all kinds of equipment on their belts, shiny badges, and complex designs on their hats.

"We just have a couple of routine questions for you so we can get the case going," he adds. I hope they're not too explicit. It was traumatic enough just being there, watching him die.

"Sure, no problem. Please have a seat. Do you want some coffee?"

"No, that won't be necessary," Ken replies, as they both seat themselves on one of the sections of the large couch. "Is it true that Ravi wanted to kill you?" he asks.

I sit on the sectional beside Samuel. "No, I don't think he would've killed me. He was just very mad at me."

"Linda said he was planning to kill you, that he had a gun. Why was he threatening you?"

Damn, I forgot that these people don't know what's going on. When I think about it, though, not even I can keep up with everything that's happening.

"I'm not sure." If we ignore Pangea, Ravi had no reason to threaten or kill me. This must look really odd for people not involved in this.

"Did you have some kind of business disagreement?" Samuel asks.

"Yes! Thanks, Samuel!"

This is a good alternative explanation, better than saying I'm from another planet trying to destroy Earth. This sounds believable, like something that happens sometimes with business partners.

"Oh no, please call me Sam, Mike." He smiles, raising his eyebrows, and I suddenly feel like I can trust him.

"Can you elaborate? On the disagreements, I mean," Ken asks.

I don't know. I just made this up. What kind of disagreements could we have? Ravi and I never had any fights, except at the beginning, before he accepted that I was not the Mike he knew, and took Harry into his heart.

"It's complicated." I'm uncertain of what to say.

"Did he want to split the company?" Sam suggests, leaning closer.

"I'll go with that. Yes." I smile thinly, Sam grins, and we nod in synchrony. Ken takes some notes. Okay, this is the right answer. I'm glad Sam's here to help me. Ken is starting to scare me.

"But you didn't want to let him," Ken adds.

"Correct." I take a sip of my now lukewarm coffee, twisting my face.

"And you were really mad about it. You would've done anything to stop it," Samuel says, narrowing his eyes.

I rest my mug on the table. The coffee is undrinkable now.

"Yes. Wait, no." I don't like where this is going.

"Why did you leave the house after the shooting?" Ken presses.

"I feared for my life." This is not a lie. I was afraid, but not because of Linda. The protectors and the messengers were in my mind when I fled.

Ken looks at his notebook for a moment, but I don't think he's reading anything. He turns to face me again.

"Didn't you take a shower after Ravi was dead?" Sam asks.

"Yes, Sam. I was naked and covered in Ravi's blood. I couldn't walk on the streets looking like that." I mean, isn't it obvious? Ken tilts his head, as if he doesn't believe me, but Sam nods, showing empathy.

"Let me get this straight," Ken begins, dropping his notes by his side. "You were having disagreements with Ravi, your business partner. Your ex-wife comes to your house and kills him. You take a shower, put on some clothes, and just go about your business?"

"Well, when you say it like that, it does sound suspicious," I concede. Wait a minute. I know what's happening here. I've watched enough cop shows. They're setting me up.

"Dr. Pohlt," Ken says, "would you mind accompanying us to the station?" He rises to his feet.

"Am I being arrested?" I ask, standing up almost at the same time. Ken is slightly taller than I am, and stronger. There's no way I can run right now.

"No, we just have a few more people who want to talk to you," Ken says, extending his arm so I can follow him.

"I'm sorry, detectives. I need to speak with my lawyer first."

This is what I should have said from the beginning. My mind is not on this Earth anymore. There are bigger things going on.

Sam and Ken are not happy with my answer, but there isn't much they can do, so they leave after trying a few more dirty tactics. I'm sure they'll be coming back, but my lawyers will take care of it for me. Sometimes, being rich pays off.

However, the messengers may still kill me here before I go back to Pangea. It's time to make a call to John. I need his help, again.

"Yes, Mike?" John answers. "I mean, Zeon." I hear the noise of traffic in the background.

"I want you to come to my hotel room as soon as possible."

"I'm on my way there already. Sorry, I have another call."

Ten minutes and another stainless-steel carafe of hot coffee later, he shows up. Clearly, he's staying nearby to keep tabs on me. At least I have a good grip on what the protectors want from me now. Unlike the cops, he accepts when I offer him coffee.

"I heard you had visitors today."

Bad news travels fast on any planet, it seems.

"Yes. They wanted to arrest me. My lawyers are on it," I say. John sips his coffee as if we're two old friends catching up.

"My sources tell me you incriminated yourself. Is that true?"

He still doesn't believe that I had nothing to do with Ravi's death, and I just made it worse when talking to the police. Nice job, me.

"I was trying to fabricate a convincing story. I can't tell them about Pangea. They'd arrest me, and I'd have to claim insanity, which is what they'll do for Linda anyway." I look at my warm coffee mug. This is already my third today. Perhaps I should stop. "But I do realize I screwed up."

He shakes his head.

"John, you have to trust me. I didn't kill Ravi."

The messengers are wrong. You're a murderer even if you don't do the deed yourself. They're as guilty as the people who murdered for them.

With his free hand, John turns his chair and wheels himself smoothly to the window. He must have years of practice.

I get up and join him. We're both staring at my fans outside. Someone there carries a sign that says "Mike for President." A woman flashed me earlier today. However, most of them are here to accuse me of murder, or worse.

"I thought you were bluffing yesterday," John says, restarting the conversation. "You know, about controlling our nuclear weapons. But do you know what happened this morning?"

I nod. Of course, I know. I was the one who did it. I set it up yesterday before I went to Pangea.

"Before you called me today, I was pinged by one of our missile sites. Somehow, it contacted me directly," he says, staring at his black coffee.

There's no direct communication between a missile silo and the outside, by design, but somehow, I did it. I'm particularly proud of this achievement.

"I asked one of my staff to look at it, and they confirmed its origin," he continues.

"I guessed you'd need more proof than what we saw yesterday on the news. The missile software contacted you so you'd be convinced."

John sighs.

"Zeon, I have something to ask of you. We'll battle the messengers tonight. And I agree with you, they are the real enemy. I never thought otherwise." He turns his wheelchair so he can face me. "People die in battle. You may die tonight. We all may die."

"Sorry, I can't give you the codes to deactivate the missiles, John."

He sighs and closes his eyes, looking livid for a second. Taking his time, he inhales and exhales. This is as good a time as any to make my request.

"And John, I have something to ask of you."

He gazes coldly at me. "I can't believe you have the nerve to ask me for anything."

I walk back to the couch and put my coffee mug on the little table so I can rub my eyes with the palms of my hands. He wheels himself after me, still steaming mad.

"I'm afraid for my life, here," I continue. "The messengers tried to kill all of us yesterday. They want everybody to die. They want me to die." I pause. "Can you give me military protection?"

John shakes his head.

"You're rich. Can't you just call someone?"

"Yes, but I can't assemble a SWAT team in the next hour. It'd take at least half a day, and by then, it may be too late."

John is the type of guy who likes to be in charge but he can't control this. Not yet. And, worst of all, he'll have to do as I asked because he doesn't have a choice. He can't afford to let them kill me—unless he's working for the messengers.

He puts his mug on the table next to mine, deep in thought. Then he leans back and clasps his hands behind his head.

"Okay, Zeon. I'll do what I can." He nods. "But this ends tonight, one way or another."

40

ANGEL

Tonight is the night. Yes, I may die, but I'll do everything I can to keep Jane safe. As always, I feel nothing during the transition from Earth to Pangea, and only realize I'm there when I open my eyes and see the soothing white ceiling.

I almost chuckle when I remember how everything started—when I first saw the outlandish place I mistook for Heaven. I thought I was dead and some new kind of life was starting. I wasn't wrong, per se, but I was so very far away from the truth. I can't believe I'm feeling nostalgic about this place.

Someone's in the room with me. I knew this would happen; I didn't truly think they'd let me go without a fight. To my surprise, it's Jane who's nearby, watching me as I sit up. I smile. I definitely didn't expect to see her here. But then I frown—she has a capacitor in her hand—another thing I did not see coming. Sometimes, it seems that the messengers are omniscient. They did say that no one here was my friend.

I try to laugh, but I just feel empty.

"Jane, what are you doing?"

I'm the one asking this question, for a change. I watch her beautiful dark eyes, and the pain I see there makes me feel worse. They're swollen, as if she's been crying for a long time.

"I didn't want it to end like this," she begins in a choked voice.

"What do you mean, Jane?"

She wears a long black jacket, and her hair is again arranged in a ponytail.

"Zeon, I'm an angel," she replies. My heart drops, and I feel in my guts the same sensation I had when I learned that Nia cheated on me—the crushing blow of betrayal. I thought that nothing could blindside me like that ever again. But once again, all the signs were there, and I missed them, just like I did with Nia. So much for learning from your mistakes. This is the price I pay for being an optimist.

She tries to smile at me, but fails. There is some hope, then. Maybe she's not sure about what she has to do, just like when Linda was told to kill her daughter. Jane and Linda. Who would've thought—two sides of the same coin.

"An angel?" I ask. I know what she means, but I want to hear her say it.

"I was raised by the messengers," she explains.

"They brought you to Pangea when you were a child?"

"I didn't know it was called Pangea, but yes. They showed me fairies, dragons, space ships, castles, everything."

If I mistook this for Heaven, imagine what an impressionable little girl would think. This is a battle I lost the first day she came here. No one can compete with Heaven.

"They wanted me to be one of their angels," she continues. "Angels learn about love, and about sacrifice." She closes her eyes for a second. I could've taken her down at this moment of weakness but I want to hear the rest of the story. "All I learned while I grew up was the love part. I knew that some kind of sacrifice was coming, and I was ready." She sighs. "At least, I thought I was ready." She rubs her eyes with her free hand.

"Jane, they brainwashed you."

I always find it fascinating that this is so obvious for someone on the outside but it sounds so absurd if you're the one who believes in it.

"No, I can't believe that," Jane says in a low voice, but she sounds conflicted, not mad. "They want to save us, even if we have to die."

"So, killing Ravi was part of the plan?"

"Linda killed Ravi. The messengers wouldn't do that. He's a protector. You're just trying to make them look bad."

The messengers have layers and layers of lies. Of course, why tell the truth? Some people might not go all the way if they know what's going on.

"Did you know that they ordered Linda to kill her daughter, as well?"

"I do not believe you!" she yells, losing her temper for a second. Then she visibly reins in her emotions. "I'm sorry. This is so difficult for me. They said you'd tell me lies."

"Do you think I'm evil?" I know it's hopeless but I have to try to change her mind.

She avoids looking directly at me for a moment. "No. I've known you for some time. You're not evil. You're just... misguided." Her lips tremble as she says this.

"You think they know better than us."

"They have to. They're the messengers of the gods!" She glares at me.

How ironic. Her relentless faith is one of the reasons I'm

attracted to her, and now it's what will kill me. She's faithful to the end, and I almost envy her naïve trust. I miss that. I used to be like her, but that part of me died when I was betrayed by my two best friends.

"What if they're lying?"

"No, Zeon. I know, in my heart, that they're not lying. I don't know how to explain it. I just...trust them."

I can't reason with that. People have done horrible things when following their hearts. Sometimes, the truth is too hard for them to accept.

"Is this why you understand Dïnisc?"

"I'm an angel," she replies and pauses, as if that explains everything. Finally, she adds, "We speak all languages in Pangea."

In a way, this is amazing. There is so much we could do with this technology and, instead, they use it for this.

"It's funny." She laughs a little. "I was under the impression you were an angel for a while because of everything you can do here." She frowns. "But you're not an angel. You're not like me." Jane strengthens her grip on the gun.

"You know you can't kill me here with that," I tell her, gesturing at her capacitor. By the time she pulls the trigger, I'll be there, stopping her. "You can't stop me, Jane."

"You're right." She nods. "But the messengers told me about your weakness."

Wait, what?

"My...weakness?" I frown. Is it my hair? I can't think of anything. "And what is that?"

Jane crouches down and slowly places the capacitor on the floor. The weapon was only there to keep me away for a while. Then, she stands again and opens her jacket so I can see what's underneath. Dozens of little interconnected black boxes cover her chest, a red sleeveless tank top below them. She's wearing a suicide vest.

Jane is my weakness. And I believed I had thought of everything.

"No, Jane." Tears fall from my eyes. "Why would you do this?" I can see her tears as well. She knows how stupid all of this is, and yet she goes through with it. I know in my heart that she somehow realizes that what she's doing is wrong.

"Sorry, Zeon." She looks down and her voice quivers, as if asking for my understanding. "The messengers asked me to do it. How could I say no?" Jane bites her lip and more tears fall.

Perhaps I can jump on her and disable the vest. She won't have time to react and detonate it. I'm that fast here; there may be a chance. I close my eyes. Come on, Zeon, concentrate! I can't screw this up. This is for Jane.

Even from here, I can see and feel her body in my mind, just like the time we made love, except now, she has bombs and wires around her. There is one single point where the circuits converge. If I'm quick enough, I can deactivate everything in one swipe.

"I know what you're thinking," she says, stopping my thoughts. "Please, don't. If anyone gets close to me, it'll go off automatically."

Damn it.

I open my eyes, defeated. "Jane, everybody on Earth will die if you do that."

"The messengers have made their choice. They want Jora to survive." I think I cracked her façade a little because she lets out a sob. It's not enough. "It has to be done. At least we'll save one of our planets, even if it's not mine." She pauses, clutching at her arm. "And if this doesn't work, they can try again."

There's no need for this. She could've finished us already. I didn't want to see this before I die. There's no way out if Jane is not on my side.

"And you don't think that beings who use you like that are evil?"

She looks away. It's a hard question, and it doesn't look good for her, the messengers, or their gods. At least part of her must realize that.

"The gods work in mysterious ways," she concedes. "Who am I to judge them?"

Well, she doesn't know the whole story, and I'm still alive, so there must be a reason she hasn't killed me yet.

"Jane, what are you waiting for?" I stand up, and she steps back, giving me space. Now more than ever, everything feels surreal. Unreal. This is not real, I think. But it is. People died.

"The messengers want to talk to you first."

She turns around and walks toward the wall facing the outer ring. I watch her go. When she gets close enough, the wall opens in the form of a circular passage. After that, she walks out into the white hallway and waits, so I can follow her.

The corridor is already swarming with protectors bearing football-powered guns, ready for the fight they thought would happen. It's already been lost. John carries the largest single-barreled capacitor we have in our arsenal, with four circular arrays of footballs. It's so big he has to carry it by wrapping both arms around it.

No one knows yet that weapons won't help us. John sees us and sprints in our direction. If he gets near enough, he'll detonate Jane's vest. Startled, she tries to move away from him, but her body language doesn't slow him down.

"Get away from her!" I shout, reminding myself of my favorite Mexican soap opera that I'll never watch again. John looks at me, confused, but he stops walking and gives Jane some space. "She has a suicide vest!" I yell, making sure that everyone hears.

"What the hell are you thinking, Jane?" John shouts, staying a couple of meters away from her. Her face is hollow when she looks at him. Her dark eyes must be trying to comprehend the horrors she's about to unleash on her own planet.

"It has to be done, John."

He gives me a quizzical look, which is weird. I'd expect panic or anger. I warned him that we don't know who to trust but Jane was the last one I thought would betray us.

The protectors around us get the message, and we all walk behind her, not too close, as she leads us to the south of Pangea, in the habitat rings—the entrance to the messengers' hypersphere.

No plan survives contact with the enemy. I tried to play all kinds of scenarios in my head as to how this would happen. In all of them, I was expecting some kind of a battle. Instead, we're all going like sheep to be slaughtered. The protectors follow us in silence to meet our demise.

41

REDEMPTION

Hermes waits for us at the end of the hall, in front of the five entrances to their hypersphere, and Jane moves to stand next to him. The messengers must not affect the bomb. Mike's on the other side, hands up, and Bodan has a gun to his head. Jora's protectors are there already, waiting. Some of the Jori carry weapons, but they seem unsure.

When most of us are here, Hermes finally speaks.

"You have failed the gods. They were just trying to help you. But instead, you rebel against those who guide you." He looks first at Mike, and then at me. "Because of your heresy, because of your rebellion, both of your planets will die." He says this in a warm, fatherly voice, almost convincing us that it's the right thing to do. We, the children, misbehaved, and he's punishing us.

Everybody talks at once. The Jori must've heard his speech in Dïnisc, for they are also shouting. My heart breaks again, but this time for Jane. Once you experience betrayal, you hate seeing your loved ones go through it.

"What?" she says. Her face goes dark and scared at the

same time. Her lower lip trembles. This is the moment her trust is broken; a trust that goes all the way back to when she was a kid. Jane is finally realizing that there are no gods.

Hermes extends his arm and touches Jane's face, wet with tears, as if drying them.

"You have done well," Hermes says in a condescending tone, and I flinch. "Your work here is done, my angel."

"But...we must save one of our Earths," Jane pleads. "You're telling me that everyone...all of us..." She stops and looks around in horror. "All of us will die?"

"We don't always tell the whole truth, child. You wouldn't understand it," Hermes replies. "Would you have done it if you knew?"

"Of course not!" Jane says, raising her voice and slapping Hermes's hand away. As always, he takes it in stride, as if nothing out of the ordinary happened. He brings both of his hands together and turns to face us.

"We know each and every one of you, every hair on your head, how many breaths you take, how you think, your deal breakers," he says, then turns back to Jane. "We never ask you something that you're not able to accomplish."

"Why did Linda kill Ravi?" I ask, trying to delay the inevitable. They seem to be willing to tell the truth finally, since this is the end, so I might as well make them talk.

"She was told to protect you, Zeon," he answers, looking directly at Jane and not at me. Jane shuts her eyes firmly for a second, perhaps hoping to wake up from a bad nightmare. She's learning how far the rabbit hole goes. "And she did well, just like Jane."

When Jane finally opens her eyes again, she looks at me, blushing and shaking her head. I nod slowly, accepting her implied apology. I hope she knows I don't blame her for this. Jane has reached her limit, but it's too late.

I glare at Hermes, clasping my fist.

"Why did you lie about the portal?" I say.

"You needed motivation, so we gave it to you," Hermes explains. "Your minds are too small to understand the big picture."

"I think you didn't want us to join forces," I accuse him. "You're afraid of us." But why?

He smiles. "You have no idea what's out there, Zeon. Your world view is so small."

"What's going to happen now?" Mike interjects, and Bodan presses the barrel of the capacitor on his temple.

"As soon as I disconnect from Pangea, Jane's bomb will explode. Everyone in the habitat rings will die, regardless of where you are," Hermes explains. I wonder why it hasn't happened yet. Jane could've killed us earlier and spared us from this horror show.

"And you know what will happen once Zeon and Mike are dead, right?" He looks at the two of us, and I finally understand. He wants confirmation. They're not omniscient, after all. "Mike's Earth will end in a nuclear holocaust. Zeon's Earth will die by a rain of rocks."

For a moment, I forget that we're all going to die and I chuckle. It's so out of place that everyone stares at me in disbelief.

"You are so wrong," I say, clenching my teeth. "You may think of me as superhuman, but I'm nothing of the sort." They must think I'm crazy, and perhaps I am. "I deceived you all."

"What do you mean?" John says. Bodan and Hermes exchange glances, but they don't say anything. It's my show now.

"You gave me an impossible task. It would take more than five years for me to take over Earth's nuclear arsenal, and people would've figured it out by then. In fact, I only have two Russian warheads and one American under my control. That's it." I smile at John. "And I only kept them in case I had to do an extreme demonstration." I was looking for a deserted place where I could do it, in case the submarine ploy didn't work out, but in the end, I didn't need it.

"How did you fire a missile from a Russian submarine?" John asks.

"That was the easy part. I'm rich, so I just bribed the captain." I chuckle again. "He knew it would be harmless, just for show. He could blame a malfunction, or misunderstanding. His career has ended, but he'll be comfortable for the rest of his life." Vladimir frowns at me in anger. I look back at him, trying to save face. "It wasn't easy, Vladimir. It took forever for me to find someone who would do it." He mouths something under his breath that's probably not a compliment.

John grins. "You don't have a dead man's switch, then?"

"No, John. No matter what happens here, Earth is safe."

And for the first time ever, John laughs. Not only that, he starts what seems to be an uncontrollable outburst of laughter, as if I had told him the best joke of his life. Paulo and Louise are crying and hugging, while Vladimir and Carmen look at us as if they didn't understand a joke.

Jane still appears distraught, but watches me thoughtfully. Even if we all die here, she won't be responsible for any deaths on Earth.

"I'm disappointed," Hermes says, spreading his arms, making me feel bad for a split second. "It turns out that only one planet will be destroyed. Humans are so unreliable." He shakes his head. People stop talking when they hear him. "It's not what we wanted, but it'll have to do."

"Ahem," Mike clears his throat and we eye each other.

"What now? Are you going to tell us that your rocket is unable to destroy Jora?" Hermes asks.

"Oh no, it's perfectly capable of destroying their planet. It's ready to go at any moment." Of course, Mike would make his plan perfect. I'm not even surprised.

"What happens if you die?" Hermes asks, hands on his hips.

"If I don't contact the rocket after some time, something will indeed happen, but not what you're expecting." Mike keeps his arms up because of the threat of Bodan's capacitor. "My trigger will only activate the self-destruction system on the rocket." I almost give him a thumbs-up, but manage not to do it just in time. He might not take it that well.

The mood changes around us, and people chat amongst themselves with a mixed sense of dread and relief. Nia and the other Jori don't understand anything Mike and I say, but they must be figuring out at least part of it by our body language.

Game over. The messengers have lost. Too bad we'll all die because of Jane's vest.

All of a sudden, a sphere the size of a baseball flies in the middle of us, and everything slows down inside my head. I don't know why this is happening, but I'll take advantage of it. Time comes to a crawl. Not even the messengers can think as fast as I can in this mode.

Nia is the one who threw the sphere, which is an AED bomb. Where did she find one? It's the same type we used in the underground tunnels to conquer the pyramid. Jane's suicide vest is rudimentary, so it'll only be offline for a short period of time.

As I crouch, Mike punches Bodan in the arm and the AED explodes. Almost everyone is knocked to the ground. Bodan's capacitor flies into the air for a moment and falls near Jane. Mike's not as fast as I am, therefore he must've known this would happen.

I count the seconds since the explosion.

One. It's obvious what I have to do, so I jump toward Jane. Like the others, she's on the floor due to the shock wave. I must get to the vest to disable it. Nothing else matters.

Two. She's lying down on her side, trying to get the gun that Bodan dropped. Slipping in right beside Jane, I turn to face her. She's not looking at me. She's focused on the capacitor nearby, but she won't be able to grab it. It's too far from her hand.

Three. My hands touch her near her stomach and I concentrate, finding the point of convergence in the vest. She ignores what I'm doing. The weapon on the floor flies to her right hand as if by magic. I don't have time for this. My mind keeps working on her vest.

Four. Again taking me by surprise, Jane points the capacitor in my direction and pulls the trigger, trying to kill me, but it's not operational yet due to the AED bomb.

Five. Her vest is disabled. The bombs will not go off. Still, the explosive is made of small parts that can fix themselves, so I must disable all of them before I let her go.

Six. I must have successfully disabled the vest, because otherwise we'd be dead, but the gun in her hand is operational. I won't be able to stop her from shooting me. At least I saved her. I close my eyes as I disable the remaining explosives in her vest.

Seven. She pulls the trigger again, activating the capacitor. The gun fires.

Someone is shot but I'm not dead yet. I don't understand. She couldn't have missed me this close. When I open my eyes, Jane's whole body is shaking with deep sobs.

Without saying anything, she pulls me into her trembling arms. I hug her back, soothing her.

There's no need to look behind me to understand what's happening, since I can use my mental map. Jane killed Hermes by shooting him in the head. He'll never come back from this the way he did when I shot him in the hypersphere.

She feels so fragile as I embrace her, but what she did was courageous. It must've been inconceivable for her. She killed someone she worshipped, out of rage for the betrayal. As we all do in similar situations, she must be second-guessing herself. Nothing I say will make this better, so I stay quiet while she cries.

She drops the weapon on the floor, and I can't help but let some of my own tears out. In her distress, she somehow managed to connect with Pangea like I do, calling the capacitor to her hand. Impressive. I was only able to move things when I was under distress, too. It's way easier for me to fly and to explore inward.

After a few moments, I help her up, placing my hand on her side. I can't let this vest explode. Meanwhile, the others hold Bodan, while a few protectors disappeared into the habitat rings like cockroaches. I wonder how many others are traitors.

Mike comes next to me and gives me a side hug.

"Thanks, Zeon."

"We should thank Nia," I say, glad I wasn't alone all this time.

Without warning, the middle door to the hypersphere opens, and we turn toward it as Mike grabs the gun on the floor. Iris enters the habitat ring looking at us in contempt. For the first time, we see a messenger wearing clothes—a red robe with white diamonds, as if she's ready for some kind of ceremony.

John isn't taking any chances. He points his large capacitor at Iris, ready to shoot, but all our weapons fall to the ground, moved by an invisible force.

The messengers are stronger than I am.

"At ease, children," she says in a somber mood. "I won't hurt you." She's not technically lying, but I'm worried about her human friends.

"Pangea is the home of all minds, and the home of the gods, but it is not limitless. If it becomes lawless, all life in the universes will eventually perish," she begins.

John shakes his head. "Iris, stop with all the bullshit. Why did you want to destroy our Earths?" He tries to pull his gun from the floor, without success.

"We're in a war that's been raging for thousands of years for the control of Pangea, and the gods cannot afford to have any species falling into enemy hands. Like a cancer, you must sometimes destroy healthy tissue to get to the tumor."

John stands up, resigned to his lack of weaponry. The capacitors are glued to the floor.

"But why the games? And what about the portal?" he asks, as if continuing a conversation by the office kitchen.

"It's rare, but once in a while, we find a race that can face this enemy. Humans have a violent spark, ingenuity, and the ability to fight, while having empathy for their enemy. A perfect balance. The 'games,' as you call them, are just a training area for the real war, and the threat of destruction by the portal was a ruse to force you to participate." Iris frowns and smiles at the same time.

As Mike and I guessed—mostly Mike—the portal story was bullshit. We can create a portal between our planets and they won't be destroyed because of it. But what the hell does any of this have to do with what happened in our hypersphere?

John walks toward Iris with both of his fists up. He should know, though, that punching does nothing to them. However, an invisible wall stops him in his tracks.

Resigned, he takes a deep breath and glares back at Iris.

"A training area? Fuck you!" John yells. "People died. There must be a better way. Why didn't you just tell us that?"

Iris extends her arms, as if encompassing everyone with her gesture.

"This experiment has failed. It's such a shame. You even killed a messenger," she says, and I get a feeling of disappointment in my mind. Looking around, it seems that I'm not alone in my feeling. They're also telepaths, it seems, these messengers. That's how we all understand her, regardless of which language we speak.

"Perhaps we can still discuss terms?" Jane interjects. "Maybe we can willingly help the gods, without all the lies."

"Oh Jane." Iris laughs, but the sound of her laughter is out of sync with her mouth. "You don't know what you have done. Yes, the gods are always searching for strong, empathetic races, but the most important value we look for is loyalty. You failed miserably in that aspect. Humans do not respect the gods, or the messengers."

She shakes her head, but it moves too far on both sides of the gesture. It's hard to respect the messengers when it looks like they're trying to unscrew their heads.

And then it dawns on me—the real reason they wanted to destroy our Earths.

"The war, Iris," I finally say. "The messengers started it because the gods want Pangea for themselves." I smile thinly. "This is why you wanted to kill us."

Iris stops in her tracks for a split second, and tilts her head. Again, their desire to copy humans gives their emotions away. Maybe they can't control who shows up in Pangea, and they want us—and any other intelligent beings —gone. Clearly, whatever the gods created before the messengers to purge Pangea has rebelled against them, like a weaponized virus, and they were counting on us to help them fight it.

She finally takes a step closer, her red eyes locked with mine. Meanwhile, Jane embraces me, her arm behind my back, indicating where her loyalty lies. Or maybe she's going to kill me. I'm not a good judge of character. Regardless, I embrace her back.

"Goodbye, former protectors. You will never see the messengers or Pangea again."

"Wait!" John yells, but it's too late. Jane and I look at each other one last time. At least we'll die together.

Everything goes black after that.

42

JORA

There's a lot of noise in my brain when I wake up, like the whole world is talking inside my head, hurting and overwhelming me. I scream. The connection I had with Pangea was smooth, strong, and straightforward. The one I'm feeling today is rough, invasive, and paradoxically weak. I forgot how I used to live like that. It'll take some time for me to get familiar with this again.

After a while, the explosion of sensations goes away. Someone noticed my distress and dialed it down for me. No one comes to my room. On Jora, almost everything is automated. You just have to think about what you have to do and it happens. I'm back home.

This is one of our hospitals. I don't recognize the place but it's not like I toured hospitals in my previous life.

As I start getting used to my senses again, all the data comes back to my brain. Gradually the information trickles in. So much has changed since I left. When I'm strong enough to be able to handle it, I check my logs, and they indicate I've been here for almost three weeks. This was the time it took me to wake up on Mike's Earth the first time. It looks like we can't just go back to our planets like the other protectors. Unlike them, our brain must be reconstructed. We were in the wrong body for all this time, after all.

Iris told us that we're never going back to Pangea. My stomach churns as I realize that I'll never see Jane again. The silver lining is that she must be alive, and for a moment there, I thought she wouldn't survive. Jane will most probably struggle to make peace with what she did, but she'll thrive. She's tough. That's what matters. This brings me conflicting emotions; I feel both sad and happy at the same time.

There are several messages in my queue—people everywhere want to talk to me. Based on the contents of the messages—mostly physics stuff—most of them assume that they're speaking to Mike, the genius physicist, not me. They'll be so upset when they realize I know nothing about particle physics. I'm so good at disappointing people. It really should be some kind of profession. What do you do, Zeon? I'm an expert in letting people down. Nice to meet you.

A message from Nia distracts me from feeling sorry for myself. She tells me she wants to be there for me when I leave the hospital. The protectors came back as soon as we left Pangea, but it's taken weeks for Mike and me to go back.

Nia's the last person I want to see. I just want to go home and cry, but I'm not sure if I'll be able to leave yet. My muscles are weak. This is what happens when you spend three weeks in bed.

Akiva comes into the room. I've never seen her before, but my sensors tell me she's my assigned doctor. For some reason, her face is tense, and she's sending angry emotions toward me. She's not in a good mood.

"<Zeon, I'm glad you're back with us,>" she lies. I sense

her lying emoticon at the same time I hear her greeting. I hate when people do that. "<Unfortunately, we don't understand what happened.>"

"<Did you check my MRI scans?>" I ask.

Akiva wears special glasses made of see-through glass that allow her to do special exams, such as instant MRIs, or visualize circulatory or nervous systems; they connect to her mind through her temples. Due to this kind of equipment, doctors and nurses often don't wear any temple jewelry.

"<Yes,>" she says, and as soon as she tells me this, I get a message containing all the scans that were ever taken when I was in this hospital. "<There's something wrong, though.>"

"<I know. The brains are different, right?>" I laugh, but it hurts, and I look at her with a grimace.

"<Right. How did you know that?>" She removes her examination glasses to take a better look at me.

"<I'm a neurocomputer scientist.>"

"<I know,>" she replies, annoyed. "<How did you figure it out without even looking at them?>"

"<It's a long story. And you wouldn't believe me, anyway.>"

She presses me to tell her what I know, but I refuse. It won't do me any good and she may send me to a mental wing or something. No need to complicate my life any more than it already is.

"<Akiva, I want to go home.>" I try to send the goodbye emoticon, but fail. It'll take me some time to relearn all the communication tricks we have here.

"<No. We'll observe you for one more day.>"

There isn't much I can do. Once I'm in one of our hospitals, the doctors are in charge of my decisions. Usually, they ask us, pretending we have a choice. We also have social games here, but she didn't do that. Her people skills are lacking, which is not an ideal trait in a doctor.

THEY KEEP me one more night for observation. I didn't realize how much I'd missed real sleep, and it's so good to be able to do it again, but I'm still depressed. We saved both worlds, but many died. Ravi died. And Jane is gone forever. I don't have much incentive to be happy.

Akiva comes into my room and based on the data I'm receiving, she's discharging me, though she's still angry at me for some reason. She's a bully.

"<You should be happy you can go home. Most people want you in jail. You have powerful friends.>"

"<What?>" I ask, confused.

"<You know what I'm talking about. You sabotaged our mission to Mars.>"

Oh yeah, I forgot about that. So that's why she's so moody. Mike left a nice parting gift here for me. At least I'm not being charged with murder, or tampering with nuclear weapons. I can't help but chuckle, even though everything else is sad. At least in this aspect I have outdone him.

"<Laugh all you want. It doesn't mean you'll be free. There'll be a trial. I hope you rot in jail for the rest of your life.>"

After she leaves, I get ready to go back to my house. It takes me some time to have the courage to wear a skirt. But this is normal here, or so I keep telling myself. Resigned to the way I look, I ask the network for a ride and soon an automatic car picks me up at the hospital and drives me home. I forgot how smooth it is riding in a car here—no traffic jams, no near-death experiences. On the other hand, there's no American football, either.

It's afternoon when I get to my house. The last time I was here, my heart was broken, and now it's broken all over again, but for a different reason. This is better than everyone dying but it still sucks.

The house sensors recognize me, so I walk inside as the doors open. Everything is fluid on this planet. As I walk down the main hallway, my calico cat, Bebe, watches me from under the dining room table. At least someone loves me. While she ignores me, and tries to flee, as usual, I grab and hug her. She meows a complaint, so I let her go, and she disappears into the laundry room.

All of a sudden, the smell of sewer hits my nostrils, and my senses alert me that I should be angry, startling me and, indeed, making me angry. Worse, someone else is in the room, and I'm caught like a deer in the headlights.

"<Mike? Are you back?>" Nia smiles as she comes into view. She's here, inside my freaking house. "<Why didn't you contact me to meet you at the hospital?>"

Oh yes, of course, she lives here. I forgot. Also, perhaps it wasn't a good idea to assign Nia's presence to sewer anger. I immediately turn it off, and the smell goes away.

Anyway, in my fantasies, she had moved out to live with her prince, but maybe she stayed to take care of Mike and his pretend amnesia.

"<I'm not Mike. I'm Zeon again. I'm back, Nia.>"

I forgot how she used to look here. Older, but still beautiful. And the way she's dressed makes me flinch. Unlike Earth, the planet of the prudes, here people couldn't care less about nudity. She's only wearing a teeny tiny cêlcinhê with no sîtoe, covered by a see- through night pêlê. I guess I got used to the prudish behavior of Mike's Earth, and the sight makes me wince.

"<Oh.>" She frowns, unable to hide her disappointment. She was expecting Mike, not me. Really, I didn't have to see this.

"<Sorry about that,>" I blurt. "<I'm sorry I disappoint people when they see me.>" I keep forgetting that this is my expertise. She stops me with a hand on my chest when I try to get into my room.

"<Wait. It's not that, Zeon. I just miss...Mike.>" She hugs her arms and leans on the wall.

"<Well, Jane ended up not shooting me. Perhaps you want to do it instead and take me out of my misery?>" I open my arms. I know it's unfair to say this to Nia, but for me, everything only just happened. It's been three weeks for her. She's had more time to process it.

"<I said I was sorry.>"

Yeah, she's always sorry. Everybody's sorry. Sorry they didn't love me enough not to cheat on me, sorry I'm not Mike, sorry that they're nuts and trust the messengers. I shake my head and walk into my old room. Nia looks at me, a confused look on her face for a second, but quickly looks down. She's lived with Mike since the early days, so she must've realized that I'm not suggesting anything.

Mike has left his touch here. My private quarters were never this tidy before. Unexpectedly, Nia follows me, breaking one of our society's unsaid rules—that you cannot just enter someone's chamber without asking them first, even if you're married.

"<Zeon, will we ever see them again?>"

I miss Jane, she misses Mike. We're all hurt here. I should have some compassion.

"<I don't think so.>" I'm not sorry, though. For a change,

I have nothing to do with that. "<We won't go back to Pangea, and we can't open a portal. Both planets would need to agree on a specific place and time to do that. We didn't, so it's impossible.>"

One thing is certain, though. Nia and I can't both live in the same house. True, we bought this house together, but we'll have to split and search for another place. I can't keep seeing her every day. Even if I'm over her, I'll never be over her betrayal.

Walking over to the largest window in my bedroom, I look up at the Ring one more time. The rocks that are farther away reflect the afternoon sun, which makes the planet look like it's wearing a giant bracelet. I forgot how much I missed it. Even though I feel misplaced, it feels like home for a second.

And then I turn around to face Nia.

"<Nia, you threw that bomb in Pangea. How did you know what was going to happen?>"

Her gaze drops to her hands.

"<I told Mike that we needed to have an escape plan if something went wrong,>" She gives a dismissive hand wave. "<So I suggested taking an AED bomb with me the next day and wait for my signal.>"

"<But how did you have an AED bomb in the first place? I thought they were all gone!>"

Nia stiffens. "<I had a bunch of weapons stored in my quarters.>" She frowns.

"<But why?>" I press. She runs her hand through her still unfamiliar-to-me short hair, thinking.

"<Well, you know, Bodan started to freak me out. When we broke up, I thought he was going to hurt me.>" She sighs.

Nia had a plan B, and Mike trusted her with it. After what Linda did, Nia was the only one who could be trusted.

How ironic. She and Mike saved us in the end. And Bodan, too, indirectly, because he's an ass.

"<Thanks for saving us, Nia.>"

She accepts my gratitude by pinging me through our biosensors, while also staring at the Ring.

"<After I broke up with Bodan, Mike and I got really close in Pangea.>" She blushes, avoiding my eyes. "<You know what,>" she begins, and yes, I know what she's going to say. If you recall, I have all the hits, and there's one in particular that's always in the top three.

"<He reminds you of me?>" I interrupt, trying to hide my sarcasm but not succeeding, especially because I accidentally send the sarcasm emoticon to her. I'm still getting reacquainted with our systems.

We have to sell this place as soon as possible. In fact, I'm going to put it up for sale on the net today. Better yet, maybe if I grab a random person off the street right now, they can just take it for free so I can leave.

"<Yes,>" she admits. "<And I'm glad for that. Of course, Mike's the smartest person on either of our planets, and you're too 'in your face,' while Mike's— >"

"<I know, Nia, I'm an oaf. No need to rub it in.>" I forgot how blunt people are on Jora. I wish they had more tact.

"<Sorry, I didn't mean it like that. I just meant that you both have a great heart. You may say otherwise, but you care about people, and that's what matters. That's what saved our Earths.>" She sighs. "<Thanks, Zeon.>"

Everyone is the good guy in their own minds, and I was never sure if I did the right thing, so I'm glad that she said that. I'm tired of second-guessing myself.

"<Thanks, Nia, I think,>" I say, still a little bit offended. "<We all helped. I'm just glad it's over.>"

Nia touches the fractal flame on her temple and catches me looking at it.

"<I forgot to ask,>" I say. "<What is it?>"

Nia pops it off her temple and holds it on her palm, showing it to me. The interlocked rock pattern is more discernible up close.

"<They're ring flames. It's my own design.>"

Every day, our planet creates a shadow on the ring, and the farther away you are from the equator, the more impressive it is. When the sun is lower in the sky, near the horizon, and there are only a few clouds, part of the Ring reflects and redirects the light through the atmosphere, making the border of the Ring eclipse—the penumbra—flash with several colors. As the shadow of Jora moves, it looks like the darker and lighter border is made of flames consuming the rocks. This is where the tradition of eating guardian angels at the Church of The Ring comes from.

Both on Jora and on Earth, the sun setting and rising has the meaning of beginning and end, birth and death. Ring flames also have a specific interpretation, regardless if you're religious or not.

"<It means hope,>" she says, stating the obvious.

After that, there's nothing more for us to say. Nia leaves me alone in my room, and I throw myself on my bed, turning off all communications in my head. Curled into a ball, I cry.

I cry because I'm happy we survived, sad because Jane and my life there are gone. I even cry because of Nia. No, I don't miss her anymore, not after Jane. What I miss are our shared dreams, now destroyed. And for once, I have time to grieve for Ravi and think about what his death means to me, to Louise, and to his loved ones. My head tries to process the sadness of his loss, the shame that I'm somehow responsible for it, and the guilt that I couldn't save him from myself. Damn it, even delusional Linda and her daughter whom I never met make me sob.

On top of that, there's no real home for me anymore. I miss Earth, but when I was there, I also missed a lot of the things from Jora. I'm a citizen without a country. I belong nowhere, and to no one.

After several minutes of feeling sorry for myself, I decide to do something with my life. No need for self- pity anymore. This is what I do—I'm resilient. It's all just water under the bridge. Tomorrow, my new life starts. And I'm used to starting from scratch.

As I reconnect to the network, something in my message queue catches my eye. This in itself is not out of the ordinary, since we get a ton of messages all the time. In fact, I often get in trouble because I ignore so many messages, even if they're important. However, this one stands out, because I was the one who sent it, minutes ago.

Understanding fills my mind when I open it. It was a time-delayed message. Mike created it three weeks ago to be sent twenty-four hours after I contacted the network. I ping Nia through the net—we don't have to shout here. Yes, I could've forwarded the message to her but I know she prefers to see things with her own eyes. This is what makes her a great artist.

When she comes in, I use the mind-projector above my bed for more impact. Her eyes are wide as she reads the text projected in the middle of my room.

<Dear Zeon,

I look forward to seeing you at 9035.07.23.20.20

at Fire Woods Park.

Best regards, Mike>

Fire Woods Park is the place where I proposed to Nia, so

they must have talked about it. I smile. Mike truly is the best of us. Nia lets her sobs out.

Jane and I will meet again. In truth, she'll probably have moved on by them, but it doesn't matter. We'll meet again.

Sometimes I wonder how someone can be so happy and so sad at the same time. Holding Nia as she cries, I watch the late afternoon sky. The always rotating rocks of the Ring are now burning in red, yellow, and orange colors.

The Ring is in flames.

A word about the author...

Originally from Brazil, Christian Hofsetz has a Ph.D. and an M.Sc. in Computer Science. After working for several years as a professor in Brazil, he moved to the United States and changed careers. Currently, he is a Software Engineer Manager at Microsoft by day, and a writer by night.

Software engineering and computers have been his passion since he was a teenager, but he's been reading novels for longer than writing code.

One day, he couldn't help it anymore. He wrote the first chapter of a book. How bad could it be? But things escalated quickly. Next thing he knew, he was writing yet another chapter, and then the next. He tried to hide it, but his family knew he was up to something.

When they figured out what he was doing, it was too late —he accidentally had written a whole book.

The result of this journey is Challenges of The Gods, a story about a fantastic world of gods meddling with humans.

For more info, check the link below:

https://hofsetz.com

www.ingramcontent.com/pod-product-compliance
Lightning Source LLC
Chambersburg PA
CBHW061925170626
46813CB00006B/2297